THE
LANTERN

Book Three in "The Hidden" Series

Callie McFarlane

DEDICATION

To all the women of history who have contributed so much
to the lives of those they loved; to the lives of many they did not know;
to the march of civilization, change, and life, as it moves ever forward;
for being loving, courageous, and tenacious enough to turn
the "ordinary" into the "extraordinary."

Love's Lantern

Because the road was steep and long
And through a dark and lonely land,
God set upon my lips a song
And put a lantern in my hand.

Joyce Kilmer

I celebrate you!
Callie McFarlane

TABLE OF CONTENTS

PREFACE

In times of darkness
Love sees
In times of silence
Love hears
In times of doubt
Love hopes
In times of sorrow
Love heals
And in all times
Love remembers

CIRCLES by Katrina Wood [2006]
p. 104; 1-60034-585-9; Xulon Press

What will survive of us?

It matters not whether one believes in the concept of the God of Abraham and Isaac – the God of all Christendom and Judaism–or Allah, or God by any name in any other culture or religion. All have a central tenet of obedience to a Creator God, the source of all love and power, whose laws we must obey to live an acceptable life on earth with the promise of eternity in spiritual form. (By definition, atheists exclude themselves as death means everything is over, dead, and finished.) None of us has proof of heaven or hell. We continuously grasp for an understanding of that which follows after death, or some sign that reassures our choice to faithfully believe that there is "something." What does 'life after death' mean? Many different things to many different people. One thing among many I have come to know with certainty that can have plain meaning to all those living left behind (believer and nonbeliever alike) is that life after death in terms we can understand means **remembrance:** the feelings we experienced from the touch of love expressed or given by the person who is now dead. Love never dies; it lives in the hearts and memories of those left behind. What will survive of us in the *earthly life* is **love.**

From the "ordinary" to the "extraordinary."

Everything we do and how we do it conveys "who" we are. Hopefully, that expression changes from time to time as we mature and grow in understanding. One applicable truism of life is that individuals choose to respond or act, and that their choices, responses, and actions, define them. Another axiom of life is that right or ethical decisions and reactions, do not always result in right, positive, or acceptable consequences.

Despite that we all experience and have to live with the effects of unfairness and injustice, as well as random incidents, the difference in outcome can be startling if consistently impelled by one, indestructible force: **love.** It is through love that all of us as "ordinary people" can accomplish "extraordinary things." **THE LANTERN** focuses on some representational lives of women throughout some of the eras of humankind's past rooted in historical record. These ordinary women (and many more like them who remain unheralded) accomplished extraordinary things in their lives. I celebrate them!

Love never dies. We die. **What survives of us is love:** the love that emboldens us to choose, respond, and act, making the ordinary into the extraordinary in thought, word, and deed. **Love** is a **lantern** casting its light into the dark corners of our existence. With each act of love, the lantern burns brighter and brighter; and the lantern burns bright; and the lantern burns... with the unfolding of time into forever.

Blessings and Smiles,

Callie McFarlane

PROLOGUE

She walked onto the veranda her feet silent on the stone. Music wafted from the open doors muffling the drone of voices within. "Can I talk to you for a minute, Auntie Lauren?"

The older woman was gazing intently at the night sky littered with stars. "Of course, you may, Bethany; I don't know if you *can*, but you *may*," she quipped, easing the young woman's tension with a kind smile. "Beautiful, isn't it?" she said, nodding toward the heavens.

"Eternity is too short," Lauren whispered wistfully. "That's something my husband wrote to me once. Those were also his last words to me. Take a seat; there's no charge."

"I need to sort out some things, and it always helps to talk to you." The young woman hunched on the garden bench, swinging her bare feet and legs. The older woman remained silent.

"It's just that I'm not sure; there are things I love about him. I mean, I'm fairly sure I love him, but there are also some things I dislike about him... about our relationship, I mean. You know, things I have to put up with, times when he's completely unreasonable and temperamental over nothing. That's when he makes me miserable. Then when we fight over it, he cries, says he's sorry, and I end up forgiving him because I don't want to be alone again. When I think about it afterward, I tell myself to concentrate on the good parts, but I always have this nagging, unsure feeling, you know? Am I making the right choice, handling things the right way, you know? It's all come to the fore with James' relationship with Rachel. He seems to know for sure; why can't I?"

The older woman nodded. "There was a movie I saw years after my husband died. It was something written by the American actor/producer, Tyler Perry. He was a genius who also played several parts in the movie, but that's neither here nor there. The point is that one of the characters was talking in one scene to a young woman about your age, who herself was unsure about her upcoming marriage. Cicely Tyson was the actress, I think; she played a woman more or less my age.

"The lines she said in the movie moved me to tears because

they perfectly described my relationship with my dead husband, who I miss with every breath I have drawn since his death."

Sighing, the older woman continued. "She told the young woman—and I've never forgotten it—'*I have had an opportunity that few people ever get on this earth. God has blessed me to share time and space with a man that He designed Himself just for me. I have not only been blessed, but I have also been divinely favored.*'

"I remember weeping for several minutes. It was the late evening of New Year's Day, and I was missing my husband and our life together, reminiscing over snippets from years past. Somehow, that sweet soliloquy gave me peace because it so perfectly framed our relationship from a different perspective."

Standing, Lauren reached for the younger woman's hand. "Walk with me." Taking a turn around the lovely, fragrant summer garden, she said, "Look up, honey. You need grounding." As Bethany lifted her tear-filled eyes skyward, the older woman gazed up as well, smiling and rested her arm on the young shoulder with a light hug.

"I can tell you that real love... the kind that lasts... is not unsure. It stands firm in the face of adversity; it's loyal, trusting, and patient, no matter what happens and despite what the world throws at you. It doesn't matter if it's stress, financial pressure, a hardship of any kind, sadness, betrayal, loss, or failure. It stays sure, without doubts and with an inner sense of peace through it all. It makes your heart flutter from beginning to end." The older woman chuckled. "Why, would you believe that my heart still trembles when I look at his photos?"

"You were so lucky," the younger woman said. "Your face always lights up when you talk about him. You must have had a perfect life."

"Lucky? Yes, I was lucky or, as the actress in that movie said, 'divinely favored.' But perfect? Ah, no, far from perfect. Our life together had many burdens, years of soul-destroying trauma, and ultimately the cruelest ending to endure. I thank the good Lord for peppering my life with so much goodness and continuing happiness. Someday, I'll tell you the full story. But for now, ask yourself if your relationship comes close to that movie's soliloquy. Ask yourself if your heart feels as if your young man is the other half of your soul. Listen well, and if your heart flutters, you'll have the right answer. And always remember to clear your mind by looking at the purity of God's starlit heavens."

The younger woman smiled and kissed the elder on the cheek. "Thank you. You always seem to be able to clear things up for me. It's just so hard being a woman in a man's world. Women have been clawing for freedom from expectation and limitation of their roles for the whole of history! How did you manage to have a successful career, Auntie Lauren?"

"Oh, that's a tough one, Bethy. I had a man who believed in me... no, two men who believed in me. That bolstered my courage and belief in myself. And equally important, we shared convictions. Love encompasses much more than simple compatibility and suitability. Then, there's my innate stubbornness: I don't 'give up or give in' easily, as your Uncle Nick would be happy to explain!

"But you need those three ingredients: your man must believe in you; you must have the courage to believe in yourself, and you must have shared convictions about life. Without that formula, there's little chance of living your dreams if you choose to marry. Do you?"

Bethany inhaled deeply. "Do I what? Choose to share my life with a man or have the ingredients to the formula for success?" She looked forlornly at Lauren.

"Both, as well you know. Question posed and unanswered; your move." Lauren sighed, looking skyward.

A tall and handsome blonde man called to them from the veranda. "You two out there, Mum says to come inside! Dinner is about to be announced," his smiling face declared.

"How lovely of you to fetch me, James," she called out, as the two made their way back to the veranda. Winking at the younger woman, she said quietly, "I expect there will be a surprise announcement over dessert. Just look at that brother of yours, he's almost bursting."

As she topped the steps, her godson offered his arm and lightly kissed her cheek. She looked over her shoulder. The younger woman stood at the bottom of the steps bathed in moonlight, her face tilted to the glittering night sky. Lauren remembered a time long ago when she stood in the same place as Bethany stood now, contemplating her future, and searching for answers.

Smiling, Lauren said, "Now then, James, are you going to show me the ring before you present it?"

"What?! How did you... I've told no one, not even Bethy, Mum, or Father!" the young man spluttered.

"Never mind, love, just chalk it up to the wisdom of the ancients! Quickly now, let's have a look!"

Chapter One
Waverlee: After the Dig

The family gathered around the dining table. Nick flourished a bottle of champagne as he said, "We've come a long way together. I propose a toast to our success. What say you, James?"

Standing with glass raised, James looked at each member of the team. "To you: stalwart, fearless, crew. Bravo, and thank you. All we accomplished is due to the role each of you played individually and together. It was a rough one and almost ended in disaster, but we came through, thank God. To God's faithfulness and your loyalty and excellence!"

Everyone raised glasses and offered various accompanying cheers. Everyone celebrated, that is, except Alistair. It did not escape Bethany's notice.

"Alistair, you haven't toasted the completion of our project and its success," she said with not a little denigration, staring at him with raised eyebrows.

"Look here, I'm glad you all escaped more serious repercussions, but there's no use pretending or whitewashing this entire affair. You all know I was never in favor of it, or rather, of Bethany's participation. So, with all that's happened, I'm amazed you can all be so cavalier about it."

"We're not 'whitewashing,' Alistair; we're expressing thanks, relief, and celebration," said Nick evenly.

"Whatever," mumbled Alistair with a frown.

"Well, I, for one, am thrilled you are all back!" said Lauren, giving Nick a bright smile. "I'm starving. Who wants rare and who wants medium?" she said to break the tension, taking up the serving fork from the lamb platter.

"Can you not for once acknowledge that there are other

choices in life besides yours?!" exclaimed Bethany. "James has accomplished something huge, and I would think you might congratulate him instead of being so obstinate in your views, despite that you didn't approve of my going."

"Yes, that's right, Bethany. Praise the golden-haired brother and take his side against your husband. That's the way it is with you, Brandons, isn't it? You close ranks when you come up against something you don't like. Well, I will not be cowed, despite your disrespect!" he said, glaring at no one in particular.

"Ah, Alistair, let's not argue. You have it all wrong. No one's ganging up on you. We're just thankful everyone is home and safe. Let's just enjoy this blessing together with a quiet, family dinner, shall we?" said Marcy, placing a hand on his arm.

"The Mother of It All has spoken! You whelped these two, Marcia. Don't tell me you bear no responsibility for their way of going, always chasing this dream or that, never following the status quo or normal pursuits. Why, I..."

"THAT will do, Alistair," said Thomas interrupting sternly, as head of the family. "Keep your opinions to yourself if you please. Either join us in the spirit of this dinner or excuse yourself. I will NOT endure any further insult at my table."

"How dare you speak to Mum that way, Alistair!" cried Bethany, in chorus to several other comments of protestation.

In a flurry of frustration, Alistair pushed back his chair and threw his serviette on the table. "It is clear that no opinion is acceptable in this house that does not toe the party line, so I will spare you all what you perceive as my unpleasant company." With that, he strode out of the room.

"I'm so sorry, everyone, but to you, James, my deepest apologies," said Bethany, wiping her eyes.

"Not to worry, Bethy. I'm just sorry that my invitation to you to accompany us and document our work caused such a rift between you. I had no idea it was such a problem or that you and he were having problems, as it appears you are."

Unable to speak, Bethany just shook her head.

"Well, let's just leave it there for the moment, all right?" said Lauren brightly, with a calming hand on Bethany's shoulder. "Now, who wants what?" she said, brandishing the fork. Her gaze settled on Nick, who blew her a kiss.

"I want medium, and Marcia will have rare," said Thomas, "and I propose a second toast:

To the Brandons--extended family included—may we always be strong and united!"

After dinner, when everyone had retired to the veranda, Bethany walked into the sitting room. "Alistair, there you are." She approached him confidently. "We need to talk."

He looked up from his phone and sighed. "What is it you wish to say now, Bethany? I would have thought your offensive performance at dinner was sufficiently clear."

Bethany shook her head, chuckling. "You simply cannot resist making me the bad guy, can you?"

"When the shoe fits..." he retorted.

"Seriously, Alistair, we ought to be able to speak without further argumentation; we need to do so if for no better reason than the sons we have together. I'm asking you to set aside your displeasure with me for their sakes." Bethany plopped onto the loveseat opposite him, leaning forward.

"Fine, Bethany, carry on," he said, with a sarcastic tone and wave of his hand.

"Neither of us has been happy for a long time, Alistair. At least, that's my perception. It's not fair to either of us; it certainly is not fair to our boys. I..."

"Not fair! That's priceless!" he interrupted. "I'll tell you what's not fair!" he spat, rising. "It's not fair that I have a wife who does nothing but complain about me and has no hesitation in doing so in public like tonight's display! It's not fair that I have a completely ungrateful wife for all the benefits she enjoys, thanks to my hard work! It's not fair that my wife disregards my opinion and goes skiving off with her brother to parts unknown on some lark of a journey and then expects me to partake in a celebration of the fact! It's not fair that my wife cannot manage to be civil most of the time! It's not fair that after all these years of marriage, I feel as if I've wasted time and energy, yes, even my marital life! That and a host of other things is what's not fair!" He pointed his finger in her face. "YOU are the one who's not been fair, Bethany... YOU!" He turned, seething, and walked to the windows overlooking the veranda and garden where the family's balance shared evening coffee.

She shook her head. "Do you feel better now?"

"No, I don't feel better. I'm very agitated, but I feel as if I've said what had to be said and what needed saying for a long time." Alistair was breathing heavily.

Bethany rubbed her face with her hands. "Alistair, I'm sure from your point of view that you feel justified. I'm asking you to consider the other side of the coin: the way things are and have been from my perspective. Do you think you can do that? Will you do that for just a few moments?"

"Go ahead, Bethany. I gather that was your intent all along anyway." Alistair turned from the window, looking at his wife with anger and disgust. "For now, I shall agree to be a captive audience."

"Alistair, when we married those many years ago, it seemed as if we had the world by the tail. We got along well; you made me laugh; we shared mutual hopes for the future; we were compatible; you seemed to like who I was; you even expressed pride in my professional accomplishments, such as they were at the time. I thought you loved me, and I thought I loved you. Agreed, so far?"

"Yes, yes, Bethany, but that was then, and this is now." Alistair sighed, shaking his head in disdain.

"As time progressed, your business life expanded, as did the time you spent away from home. I made a home for us at Red Leaf, attended various events as a corporate wife when required, and raised our boys. I completely set aside my profession and dedicated myself to being your wife and the boys' mother. Correct?" Alistair nodded.

"You and I spent less and less time together as a couple. You were always distracted or dealing with a business call or work even during the short times you were at home with us. You were either traveling or at the London flat for over two-thirds of the time. When we attended any kind of meeting, event, or dinner together, I was more or less on my own to play a good corporate wife. I felt like a show thing, an appendage. Even when we were driving home to the flat, you were uncommunicative, claiming exhaustion or disinterest in anything I had to say. More often than not, I had the feeling that the unspoken words were 'Just sit there and look pretty, Bethany, and don't bother me.'

"Any time I tried to share concerns or interests with you, half the time you never even heard me, much less responded with even a modicum of interest. I don't think you even realize that your pat response to me was, 'Whatever you think, Bethany; I'm off. I'll phone when I can.' That increasingly deteriorating life was very depressing for me because everything I tried made no difference in your attitude." She dabbed at her eyes and snuffled.

"Then you took my boys away at the tender ages of 6 and 8, despite that you knew I was against their attending boarding school. You never even considered the reasons for my objections; what I said didn't matter to you. That's the way it was with everything. What I thought, needed, or wanted was of no concern to you. In your view, my existence should be seeing to your occasional needs, playing the corporate social wife, and acceding to your every wish. You never accepted my having an opinion about anything. You wanted me to set aside any need I might have and occupy myself with luncheons, tennis matches, garden parties, and the like. You wanted an automaton with no mind or thought, an android or a robot!"

As she spoke, Bethany colored and became more animated. "That is what wasn't fair from my perspective, Alistair! You have spent the majority of our marriage in total disregard of me as a person. I could give a thousand other examples over the last ten years, but there seems no point. I don't believe you are happy, and I certainly am not. We need to determine if there remains *anything to salvage* and whether we *care to salvage* our shattered relationship.

"And lastly, just to let you know, I bear some of the responsibility for not facing this off before this. It's just that I kept trying to get around things, make it better, all the while hoping that you might reach whatever pinnacle you sought, and we could have a life together again. When it was clear that wasn't going to happen, I accepted the opportunity to work with James on the dig, to do at least something in which I had an interest and could feel valued for my contribution and abilities. I make no apology for working with my brother, which is far better than having a full-blown affair like other women might have done and do. You'd be surprised just how many of your associates' wives engage in extracurricular activities!"

With that last statement, Alistair gaped at her. "You surely would not have brought that kind of scandal into our lives, Bethany. That would be the lowest of the low."

"Oh, were I cut from a different cloth, I might have, Alistair. You did nothing to prevent it. But I love my family too much to hurt them that way, and I love myself as well. Although I must say, I have come close, if you want to know the truth of it."

"Bethany! I am shocked and appalled!" Alistair was breathing heavily and began to pace. "Your description of our lives dismays me. I cannot believe that is the way you saw things. I have worked hard to provide you a good and decent life. I thought you enjoyed the corporate side of things. Why all the men thought how lucky I was to have such a charming and intelligent wife; they all said such time and again to me. I felt quite proud of you!"

"Wouldn't it have been nice for you to tell me that even once? Wouldn't it have been nice, much less enjoyable for you to sample the 'intelligent wife' part even occasionally? Wouldn't it have been nice to ask me about something, *anything*, as distinct to always giving me marching orders, or *your* agenda, or an 'I'd appreciate it if you could...'? You forgot about the living, breathing person who had limits, interests, needs, and opinions. You treated me like just another belonging, a minion, a pet horse you trotted out when you wanted to impress. After I served my purpose as an egg donor, nanny, wife—and performed whatever tricks you required—I got locked up in the stable again. Do you know that once one of the boys said that I reminded him of Rapunzel when I was reading them the story? That's how pathetic my life was: even the boys saw the emptiness... the isolation."

Alistair paced with his hands behind his back, looking alternately at the floor and at Bethany. "I don't quite know what to say. I shall have to think about all this. We are miles apart in our view of things. It may be that we are miles apart in what we want from life as well, but we should both devote some time to determine that before speaking further."

"All right, Alistair, that's sensible, so long as we don't let it go too long. But I think you should have a word with James. Your barbed comments at dinner that elicited my outburst spoiled the dinner celebration and warrant your apology. He didn't deserve what happened; neither did the others who were a part of the enterprise. As for Mummy, I can't think what possessed you to show such nastiness, given the Love she has shown you. You were beyond malicious. I demand you apologize to her tonight. I'm sorry, Alistair, but your expressed wrath made you look like an ass and a vicious one at that. I cannot speak with you again unless you apologize to my mother. I mean it, Alistair." She stood and began walking toward the door.

"Bethany..." Alistair called after her. She stopped without turning around. "I don't know if we can fix this, but for what it's worth, I'm sorry. If things are as you represented, you haven't deserved the last several years or tonight either. I will speak to Marcia tonight. I cannot promise to speak to James or anything more; this evening has been quite trying, and I have my limits."

She didn't speak as weeping closed her throat as she proceeded into the hall.

Bethany went to the stables and bridled one of the geldings she usually rode. The idea of sharing chit chat and coffee with the family after her stand-off with Alistair seemed ludicrous. She needed time away from everything and everyone. Serious situations had bubbled to the surface. As usual, her reactions were head-on and not the most diplomatic of choices. She never had an easy time standing down when she perceived glaring wrong in front of her. There was no question in her mind that Alistair was wrong. Wrong, wrong, wrong -- now and in years past!

As the gelding walked toward the river beyond the stables, she reviewed many different times over the years when she had attempted to bridge the gap between them. Always, the result had been the same: an impervious shield, a brick wall; no satisfaction; no acceptance. She scoured her memory to identify a time, just once over recent years, when Alistair encouraged her about anything, much less showed any interest in her or what she did or thought. As usual, she came up empty, sadness flooding through her. They were well and truly "over."

She touched the gelding's flanks lightly, and he cantered over the field, drawing them closer to the river. As she gazed on the water moved along by a lazy, almost invisible current, her thoughts returned to Syria, when she and Amir hid behind the waterfall beyond the dig, having escaped the bandits (for lack of a better word). In three days, Amir learned more about her than her husband knew after ten years.

Despite their precarious circumstances, she felt alive and valued during that time more than she had in many years' past. Amir had been patient, respectful, and caring, asking nothing in return. As a result, they shared more than either of them intended, about which she had no regrets. Their immediate future was unknown during their time of hiding and not particularly hopeful; their circumstances separated them from their past; their present was unsustainable. All that mattered in those dangerous, insecure days was surviving from moment to moment, living in the "now" because of awareness that tomorrow might never be. Still, she pulsated, feeling alive, happy, and at peace. An unusual, surreal circumstance far from the monotony of ordinary life and its distractions? Indubitably! But perhaps she was so numbed that the restoration to feeling required extreme conditions and a highly unlikely partner.

'My God! A Muslim!' she thought to herself. His relationship with her defied cultural practices intrinsic to him, much more, violated some of his faith's tenets. She did not want to cause him harm or unhappiness, but she had unintentionally done so. He was complicit, as well, and would have to bear the burden of his share of responsibility. He was honorable, and she knew he would do so without any prodding. They needed to discuss this together, but not now. Now, she had to concentrate on her immediate steps for the coming weeks, her boys, and her future. Baby steps; one step at a time; remain calm; focus on the end goal: she could do it. She was a "Brandon."

"There you are, Bethany! I was getting concerned," James said as he bounded out of his chair to hug her. "Things ok?"

"Yes and no," she responded, "but they'll get better with time. Alistair and I had a dress-down, not the productive type of argument that arrives at solutions, but we at least cleared some very stale air between us. I'm somewhat relieved, even if I hate myself for losing composure over his shenanigans."

"Don't be ridiculous," her father said, "come here, you. You are entitled to disagree with anything or anyone if it is hurtful, whether it's your husband, your brother, your parents, other relatives, or your friends." Bethany walked to her father and sat on the veranda between his legs while he stroked her hair.

"Look, all of you, I know I can be insufferable at times. I know my tongue can be sharp. I have no excuse, but I do have an explanation. I have been singularly miserable for several years. All that pent-up emotion colored all my exchanges in relationships, depending on my stress levels. I felt like I was suffocating or drowning and had to claw my way to a breathable space just to be heard, to survive. Sounds crazy, doesn't it? Well, I'm not certifiable yet! I've told Alistair that things are over unless we can find a way to resolve the pattern of our life and relationship."

"What did he say?" asked her mother. "Don't share if it's

too personal or painful, darling."

"No, Mum, it's ok. He's going to 'think' about it, and we'll talk again. He wasn't pleased with me or the fact that I didn't give in and defer to his demands. He acted viciously; I told him he was nasty, and I demanded he apologizes. He promised he'd consider one for you, Mummy, but not James, me, or anyone else."

"What a condescending, sanctimonious ass! He needs and deserves a good throttling, that's what!" Nick spat.

Lauren smiled, calmly refilling everyone's cup. "Not everyone acts with good sense or reason all the time." Nick looked at her and blanched.

"I couldn't help but think of our chat so long ago, Auntie Lauren. Do you remember? We were on the veranda the night of James' and Rachel's engagement? You gave me a formula for knowing when one is in love. I have recalled that conversation many times over the last ten years and realized that your formula clarifies when you are in love and when you are not. I owe you a belated 'thank you.'"

"Love has a way of echoing through the years, honey. I'll always be here for you," Lauren said softly. "All of us will."

After the team attended a series of meetings with the British Museum and several associated authorities to submit verification of provenance and all related aspects of their expedition and its composite "finds," James and Bethany stole away. They needed some precious "down" time alone. Driving through the impossibly green countryside toward Cambridge, Bethany felt freer than she had in years.

"James, I'd like to share something with you for an honest comment, ok?"

Quickly turning his head to assess her, James said, "Of course, Beth. Is it the kind of sharing that will go down better with a pint?"

She grinned. "Sounds wonderful to me, but no, you don't have to stop if you'd prefer driving on. I just need a sounding board, is all."

"There's a quiet little place not far from here and, as we're not due to Auntie Lauren's until sevenses, we have time. I think you'll like it: they have a rough lawn set up with tables under the trees, and the ducks walk by on their way to the pond. Just mind where you walk! I don't fancy duck droppings on my car mats."

Once seated at a table in the shade and sipping their chosen brews, Bethany began. "It's been a while since that dust-up at Waverlee with Alistair. In the interim, we've chatted privately and with our solicitors. I expect proceedings to get down to earnest in a few weeks."

"Ah, I'm sorry, Bethy, unless that's the way you want things to go," her brother offered sincerely. "Whatever the path, please know I'm here for help or advice. I want you to be fairly treated, Bethany. Don't walk away from this without your just dues."

"Thanks, James, but the solicitor Father recommended has things well in hand. That's just the preamble to the meat of what I wanted to run by you."

James reached for her hand. "Go on, Bethy, there's nothing you can't tell me."

"We've agreed that the boys' lives should not suffer dramatic change, so they will stay at boarding school for the present unless the news is so troubling to them as to demand an alteration. I suspect they will not be all that surprised. So long as I can see them and explain the situation, I think they will prefer to stay at school because it, at least, is stable and continuing. They've made some friends and are doing well in their studies."

"Good lads, they are, Beth. It will still be a bit tough on them as they're young, but their relationship with you is strong enough to get through this; I passionately believe that. Please ensure you tell them they may speak with me at any time. I'll drive there, or they may come to us. I will accept phone charges at any time of the night or day. Father and Mum feel the same. I find children react more openly when they know there's a backup plan on which they can rely if a situation seems too much to bear on their own. Rachel is on board, too."

"So, the family has been speculating about my circumstances, eh?" Bethany laughed. "I suspected as much, knowing you lot. No, it's ok with me, James," she said, shaking her head when it was apparent that her brother was troubled by her remark. "I expected that to happen. I know you have my best interests at heart, as well as my boys' secure future. Has Amir spoken to you as well?"

"Only to inquire about your well-being and to ask if I knew of your forward plans. Why?"

"Just wondered. We got remarkably close in that hideout,

talking for hours and hours. I shared my unhappiness and history with Amir. Not knowing if we'd ever make it out safely and alive or get discovered and left for the vultures changes the way you live every moment. I would have been dead without him, James." She tipped her mug to drain it, looking steadily at her brother to monitor his reaction. "He kept me alive; he made me want to live. I'll never forget him for that and other reasons, as well."

"Yes," he softly whispered. "I still carry guilt about leaving the two of you there. But none of us imagined that Abed was a 'plant' in our expedition and was in league with that group. He checked out fine and had known Moha and Hasan for years. I often wonder if he took part in their killing. To all intents and purposes, leaving you and Amir at camp with three men seemed safe. Nick and Andy were more concerned about Nigel and me being on those long stretches of desert roadways alone. Once we unveiled things at their ministry in the city, unstable at the best of times, the associated risk would put us in very tenuous circumstances. That place leaks like a sieve, and the news would spread like wildfire—and did—placing us at risk. Nick and Andy did their jobs well. I'm not sure we would have made it back to you on our own, much less be able to stabilize the situation once back at camp, as they did."

"We all know Nicky is used to that sort of thing, even though retired. But Uncle Andy? He's retired CIA, but as I understand it, his job was more intellectual than hand-to-hand, according to Mum." Bethany leaned forward, "Do you know any differently?"

"He shared with me a long time ago that his job dealt more with posing solely as an academic in scientific circles and either getting or dropping information or messages than as an active operative. He told me about a hilarious incident when he was running from someone after his cover was blown. He ended up in Port Grimaud in the south of France on a nude beach. He shed his clothes and swam out to a windsurfing group and, as typical to Uncle Andy, charmed the ladies straightaway, thereby looking like any other swimmer in the surf. His pursuers thought they lost him and left to search elsewhere. As Uncle Andy tells it, that little detour—despite that, it saved him—caused the loss of a week. He said he caught hell once he reported back in. He claimed he had to stay a week with one of the women to solidify his cover before he deemed it safe to move on!" Both James and Bethany laughed at their uncle's antics.

"I wonder if that was 'before or after' Aniela," Bethany quipped.

"Oh, well before. Those two are forever solid. But Mum did share that they had an ugly encounter during their European operation when they smuggled The Message to the free world. Both he and Aniela had to fight for their lives, and each of them killed someone in the struggle. I understand there were several assassins on their trail, each representative of different factions. There was more to it, but of course, it is classified. Aniela suffered PTSD, and Uncle Andy struggled a long time because of taking a human life. After all, he's an academic at heart and takes his faith very seriously. On another note, I do sometimes feel that Aniela longs for Europe, so I wouldn't be surprised if they move back to spend their golden years here or somewhere on the continent."

"It would be nice, James, to have easier access to them. I know Mum would love it, and Auntie Lauren and Aniela clicked with each other."

James paid for their tab when their second-round arrived. "Now, back to you, love."

Smiling at him, Bethany took a breath and sighed. "I am considering putting together a volume in celebration of women, short on text and heavy on representational photographs, from cultures around the globe. The theme is 'ordinary women can and have accomplished extraordinary things.' I've already had preliminary conversations with Nat Geo, and they are fundamentally on board. They know my photographic work from the past.

"I need and want to do something of value, James. I'm a reasonably good and successful photographer. Still, I don't want to do horse shows, weddings, or formal portraits, and to repeat the type of shoots I did for Nat Geo in the past would seem like replays of 'been there, done that' sort of thing. Do you understand?"

"Yes, I take your point, Bethy, and I think the idea sounds splendid! When do you hope to begin?" James asked excitedly.

"I don't know exactly, but certainly not until this mess is over with Alistair. In the meantime, I'm busy researching. I want to ensure that what I identify will impact people's consciousness. I hope to create a new awareness with all that the book presents. After what we found on the 'dig,' I was so inspired, James! And after all my woes, doing something worthwhile that I have an affinity to, that I feel a synergy with—well, it all just seemed to come together. It's the kind of thing that could also be a photographic exhibition or a coffee table book. So, I need all the help and suggestions I can get!"

Thoughtfully, James said, "Look here, Beth. I think you should share this with Lauren. She's an artist and has had exhibitions. I'd bet she would have some solid advice for you."

"You're right! Isn't it lucky we're on our way to the Tower to meet up with her and Uncle Nick? Capital! And I'll bet Nicky can fill me in on the right way to proceed with authorities, particularly in touchy countries. Foreigners are not always welcome, much less foreign women! Truthfully, I'm not eager to visit the Middle East any time soon after our last junket."

"I can fully understand that. But there's a big world out there, Love, so you have your pick and choice, as they say." Taking his sister's arm, James and Bethany walked to his car, animatedly chatting about her prospects. Opening her door, James said, "Good to have you back, Bethy."

Looking up, she said, smiling, "Good to be on the road back. I remember what it feels like to be happy, and I'm holding on tightly!" James nodded.

Chapter Two
The Dig: Part 1

They had been driving for hours, the view beyond the dust clad vehicle's windows a monotonous, barren beige with only an occasional outcropping of windswept, bleak stone.

"Are we there yet?" quipped Bethany in a child's mocking voice.

"Almost," said James, joining in with the laughter. "It should be just around those next hills with the flat top between two rounded crests. The cave entrance is at its base. Nigel said they'd have a decent dinner waiting for us. I suggest we all relax this evening and get a fresh start in the morning. No need to be up too early, as we'll be inside the cave where the heat of the day won't intrude. So, let's say, breakfast at 8:00 AM?"

"Copy that," said Nick.

"Roger," chimed in Andy.

"I thought you said no need for an 'early' start? Eight o'clock in the morning isn't exactly what I'd call 'sleeping in,'" chimed in Bethany.

"Bethy, you have my assurance, you'll not find it difficult to awaken with the heat and the uncomfortable cot! We're not in Kansas anymore," jibed James to the other men's chuckles.

"Yeah, yeah, smarty pants. Just don't forget, I can rough it as well as you lot, and have on my previous photoshoots!"

"Touché!" said James, pointing to a spiral of smoke beyond the nearing hills. "That's our camp, I reckon."

As they veered off the dirt track toward the clearing, a tall, lanky man in a broad-brimmed hat approached, waving. "Hail, hail, the gang's all here!" called Nigel, with arms outstretched. The team hopped out of the Land Rover, and James did the introductions.

"I'm so glad all of you could come. I can use the help. My

benefactor is generous, but he has no real idea of what we do for a project. He's more used to an African safari! But we have a decent cook and other men to help with the grunt work. So, let's get you settled in."

Nick and Andy helped Amir unload the second vehicle laden with tents, equipment, and sparse personal gear. At the same time, James and Bethany followed Nigel to the center of the area to meet the waiting Jordanians and discuss the camp layout. There were three small sleeping tents adjacent to one another and an adequate short supply and cook tent several paces away in front of a good-sized campfire surrounded by a stone perimeter.

"There's only scrub wood out here, but it burns well enough. We got here only late yesterday, so I'm afraid we've done only the bare minimum," said Nigel apologetically. "My first trip was a month or so ago. It took forever to jump through the hoops for a second foray, so you'll find things a bit less than ideal to begin. But once we send verification back, then things will change, I'm certain of that. At least the authorities have closed the site and surrounding area to the public."

"That was no mean accomplishment on its own, Nigel. Congrats, mate!" complimented James.

"We saw a slight bit of smoke as we approached," said Bethany. "I presume you keep the fire going only in the late afternoons and at night?"

"Yes, that's right. We shall need to conserve what few natural resources are available to us, but there are a small waterfall and pool on the side of that hill that rings this plain," Nigel said, pointing, "so we've got water, which in this terrain is a huge bonus! The surrounding ground there is where we gather downed wood and scrub for the fire. Once you're unloaded and set up, we'll all have a stroll around, so you get the lay of the land. Sound good?"

In short order, they erected tents in an area surrounding a central communal campfire. The shared work tent contained each team member's equipment. Its position in the center of the sleeping tent area provided protection and immediate access. Familiar with the region, Nick brought two satellite phones, electronic and defensive gear, which he and Andy were busy cleaning, assembling, and testing. Bethany worked at checking and cleaning the photographic equipment, setting up a small folding table to hold various plastic containers, cameras, supplies, notebooks, and journals.

Outside the work tent, porters busily engaged in setting the perimeter with motion detectors and night cameras, filling water tanks and containers, and stacking firewood. Two men dug a small, secondary firepit close to the cook tent from which wafted scents promising dinner. The hired help's sleeping tents were beyond the tent housing tools and other equipment, all neatly stowed within. The sleeping area of the principal parties formed the left flank of the semicircle, the hired help tents creating the right side with work and equipment tents at the center. A third, small, stone encircled area for a campfire was at the semicircle's center. The watch guards would keep this campfire burning throughout each night, while the other one outside the cook tent would smolder to hot coals to await rekindle in the morning for breakfast preparation.

When all were awake, breakfasted, and briefed, the work party walked excitedly to the hillside cave opening. Hasan, Abed, and Moha (who doubled as a cook) supplemented the team. The core team amply covered the needs of this phase of the project and was comprised of:

- Nigel Rutherford (the "official" overall head of the expedition on behalf of his collector-benefactor);
- Nick Lawson (as unofficial team leader overseeing everyone's safety);
- Andrew Stanton (Nick's security counterpart and assistant linguist well-versed in ancient languages);
- James Brandon (co-archaeologist with Nigel, famed in his own right for legitimate and accepted ancient discoveries and translations);
- Bethany Brandon-Maxwell (photographer, whose task it was to document every aspect of the expedition's undertakings as well as photograph the inscriptions for the overall presentation and up-close version); and
- Bin Amir Najjar (archaeologist and Andy's associate on many "digs").

Accompanying the team for their first entry, Hasan looked back at his companions, stacking the wood at the entrance for the platform they planned to build to enable better scrutiny and photographic documentation. He, Abed, and Moha had drawn straws for their participation. Hasan shivered slightly, wishing that he had not picked the long straw.

The group made its way carefully down the long and winding tunnel, the air more humid the farther they penetrated. The lanterns cast an eerie glow on the tunnel walls, glistening with moisture and muted, striated colors. An hour's trek with each member of the team carrying equipment took its physical toll. No one talked; all were moving more slowly and breathing heavily.

"It seems you left out a thing or three about this expedition, Nigel," Bethany said sardonically. 'A short walk down a tunnel' hardly describes this trek." Her remark was joined by a few quiet snickers and some mumbling.

"Now, now," retorted Nigel, "one cannot expect a prize such as this to be around a corner for the plucking, can one? Otherwise. It would have been plundered years ago."

They came to what seemed the end of the tunnel. A towering wall of rock reached upward from the open space at the tunnel's end, beyond their line of sight.

"Ah, here we are at last," Nigel told the group. "Let's take a short break for rest and water. Then we'll take the path and one last hop, skip and jump, and we'll be there!"

The team looked at each other in confusion. Nick spoke up. "Nige, what path?"

"Why, this one, of course! Can't you see it?" he said, pointing upward. "Look for the depression under that ledge about halfway up and trace down backward." The man was clearly excited.

Looking up, Bethany said derisively, "I hate heights, Nigel. You could have warned me!"

Approximately 100' above them, a narrow, cantilevered ledge protruded from the wall. Immediately beneath it, the stone looked dark and dimpled. Apparently, that was the continuation of the access to the cavern about which Nigel spoke. The "path" to which he referred angled diagonally from the rock wall base to the depression above them. Unless one knew the path was there, it was virtually undetectable from the perspective of someone standing at ground level.

"Will we need climbing gear?" Nick asked brusquely, not at all pleased at being deprived of what he considered critical information.

"Oh, no, not at all. The path is sufficiently wide for human passage. You'll see. But, uh, we might wish to rig something to hoist some of the larger bags and bulky equipment. I had none of that when I was here last, just my rucksack." Nigel said meekly, sensing the simmering displeasure among the team.

"Lovely," muttered Nick, rifling through one of the bags. Andy joined Nick in placing the bags in some harnesses and readying coils of rope, one of which was rigged with a large pulley. "God damned academic! All he sees are rainbows!" Nick mumbled. "What if we hadn't brought any of this gear with us? Idiot!" Andy said nothing but silently agreed with Nick. He, too, was an academic, but one whose experience and background was steeped in practicality and logic.

When the team was rested, and the gear readied, Nick took charge, saying, "Nigel, you will lead the way; I'll follow with the ropes and set some bashies[1] and anchors. The rest of you wait for my ok, then come by pairs, maintaining the 5'5" single rope distance allowed between you. Check with your partner before unclipping your carabiner and moving to the next one. Slowly but surely, using this method, everyone will get to the ledge safely.

"Bethany, you and Andy will be the last pair. Andy, make sure her chest harness and carabiner are correctly fastened; I suggest a figure 8." Directing his last comment to Bethany—knowing she would fare better with "knowing" what was planned, he said, "It's a climbing knot used for tying the climbing rope to a climber's harness, as in belaying or rappelling, Bethy. That will keep you safe and secure, I promise.

"Hasan, you attach the equipment parcels to the ropes I cast down. You and I will pulley them up. Then you can climb using the bashies for your snap link and the single rope safety line I'll rig on the ascent.

"A few last things, so listen up: These are only precautions; you can all do this. After all, Nigel, here, did it without any aids on his own. That alone should give you confidence." Everyone laughed, including Nigel.

"But we're taking these measures to account for the unforeseeable. If someone should sneeze, take a misstep, or lose balance, the single rope to your partner will halt a fall because each of you will have your end of a Kevlar rope clipped to the wall anchor with a carabiner. So, nobody can go over the side and pull another with him, got it? Use the single rope I'll set into the rock face for extra confidence if you like. It's there for a purpose and is around 11 mm in thickness, so it can support a fall. We'll leave everything in place for our safe descent. Right, then, let's move out."

---

1 Bashies are malleable anchors "bashed" into small cracks for use in aid climbing; tough to remove.

Nigel and Nick reached the ledge without so much as a pebble falling to the waiting group below them. Nick set a bombproof anchor[2] around a huge boulder a short way down the passage near the ledge. Next, he uncoiled the long rope after securing the pulley to the bombproof anchor rope with a closed-gate carabiner and dropped it to the waiting Hasan. Nick called down to Andy to get the group moving.

"And Andy, I figured you'd know, but just in case... I want you to belay[3] Bethany. I suggest a clove hitch[4]. "

"Yeah, bud, I figured that out when you unpacked the rack[5]. Same page and all that."

"What? Andy? Don't you think for a minute that you're going to keep me back from scaling that puny little hill!"

"No, honey, I'm not, and I wouldn't. It's a climbing term, that's all. Just for safety. You know you're 'precious cargo' to Nick as well as to me." Assuaged, Bethany smiled and nodded, oblivious to the meaning behind the exchange.

After ascending the steep path to the ledge and the narrow passage beyond, the team removed and coiled their ropes, repacking the waiting gear bags. Ahead lay a narrow crevasse which showed bare evidence of a decayed bridge of sorts. Using short ropes and carabiners, each team member leaped across the 3' gash safely without incident, the bags of equipment tossed to the cavern side. The tunnel's end was in sight, the opening dark, providing no hint at the space beyond. They reached the large cavern, and Andy shined the light diffuser inside as one by one, the team members walked forward, panning their lanterns around the space. No one spoke; everyone's eyes scanned the walls, ceiling, and rock formations in awe.

"This is truly one of the world's wonders," whispered Bethany, breaking the silence.

"Deus Magnus est! Allah' Akbar! Dieu est grand! Gott ist großartig! Dio è grande!; Mae Duw yn wych! Tá Dia go hiontach! Unkulunkulu mkhulu! God is great!" chanted Andy as he took intrepid steps to make a complete circle within the cavernous space.

"What the hell was that Uncle Andrew?" laughed James.

---

2   Bombproof hold or anchor is a top rope anchor around a large, immovable boulder or stable tree trunk, providing the maximum security possible
3   Body belay: technique using the friction of the rope passing around belayer's body to slow and hold a fall; often painful for belayer and not effective in all situations but used in emergencies where no belay device is available.
4   Knot for tying a climbing rope to an anchor to belay the next climber.
5   The selection of gear used for a climb; also, a sling full of climbing gear.

"It was, oh, about eight ways to say, 'God is great,' I believe, James," said Amir softly. "People pray and praise in different ways. Let's see, I think Latin, Arabic, French, German, "Amir said, pausing to recollect, "Italian, Welsh, Irish, Zulu, and English!"

James just shook his head in amazement. "You two are 'peas in a pod' sometimes."

"To be sure, an odd combination, but then, your Uncle is not what one would call a 'typical' man, is he? I've always found him intriguing, a study in opposites. 'Odd' some would call him." Amir said quietly. "I think he's as close to a genius as I've ever met."

"If we encouraged him to go on, I'll bet he'd start on ancient languages or..." James joked.

"All right, enough, boys. It's his way of inclusive praise, ok? That brain of his goes through languages like lightning. It's some sort of genetic wiring anomaly. Mum told me about it once. Maybe he's just got a touch of autism; who knows or cares? What counts is, it works and works well—for us and the world. So, zip it, guys; he might hear you." Bethany scowled at the two men, who looked suitably contrite.

Meanwhile, Andy's voice decreased to a whisper, his lips still moving in unfamiliar syllables, his eyes full of wonder, a soft sheen of sweat covering his face.

"Is he ok?" inquired James.

"He's fine; just give him a minute, mate. He's having one of his' moments,' that's all. Whenever he encounters something wondrous in humankind's history, it turns spiritual for him. Nothing to concern yourself with; he's just 'different' to you and me, that's all. Perhaps we ought to take a page from his book, yeah? Enough with the chatter," said Nick, allowing his military side to show slightly. These days, Nick had a way of delivering the final word. He learned his lessons well from his relationship with Lauren, who always bested him by getting in the last word to close a discussion... *every time* about *everything*.

Intuitive and outspoken to a fault, the unkempt, unruffled Bethany said, "And wouldn't Auntie Lauren be proud of you, Uncle Nicky!" She smiled mischievously when he looked at her with surprise.

Nick scratched his head and wiped the sweat from his face, realizing the import of her remark. "Enough from you, too, missy!"

"I knew this would affect you all, as it did me, but I say, I didn't quite expect this! Still, let's get a move on, shall we? We all have our list of tasks--chop, chop, time is money, you know!" Nigel kneeled to begin unpacking his knapsack, and Hasan snapped the portable table together where Nigel wanted it placed off to the side.

"Glad you're back with us, mate," said Nick. "Let's get to it then, shall we?" Andy nodded, smiling sheepishly, and joined the others, each doing his/her assigned tasks. In short order, the generator whirred, and light bloomed, eliciting even more exclamations as the ancient petroglyphs and paintings came to life all around them.

Nigel rocked on his heels delightedly. "I told you it was magnificent!"

"How did this go unnoticed for so long?" queried Nick.

"It's a simple matter of geology, my friend. The caves in this region have been heavily explored and excavated since the early '90s, only thirty years after their discovery. Full exploration had to await political stasis as no one was permitted anywhere near them for years. Nobody wanted to be in the country with such unrest unless they had a screw loose or a death wish. So, they sat. Then when the categorization and mapping began, it was discovered that the cave system—much larger than originally thought—had undergone the rigors of seepage, erosion, collapse in some places, and a revelation in others. But the definitive mapping and continued exploration were halted because of dangerous conditions. My guy got hold of some of his cronies in our field, got hold of some original sketches and maps, hatched this idea, talked to me, I talked to you, and here we are! What? Bloody marvelous, yeah?" Nigel beamed.

"Before I start clicking away, Nigel, will you and James demarcate the sections in order of catalog importance? It's helpful from a frame ID perspective to have everything for a full section's mass representation and the in-depth study of individual marks or pictures. Of course, you'll want to take care not to insinuate on any image too closely." Passing him several rolls of tape (which left no residue), she fiddled with her equipment bags.

Bethany was offhand in the delivery of her request, unaware that the others were staring at her. "What?' she asked after a minute or so passed when she noticed they were all staring at her silently.

Nigel cleared his throat noticeably. Nick looked at the ground. Andy grinned, and Amir slightly shook his head.

James said, "Bethy, why, of course, yes... we were just about to do that. We know what we're doing, but I think the problem might be that these others here don't realize that you know what we've got to do, as well—you know, from hanging around with me for so many years and listening to my stories. Plus, it's considered more usual and protocol for the head of the expedition to give the go-ahead and assignments unless announced otherwise. Ok, sweetheart?" Silence.

"Well, don't look so bloody embarrassed, all of you! Sorry I made a blunder, Nigel. I'm just eager to get on with it. And in the future, James, first and foremost, do not 'sweetheart' me! A 'shut-up, Beth' will suffice." She motioned toward the wall in a propelling motion, and everyone laughed.

"You are truly 'one of the guys,' Miss Bethany," smirked Amir.

"Right! Now, James, if you'll assist me with the markers and string, Amir, hold the quadrant labels in place as we go along. Nick and Andy skirt the perimeter assessing all faults or concerns in the topography, geologic structure, etc.–you get my meaning, yes? Hasan, head back out, gather your mates, start carrying in the lumber for the scaffolding and prepare the tools and other materials. Bethany, I'd like you at the ready to snap when I tell you so we can make rapid progress, if you please. Chop, chop, lads... and Lady!" said Nigel, clapping his hands. It was a long, long day of work.

When they were relaxing around the campfire after dinner in the late evening, Nigel shared, "For those unfamiliar with pre-historic art, we've come to dub cave painting as parietal art. That label means any artwork on walls, floor, or ceilings of ancient shelters to which colored pigments were applied. At Chauvet, they used only one color ...black... making a monochrome image, whereas at Altamira and Lascaux, polychrome images—using two or more colors—were found. That pretty much defines 'cave painting' in a nutshell.

"Then we have cave drawing. That refers to an incised or engraved picture usually thought to occur by cutting into the rock surface with a flint or stone tool. The artist would draw a line onto the rock with charcoal or manganese in the painting. With the drawing—sometimes thought to be the forerunner of bas relief or sculpture--the line is clear-cut or chiseled.

"Do feel free to chime in with questions, you lot. Anytime is fine with me." Nigel poured himself more coffee, spiking it with a splash of Scotch. Bethany inquired when science believed cave painting first began.

"We don't have a clear idea, Beth. Some posit that the arrival of anatomically modern humans during the Upper Paleolithic period starting around 40,000 BCE began the process. That coincided with the displacement of Neanderthal Man. That was also the time when the earliest rock art began to emerge.

"Generally speaking, cave painting and its related techniques began to improve century by century; again, the time frame is uncertain. Then, during the Late Magdalenian period, when the Ice Age ended and a time of global warming occurred, we lost the reindeer habitat, associated human culture, and cave art. That was in the neighborhood of c15-10,000 BCE at Lascaux, Altamira, Les Combarelles, and others.

"I'm particularly encouraged by the excavations at the Cave of Manot in Northern Israel, where they found a partial skull, the oldest modern human remains ever seen outside of Africa. Subsequently, a comprehensive analysis by two dozen researchers from Israeli universities and abroad determined the skull fragment to belong to a young adult who died approximately 55,000 years ago. They also uncovered a treasure trove of artifacts and writings on the cave walls. You see, we had finds from Africa and Europe, but we were missing the connection between them that would confirm what geneticists have been predicting. That find is the connection between the older African populations and the later European people. It supports the theory that humans left Africa around 60,000 years ago and traveled through that region on their way to Europe. The cave writing also helps reinforce that theory, so perhaps you can more clearly understand why I get excited about cave painting and drawing."

"So, our being in Syria with proximity to Israel and this latest find of yours may have more significance than we were aware?"

Looking cagily at Nigel, Bethany raised her eyebrows.

"Perhaps so, Beth, perhaps so. Only time will tell through our exploration of this cave, and it will rely heavily on your documentation, I might add," said Nigel, raising his own eyebrows to her.

He continued, obviously directing his conversation to the men. "What most people don't appreciate is that the preponderance of prehistoric cave paintings displays animals—99% of those discovered, in fact. Initially, predators like lions, saber-toothed felines, and bears were depicted. They stand at roughly the same percentages as reindeer and bison, which science labels as 'game' animals. The animal figures were quite naturalistic, whereas when

23

pictures of humans appeared, rare as it was, the characters were stylized. Then we must include symbols and geometric signs, which are also common, and the oldest type of Paleolithic art found in caves. I'm sure you recall the cave hand stencils."

"What I find fascinating," said James, "is the amount of time and patience each cave painting and drawing took. Take a bison, for example, if I may, Nigel?"

"No, no, go ahead. And when your throat becomes parched as mine is, handoff to Amir!" They laughed together.

"Right then, a bison: first, the drawing of the outline and rudimentary features on the rock wall, for instance. Now, this first stage is done with charcoal or manganese, making a dark outline. The surface rock scored with a sharp stone is destined to be a drawing as distinct to a painting. Then, the animal's figure is colored with pigment—usually red ochre. Third, the figure's edges are shaded with black or another dark pigment to add dimension, just like using light and shadow in the oil paintings or watercolors we hang on our walls today. If the cave wall's contour required it, another stage of engraving or sculpting takes place to give the figure a sense of volume and relief, as in bas relief. Given the tools available, the man had to devote a helluva lot of time to one image between hunting for food and attending to everyday life tasks. That's a sure sign to me of something compelling within, something driving him to make the image, to make time to leave his mark. What do you think?"

"I agree," said Amir. "Mankind's art and music have evolved as his soul has evolved."

"I think you meant to say, 'humankind's soul,' Amir." Bethany smiled at him. "We don't know that the artists were exclusively male, do we?"

"Beg pardon, Miss Bethany," Amir bowed his head, "some habits are difficult to rein in after so many years. In the desert, we tend not to worry too much about 'political correctness' as we do in other civilized places... places like England."

"Really? I thought a major aspect of desert culture was traditional courtesy and hospitality practices, no? 'Mankind' is, you must agree, an exclusive term. Its usage evolved from history's male-dominated societies. The world has changed, has it not? It seems altogether too evident—knowing what we now know from the historical record--that it is discourteous to discount females of the species." Bethany leaned forward, eager for his answer, like a mongoose ready to strike at a cobra.

Amir bowed his head, saying, "Miss Bethany, do not attempt to bait me. As you have said: courtesy and hospitality are essential to the Arab world, especially to Muslims like me. We do not seek deliberately to offend in friendly discourse. It was a simple mistake borne of colloquial language habit and my culture, in which males dominate to this day. That is all. Hereafter, I shall try to remember to speak inclusively by using the word 'humankind.' I sincerely beg your pardon. I had no intention of offending, as I have said." The gentle man spoke these words with his eyes downcast, as was the proper demeanor in his culture when addressing a female.

Ashamed, Bethany said, "I accept your apology, Amir. I didn't intend to offend, either. I seem to be too used to dismissive, demeaning behavior from men."

"No, Bethany, darling, not 'men'; only one man, who has relinquished his right to influence your life, as I see it," said James in support.

"Right, well, I suggest we pick up this discussion on the morrow, what?" Nigel stood. "Good night, all. We leave for the cave at 7:00 AM sharp!"

Sitting with his sister after the others had retired, James asked, "What's up with you, Bethy? This snarky behavior isn't at all like you. You've never been a confrontational bitch by nature. Spirited, independent, a bit sharp in tone sometimes, and capable, yes, but not antagonistic and stroppy."

"Thank you so much, James Brandon!" Bethany emptied her cup and poured a bit of Scotch into it, taking a few deep breaths. "No, forgive me, James, you're right. I've got a lot of mental crap to sort from my last meeting with Alastair just before we departed. I'll bounce back, never you worry."

"You know, you've got a brother here who's got your back, Bethy, don't ever forget that or to use the shoulder that stands waiting." James stood, saying, "Get some sleep, old girl."

The desert's absolute stillness seemed to radiate in concentration and focus of the "now" without any interference. Staring into the fire, Bethany dissected herself: her behavior, her beliefs, her character, her responsibilities, her dreams, and her future for another hour. Finally, feeling somewhat purged, she arose and walked toward her tent.

"I am not going to let you spoil this for me, Alastair," she whispered. "I'm Bethany, the one and only, not the Bethany you turned me into to survive marriage to you!" she said to herself with all the conviction she could muster.

She did not see Amir standing to the side of the work tent.

He remained very still, not wanting to startle or embarrass her, but he heard every word. He smiled.

Chapter Three
The Dig and the Cavern: Part 2

Nick and Andy pulled on their respective ropes to hoist Bethany and her equipment to the top of the scaffold. She clambered over the edge, reaching for her expensive cameras to secure and prevent any banging against the wooden frame.

"Picked up a pound or two, missy? You feel a stone heavier," teased a perspiring Nick.

"Ha! I suspect it's just your age, Uncle Nicky. Whoa, this is really high!" Bethany said, feeling a touch of lightheadedness.

"You ok up there, honey? We don't need you fainting!" Andy called to her.

"A-Okay, Uncle Andy. I'll be fine; I just have to acclimatize my tummy! Now get back to work, you two. I have twenty-four feet of the ceiling to photograph. I shall expect that the next section is ready by the time I finish up here, and we can move the scaffold frame along for tomorrow's shoot."

The three workers built a reasonably stable wooden scaffold under Andy's direction to hold Bethany while shooting various ceiling parts. Nigel and James placed the appropriate markers to identify sections that she would photograph both with and without tags to facilitate two types of presentation with cross-verification. She was determined to put together both a photographic representation in individual shots of various magnifications along with a broad, sectional panorama, followed by a slide presentation. In one of her journals, she carefully cataloged each frame with its digital ID, as well as a figurative description. In another of her diaries, she documented dates, times, and tasks in detail of all participants, including verbal comments as nearly as she could jot them down, with candid photos to accompany her notes. She reviewed this journal with Nigel each evening for the accuracy of the descriptions.

Lying on her back on the edge of the platform after completing ceiling photos from opposing ends to the center, Bethany felt the structure begin to sway.

"Hey, someone! This thing is rocking! Whoa, whoa, now it's wobbling terribly!" she called out. Hassan and Moha rushed to the scaffold, each man reaching toward a vertical strut on opposite sides to stabilize the frame. Abed ran to them, carrying two longboards and tools. Amir joined the group and agreed that the planks might help increase the balance for the teetering top-heavy frame.

"Remain perfectly still, Bethany. Do not change position until we say. Can you do that?" Amir called to her.

"Yes, I'm not going to move a muscle except to lower my camera. Is that ok?" Bethany began to perspire and had the urge to ignore the instruction and scurry from the scaffold's edge. However, she trusted Amir, obeyed, and steadied herself. Slowly, the frame's swaying lost momentum, merely creaking and shuddering. The wall section against which they intended to lean the support planks contained no images or writing, but Amir called the others to assess the situation.

"I think it will work, Amir," said Nigel. "If you place them at a 45-degree angle on this side and that end, it should do the trick. What do you lads think?"

"It wouldn't hurt to have more than two, Nige, together with some cross beams to tie it all together," offered Andy, who was familiar with construction from the past helping his father repair their barns.

"We could fit the structure with guide wires or cables on both sides, anchoring them to the floor with stakes. Then we just pop them and reset as we move along the ceiling." James inspected the floor of the cave to determine and recheck its composition.

"I just hate to deface this treasure in any way, James, even if it's the floor we stand on. I give you that we've already examined it for anything of value archaeologically. I know Amir took samples earlier just for verification, but I don't know if I approve of the idea of hammering or drilling into it." Nigel walked around, looking up, down, and beside the scaffolding. The men kept discussing and sharing ideas to solve the situation. With every passing minute, Bethany grew more anxious.

"Hello! Remember me?" she called out, her words bouncing off the ceiling back at her.

"Hold on, Beth, we're working on it," responded Andy.

28

The consensus was to steady the frame by placing stabilizers at an angle on the long sides and end closest to the cave walls while creating an opposing force using additional boards placed against free-standing boulders on the cave floor. Andy's assurance that the 12'x24' frame could not go against the laws of physics and topple end over end, particularly with stress placed against the long sides for solidity and strength, fostered unanimous agreement. The plan also allowed for minimum interference with the entire site to Nigel's relief, who barked orders to the men to begin the process.

Abed used the sledgehammer on the last of the placed struts at the narrow, 12' end of the frame. With a mighty swing, he hammered home. Everyone heard groaning and a rumbling sound. Then the floor began to vibrate, and the frame shivered. Bits of the undecorated ceiling close to the tunnel entrance fell to the floor. Bethany screamed. The rumbling became louder; the grinding increased without its previous intermittence. Someone yelled, "Cave in!"

Nigel and Nick yelled orders to the men to secure and protect the equipment by moving it into the tunnel. James called to Bethany. "Jump, sweetheart! Jump to me; I'll catch you!"

"But I took my harness off, James! You told me to take it off! It's too high; I'll kill us both!" she wailed. "Go on, you go, and I'll try to climb down!"

"No, Bethy! Do as I tell you: jump to me! I'll catch you, and we'll roll together; it'll work!"

"My cameras!" Bethany cried. "I can't leave my cameras and all we've got!"

"God damn it, Beth, stop wasting time we don't have! Jump!" James yelled desperately.

"Drop your cameras to me one at a time," yelled Amir, who had run over to the scaffold to assist James and Bethany. "I will catch them!"

Bethany looped her mid-sized digital around her neck, dropping the larger one with the large, unique lens, her small 35mm camera, her bag of lenses, and her bag of journals one by one to Amir in quick succession. Fortunately, the cameras and lenses were still in their cases, making it easier for Amir to grab them as they fell to him. She looked at James amid the dust and falling debris, struggling to muster her balance as she crouched atop the shimmying platform. Bethany closed her eyes and...

The next thing she felt was James' arms closing tightly

around her and rolling her over and over. She fought to catch her breath; she was having difficulty seeing through the cloud of dust.

"Come on!" James said, yanking on her arm until she was standing. At the run, James, Bethany, Amir—loaded down with Bethany's equipment bags--headed for the tunnel opening. The noise level was deafening in the confined space. Once inside the tunnel with a dust cloud following them, the trio ran, retracing their entry steps on the heels of those in front, struggling with the equipment they rescued. As the group exited the tunnel to the ledge and wall path, they hastened in their descent.

"Careful as you go," intoned Nick. "Trust yourself and the process, and be sure to hook your carabiners. We've got time to make it. Slow and steady, now, everyone!"

Finally, they exited the extended access tunnel leading from the rock wall with its precarious descent into the oppressive heat and blistering sunshine. They fell to the ground in a mixture of relief and exhaustion. Temporarily blinded by the light differential, they slowly sat or stood, checking each other's status verbally.

"I say, that was a bit exciting, what?" exclaimed Nigel. For a moment, everyone looked at him in disbelief, and then they laughed in amazement and release, celebrating the fact they had survived.

"I don't know about you boys, but I could use a double Scotch!" said Bethany to a chorus of "Hear! Hear!" from all the men. Later, sitting around the campfire, the team discussed their adventure.

"I must say, I'm a bit surprised at the instability of that cave. We had no indication from the authorities, and you lot didn't find anything worrying with the scans, did you?" Nigel directed his question to Nick and Andy.

"No, or else we would have flagged it to you," said Andy openly. "Nick and I have spent far too many years in dangerous circumstances not to recognize the downsides of most situations and the need to share that info with our team. This may not be war or a skirmish or a black op, Nige, but it's still hazardous to life and limb. I'm mystified, though, that our equipment didn't reveal any fissures."

"It must have been the percussion of stabilizing the scaffold that carried through a fault from all the erosion buried and unseen behind the walls," James said. "That's the only thing that makes any sense."

"Whoa! Wait a minute!" shouted Bethany. "I cleaned up my cameras when we got back to camp, but I didn't notice this then. Look at this!"

The men gathered around, looking over her shoulders as she flicked through the last of the digital frames from the 35mm camera she had strapped around her neck as she leaped toward James. She recalled she released her grip on the camera to stretch both arms toward James. The images were clear enough to ascertain what was photographed if a bit skewed in terms of angle.

"I had a high-speed setting on this one, and it must have gone off in auto mode sequence either as I jumped or as I landed. The camera was programmed to take several shots in a row. Is that a doorway?" Bethany asked incredulously.

"Oh, my God!" bellowed Nigel excitedly. "It looks as if it is!"

"Could it be anything like those Egyptian pressure doors in pyramids?" Andy asked, feeling a bit foolish. "I've read accounts of them. You know, the ones that are invisible until the right spot is pressed? Bookcases that move to reveal secret passages in castles or old mansions were built on that same principle, right?"

"As far-fetched as that sounds, Uncle Andy, you may have a point. I certainly didn't see any indication of a line in the stone wall when we first examined the room, did anyone else?" James looked at the others, who shook their heads almost in unison. "And the scans showed nothing, either."

"I'll bet that brute, Abed, swung that hammer so well that the strut against that wall took the percussion applying just the right amount of transferred pressure to initiate the door to swing!" Nick offered speculatively. "Sort of a combination of what I said before and what Andy just said. And the grinding and groaning we heard was the shifting of that door!"

Warming to the idea, James said, "Think about it! We began on the opposite side of the cave. During the episode, stuff fell from the ceiling, but only from the undecorated part closest to the tunnel opening, and it was only crumbling and dust, mostly. And the door is closer to the tunnel than the scaffolding. Whatever mechanism is built into that wall must be on the lateral side of the door in the cave wall against which the boards were hammered into place. No chunks of rock let loose anywhere, at least not as long as we were inside, although we didn't know if they would with time, so we did right to get the hell out of there as quickly as possible. Still, it took some minutes for the evac to be complete, and no big chunks fell!"

Bethany held her camera at an angle and pointed. "See here? That door is quite thick and looks solid. I'll be that's why it didn't flag on your sweep of the walls."

"It seems possible that the wood strut against that side of the wall acted as a trigger on a pressure point engaging the door's movement. We've seen these things in Egypt and elsewhere. After so much time of disuse, rumbling and shifting would likely take place. It mimicked a cave-in to our senses and experience, but it was nothing of the sort in reality. We may not have been in as much peril as we originally thought, my friends." Amir smiled as he spoke. "Perhaps instead, we have made another discovery beyond that for which Nigel brought us here to document and interpret!"

Nigel sat down hard. "Could it be?"

The others took their places around the fire, James dribbling a bit of Scotch into each of their cups. The import of Amir's suggestion hit all of them, each eager to add comments and actions to be considered for the following day's return to the cave for inspection, assessment, documentation, and potential discovery. But of what?

Chapter Four
The Dig and the Doorway: Part 3

The team readied themselves and the equipment to re-enter the cave. Not knowing the extent of what the original space sustained or what damages they would find, unanimous agreement to complete an assessment of the wall and ceiling drawings first was determined a priority in honor of their patron. Next, they would explore the space beyond the door.

Bethany was impressed by the three archaeologists' restraint, as she was itching to slide through the narrow opening, documenting each step and disclosing on digital film the first glimpses into what was a hidden room or might be a burial area. Whatever it was, its existence and discovery alone was an archaeological boon. If artifacts were present, it would become a treasure trove, archaeologically speaking. With grudging respect for their professionalism, she documented the "after" condition to compare to the "before" shots she had taken on the first entry.

"Overall, lads," said Nigel, "things didn't suffer much for wear, would you agree?"

"Frankly, I'm amazed. With all the reverberation we felt, I was sure some pieces would shear off or get scraped, in the least." Andy inspected the western wall closely. "It seems mostly dust, which isn't problematic, even for the photography. We can remove it easily enough."

Amir clapped Abed on the back. "Looks like the scaffold you men built survived as well. You may have opened up yet another spot for exploration with that last, mighty swing, Abed." The man grinned, whispering thanks, and continued to collect the small amount of fallen debris with the others.

After a short time, it was clear that they could move on. No one spoke; all looked to Nigel for the "go-ahead." Bethany refrained from huffing after a deep, audible inhale and rolling her eyes, only because of James's stern look, a soft smile from Amir, an open grin from her Uncle Nick, and a shake of the head from her Uncle Andy.

Andy opined, "You know, Bethany, the older you get, the more you remind me of my sister." She opened her mouth to respond with sarcasm but instead gifted him with a dazzling smile.

Oblivious, Nigel clapped his hands together. "Right then, lads, are we all ready?"

"I'm ready, too," said Bethany.

"Yes, of course, Bethany, sorry. I suggest you lean in first and take a couple of shots before we enter to depict what our eyes shall see on the first entry. I will then go through, followed by James and Amir, followed lastly by Bethany. If you please, Andy and Nick, remain here in the larger cavern with the men for the moment, just in case our entry triggers the door to close. I'd hate to have us all trapped inside with no one the wiser. You blokes can figure out a way to get us out if the worst happens. Right then, here we go. Bethany?"

Inexperienced with the nuances of dig safety protocols, Bethany was initially frightened by Nigel's remarks. She had not considered a reverse trigger regarding the door. Casting a look back to her uncles, she said, "If I get stuck in here, make sure my boys have a normal childhood and tell them I'll love them forever." She then turned and stood in the narrow space leaning as far forward as balance would allow and captured as much of the interior as possible. Not realizing she had been holding her breath when she backed out, she was breathless.

As Nigel moved to change places with her, he said, "I hereby claim this place on behalf of the archaeologists here present at this moment, our benefactor, and the British Museum, noting that Bethany Brandon-Maxwell was the first woman to set eyes on this secret space!" Bethany was taken aback. A grinning Nigel turned his head back to Bethany, continuing, "I do have a sensitive side, you know." Nigel passed through, followed by the others in order.

The interior was dark but remarkably free of dust, except near the doorway. The walls were hand-hewn, sledge and chisel markings apparent here and there. While stale, the air was arid as distinct to the ambient humidity present in the more massive cavern on the other side of the door. Three large niches were carved into the north wall; the eastern wall was covered in chiseled carvings around several small ledges and niches; the southern wall free of adornment with a simple post and lintel altar or table leaning against the wall for stability.

"*Jazakum Allah khyraam*; Allah be praised," whispered Amir.

"We shall need Andy for translation. It looks to me as if these carvings are either ancient Hebrew or Aramaic. I'm not sufficiently well versed in either," James said softly, awe evident in his voice. Nigel was speechless for once, as was Bethany. The only sound for the next several minutes was the clicking and whirring of Bethany's two cameras and human exhalations.

"What do you make of this, lads... an ossuary perhaps?" Nigel walked to one of the large niches on the north wall.

"It's not big enough for bones, maybe only a few smaller ones, but most ossuaries are larger," James observed. "Careful," he cautioned Nigel as he reached toward what appeared to be a mid-sized stone box. "Beth, get a shot of this from all angles. We have to document *everything* in here as best we can, so everyone keeps hands off until that's completed."

"Of course," apologized Nigel, "I just had this overwhelming need to touch it. Quite odd, as I know better, but it's as if it magnetically drew me to it!"

"Look, Nige, I'm sorry for being so sharp. I know you know very well how to do this; I just want to make sure nobody makes a false move spurred by emotional excitement that could be criticized later. Are we good?" Nigel nodded his confirmation.

"Well, if anyone cares for my opinion, I think Nigel was sensing something. It—whatever 'it' is or whoever put 'it' here—wants to make sure we pay attention to that box. That's what I think." Bethany was breathing excitedly as she worked. "It is splendid, isn't it? Even though the carvings are a bit rough, it looks to me as if the stone of the box itself was sanded down or abraded with some tool to make the carvings stand out in a sort of bas relief with the difference in texture accentuating the images."

The stone box was approximately 42 cm long x 21 ½ cm high x 14 cm wide, including the lid or cover, which itself was about 6 cm in height, overlapping the length and width only slightly. The team thoroughly checked, measured, photographed, and documented all findings and images. Amir shone a flashlight from one side while James monitored for any glints of light on the other. Amazingly, the chiseled stone cover fitted true, effecting a perfect seal.

James called to Andy to bring the folding table and valise with materials. Everyone was already masked and gloved, but brushes, small tools, sheeting, and other materials were stowed in the valise, together with water bottles for the team. Andy passed the materials to James through the doorway, remaining on the cavern side.

"Well?" asked Andy excitedly.

"It's clearly a secret room, but containing what secrets, I don't know as yet. We'll have to switch out in a bit, as I need you to rough translate some of the markings. Stay ready. All well out there?" James asked.

"Fine. We've just got a case of the jitters, is all. The men are having a rest and a natter, which is probably a good thing. Call out when you want me. I'll be sitting down just outside the opening biting my nails!" his uncle replied with a grin.

James returned to the gathering inside the room, passing the materials to Amir. "Nige, you take the left, and I'll take the right, okay? Amir spread the sheeting on the table just in front of us. Beth, you stand slightly to my right and capture the lift, then get in front to cover the removal and placement on the table. Everyone get ready. I want this entire process fully covered. Amir, use the diffuser light next to Beth over her shoulder to ensure the light is right. That should illuminate the sheet as well, so we can place this down properly and catch any siftings that might fall from the lid's bottom. Everyone got it and set? On my mark of three... one, two, three."

The lid lifted off with relative ease, making a soft sound like a sandy footstep on a polished floor. Nigel and James slowly placed it without incident onto the sheet spread on the folding table. Inside the stone box was another box that appeared to be made of metal, approximately 5 cm narrower on all sides than the stone box. The team stood around and peered at it in wonder. The only audible sound was Bethany's camera clicking and whirring.

"This may be--and likely was--oiled before being placed into the stone box. Note the discoloration in certain spots from its aging process", remarked Amir.

Deferring to Amir, James asked, "What kind of metal do you think it is?"

"I suspect iron." The man was thoughtful, obviously sifting through knowledge stored in his mind's data banks. "Equally, it may be tin or copper. Remember the Arabah Expedition by Rothenberg in 1969? He assigned the copper mines in the Timnah area as attributable to three periods: the 4th century BCE, the early Iron Age, and the 3rd and 4th centuries CE. Raw copper was still being exported from Egypt via the Red Sea, or from the copper mines south of the Dead Sea in the eastern Arabah—the area conquered by David and Solomon, and the bulk of the metallurgical industry was located in the plain of Jordan.

"Although copper is a possibility since it was used by the Israelites for vessels in the Temple through the Time of Moses and II Kings, it was gradually replaced by iron. Copper, or "Nehoshet," appears in the Babylonian Talmud and Jerusalem Talmud as a copper caldron room in a bathhouse. We know copper was used as a covering on the Tabernacle altar with copper bowls for oil in Herod's Time.

"That covers Old Testament times for those of you who are Christians; for the others of us who mark history in terms of anthropological migrations of the nomadic tribes of the region and their development, inclusive but not limited to religion of any derivation, we know that the symbolism of metals represents the four kingdoms: Gold for Babylon; silver for Media; copper is Greece; and iron is Edom or Rome. I can tell you that in the Torah of the time surviving to modern times can be found the words, '…as wine cannot be preserved in golden or silver vessels but only in the humblest of vessels,' meaning earthen ones like clay jugs, so the words of Torah will not be preserved in one who is in his own eyes like a gold or silver vessel but only in one who is like the lowliest of vessels."

"And that has to do with your deduction that the box is iron because?" queried Bethany.

Amir continued. "Whatever people forged this vessel, as well as the carved stone box in which it has resided all these thousands of years, are a people who learned metallurgy from the Egyptians or those controlled by the Egyptian culture. They had not only developed the techniques but had a stranglehold on the employment of the technology.

"With the consistent mention in the Midrash and Talmud of how specific metals were used, when and for what, and the fact that copper was outlawed in preference for gold and silver by ancient Judaic scholars and Rabbis, I think it is iron. It is a known fact that smelted iron replaced copper and tin in most applications."

"But it could be gold or silver, by the steps in that deduction, yes?" Bethany persisted.

James interceded, "No, Beth, I don't think so and therefore agree with Amir. The skill required to duplicate this hidden portal—

as is seen only in the pyramids—speaks to a people who were used in the Egyptian construction of those edifices using like techniques. The secret may have been passed down through generations, yes. Still, the technology is flawless, and the box's carvings represent a certain period in time and specific people: ancient Hebrews, or as you would refer to them, ancient Jews.

"In keeping with their faith, for them to sequester something of this nature and go to all the significant trouble to create this tomb or hidden room, they clearly ascribed great value to it. The box and the altar are the only things here. Both the posts of the altar and the exterior of the stone box display ancient Judaic inscriptions, figures, and symbols. They would have followed the teachings of the Torah, not defied them. Ergo, they would not have used gold or silver but iron. Also, to procure sufficient gold or silver to make the box would require much wealth, and whoever accomplished this whole thing," he explained, waving his arms around the room, "were skilled laborers, not wealthy nomads."

"But a wealthy overlord could have commissioned it; that's a possibility, right?"

Nigel said, "We will know more once the opportunity for close analysis is had, Bethany. But do note your questions for later consideration. Now, are we ready, gentlemen, for the next step?"

Again, James and Nigel carefully placed their gloved fingers at the ends of the metal box, slightly overlapping the sides with thumb and pinky fingers, and lifted the metal box straight up and free of its stone box enclosure. The co-mingled sounds of heavy breathing filled the small room. The metal box was decorated on each of the long sides and lid. The lid extended to the box's side-walls, suggesting either a flat plate lid top or one with an interior flange that would neatly slide down all interior four sides.

"Who's going to do it?" whispered Andy.

"I'm shaking too much," confessed Nigel, winning everyone's grin. "James and Amir, you do it."

Both men, besides being noticeably excited and eager, flexed their fingers and adjusted their face masks. As one, they nodded and placed their fingers against the sides of the lid, lifting in a steady, sure, upward direction. The cover did not move. Again, they tried, and once again, the top remained securely sealed to its box.

"Enough. This is going to require discussion of a different method, other of our tools, and more time in a controlled environment," James advised.

Amir concurred. "And whoever sealed this box may have done so with wax or a similar adhesive for protection. We should wrap it appropriately and transport it back to the work tent."

Bethany recorded the exchanges on tape, in her notebook, and photographically.

Nigel produced material for binding the box. With James and Amir holding the box gingerly, he carefully wrapped it, placing it in one of Bethany's waterproof hold-all bags.

"Time for tea, everyone. I think we've done enough today. Hours have passed, and my ticker could use a break. Come on, lads and Lady. Back to camp!"

One by one, they squeezed through the slim doorway opening, much to Nick's relief. His face mirrored the many questions running through his mind, but he had the personal restraint to verbalize none of them, knowing that this was not the right time. James passed him the hold-all bag saying, "Guard this with your life, Uncle Nick." He was barely smiling and clearly exhausted.

Departing the massive cavern, the party made their way through the access tunnel back to the wall which dominated the first cave space, with Hasan leading the way. Andy followed next, with a pistol drawn in his left hand and rifle in his right; the three archaeologists were next; then Bethany, loaded down with her bags of gear and a bulky camera with its colossal lens hanging from her neck. With the hold-all in one hand and rifle in the other, Nick stayed close to Bethany, whose progress was slow. Finally, Abed and Moha brought up the rear, loaded down with the remainder of the equipment. In each of the team's mind hovered dread of the descent of the wall. Each in his/her own way mustered the courage to overcome that awaiting obstacle, committed to the mission of bringing their "find" to safety for analysis and ultimate provenance as one of the world's ancient treasures.

The sun was waning; the air was hot, dry, and breezeless; the only noise the team's footsteps and labored breathing. No one spoke. Once they cleared the first tunnel and reached the camp area, each stowed the equipment. The three archaeologists placed the wrapped treasure into an insulated small cargo box in the work tent fitted with a locking mechanism and a padlock for good measure. The cargo box was placed into a larger metal padlocked container for safety and temperature control, with cooling packets stuffed around the interior.

"Good," said Nigel, "now for that tea, a tot, and a good, long chat. Well done, lads. By the way, Lady Brandon, is it Maxwell-Brandon or Brandon-Maxwell? I'm unsure of the protocol."

Bethany turned toward Nigel, stuck out her tongue, and flung a dirty towel in his direction. "Just for you, Nige, the protocol is 'My Lady,'" she said with a wicked, smug smile.

Walking back to the campfire in front of their sleeping tents, Amir and James spoke quietly, Nigel having walked rapidly to his tent to wash up and change. "Between the cave drawings and this unexpected room, our find will have to be carefully categorized in terms of analysis, priority, and provenance," Amir cautioned.

"You're right, my friend. We must also predetermine our individual places as concerns the documentation and attendant responsibilities. I don't think Nigel will give us any pushback on that; he was the one to request our help. But 83% of the expedition comprises the inclusive group of professionals put together by you and me. Nigel is the remainder of 17% as originating professional, but only for the cavern paintings... not the hidden room. Had we not needed the scaffolding secured for Bethany's photographic documentation, and revealed by Abed's last swing on that stabilizing board, we would never have known the room existed!"

Amir nodded in silent agreement. "James," he said, stopping after a few steps, "you know the right and correct thing is for Nigel to share the find... officially, I mean. I'm not saying this because of greed or the need to pad my reputation, but just because it is the right thing to do and speaks to provenance. You know Nigel better than I. What will he do, do you think?"

"Don't know, mate. I've not had to deal with this sort of thing with him before. Even with this job, we all signed on under Nigel's umbrella terms with his sponsor. I'm no solicitor, but I would think those terms extend to anything and everything discovered and documented by this expedition. And remember, Nigel has his own specialty; he's not equipped to manage or oversee what we found in the room. Only you and Andy can do that, and me to a lesser extent. Let's wait and see if he mentions it, but we should settle it tonight if for no reason other than the protection of the find for posterity. Having found the thing, we have a responsibility to safeguard it.

"Most assuredly, it would be a thrill to work on it, translate it, write it up, and present it. But you and I know that notoriety is the least important thing to a true archaeologist—preservation and explanation for the world beat that every time. I look at us as

God's hand tools, simple men using trowels, scrapers, and brushes, uncovering bits of mankind's history for all the world to see and understand. In the final analysis, all of it--from the very beginning to now--is God's creation and therefore sacred." The two men shook hands solemnly.

"James, my friend, one of the reasons we continue to work together is because your heart is in synergy with my heart. You care, and you do what is right without selfish motivation. We do what we do for the world, its history, its people, and those who will come after us. We are spirit brothers in this for all Time, James. It is a rare blessing, praise Allah."

"*Barak Allah fik*[6], my brother, Allah bless you. God bless you." James embraced Amir. Bethany, Nick, and Andy saw the exchange and smiled.

---

6 May God protect you, my brother.

Chapter Five
The Dig and the Box: Part 4

After much careful but only preliminary examination and discussion, the group agreed that the first order of official business was to inform the authorities of their discovery. The Box was too valuable an artifact to subject to elemental analysis at camp. The team did not have the proper equipment and environment to ensure both the objects' safety and provenance and quantify their conclusions following detailed, structured, scientific analysis.

"Nigel, you should notify your sponsor straightaway, enlisting his support and influence. We have a satellite phone, so that shouldn't be a problem. Once we are all satisfied with his response and hear his suggestions, we must notify the Ministry to keep our 'noses clean' in their eyes. This stage will, of course, be more complicated." James rubbed his face.

"In my experience in this part of the world, whatever government one is dealing with takes the immediate position that bits of antiquity must reside within the country's jurisdiction as an integral part of their history. It follows that there is red tape to contend with and the necessity to deal with their archaeologists and hangers-on.

"I'd like to be able to limit outside interference as much as possible. Our success with this stage will rely heavily on the clout of our combined status within the global archaeological community, replete with our various specialties and the weight and sway of your sponsor. Frankly, it's a crapshoot. We risk losing majority control of the find and the site, possible total exclusion from the scientific investigation, and worst-case—expulsion from the country immediately following the handover."

Bethany stood, complaining, "Really, James? That seems unreasonable and severe. After all, you've had their permission and blessing to excavate this site. They have done nothing with it for years, likely for lack of funds or low priority, considering their political aims over the last several years. The team's funds come from outside sources, so why the Hell would they care whose money and effort brings the find to world notice and acceptance? No one will challenge its provenance, much less its ownership."

Amir explained, "We are not dealing with logical reaction here, Miss Bethany. The authorities are overly sensitive to this kind of thing, harboring many years of resentment for the West, and what they perceive is the pillage and loss they experienced in the past. Justified or not, that is something one must recognize when dealing with values in these countries. Also, none of you is an Arab, and none of you are Muslims. Therefore, you are not trusted, and your motives and guarantees are instantly suspicious. I am sorry, but that is a fact with which we must deal sensitively."

"Says the Arab Muslim among us..." quipped Bethany, "or is it 'Muslim Arab?'".

"Bethany, enough with the sarcasm, which helps nothing!" Andy retorted with annoyance. "You have no idea what can happen to people like us in these countries, no idea of the forces at play. I have similar concerns to those James raised, and from my experience, I can tell you this is not a joking matter. The possibilities he mentioned are highly likely, and he neglected to mention other ones, which I'm sure was deliberate." Nick nodded in agreement.

"We must secure the artifact at all costs until stages one and two are engaged and results determined. We should strategically leave the artifact in situ, bringing only photographic evidence with some text notes, measurements, etc. The persons best qualified to present to the authorities are the archaeologists. Andy and I will serve as bodyguard protection under the guise of associated team members." Nick's statements were made as assumptions, not as suggestions.

"Agreed, Nick, without a doubt." Andy chimed in. "My only adjustment would be to leave Amir at camp with Bethany because..."

"What?! I'm the one who took the bloody photos you'll display to verify the artifact. Doesn't my authentication count for anything? I have an impressive CV too, qualified by all my work with National Geographic, which is international! Why do I have to miss all the fun?"

"Zip it, Beth, and just listen for once!" Andy warned. "I was trying to explain my reasoning when you interrupted. As you said, Amir is an 'Arab' who is also a 'Muslim.' That the artifact is with him will subliminally supply confidence regarding its safety. Next, you are a female. Need I remind you of the lack of regard for women in this part of the world? Your particular style of direct exchange would be insulting and unwelcome in these circumstances. Third, I want you nowhere near any untenable or dangerous conditions, which might occur. Concern for you would possibly inhibit Nick's and my responses and influence our degree of safety. James and Nigel, as the two principal archaeologists on this dig, are perfectly capable of meeting requirements for explaining what we found and the plan for further examination. Amir's presence would be unnecessary in this regard and only icing on the cake. He is far more valuable as a guardian angel. Besides, he is well-equipped to see to your safety while we're gone."

Bethany looked at Amir with different eyes. "Do you know karate or something, Amir? You surely don't look much like a boxer or fighter to me; no insult intended."

"Amir and I have been in difficult situations together in the past, Bethy. He's saved my bacon more than once. That's all you need to know for the moment." James said quietly.

"What?! You've never mentioned anything about the danger associated with archaeology, James!" Bethany adopted an indignant tone and stance.

Nick stood with a water bottle in his hand. "Love of George, Beth. Unless you want me to dump this over your head, cool down, will you? The last thing any of us needs is challenging our every statement and plan when you don't know what you're talking about!"

"Let's all of us calm down," said Nigel amicably. "This is, after all, a planning session with nothing written in stone just now. We haven't even made the initial call yet, so all of this speculation may be a nonstarter until I call my guy in Turkey.

"But Bethany," Nigel continued in a severe tone, "you should be aware that this part of the world is rife with bandits, thugs, summary detention for an indeterminable time under bogus charges or suspicion, instant and inherent opposition to Westerners, and the like. If James and I are to be reasonably safe on that long journey over deserted tracks and isolated roads, I'd feel much better with Nick and Andy at our backs. Safety in numbers, and all that, my dear, lets old Nige live another day to tell another tale!"

Chagrinned, Bethany said to the men, "I'm sorry. You're all correct. I spoke out of turn and recognize I am a liability in some circumstances. I guess I'm overprotective of my role as a contributing member of the team because I am a female."

"So noted, Bethy." James grinned. "We're all aware of that, and you are valued."

"Yes, especially the part about being a female," Amir added meekly.

"Danger, danger, my friend," laughed Andy, pouring them all a cup of lukewarm water. "I'd never admit that. What are you thinking, man?" Everyone, including Bethany, laughed and relaxed.

Hasan, Moha, and Abed were to stay with Amir and Bethany, maintaining the camp and cleaning the remainder of the site from debris while the others were gone. They were told a minimum about the intended trip to the city and its purpose. Everyone was careful about conversation within earshot of the three men (two of which were Syrians, the other a Jordanian), keeping them as much in the dark as possible.

Insofar as they were concerned, James and Nigel were traveling to the authorities to report on the outer cavern images and the room's unexpected discovery within the cave. They remained unaware of the details surrounding the artifact's existence, other than that the archaeologists had taken a sample of some of the stone from the cave for final testing and dating, a common enough procedure in archaeological digs.

James conferred with Bethany and Nigel two evenings before their departure about which frames to develop into photographs. Although Bethany capably performed in her "rigged" dark room within the Work Tent, the environment made extended development difficult. She had provisionally brought a small supply of chemicals among her stores allowing for limited reproduction. All agreed that the remaining film and digital images should remain at camp where they could be secured. The artifacts were safe and secure in the Work Tent.

The four men packed light. James and Nigel split the pile of photographs and associated data between them in shoulder correspondence bags. Nick and Andy packed as much defensive gear as they thought provisional, planning for potential (but hoping they would not have to encounter) problems during the trip. Nigel's sponsor was already at work with the authorities in an attempt to pave their way. They had covered as many contingencies as possible.

"Well, dear hearts, cheerio! Take good care, remember to apply sun lotion, Bethany, and Amir, keep an eagle eye on everything." Nigel shook their hands.

"We shouldn't be overlong, Beth, assuming cooperation during our granted meeting. One day to get there, and one back, with a day in-between for conferences, is my guess," assured James, hugging her. "Take care of yourself, and no unaccompanied roaming about!"

"Yes, sir, younger brother! I promise I'll be good. I'll treat it as a few days at a spa!"

Amir laughed at her remark. "We will be fine, James. Do not worry. Godspeed and good luck, *Allah yuhafizuk ya 'akhi*. We have our cell phones; you have the sat phone. With any luck, we should be able to communicate with each other. I shall look after her."

"I depend on it, Amir. I trust you will keep her safe. I hate leaving you here alone, but the three men respect you and should be able to do whatever you say. Can I bring anything back for you? We will, of course, bring more food and drink. That is, presuming we are allowed to stay on the site. Pray for the desired outcome, my friend." Amir and James embraced; Bethany kissed her uncles and brother, and Amir shook hands with the departing men and bowed.

"Right then! We're off! Bye, bye, kiddies!" called a jolly, excited Nigel, waving to the five figures standing in camp as the SUV slowly rolled away.

"Dear, sweet, oblivious Nigel," said Amir to himself, walking away, unaware that Bethany heard him.

Following behind, Bethany said, "I'd kill myself if I had to live with him."

Amir just shook his head.

The next morning, Bethany decided to bathe in the small pool at the foot of the waterfall. As was her habit, she brought her cased cameras with her in their water and weatherproof carry-bag and a towel. Removing her boots and tying the laces together, Bethany mumbled to herself that the men should be grateful she wasn't a 'typical female' requiring shampoo, other toiletries, or conveniences. She could hold her own living 'rough.' Peeling off her shirt and shorts to wash in the pool after her swim bath, she dove into the water. Rubbing her body all over, Bethany held her underwear away from her body to allow the cleansing water to reach crevasses and scrubbed at her underwear to remove salt and grime. Floating in the sunshine feeling refreshed, she uttered a squeal of surprise as Amir's head appeared from the water right next to her.

"Amir, my God! You scared me to death!" she complained.

"Bethany, be quiet now and do exactly as I say as quickly as you can," he whispered levelly. "I'll grab your cameras; you get your clothes and boots. Stay in the water and follow me. It is not hard, but you must dive and follow me under the water."

"Whoa..." she began to question.

"No time, do it now; I'll explain later," said Amir breathlessly. He swam the short distance to the pool's perimeter and grabbed Bethany's carry-alls with her expensive cameras. She followed his instructions and looped her boots around her neck, quickly grabbing her shirt and shorts, knotting them together. They swam to the middle of the pool near the cascading waterfall and trod water while Amir moved in a full circle, surveying all around them.

"Follow my lead," he said softly and dove beneath the surface. Bethany followed him beneath, the underwater visibility allowing her to see Amir's form several feet in front of her. In only a few minutes, they both surfaced behind the waterfall.

"Come," he said to her, spluttering. They swam several feet to the stone periphery behind the waterfall and climbed from the water onto a ledge.

"Amir, explain yourself!" Bethany demanded.

"Sit here, Miss Bethany," Amir pointed to a blanket, handing her a small towel to dry herself. "All will be clear in a moment."

Amir spread out Bethany's shirt and shorts on a boulder on the ledge side and unzipped and untied the carry-all bags and their liners without opening them fully to the humidity behind the waterfall. "Are you chilled?" he asked her. She shook her head.

"I am sure you have a million questions, knowing you. But allow me to speak and explain, and then you may ask me anything. Agreed?" Bethany nodded assent but tilted her head, assessing Amir, different scenarios flitting through her mind.

"Each morning, I walk the periphery of our campsite from high ground, using the binoculars to survey 360 degrees. It is merely an ingrained habit. This morning, I noticed two SUVs throwing up a massive dust cloud far away in the distance. They were traveling fast. There is nothing out here except our campsite. The SUVs appeared to be black, not the olive drab vehicle James and the others took, nor the rattle trap muddy color with canvas available to the Ministry.

"That could mean only two things: 1—that the SUV's were bound for our campsite; and 2—that they were in a hurry and up to no good. Locals do not have fancy black SUVs; neither do government employees–the only two alternatives that would not encourage a strong sense of fear. A government employee might be dispatched to let us know our team is unavoidably delayed. Since we have not heard from them via phone, I must assume there is a service problem. Locals may have heard about the dig and might seek employment as it is commonplace in these places where people have little and money is scarce. But new, fast-moving SUVs speak to a well-funded and supplied group—likely bandits, intent on stealing, overtaking us in the least, doing grave ill at the worst. I promised I would see to your safety. That is what I have done."

"All of it makes sense now, Amir. Thank you. But bandits? Are we really at risk from that?"

"Bethany, because the others did not want to alarm you, we spoke of 'situations about which you were unaware' only in general terms. It is not unusual for digs to be overrun, vandalized, or robbed in certain areas or countries. There are also occasions of beatings when the excavation is lightly manned and equipment or artifacts are stolen. There have been some murders, as well, but the lid is kept tightly on these matters. We are currently only lightly manned when everyone is on-site; we are significantly understaffed in our current condition. We can depend on our three natives to an extent, but they are no match for well-armed, experienced, professional mercenaries. In the interests of prudence, I must assume that is the type we would face. Two loaded SUVs with perhaps four passengers each make me little of a deterrent in a face-off.

"Perhaps I am wrong and overreacting. We will see when I check on things after their arrival. But in the meantime, you must remain here and safe. I have some modest provisions in my knapsack over there," pointing to the back of the ledge, "but use what you need only sparingly in case we are here for longer than anticipated. I did the best I could with the limited time available."

"What about all of our supplies and equipment? Do you think they'll raid that?" Bethany's mind was spinning. "I left my smallest camera on my worktable, but we've at least got the major images with us and all the sim cards. But the small camera does have images that give away what we found, but only of the walls and ceilings on that first day—not the room."

"That much is good. No one can take the wall drawings. They

also cannot take the stone box, as I removed it early this morning to an off-site hiding place," Amir bowed, saying, "I praise Allah for giving me the foresight, may His name be praised."

"That's a relief, at least, Amir. But you should show me where you put it, just in case." She left further explanation unverbalized, knowing Amir would understand her meaning. "But I'm sure we'll both get out of this in one piece. Anyway, the guys should be back in time, yes?"

"If all goes well, yes, we said three days in the least, remember? But I warn you, Bethany, that did not allow for any unexpected complications or delays. Let us not borrow trouble. We are safe for now. But we must maintain quiet without light during the nighttime, in particular. Daytime will give us muted illumination through the waterfall. But the nighttime reflection of the flashlight through the waterfall would be dangerous, and sound carries at night. We must play the hand God has dealt us piece by piece, moment by moment. Please remember these things." He patted her hand.

"I'll do my best, Amir, but I don't understand how anyone found out! Our team got there only yesterday, with their first meeting this morning."

"You heard your brother: that place leaks like a sieve. We do not know if someone in the Ministry is in collusion with those who thieve and steal. In any case, they will be upon our camp in less than an hour, more likely half an hour, judging by how long it took us at normal speed versus their speed of travel. Excuse me now; I must pray for our men. I did not have the time to warn them *and* get you to safety. I had to choose."

"Thank you for choosing me, Amir," Bethany said sincerely. "Although I feel bad for the others. They are men and only workers, so I think they may be all right. They know nothing of our find, after all. Here's hoping," she said, crossing her fingers.

"All is in the hands of Allah," he said, turning from her, walking the few steps to the rear of the ledge where he bowed and whispered prayers.

Hours passed with muted sounds and men's voices coming from the campsite. There were a few gunshots, but the bulk of the sounds were crashes, laughter, and orders. Neither Bethany nor Amir were able to make out what was said or happening. Then they heard a high-pitched wailing and scream, ending with a gunshot. Bethany covered her face and wept. Amir sat with his arm around her, his face an unreadable mask.

They could see the distant glow and smell of a campfire through the veil of water. It occurred to Bethany that the small waterfall and pool had initially seemed only a convenience; now, it represented their single cover and haven of safety. Amir placed his hand over her mouth, looking directly at her and shaking his head. They heard scuffling noises over the sound of falling water, then a splash, then a muttered curse. The minutes seemed to meld into hours until they heard more mutterings accompanied by scrambling and scraping in the scrub bushes. "Ok," they heard a voice call out. "Sa'aeud, la shay' huna, la vujad 'lisharat." [I'm coming back, nothing here, no sign.]

"He is leaving," said Amir. "He saw nothing of interest and no signs of us." Bethany breathed in relief. "We should try to rest." Amir eased her down onto the blanket, lying down beside her, and covering them with the space blanket he had brought. "God, be with us."

Bethany awoke to a sensation of warmth. Opening her eyes, she focused on the interior side of the waterfall's scant light filtering in. Amir was lying beside her, his body warmth steaming in the cold but humid atmosphere.

Eyes still closed, Amir said, "There appear to be six of them, not eight. They are well-armed and dressed in black."

Bethany scoffed, "So, they match their SUVs! At least they have a sense of style!"

Amir turned his head to look at her. "You use humor or denigration to mask your discomfort. I understand, Miss Bethany, but do not allow yourself complacency about our circumstances. For now, we appear to be safe. What will come, I cannot say. I will check again later."

"Roger that," a penitent Bethany replied softly, accepting the offered water bottle and energy bar. "Are there signs of any damage or looting? And what about our men?"

Amir reclined after drinking, closing his eyes. "I can identify only two men—Hasan's tall lankiness and Moha's bulkiness. The shorter and smaller Abed was not in evidence when I surveyed the camp with binoculars. I had to limit my viewing time so the rising sun did not reflect in the binocular lenses. The tents remain erect, although the flaps are open on all of them. Several stacked boxes and tubs are outside the work tent. I presume the containers hold equipment they plan to load into the SUVs. They will make use of all of it elsewhere or sell it on the black market. In any case, whatever they take is lost to us."

"That's the least of my worries, Amir. But what about the men? You saw two of them: were they all right?"

"They were prone. I do not think the men were asleep."

Bethany stifled a scream, breathing rapidly to try to relieve her distress. "You mean they might be dead?!" she whispered between gasps.

Amir reached for her hand. "I cannot say for sure, but it looks likely."

The hours passed in silence, the only activity Amir's calisthenics and Bethany's pacing. At last, they heard sounds of movement and muffled voices from the campsite. As the second night behind the waterfall approached, Bethany shivered uncontrollably, tears cascading down her cheeks. "My body seems to be in synergy with our hiding place, Amir. See? I'm making my own waterfall! Isn't that funny? No? Well, I think it is. At least it's a sign that I'm still alive, even though I feel numb. Is it only a matter of time before we die, too, Amir? You can level with me; I'd rather know than not."

"Piece by piece, moment by moment, Bethany. We breathe, and we wait," Amir replied with a calm that both mystified and impressed her.

"How can you be so 'in control,' Amir? We're in incredibly precarious circumstances here. Even if we remain undiscovered, we could die of pneumonia in this damp cold or hyperthermia! God only knows when James and the others will return!" Bethany huffed and shifted to find a more comfortable sitting position on the hard, stone ledge. "And would you believe it? I saw a spider this afternoon... a spider! Who'd have thought a spider could exist in this wet?! I hate spiders; in fact, I hate all bugs. Are there more, do you think?" She continued to mumble to herself.

"I remain as in control as Allah allows, Bethany." He chose not to address the subject of insects as he knew the answer would only augment her aversion and add to her increasing stress. He needed her to remain patient, stable, and cooperative to maximize their survival chances, whatever the future brought. "Tell me about your boys," he encouraged.

"My boys? Ha! What, are you using reverse psychology on me because you're afraid I'm losing my nut? I'm not stupid, Amir. And I'm not about to lose my mind, either. I'm just angry and upset with everything in this lousy life of mine. Not that it wasn't good for part of it, it was. But the last several years have been Hell. Now, just when it seemed as if I had a new lease on life, this happens! It sucks; it really does. And it's jolly unfair, that's what. I don't deserve this."

Amir split the next to last energy bar with her. "Your dinner, Madame," he said with a smile.

Chewing in silence, they lay down on the blanket covering themselves with the silver space blanket to face another night behind the endless sound of the waterfall. They talked for hours, each sharing details of their histories and feelings about life and the world in which they lived. Their conversations spanned as many subjects as their minds were inspired to raise. It seemed as if what might have been months of dates or outings in normal circumstances were covered in those several hours and days of their free, constant, and unhampered exchange.

In the wee hours of the 4th night, Bethany whispered, "I wasn't always such a pushy, ill-tempered brat, you know. I can behave properly in almost any situation. Mum made sure of that, and Grandmother was implacable on propriety. James and I are the respectable products of their lessons in decorum and decency. Father—whom *only* I call 'Papa'—was the perfect example of fairness, hard work, personal strength, and accountability. When I think of all he and Mum went through before James and I were even a passing thought, it amazes me. Their relationship stands as tall as Everest for me, a beacon as to how things could be. Does that sound childish?" Bethany blushed, but Amir could not see it because of the ambient blackness.

"Not at all," he responded. "Everyone should have someone to hold as an example to which one aspires. That's normal and healthy, despite your ethnicity or culture. You see X as a shining example in one person and Y in another. Or maybe a lot of Xs and Ys, but we all need a lantern to show us the way in life."

"Who were yours?"

"My mother died giving life to me; my father in a village skirmish while trying to gather some children to safety from the shooting. My grandmother and grandfather raised me as a faithful Muslim, but one who understands the world and the ways people get it wrong. My grandfather's connections allowed my placement with a family in England, where I completed my studies and postgraduate degrees.

"It was years later that I met James on a dig in Egypt. It wasn't an exciting time, just drudgery, really, so we had hours and hours together to talk while we were sifting and brushing. We found we had much in common insofar as our hearts and minds were concerned. I knew much about you and your earlier family life before our first meeting."

At that last phrase, Bethany turned, propping herself up on her elbow. "What did he say about me? I insist you tell me!"

Amir laughed, saying, "It was all good, Bethany. He adores you and is immensely proud of you."

"But what did he say... specifically?!"

"It was a long time ago, and we've had many conversations since. You don't always come up. But James thinks you are the more capable of your twinset, that you can charm anyone when you put your mind to it, that you're smart, witty, full of grit and capability no matter the challenge, forthright, and..." Amir hesitated.

"And what else? Come on, Amir," she interrupted at his pause. Punching him lightly, she demanded, "Give!"

"Well, he has said that you can be stubborn, but he sees that side of you manifest itself in tenacity, perseverance, and determination. He was clear that you are not the side of stubborn that shows inflexibility or immovable obstinacy."

Bethany lay down again, asking pensively, "Do you find me pig-headed, Amir?"

"No, I do not. When you see you are wrong, you meekly apologize. That is a nice quality."

"So, you think I have other qualities?" she teased.

"Yes, I cannot lie. You have a good and caring heart from which I am sure your boys benefitted. You are not a whiney, weak woman and can do without the creature comforts that modern civilization provides. You are a self-sustaining professional woman in a man's world, which takes the ability to overcome challenges and prejudice. You are willing to try anything, even if you fear it, if it helps accommodate the end goal. And you can cook—a particularly desirable characteristic from one who has eaten your brother's prepared meals!"

They chuckled companionably, ever aware of the need for relative quiet. Tentatively, Bethany asked, "And what about not-so-attractive characteristics? What do you see them as being?" She felt, not saw, his hand stroke her cheek tenderly.

"I am not your counselor, Miss Bethany, only a man who..."

"A man who what? And let's drop the 'Miss Bethany' shall we? After everything we've been through, a simple 'Bethany' or

'Beth' will do. I repeat, a man who what?"

Protracted silence, and then Amir spoke softly, sitting upright. "I am merely a man whose opinions and observations do not matter."

"I insist you tell me about my downsides, or else, or else I shall yell out something X-rated, an expletive or something, and give away where we are hiding!" Beth whispered animatedly. She could tell he was amused and chuckling to himself by the crinkling of their covering.

Without preamble or excuse, he said, "You sometimes use biting sarcasm or sardonic humor to show your disdain or cover your hurt. You hate it when you are driven to tears because you feel that others expect a woman to cry, and you view it as a sign of weakness. You are sometimes too outspoken, and you don't think before you speak. You rarely appreciate that your actions to forge ahead place you at risk. Though you don't consciously intend to do so, sometimes you are inconsiderate of other people's feelings and hurt them with your words. I recognize that all of the above is rooted in your desire 'to do, get things going, and done.' I don't think that when you act headstrong, you realize that you are doing so because when you become aware that you have delivered hurt, you are sorry and genuinely apologize."

"Huh! Well, that's an enlightening summation of my character, I guess. I asked for it, so thank you. I shall have to think about what you've said. My only disagreement with you is that your opinions do matter. They matter a great deal to me." With that, she turned on her side away from him and swiped at her leaking eyes. Bethany sensed that Amir had reclined and turned toward her. After a few moments, she felt his arm tentatively, pulling her close.

The warmth of Amir's body was welcome, as was his soft embrace. Until she heard a quickening in his breathing, Bethany felt he meant only platonic comfort by his encircling arm. She slid her hand to grasp his. Gently, he began kissing her neck.

"Amir? What about your faith? I don't want to be the cause of later recriminations."

"Beth, I have decided to call you 'Bayth,' by the way, which is 'Beth' in Arabic. I think it suits you and will be a term of endearment between us."

"That's lovely, Amir," said a breathless Bethany, reacting to his gentle kisses, "but you haven't dealt with my concern—you are a faithful Muslim. Think about what you're doing and where it might lead. Please, Amir."

"Allah and the Imams say premarital sex is immoral and punishable by Islamic court by receiving a hundred whiplashes with a scourge with witnesses to the shame and punishment of the guilty. If couples indulge more than once, they receive three times the sentence, with a fourth committed instance punishable by death. Though there is no one here to suspect or witness, you and I would know.

"That many couples indulge themselves as an expression of attraction or love does not address their spiritual commitment before their Creator. You are a Christian woman and subject only to your Christian beliefs, not to Muslim law except as a participant, should we engage in sex with each other. Those are the facts, Bayth."

"Then we must not allow our feelings and circumstances to influence us, even though we may never get out of this place with our lives. But I confess, I haven't experienced such tenderness in many, many years, Amir. Having had a taste, I long for more, to be honest."

Tenderly, Amir stroked her face, neck, and shoulders, and Bethany moaned. She could feel his passion mounting to meet hers.

"We must not, Amir. I will not be the cause of your sin against Allah and all you believe. But there are other ways... ways to ease our physical needs. I'm willing if you are. But we must both agree and want the same thing, making our choice independent of the other. And by the way, I'll give you an hour to stop doing that while you decide," she said teasingly.

Amir laughed softly. "I'm sure you don't want to hear it, Bayth, but my religion says masturbation is indecent, and while physically relieving, it is labeled as psychologically depressing and spiritually weakening. I do not do that either," he admitted.

Continuing, Amir said, "But since sex involves two people with penetration and release, there is no reason I cannot help you by showing my feelings, so long as we do not have sex together. And I realize I am skirting the intent of Muslim law because of the intimacy my suggestion proposes, but so long as I do not have sex or masturbate, I can live with walking the line.

"My feelings for you are pure but have snowballed and surprised me. These hours and days together make me know you as if we have been walking in your meadows for years. I have seen your heart; I have laughed at your spirit and humor; I have seen your bravery; I have seen your genuine tenderness and concern for my beliefs. I truly see the real you, Bayth. That is the Bayth for whom I have tender feelings, and I want our hearts to join more intensely. I am in charge of my life; no one else can make this decision for me. I make it freely and willingly. All I need to know is how you feel."

He had stopped stroking her and merely held her close, awaiting her answer. After several minutes of silence, Bethany spoke. "I've shared my soul with you behind this waterfall. You know my fears, ugly side, dreams, needs, and so many other things. I won't pretend to be as spiritually connected to God as you are to Allah, even though I think they're one and the same, just called by a different name. But I do have a strong morality. That said, despite where we find ourselves, I am still a married woman in the throes of divorce. I don't take the concept of adultery or carnal knowledge casually, probably because of my upbringing.

"But I confess I do want to be with you; I want to satisfy my physical needs and feel intimately loved by you. While our options are limited, I will meet you halfway, accepting sole responsibility for my choice and actions." She turned on her side to face him, placing her hand on his bare chest.

Smiling at her, Amir relaxed. "It seems as if this fragile moment in time has endless possibilities. It's as if we have all the time in the world, doesn't it? There is nothing pressing we must or can do; no one to interrupt us with a telephone call or a task to complete. We have the orchestra of the waterfall and the lapping of the water against our stone bed. And we have each other to love freely in ways that do not compromise who we are in our hearts. Will you accept me, Bayth?" As he said that last phrase, he moved his hand to her buttocks, pulling her close.

"I accept you, Amir. Will you accept me?" she asked coyly, just able to make out his face in the rapidly failing light. She raked his hair back and toyed with his ear.

"I accept you, Bayth," he said, kissing her deeply with more urgency. "Now, let me give you a small taste of flying on the wings of eagles," he whispered, moving hands and lips to her throbbing body.

Bethany's eyes opened wide to the utter darkness, her breathing rapid, interrupted only by her soft moans, which matched the rhythmic sound of falling water and the pulse of lapping water against their stone ledge.

Chapter Six
Miryam the Migdalah

To help keep Miryam of Migdalah[7] and her time in perspective, it is helpful to bear in mind that the great kingdoms in the ancient world were Persia, Greece and Rome, Egypt, Babylon, and Assyria. At one time or another, they were all world-governing empires. Israel is located right in the center of them all! It was through Israel that travelers passed: from Egypt to Greece, from Babylon to Rome, or from Persia to Egypt.

Israel has no natural harbors on its coast due to the constant stream of Nilotic silt, which comes from Egypt. The great harbor city of Tyre (the capital of the great Phoenician civilization at one time) had a southern and northern harbor; the southern harbor does not exist anymore. The harbor that created the port city of Joppa (Jaffa) is now completely silted up and forms a flat plain. All of the rains that fall on Israel's hills and valleys come from the Mediterranean Sea. During the rainless season, Israel experiences heavy dews with the consistency of clockwork in the cool of the evening for three-quarters of the year, which dews nourish the grain and fruit harvest.

Israel, during the time of Jesus, was around 160 miles from north to south. At its broadest measure, it was about 85 miles wide but averaged only 50 miles wide east to west. Its primary **geographic** regions were:

The Jordan Valley: the Sea of Galilee was in the north; the Dead Sea was in the south. The valley is a low point because it sits in a geographical fault called the Great Rift Valley, which begins

---

7   Miryam of Migdalah also referred to as Mary of Magdala, Mary Magdalene, the Magdalene, the Beloved
Companion, etc.

far north in the Taurus Mountains and extends southward into the African continent. The Sea of Galilee is appro-

ximately 680' below sea level, and the Dead Sea is about 1275' below sea level (and currently evaporating rapidly because of climactic and modern environmental reasons). The entire region of Israel is subject to seismic activity and earthquakes.

The Mediterranean Coastal Plains: these are on the western side of Israel and are lush for cultivation and beautiful.

The Shephelah: an area of land farther up the coast (but not as high as the Hill Country) and was fertile land used for farming.

The Hill County: a beautiful area with many cliffs with Jerusalem placed on a large plateau high up and visible from many surrounding valleys separating the hills.

The major *territories* in Jesus' time were Judea, Galilee, Perea, and the Decapolis. The Mediterranean Sea was the western boundary; the Jordan River was the eastern boundary; the mountains of Lebanon and Mount Hermon were the northern boundaries; the great Negev Desert was the southern boundary. A land of opposites in Jesus time, Israel remains so to this day: a land of plenty and a land of want.

Historically, Israel was the "promised land" given by God to Abraham, the first Hebrew. The Hebrew and Christian Bibles tell us that Abraham was called by God to leave his country to journey to a land he had never seen, and God would give that land to him and his descendants.

Nazareth (called "the guarded one" in Smith's Bible Dictionary) was the city of Jesus' residence situated in the hills of Lebanon's southern ridges. In Merrill's *"Galilee in the Time of Christ"* (1881), it is a place of antiquity not so insignificant and lowly as has been previously represented. The identification of the ancient site is in no doubt. The name of the present village is en-Nazirah. It is formed on a hill or mountain [Lu 4:29]; it is within the limits of the province of Galilee [Mr 1:9]; it is near Cana, and by implication, in Joh 2:1,2,11 a precipice exists in the area of the city. [Lu 4:29]

Jesus grew up in Nazareth, then a small village, which was near the Plain of Esdralon in Galilee. Although it is not mentioned in the Old Testament, archaeological excavations reveal settlements dating back to the Bronze Age and tombs dating from the Iron Age to the Hasmonean period. The Biblical account says that

Joseph and Mary lived in Nazareth after their betrothal, and the announcement of Jesus' birth came to Mary in Nazareth (Lk 1:26).

It is widely accepted—possibly due to so many translations and transliterations—that Joseph was a carpenter. It is more likely that he was a stonemason or builder, as the area did not and does not have a ready source of timber but is located in the rocky hills with houses of stone and mudbrick. Further, Joseph could have been akin to our modern-day general contractors or artisans, capable of dealing with stone, wood, or the technical aspects any "builder" would have to know. But the facts are that the Greek word "tekton" (as found in the Greek text) does not exclusively mean carpenter.

Professor James D. Tabor, a biblical scholar at the University of North Carolina, has suggested "builder" or "stonemason" would be a better translation for the Greek téktōn in Jesus' case, for particular reasons: Jesus' preaching often uses metaphors inspired by construction; frequent references to "cornerstones" and "solid foundations" might suggest Jesus was familiar with the details regarding how to plan, finance, lay, and build a house; also, the fact that the region where Jesus lived and died is not exactly abundant in trees, and that most homes in his day were built with stones, thinking that Jesus and Joseph might have worked in the building business makes sense.

Without a doubt, the village of Nazareth was a nondescript dot on the landscape with not much to offer, overshadowed by the nearby city of Sepphoris. Since Nazareth was a small village, Joseph would have walked the scant 4 miles to the larger city where there would have been work aplenty, as Herod Antipas' plans were elaborate for the creation of his luxurious Greek-style capital. Small Nazareth could hardly supply sufficient work for Joseph to support his large family. It is appealing to imagine Joseph and Jesus, as builders, walking to Sepphoris to work on the new buildings.

All the Galilee inhabitants were looked upon with contempt by the people of Judea because they spoke a ruder dialect, were less cultivated and were more exposed by their geographic position to contact with heathens.

Archaeological excavations show just how small it actually was, but every bit of space was used effectively. It was built on porous rock with buildings above the surface and underground cisterns for water, vats for oil, silos for grain, and underground tombs chiseled into the soft limestone bedrock. There was a single, ancient spring for water. It was a conservative town, clinging to traditional Jewish culture in a world that had been radically affected by Greek thought and culture. It had a population of about 400, so everyone knew everyone else. The people of Nazareth were essentially farmers, so they needed space between the houses for livestock and their enclosures and land for plants and orchards. They were physically robust, strong-minded, practical, respectful of tradition, and loyal to family. They spoke Aramaic, a language with a strong poetic tradition. [Being able to communicate well was a valued skill, and young Jewish men were expected to be literate. The Jewish queen Salome Alexandra made reading and writing compulsory for all Jewish boys to study the Torah.] The peasant families who lived there eked out a living, paid their taxes, and tried to live in peace. They were observant Jews, circumcised their sons, celebrated Passover and other feasts and holidays, did not work on the Sabbath, traveled as pilgrims to Jerusalem, and valued the traditions of Moses and the prophets.

The limits of the village's perimeter to the west, east, and south (since burial was always done outside inhabited areas) would have been 2,000 feet at its most generous east/west length and around 650 feet at its most generous north-south measure. However, the actual area inhabited in the first century was much less, perhaps only around ten acres. Steep ravines and ancient terraces on the northern slope confined the oval-shaped settlement. Above the town were several rocky ledges, over which a person could not be thrown without suffering almost certain death. There is one very remarkable precipice, nearly perpendicular and forty or fifty feet high. It is speculated by many to be the place an infuriated fellow-townsman attempted to hurl Jesus. Nazareth is famous for one thing and one thing only: it is the hometown of Jesus. It was here that Jesus spent his boyhood, living with his mother, father, and siblings, and here that he faced the skeptical townsfolk of Nazareth.

The tombs surrounding Nazareth were also very modest, characteristically placed at the village or town boundary. Each of them was typically Jewish. The body was first buried in a body-length shaft cut at right angles into the rock tomb chamber walls, then sealed with a large stone rolled into place. When the flesh had decayed, the remaining bones were gathered together and usually placed in an ossuary or bone box.

Ritual bathing pools or mikveh were also found at Nazareth. Used for ritual-purity immersion, they were found at virtually every Jewish site in Galilee, the Golan, and Judea.

The people of Jesus' time would have been shorter than modern people: five feet tall for women and a bit more for men. They were robust, sturdy, with strong brown hands calloused from work and glossy black hair.

Peasant women often painted a red or purple line down the center parting of their hair and wore modest jewelry pieces. Their clothes were homespun, loose-fitting wool or linen, in one of the soft colors of natural dyes—cream, a deep faded pink, or a pale grey. Both sexes wore leather ankle-length boots in winter, sandals in summer, and cut their dusty toenails with a sharp knife. Young Jewish women like Mary of Nazareth lived with extended family or with the family of their husband(s). Homes were of stone and mudbrick. Though not beautiful on the outside, the insides were cool, comfortable, and pleasant. Mary would have performed traditional woman's work—preparing food, washing, fetching water from the well, working in the fields owned by her family, helping other women raise their children:

washed clothes in an open-air communal water-trough. These wash-troughs all over the Mediterranean world were scenes of companionship and gossip.

carried water from the ancient spring that served everyone in Nazareth.

cooked food—steaming bread cakes were a daily item. A primitive sort of popcorn, made by putting fresh grain on a hot metal plate, was also popular.

preserved food--at certain times of the year, the women were inundated with the task of drying grapes, dates, and figs. Olives were eaten fresh or pickled. There were many vegetables, eaten fresh or dried: beans, lentils and peas, onions and leeks, melons, and cucumbers. These were made into spicy soups. Goat cheese and yogurt were eaten fresh because of the heat. Dried fish and eggs were protein sources, with chicken, mutton, and lamb for special occasions. The food may have been simple, but the taste was strong, seasoned with rock salt, vinegar, mint, dill, and cumin.

made clothes; the clothes of the day were simple, but they were made from scratch by each family's women.

tended the goats and sheep who grew the wool, clipped the animals, carded, spun the yarn, wove the cloth, shaped and sewed the clothes, and mended them when they showed signs of wear. Each house was a little self-sufficient center.

Every Jewish woman, young and old, knew the small tasks involved in **caring for the elderly, and for family members who were ill,** sponging their face and hands, combing their hair, keeping the room where they lay as quiet as possible, etc.

The work may have been shared among all the women, but it was still heavy work. At the day's end, women ate with a hearty appetite and then fell to sleep, exhausted by their routines.

As far as we know, Jesus' family lived an everyday life in Nazareth. They were devout, traditional Jews, often traveling to Jerusalem for the major religious festivals. Jesus was taught building skills by his father, Joseph, and was expected to carry on the family trade. Their lives were simple and ordinary.

1894: The spring of the Virgin in Nazareth, 19th-century photograph

Women in rural communities like Nazareth did not read since it was unnecessary. Instead, stories were memorized. Mary of Nazareth and Mary of Magdala were part of an oral society of storytelling. The great enemy in ancient civilizations was boredom, and talk kept boredom at bay. People in the ancient world told stories and acted them out for pure enjoyment. It was not only the passing-on of traditional tales, but a challenge to the audience to make judgments about what was right and wrong. It was the woman's responsibility to teach her children about Yahweh and Judaism until the age of seven, when boys were then instructed by a male teacher at the synagogue and taught to read.

When he was perhaps two years of age, Jesus was brought to Nazareth by Joseph and Mary. The available historical record reveals that at this time, he was their only child. Later, however, his half-brothers, James, Joseph, Simon, and Judas, were born. Joseph and Mary also welcomed and parented girls, Jesus' half-sisters. Thus, Jesus had at least six younger brothers and sisters.

Jesus had other relatives, as well. We know about Elizabeth and her son, John, who lived many miles to the south in Judea. Living close by in Galilee was Salome, who was Mary's sister and Jesus' aunt. Salome's husband was Zebedee. Their two sons, James, and John, were Jesus' first cousins. We do not know whether he spent much time with these boys while growing up, but eventually, they become his close companions, serving as two of Jesus' apostles.

The life of Joseph's family as good Jews was centered on the worship of Jehovah. In keeping with God's Law, Joseph and Mary gave their children spiritual instruction. There was a synagogue in Nazareth, and it is almost a certainty that Joseph regularly took his family along to worship there. Later, "according to his custom on the Sabbath day," Jesus went to the synagogue. (Luke 4:16)

We can reconstruct from scripture and other historical writings that Jesus left Nazareth at age 30 to be baptized by John (Mk 1:9) and returned to Nazareth before beginning his public ministry (Matt 4:13). He was violently rejected by His town's people and moved on to Capernaum (Lk 4:16-30). There is no mention of Him ever returning to His hometown of Nazareth, but he was always identified with it (Matt 21:11). He was called a "Nazarene" (which comes from the Hebrew root meaning "branch," per the promises made to David that the King or Messiah would be a descendant (branch) from the royal line of King David).

[External attestation of Jesus' existence emits from more than the Jewish or Christian scriptures. Eusebius of Caesarea[8], a church historian; Tacitus[9], the non-Christian, Jewish historian (who-

---

8   Also known as **Eusebius Pamphili,** was a Greek historian of Christianity, exegete, and Christian polemicist. He became the bishop of Caesarea Maritima about 314 AD. Together with Pamphilus, he was a scholar of the Biblical canon and is regarded as one of the most learned Christians of his time.
9   **Cornelius Tacitus** was a Roman historian who lived during the reigns of many Roman emperors, from about AD 55-120. He has been called the "greatest historian" of ancient Rome (Habermas, VHCELJ, 87).

chose to live in Rome in later life), Josephus[10]; and the 3rd Century Origen of Alexandria[11] all refer to Jesus' existence, his ministry, and death. Equally, the Apocrypha Books shed light on his life and teachings [though not chosen for canonization].

By understanding Jesus' home life and complexion, one can garner insight into Mary of Magdala's daily existence as a growing child to a somewhat rebellious young girl and the precariousness of her development into an independent-minded, contemplative woman of opining. Although Magadan[12][13][14] was a larger place than Nazareth, the life of a typical female Jew in that time—as depicted above—was the very sort of limited task-driven existence that had no appeal to Mary Magdalene [Mary of Magdala; Miryam of Migdalah] nor satisfied her intellectual curiosity and awareness.

---

10   **Titus Flavius Josephus,** born **Yosef ben Matityahu** was a first-century Romano-Jewish historian born in Jerusalem—then part of Roman Judea—to a father of priestly descent and a mother who claimed royal ancestry. He initially fought against the Romans during the First Jewish–Roman War as head of Jewish forces in Galilee, until surrendering in 67 CE to Roman forces led by Vespasian after the six-week siege of Jotapata. Josephus claimed the Jewish Messianic prophecies that initiated the First Jewish–Roman War made reference to Vespasian becoming Emperor of Rome. In response, Vespasian decided to keep Josephus as a slave and presumably interpreter. After Vespasian became Emperor in 69 CE, he granted Josephus his freedom, at which time Josephus assumed the emperor's family name of Flavius.

11   **Origen of Alexandria** (c. 184 – c. 253), also known as **Origen Adamantius,** was an early Christian scholar, ascetic, and theologian born and spent the first half of his career in Alexandria. He was a prolific writer who wrote roughly 2,000 treatises in multiple branches of theology, including biblical criticism, exegesis and hermeneutics, homiletics, and spirituality. He was one of the most influential figures in early Christian [9] cont'd: theology, apologetics, and asceticism.[8] He has been described as "the greatest genius the early church ever produced."

12   **Smith's Bible Dictionary:** Magdala (a tower). The chief MSS. and versions exhibit the name as MAGADAN, as in the Revised Version. Into the limits of Magadan, Christ came by boat, over the Lake of Gennesareth after his miracle of feeding the four thousand on the Mountain of the eastern side (Matthew 15:39), and from thence he returned in the same boat to the opposite shore. In the parallel narrative of St. Mark, ch. (Mark 8:10) we find the "parts of Dalmanutha" on the western edge of the Lake of Gennesareth. The Magdala, which conferred her name on "Mary the Magdalene," one of the numerous migdols, i.e., towers, which stood in Palestine, was probably the place of that name mentioned in the Jerusalem Talmud as near Tiberias.

13   **Easton's Bible Dictionary:** A tower, a town in Galilee, said only in Matthew 15:39. In the parallel passage in Mark 8:10, this place is called Dalmanutha. It was the birthplace of Mary called the Magdalen, or Mary Magdalene. It was on the west shore of the Lake of Tiberias and is now probably the small, obscure village called el-Mejdel, about 3 miles north-west of Tiberias. In the Talmud, this city is called "the city of color," and a particular district of it was called "the tower of dyers." The indigo plant was much cultivated here.

14   Strong's Exhaustive Concordance: castle, flower, tower. Also (in plural) feminine migdalah {mig-daw- law'}; from gadal; a tower (from its size or height); by analogy, a rostrum; figuratively, a (pyramidal) bed of flowers -- castle, flower, tower.

But these very developed character traits underwritten by her later financial security were the cornerstones of her ability to act supportively to Jesus' brief ministry, as well as interaction with His other apostles.

To help understand the dynamics of the time, it is essential to try to walk in the footsteps of the people of the time.

Sadducee, Hebrew **Tzedoq,** plural **Tzedoqim,** member of a Jewish priestly sect that flourished for about two centuries before the destruction of the Second Temple of Jerusalem in AD 70. Not much is known with certainty of the Sadducees' origin and early history, but their name may be derived from that of Zadok, who was a high priest in the time of kings David and Solomon. Ezekiel later selected this family as worthy of being entrusted with control of the Temple, and Zadokites formed the Temple hierarchy down to the 2nd century BC.

The town of Magdala (Taricheae) on the Sea of Galilee's western shore was a vital salt source, an administrative center, and the largest of ten significant towns around the lake. Magdala was about 3 miles north of Tiberias. "Taricheae" was its Greek name, and in Hebrew, it was called "Migdal (Magdala)," taken from the word "taricheuein," which means to "smoke or preserve fish," and "pickling place." The pickled fish of Galilee was known throughout the Roman and Greek world. Large quantities were taken to Jerusalem during the yearly feasts because of the multitudes of people who would gather there. Barrels were also transported around the Mediterranean. It was also known for its purple dye.

Josephus—the famous ancient Jewish historian--also describes Tarichae as a place "full of materials for shipbuilding, and with many artisans." (iii Wars, 10:6). Recent excavations have uncovered remains of a Roman city and a small Galilean style synagogue.

Migdal/Magdala/ Taricheae was the birthplace of Mary Magdalene (Matt 27:56, 61), and we are told in the gospels that Jesus most likely visited there. (Mk 8:10)

Palestine is also known as Israel or the Holy Land. There were three main areas in Jesus' time: Galilee, Samaria, and Judea. To jump-start your recall:

In the main, Galilee was a rural area farming area where Greek and Roman cultures were popular. Nazareth—where Jesus spent his childhood--was a town in the hills of Galilee. Much of Jesus' public ministry took place in Capernaum, a town near the Sea of Galilee. Cana was a town in Galilee where Jesus performed His first miracle.

Samaria was in Central Palestine, and its inhabitants avoided the Jews because they were viewed as heretics (against the established religious beliefs). Remember references to Samaritans?

Judea was a hot, dry area in Southern Palestine. The town of Bethlehem—where Jesus was born—was in Judea, as was the city of Jerusalem, where Jesus died.

The Jordan River runs between the Sea of Galilee and the Dead Sea. Jesus was baptized by John the Baptist in the Jordan River.

Gentiles were non-Jews. Religious laws did not permit these people to mix with Jewish people. It is noteworthy that he said his message should be preached to the Gentiles and all peoples of the world, not exclusively to the Jews.

Publicans were the Jewish tax collectors. These men were unpopular and often corrupt, keeping money for themselves. Publicans were considered to be sinners. It is noteworthy that Levi—a tax collector—became the Apostle Matthew.

Scribes were the scholarly teachers among the Pharisees who could read and write. The bulk of religious scrolls and documents archived today (most reputed to be in Vatican archives) are the result of scribal work, as are the official forms and communications of the time. Scribes were copyists of the Scriptures and, because of their detailed acquaintance with the law, they became recognized authorities. They were sometimes called "lawyers." Scribes and Pharisees were the religious leaders of the Jewish nation.

Pharisees were middle-class Jewish people that were laymen (not priests) who controlled local synagogues. "Pharisee" is from a Greek word (*pharisaios*) taken from the Hebrew/Aramaic "*Perisha*," meaning "separated one." In Jesus' time, the Pharisees were one of three chief Jewish sects; the others were the Sadducees and the Essenes. Of the three sects, the Pharisees were the most separate from foreign persuasions that were assaulting Judaism and from the ways of ordinary Jewish people. It is believed that Pharisees originated in the 3rd century BC, preceding the Maccabean wars when there were strong tendencies among the Jews to accept Greek culture and pagan religious customs (as they were under Greek domination). The rise of the Pharisees was in reaction to and protest against this shift. Their aim was to preserve their national honor and strict conformity to Mosaic law. (Later, they developed self-righteous and hypocritical formalized positions.) They were among those who condemned Jesus to death.

The Pharisees were the most numerous and influential of the religious sects of Jesus' day. As strict legalists, they stood for the rigid observance of the law and traditions in all their forms. There is no doubt that there were some good men among them, but for the most part, they were known for their self-righteousness and hypocrisy. The remarkable influence of the Pharisees among the masses *should not be discounted*. They were the most honored socio-political, religious group in Judaism at the time of Christ. When He won the people's interest with his broad message of equality, redemption, and life after death, they became his natural enemies because, in their view, he flagrantly violated the law and endangered the preservation of the Jewish religion and nation by his revolutionary preaching.

The category name "Pharisee" means "separated." Dedicated to preserving the Jewish religion's purity, they kept themselves apart from ordinary Jews whom they judged not as devout as themselves (the Pharisees). Unlike the Sadducees, they accepted oral tradition (collected sayings) and guidance from the Torah, believed in angels and life after death, and were open to developing new religious ideas. However, they clung to the concept of the arrival of a Messiah to free them from Roman rule and the establishment of a kingdom along the lines of the days of King David. Because the Pharisees also accepted the "writings" and the "prophets" as canonized scripture, they believed in an afterlife where people received reward or punishment. Rather than emphasizing free will like the Sadducees, the Pharisees believed God's sovereignty could essentially cancel out free will, though free will still affect a person's life. While the Sadducees controlled the high priesthood and the Sanhedrin in Jerusalem, the Pharisees were the teachers in Israel's synagogues.

Jesus criticized the Pharisees for elevating tradition as equal to scripture, saying, "You leave the commandment of God and hold to the tradition of men…You have a fine way of rejecting the commandment of God to establish your tradition!" (Mark 7:8-9)

Both the Sadducees and the Pharisees, like religious sects within Judaism during the time of Christ (originating more than 100 years before His birth), were essentially the ruling class of Jews in Israel. Both sects had members in the Sanhedrin (the Jewish ruling council), and both valued Mosaic law as written in the Torah. Despite these similarities, there were some significant differences between the two groups [see Pharisees and Sadducees.]

The Sadducees[15] were the wealthier and more sophisticated group. They were politically minded and often compromised with secular leaders in exchange for more power. The Sadducees were not in total opposition to Roman rule but chose to work with it to enhance and maintain their position. They controlled the high priesthood and held a majority in the Sanhedrin. The Sadducees subscribed to a more literal interpretation of Mosaic law and were exacting in keeping Levitical purity. They viewed only the Torah (the five books of Moses) as canonized scripture and did not view oral law or tradition as authoritative or binding. They did not believe in an afterlife or any spiritual realm with angels or demons and placed a high priority on their belief that people have free will.

The pastoral responsibilities of the Sadducees included the maintenance of the Temple in Jerusalem. Their high social status was reinforced by their priestly duties, as mandated in the Torah. The priests were responsible for performing sacrifices at the Temple. This included presiding over sacrifices during the three festivals of pilgrimage to Jerusalem. Their religious beliefs and social status were mutually reinforcing, as the priesthood often represented the highest class in Judean society. However, Sadducees and the priests were not wholly synonymous. Not all priests, high priests, and aristocrats were Sadducees; many were Pharisees, and many were not members of any group.

The Sadducees oversaw many formal affairs of the state. Members of the Sadducees:

§ Administered the state domestically
§ Represented the state internationally
§ Participated in the Sanhedrin and often encountered the Pharisees there.
§ Collected taxes. These also came in the form of international tribute from Jews in the Diaspora.
§ Equipped and led the army
§ Regulated relations with the Roman Empire
§ Mediated domestic grievances

The Sadducees rejected the Oral Torah as proposed by the Pharisees. Instead, they saw the written Torah as the sole source of divine authority. In its depiction of the priesthood, the written law

---

15 **Cite:** The Editors of Encyclopaedia Britannica' April 03, 2020; URL:https://www.britannica.com/topic/Sadducee; ACCESS DATE: October 18, 2020

corroborated the power and enforced the Sadducees' hegemony in Judean society.

> According to Josephus, the Sadducees believed that:
> § There is no fate.
> § God does not commit evil.
> § Man has free will; "man has the free choice of good or evil."
> § The soul is not immortal; there is no afterlife.
> § There are no rewards or penalties after death.
> § Sadducees did not believe in the resurrection of the dead but the traditional Jewish concept of Sheol for those who had died.
> According to the Christian Acts of the Apostles:
> § The Sadducees did not believe in a resurrection, whereas the Pharisees did. In Acts, Paul chose this point of division to gain the protection of the Pharisees.
> § The Sadducees also rejected the notion of spirits or angels, whereas the Pharisees acknowledged them.

The Zealots were deeply religious Jews who believed violent action was justified if it was in defense of the Jewish religion. They hated the Sadducees for working with the Romans. One offshoot group of Zealots known as the Sicarii (cut-throats) engaged in a campaign of assassination. Zealots caused a great deal of unrest among the people. Not surprisingly, Jesus was viewed with suspicion for having a Zealot (Simon) among his apostles.

The Essenes[16] were communities of monks who settled in remote places. They believed they were obeying the word of God; felt that Jewish religion was being corrupted by outside influences; and thought that they alone had the correct interpretation of the Torah.

As far as religious authority went, there were two arms: the priesthood and the *Anshei Knesset HaGadol* (Sanhedrin, i.e., The Men of the Great Assembly). The priesthood was hereditary, but the assigning of the *Kohen Gadol* (High Priest), which should have been a function of Levi's Tribe in consultation with the Sanhedrin, was usurped by the Romans and their political appointees. The position was frequently sold to the highest bidder, with none lasting more than a few months at a time. The priests and the *Kohen Gadol's* role was purely the offering of the Temple's sacrifices and

---

16 Followed strict rule of life. Three-year training period. New members had to swear to keep their teachings and practices secret. Placed great emphasis on bathing. May have influenced John the Baptist.

other religious ceremonial duties.

The Sanhedrin was the legislative body. They oversaw all court cases, interpreted and taught the *Halachah*, acted as a court, oversaw the daily life of the people, and generally performed all the functions we would expect of social services and clergy today-- including managing charities, ensuring the well-being of the poor, appointing guardians and protectors for orphans, etc. The Sanhedrin was not friendly with the Romans; on the contrary, they frequently clashed, and the Romans tried to limit their power by not allowing them to oversee cases with a sentence of death.

It is also crucial to remember that the evangelists were not working in a world consisting of just Christians, Jews, and Romans. Early Christianity was not merely a radical parting from Judaism, but frankly, only another Jewish faction: The Jewish-Jesus offshoot shared the Judaic intellectual field with:

- The Pharisees in several separate and rivaling communities all over Palestine. Those of the Fourth Philosophy were possibly a Pharisee offshoot.
- The Sadducees, probably separate factions.
- At least two separate schools of the Essenes; John the Baptist possibly having been one.
- The Therapeutae; possibly an Essene offshoot.
- The Samaritans, with their own adapted Pentateuch and temple on Mount Gerizim.
- The Zealots, a theocratic group with a robust militant dominance. They believed that they should pay tax only to God and not to Rome.
- The Sicarii, a Zealot offshoot, specialized in close-quarter assassination.
- Several other minor groups.

Those who professed forms of Judaism were at constant blows with Palestinian proponents of various forms of Hellenism, Zoroastrianism, possibly also proto-Gnosticism, and who knows what else (Acts 2: 9-11).

Last but perhaps most troubling, all of them had Rome breathing down their necks, demanding respect to the empire through mandatory religious rituals and emperor worship.

In the first three or so centuries of their collective lives, Judaism **in all of its forms** and Christianity **in all of its structures** were part of one multifaceted religious family, each contending with the other for identity and primacy.

The New Testament of the Christian Holy Bible, specifically Mark and Matthew's books, provides anecdotes that imply antipathy between the early Christians and the Sadducees. These clashes reveal themselves in both theological and social aspects.

Mark describes how the Sadducees challenged Jesus' belief in the resurrection of the dead. Jesus defends his belief in resurrection against Sadducee opposition, stating, "and as for the dead being raised, have you not read in the book of Moses, in the story about the bush, how God said to him 'I am the God of Abraham, the God of Isaac, and the God of Jacob?' He is God not of the dead, but of the living; you are quite wrong."

In Matthew's Gospel, Jesus insists that the Sadducees were wrong because they knew "neither the scriptures nor the power of God." Jesus challenges the trustworthiness of Sadducee's interpretation of Biblical doctrine, the authority of which implements the Sadducee priesthood's power. The Sadducees address the resurrection issue by using marriage as their conveyance, which upheld their real agenda: protecting property rights through *patriarchal* marriage perpetuated by *male* lineage. Further, Matthew records John the Baptist calling the Sadducees a "brood of vipers." The New Testament thus clearly positions the identity and tenets of Christianity in unquestionable opposition to the Sadducees.

Therefore, the early Christians led by Jesus Christ found themselves in a fractured society, having to meet under the threat of exposure to powerful antagonistic groups, endure challenge and argumentation when they or Jesus attempted to preach His message to an already beleaguered, confused populace who were desperate for a leader to change their lot in life and their world at large, and who were an "occupied" people under Roman control. Hundreds of years of tradition were also at stake. Those in positions of relative influence fought to maintain their tenuous hold on infrastructure by their opposition to Jesus and His message that threatened to topple their society and religious beliefs. And yet, this man, Jesus, a peasant by the world's standards, met every assault and challenge, culminating in his confrontational public entry to the city of his trial, torture, and ultimate death.

Handel's MESSIAH said it best: "He was despised and rejected of men; a man of sorrows and acquainted with grief."

Into this cauldron of roiling points of view, that encompasses societal, political, governmental, historical religious structure, and theological beliefs enters Miryam of Magdala. How and why?

The unchallenged facts about her life establishing that Jesus cleansed her of seven demons (Luke 8:2 and Mark 16:9) are most recently accepted as Jesus curing her of either a physical disorder or mental attitude, rather than the previously popular notion that he freed her of evil spirits. Through the lens of historical, archaeological, and theological scholarship, this has been shown to be an erroneous, power-driven, and deliberate fiction that served prevailing agendas. Pope Gregory put forward to the world this blighted reputation, though unsubstantiated, which sadly shadowed her historical character for many years.

One wonders: if it takes thousands of years to right such a wrong on behalf of Miryam of Magdala—undisputed by the historical record as one of the most faithful and operatively valuable disciples of Jesus Christ, and a *woman* **before her time**—how many others have suffered the stigma of a similar fate before and after her life with or without exoneration? That it has taken so long for justice to prevail is a sad barometer on humankind's desire or ability to right wrongs and pursue comprehending interpretation.

Can you hear the Eternal sigh?

She was one of the women who accompanied and sustained Jesus in Galilee (Luke 8:1–2), and all four canonical Gospels attest that she witnessed Jesus' crucifixion and burial. John 19:25–26 further notes that she stood by the cross, near the Virgin Mary. Having seen where Jesus was buried (Mark 15:47), she went with two other women on Easter morning to the tomb to anoint the body according to custom. Finding the tomb empty, Mary ran to the disciples, returning with St. Peter, who, overwhelmed, left her there. Jesus then appeared to her and, according to John 20:17, instructed Mary to tell the apostles that he was ascending to God.

The Gospels reveal her to be of a practical character. Origen and other early textual interpreters usually viewed her as distinct from the mystical Mary of Bethany, who anointed Jesus' feet and wiped them with her hair (John 12:3–7), and from the penitent woman whose sins Jesus pardoned for anointing him in like fashion

(Luke 7:37–48). The Eastern Church also distinguishes between the three, but after they were identified as one and the same by St. Gregory the Great, Mary Magdalene's cult flourished in the West as a woman of shame and disrepute. This identification has since been challenged, and modern scholars are convinced that the three women are distinct.

Luke distinguishes her as a robust, energetic woman; she had been healed of ailments, though they are not identified anywhere in the texts. "Freed of seven demons" must mean she now enjoyed health, personal appeal, physical hardiness, and generosity as the philanthropist she proved herself to be.

[In the ancient world, it was commonplace to use the word "demon" as a broad term for that which no one understood or a condition that was frightening or unacceptable. In the first century, demons were widely believed to be the cause of physical and psychological illness[17]. Think of things like ADD, leprosy, fevers, mental illness (particularly schizophrenia), rheumatoid arthritis, gangrene, plague, or merely being fractious or resistant to the constraints of one's lot in life. Many of the attitudes, conditions, and illnesses for which we enjoy modern treatment and understanding today were labeled as being "possessed of a demon."]

Mary let go of the past and was freed from everything that holds a woman back from the use of her gifts, her personal liberty, free-thinking attitude and demeanor, and meaningful service to others through identity with the greater good and spiritual purpose of the mission as proclaimed by Jesus.

She, along with other women, supported Jesus out of her means (Luke 8:1-3). Practically, this meant she and other women from Galilee, like herself, provided the financial backing for Jesus' ministry as "he went on through cities and villages." This sistership was not subjugated by family or household responsibilities—they must have allocated those responsibilities to others. No husband kept them in tow, and they evidently didn't feel tied down by traditional norms for women that hampered their accompanying Jesus and the disciples "on the road." Mary Magdalene's philanthropic support of Jesus' ministry clearly included the 12 (or more) male disciples when they were on the road or in towns, villages, and cit-

17   Casey, Maurice (2010), Jesus of Nazareth: An Independent Historian's Account of His Life and Teaching, New York City, New York and London, England: T & T Clark, ISBN 978-0-567-64517-3; Ehrman, Bart D. (2006), Peter, Paul, and Mary Magdalene: The Followers of Jesus in History and Legend, Oxford, England: Oxford University Press, ISBN 978-0-19-530013-0; Kelly, Henry Ansgar (2006), Satan: A Biography, Cambridge, England: Cambridge University Press, ISBN 978-0521604024.

ies. They had to eat; they had to have somewhere to meet; they needed a place to sleep. Clearly, sometimes they slept "rough," but from a practical view, certainly not for Jesus' three-year ministry.

While contacts or connections in other areas might be able to help with some of their needs, the complexion and size of peasant homes could hardly accommodate 15 or more people for an extended stay (feeding, meeting, and sleeping), any more than a modern-day lower or middle-class family could or would do today!

She and the others may have contributed to the daily needs of wives and children the male disciples left behind when they quit fishing (or other jobs) to follow Jesus, remembering that few of the disciples had means themselves or were from wealthy extended families. She, with the other women from Galilee, also supported themselves—lodging, food, travel—when they made pilgrimages to Jerusalem, several days' journey to the south.

These and other practical considerations cannot be ignored when considering the movements and stories associated with Jesus, his disciples, and those that followed Him during his brief 3-year ministry. They all committed to trials of differing levels, being treated as outcasts by family, friends, and the people to whom they ministered, enduring discomfort, hardship, and danger in some cases. Even the disciples argued among themselves regarding the wisdom of specific plans and actions. The women, however, remained stalwart--particularly Mary.

Consider: *if you decided to join a "cult"*—because that is what the Jesus movement *appeared to be to traditional Jews*—would your family and friends clap their hands and bid you well? Or would they find it almost impossible to understand why you were discarding and leaving everything in your life (family, responsibilities, beliefs, traditions) to follow a stranger whose message indulged and encouraged that behavior? It is not hard to imagine that your family and mine might think we had "a screw loose" or be under some sort of spell, is it? Further, would you—as an acquaintance or stranger—casually open your home to a bunch of ragged strangers, knowing that it could taint you with suspicion among your neighbors or the authorities? Mary and the other disciples certainly did not choose an easy road, nor was it a walk in the park, as we sometimes fail to consider and remember when we concentrate only on gospel accounts of that period. Much pertinent detail was not included in those writings, which begs more questions with no reliable answers, only logical speculations. Meet Mary, who was to become Miryam of Migdalah.

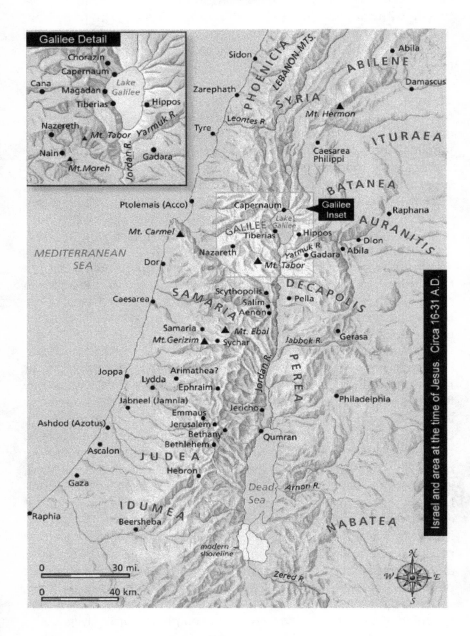

Israel and area at the time of Jesus. Circa 16-31 A.D.

Adam Clarke Commentary

Out of whom went seven devils -Who had been possessed in a most extraordinary manner; probably a case of inveterate lunacy, brought on by the influence of evil spirits. The number seven may here express the superlative degree.

Mary Magdalene is commonly thought to have been a prostitute before she came to the knowledge of Christ, and then to have been a remarkable penitent. So, historians and painters represent her: but neither from this passage, nor from any other of the New Testament, can such a supposition be legitimately drawn. She is here represented as one who had been possessed with seven demons; and as one among other women who had been healed by Christ of evil (or wicked) spirits and infirmities. As well might Joanna and Susanna, mentioned Luke 8:3, come in for a share of the censure as this Mary Magdalene; for they seem to have been dispossessed likewise by Jesus, according to St. Luke's account of them. They had all had infirmities, of what sort it is not said, and those infirmities were occasioned by evil spirits within them; and Jesus had healed them all: but Mary Magdalene, by her behavior, and constant attendance on Jesus in his lifetime, at his crucifixion, and at his grave, seems to have exceeded all the other women in duty and respect to his person. Bishop Pearce.

There is a marvelous propensity in commentators to make some of the women mentioned in the Sacred Writings appear as women of ill fame; therefore, Rahab must be a harlot; and Mary Magdalene, a prostitute: and yet nothing of the kind can be proved either in the former or in the latter case; nor in that mentioned Luke 7:36, etc., where see the notes. Poor Mary Magdalene is made the patroness of penitent prostitutes, both by Papists and Protestants; and to the scandal of her name, and the reproach of the Gospel, houses fitted up for the reception of such are termed Magdalene hospitals and the persons themselves Magdalenes! There is not only no proof that this person was such as commentators represent her, but there is the strongest presumptive proof against it: for, if she ever had been such, it would have been contrary to every rule of prudence, and every dictate of wisdom, for Christ and his apostles to have permitted such a person to associate with them, however fully she might have been converted to God, and however exemplary her life, at that time, might have been. As the world, who had seen her conduct, and knew her character, (had she been such as is insinuated), could not see the inward change, and as they sought to overwhelm Christ and his disciples with obloquy and reproach on every occasion, they would certainly have availed themselves of so favorable an opportunity to subject the character and ministry of Christ to the blackest censure, had he permitted even a converted prostitute to minister to him and his disciples. They were ready enough to say that he was the friend of publicans and sinners, because he conversed with them in order to instruct and save their souls; but they could never say he was a friend of prostitutes, because it does not appear that such persons ever came to Christ; or that he, in the way of his ministry, ever went to them. I conclude therefore that the common opinion is a vile slander on the character of one of the best women mentioned in the Gospel of God; and a reproach cast on the character and conduct of Christ and his disciples. From the full account of Mary Magdalene, she was probably a person of great respectability in that place; such a person as the wife of Chuza, Herod's steward, could associate with, and a person on whose conduct or character the calumniating Jews could cast no aspersions.

Copyright Statement

Bibliography

Clarke, Adam. "Commentary on Luke 8:2". "The Adam Clarke Commentary." https://www.studylight.org/commentaries/acc/luke-8.html. 1832

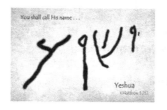

You shall call His name . . .

Yeshua
(Matthew 1:21)

Chapter Seven
The Magdalene

"You have always been the most disobedient of children," complained her mother. "Why can you not accept the rules for behavior? You bring me shame and concern. All the women speak of it, and the other girls whisper about you. Dressing as a boy and lingering about the waterside was bad enough but sneaking into the temple classes during your 'time' is unforgivable! Begone from my sight but stay indoors! And do something useful for a change."

After being chastised, Miryam ran from the courtyard and flung herself onto a pallet in the corner of the platform room above the animal quarters. 'Unforgivable?' she thought. 'No, unforgivable was that females were not meant to read, write, think, or question! There had to be more to life than the drudgery of household chores and childrearing! Who wrote the rules, why were rules so different for males, did God truly make females inferior to males? Why were there glowing lights in the night sky? Why did the sun sleep? Why was life so short? What caused sickness or death? What did the rest of the world look like? How big was the world? What did God sound like, and why did He speak to only some men?' These and many more thoughts plagued Miryam's mind as her body and intellect grew from a curious, mischievous child to a young girl to a woman on the day her monthly 'time' began when, a few months ago, she turned twelve years of age.

Shortly after her thirteenth birthday, her father announced at the dinner meal that he had agreed for Miryam to marry. Her two sisters – both younger – were immediately happy, not in the least because Miryam's betrothal meant they would be next in line without the obstacle of the eldest being unmarried.

"But I don't want to be married!" protested Miryam.

"Hush, child," warned her mother. "Your father knows what

is best."

"Best for whom? Not me! I won't do it! Did you even ask me or warn me? No!" Miryam huffed and stood in a fit of pique glaring at her father.

"You show your disrespect, Miryam. Control yourself and sit down. It is time you acted like a woman. You must cease these outbursts. No husband will tolerate them or you if you continue to behave in these outspoken ways. I give you a future and a good one at that. Your behavior threatens to throw it away," her father advised calmly.

"Sit, girl, and show some gratitude for once!" her mother whispered furiously.

"Why can I not choose?!" Miryam protested. "What if I hate him?"

"The choice is not yours to make, Miryam. You must trust that I do what is best for you and the family's future. We will meet at the next Shabbat. The subject is closed. It has been decided." Her father rose and walked from his family's presence into the court-yard to devote himself to evening prayer beneath the stars, which was his daily habit.

After the appropriate ceremony, Miryam followed her new husband from the celebrations to their quarters in his home, which was grand compared to her family's small house at the end of the town. He sat on a low, cushioned couch and signaled to her to do the same, opposite him. Nodding to his servant to pour wine, the elderly Pharisee explained to Miryam that he had been lonely since his wife's passing.

"Rebekkah was a blessing to my life except that she was un-able to bear me sons. We lost several over the years we were to-gether. I trust that with God's blessing, you and I will enjoy the gift of children. I am often harried by my work, so you will have much time to yourself. I was assured by your father that you will not be troubled by this and that you are more than capable of occupying yourself with a variety of interests." The older man sipped his wine thoughtfully. "Have some dates; I understand they are a favorite of yours."

Tentatively, she reached for a date and took a bite. "They are deliciously sweet and soft, thank you," she said demurely, keep-ing her head and eyes lowered. Soft music wafted from beyond

their room, supplied by one of the
man's other servants playing the lyre[18].

"Dance for me, my new, little wife," suggested the graying Pharisee.

Delighted by his request (as she was always chastised at home for her love of dancing, pronounced a "frivolous and useless pastime" by her mother), Miryam rose and walked to the end of the room in front of the large balcony. She began tentatively, but as the music enticed and her spirit soared, she danced and danced, the thoughts of the Psalms[19] invigorating her performance. 'Perhaps marriage might not be so distasteful' if she was able to indulge herself in pursuits such as this without punishment, she thought as she twirled.

Her husband clapped, and she stopped dancing, breathless and smiling.

"Is my husband pleased?" she asked tentatively.

"Yes, he is," said the Pharisee, motioning to her. "Come and stand by me."

Obediently, she padded to the side of his chair. "Yes, my husband?"

His hand slowly snaked beneath her tunic, and he said with eyes alight, "Ah, there it is." With the words of Leviticus[20] in mind, he touched his new wife's budding flower.

Jumping, Miryam uttered a gasp, her eyes wide in shock. His fingers began a slow stroking exploration, which, while shocking, was pleasurable. She did not know how to react, but in her mind were admonitions for a wife to be obedient and to pleasure her husband, so she remained standing next to him, braving his touch while at the same time enjoying it.

"Relax, little dove. You will become accustomed to this. It is your first lesson in marriage. Hold fast to the back of my chair, as your knees may become weak," said the Pharisee as he continued fondling her with bolder strokes.

Miryam's breathing became rapid and shallow as she stared

---

18   The lyre was the chief instrument of the orchestra of the Second Temple.F2 King David, who excelled at playing the lyre), was therefore held in particular honor by the Levites. According to Josephus, the first-century CE Jewish historian, it had ten strings sounded with a plectrum (Josephus, Antiquities 8.3.8 (94), Whiston 1957:463). The lyre is box-shaped, with two arms and a yoke, and an approximate average height of 50 to 60 cm.

19   **Psalm 150:** Praise the LORD. Praise God in his sanctuary; praise him in his mighty heavens. **2** Praise him for his acts of power; praise him for his surpassing greatness. **3** Praise him with the sounding of the trumpet, praise him with the harp and lyre, **4** praise him with timbrel and dancing, praise him with the strings and pipe, **5** praise him with the clash of cymbals, praise him with resounding cymbals. **6** Let everything that has breath praise the LORD. Praise the LORD.

20   **Leviticus 21:13:** And he shall take a wife in her virginity.

blankly into his face, becoming lost to all but the sensations of his fingers, which were unlike anything she had experienced. In a short while, her eyes closed as she moaned and shuddered in a wash of pleasure.

The Pharisee smiled. "Come and stand astride me," he said in a rasping tone she had not heard him use. Miryam obeyed as if in a trance. "Now, sit down," he said, pushing down on her shoulder with one hand, guiding her and himself with the other. "Ah, yes," he said.

Miryam's eyes flew open. She felt as if she were split in two, and all but screamed, saying, "What have you done? Oh ..." struggling unsuccessfully, as she was impaled.

"While your wriggling is pleasurable, relax, wife, and move against me," he ordered. "I will show you." And he did.

Afterward, as if by magic, a woman servant appeared with a tray of steaming towels. She took Miryam's arm and helped her dismount, handing her a towel with a knowing, instructive nod. Miryam stood shaking beside her husband's chair, his eyes closed, breathing heavily.

"Is he dying?" she asked the woman.

"No, he is fine," the woman said, placing one of the steaming towels over the man's exposed lower body. "Now, come with me. There is more to be done with you. A child should not have a child in her belly," said the woman, taking Miryam's hand and leading her from the room of her initiation to the conjugal rights of marriage. Miryam walked stiffly beside her, aware of soreness, casting a glance to her new husband, who snored quietly in his chair.

Busy with writing and teaching at the synagogue[21], Miryam's husband kept long hours, sometimes until late evenings. Thus, she had most days to herself to pursue the whims of her natural curiosity. Word spread of her swimming nude in the pool within their walled, private gardens; of solitary, unaccompanied walks in the marketplace; of unsolicited conversations with married and unmarried men about the history and the stars; of the unashamed wearing of adornments. Still, while shocking and unattractive to the expectations of the culture of the time, all of the criticisms contained no violations of her marital vows or breaking of the law. Because of her forward statements and questions about life, religion, and

---

21 Pharisees were teachers in the synagogue in ancient Israel. The Pharisees, however, went on to write the Mishnah, an important text that helped Judaism continue beyond the destruction of the temple. Thus, despite there being no sect of Pharisees today, they did lay the groundwork for modern-day Rabbinic Judaism.

societal conventions, some said she was possessed of a demon by undermining tradition. Many accused her of prideful behavior and ungodly demeanor contrary to expectations and biblical directives because of her independent attitudes.

Despite that her appearance, behavior, and deportment proved somewhat troublesome to her husband's public defense of her character, he remained charmed by and loyal to her. Mary fulfilled her role as his wife with becoming conduct laced with actions and affection that endeared her to him. So it was that when he became increasingly less virile and lively because of a growing illness accompanied by advanced age, Mary found herself becoming restless. However, she attended him with affection and constancy. Ultimately, Time had its way, and Mary became a wealthy, if still young and attractive widow. She had the same propensities as during her husband's life, but now without his powerful presence and effective defense, was subject to vicious rumor fed by covetous antagonists, many of whom were power-wielding misogynists of her day. One day these would become dangerous.

The man called Yeshua (Jesus) was amassing an ever-growing following. Surreptitiously, Miryam tried to learn more about him, to hear some of his words as people gathered when he spoke or to inquire about him. When she rose to his defense in retort to defaming comments or inaccurate reports of the message he was preaching, she was treading where angels would advise otherwise. As a result of her longstanding reputation and current actions, she was seized under a false accusation, subjected to frightening interrogation, and brought before the man himself [less in a challenge for the healing of a woman labeled as being possessed of demons with unbecoming behavior, fits of outlandish assertions, pridefulness, depravity, and other presumed sins, but more to discredit Jesus' claims and demonstrations of healing]. A tousled and desperate Miryam was forcefully thrown to the ground before Jesus[22].

---

22   Luke 8: 1-3

She looked frightened, her eyes darting fearfully around the assembled group of jeering men. Rough handling had caused her hair to come unbraided, and it was wildly askew, her head shawl hanging from one shoulder, her tunic soiled and torn. She had to yell to make herself heard above the din of complaining voices with barbed accusations. Thus, she appeared as a raging madwoman. She finally collapsed into tears, beaten down by the combined power of her accusers as a woman alone with no experiential means to vindicate herself. She had been proud; she did behave in a straightforward manner contrary to what was expected of women of her day and times; she had foolishly "bucked the system," not considering dangerous ramifications.

When she heard his voice, an instant calmness settled upon her and the gathering. Jesus did not speak loudly or forcefully. Instead, his soft tones soothed away the resounding antagonism and bathed Miryam in a sense of tranquility. He asked her accusers to clarify their allegations with examples of her supposed wrongdoing and listened carefully. Their summary suggestion that she was possessed and guilty of transgressions as they saw it, demanding that she be stoned, drew a slight smile from him. Miryam recoiled into herself when she heard them pronounce the punishment of stoning—a notoriously painful, slow, and ugly death.

While idly moving his fingers in the dust beside her, Yeshua asked her some questions that dealt explicitly with the men's accusations. She answered them truthfully and factually. Miryam was unable to muster any effective defense except to explain that she loved God and had tried her best to always follow the Ten Commandments, acknowledging that at times her actions were headstrong in response to the taunts and guffaws of her accusers. When he continued to speak with her, asking why she had spoken in ways unbecoming a woman, she felt confident in answering. She respectfully explained that it was either in an attempt to correct a wrong or because she was curious about something, not agreeing that women cannot have questions or thoughts of their own. She told him that she was unaware that God considered that a sin since the law and their society did not allow women to learn to read or write. Therefore, how could she know that asking questions was indeed forbidden before God? Miryam pled with Yeshua to explain to her why 'wanting to know' was a sin. That desire is what drove her to seek Yeshua when he spoke to the people, to learn about what he had to say, to find out the answers to her questions about life and

God. How could that be a sin merely because she was a woman?

Yeshua bent to her and placed his hand on her head, quietly praying over her. He smiled at her and whispered that God is spirit, and God does not recognize gender when taking account of one's soul. Yeshua told her that what one asks of God—if it is done with a pure heart-- will be granted in God's time. He told her that she was forgiven by God the Father for any sins she may have unwittingly committed because she was contrite and genuinely wanted forgiveness. Yeshua said that she would live a "redeemed life" afterward and experience joy and knowledge beyond her expectations because God's Holy Spirit would come to her. She would become one with the Father through His Holy Spirit. He asked for her commitment, and she gave it with her whole being, tears running down her cheeks.

Then he turned to the assembly and in a clear voice pronounced that Miryam had been freed by God from the power of any demons her accusers believed afflicted her, from previous wrongdoing, from pridefulness, and anything else they thought warranted this biased, unreasonable, and uncorroborated treatment of one of God's children. He challenged the group by saying that further pursuit of this woman would be a challenge to God himself.

"Who among you believes himself capable of challenging the forgiveness of Almighty God?" asked Yeshua to the assemblage in a clear, unfaltering voice. As he looked at them one after the other, and they either looked to the floor or backed away, Miryam felt vindicated and empowered. She made a silent commitment to follow this man in loyalty and dedication, realizing that this was the destiny God intended for her all along.

She looked up at him in reverence and gratitude, knowing in her heart that he understood her longing for deepened understanding. "Rabboni," she whispered.

With the revelations of studies of both the synoptic gospels (Matthew, Mark, and Luke of the New Testament in the Holy Bible of Christianity), the Gospel of John – considered the fourth gospel, the Gospels of Philip and Thomas (categorized as Gnostic texts), there remains one which has not received the attention it deserves:

It is the Gospel of Mary, attributed to Miryam of Magdala (Mary Magdalene), who as one of Yeshua's (Jesus) followers, providers, and supporters, was also among those faithful at the foot of His cross following the crucifixion, attendant to the anointing of his body in the tomb, lamenting at the empty tomb, and seeking information on the whereabouts of Jesus' body.

She was the sole and first witness of the resurrection, receiving a message from Jesus' transcendent form to carry to the other disciples. This was a woman of strength and faith who stood vigil with Jesus' mother and another disciple throughout the grueling hours that followed the crucifixion until they heard Him cry, *"Eloi, lama sabachtani?"* [My God, why has thou forsaken me?], whereas the other disciples hurried away out of fear that they might be arrested and put to death as well. Miryam had to wait until the Jewish Sabbath ended[23] before walking with her spice jar to the tomb, only to find that the stone had been removed.

After running to tell Simon Peter and the other disciples, they went to the tomb to inspect it for themselves, but then went home. Miryam remained, weeping in grief, answered a question put to her from inside the sepulcher, "They have taken away my Lord, and I know not where they have laid him." In utter despair, eyes filled with tears, she then saw the figure of a man standing nearby and, when he called her name, she recognized him and was likely exhilarated. What a blessing she received from Yeshua on that day: she was not only the first to see the risen Christ, but chosen to carry the news of His victory over death to the disciples. He could have chosen to reveal himself to his mother, another of the disciples, Salome, anyone other than Miryam (Mary Magdalene). Yet he chose her for this important role, which indicates his trust in her character to find the strength to seek and draw out the disciples from where they hid, comfort them, and turn their minds away from despair and darkness to the light of his teachings and words represented.

Translation taken from the scrolls discovered by Archaeological Expedition involving Messrs. Rutherford (Dr. Nigel), Brandon (Dr. James), Najjar (Dr. Amir), Stanton (Dr. Andrew), Lawson (Nicholas),

---

23   This was not to be performed on the Sabbath, so Mary had to wait until the first day of the week to anoint Jesus' body

and Brandon-Maxwell (Ms. Bethany).

All artifacts and translations filed with and currently In the possession of the British Museum with attendant provenance documentation.

[SDU = scroll damaged and unreadable]

"[SDU] "..... called Yeshua. All that I say here is true of his words, his deeds, his life, and his death.

"Many others have testified, saying the same things as I say. Their words are the same words as my words. [SDU] The law says that it is true when more than one.[SDU].

"I know as I breathe that I am with him in the beginning. I know that his testimony is true. I was with him in the end, and I know that [SDU].

"After [SDU] of speaking to many and pouring blessings and healings of people who came to [SDU], in winter at the feast of the dedication at Yerushalayim, Yeshua walked in Solomon's porch in the temple. The Pharisees   [SDU] said, 'If you are the Messiah, tell us.'
Yeshua answered them.

"He told them that he had [SDU] but they did not believe. He said that they did not believe that the works he did were in the name of the spirit and that they could not hear his voice. [SDU] He told them that those with eyes   [SDU] and ears [SDU]

"The Pharisees were angry and challenged Yeshua. He said that those who hear his words and follow them, he blesses with eternal life and they will not perish. He said that [SDU] was the one who sent the people to him, and that the spirit was greater than all men or things. [SDU]

"When he told the Pharisees that the spirit and he was one, they took up stones again to stone him. Yeshua called to them. [SDU]

"I have shown you many good works from the spirit. For which of those works do you stone me?' [SDU] They answered him, 'We do not stone you for a good work, but for blasphemy because you, being a man, make yourself God.'

"[SDU   ] and we shared bread and wine, listening as the Master spoke his words to us. Then I took a jar of pure spikenard[24] and poured some upon the head of Yeshua, my lord. [SDU   ] The other disciples called out against me. [SDU   ] Yeshua said to them: 'Leave her be. I am come to do what I must. She has done what she must.

[SDU   ] "'In truth I tell you, when they speak of me, what she has done will also be told in memory of her. You do not know or understand what she has done. [SDU   ] I tell you this: when all have abandoned me, she will stand beside me [SDU   ] From this day forth, she shall be known as Migdalah, for she [SDU   ] as a tower to my flock. The time will soon come when [SDU   ] alone by mine.' But the disciples did not understand his words.

"[SDU   ] " before the feast of Pesach, Yeshua and his disciples shared a meal in the city. He laid aside his outer garment, [SDU   ] towel and a basin filled with water and washed the feet of the disciples. [SDU   ] he said to them 'Do you understand what I have done? If I, the teacher, have washed your feet, you also ought to wash one another's feet. You also should do as I have done for you. [SDU   ]

'[SDU   ], blessed are you if you do them... [SDU   ] 'In truth I tell you that one of you will betray me.'

"I, Miryam of Magdala, whom Yeshua loved, was at the table. I asked him, 'Rabbouni[25], who is it?' He answered me with sadness.

"[SDU   ] 'It is he to whom I will give this.' He dipped the piece of bread. When he had done this, he gave it to Juda, the son of Shimon of Kerioth. Then Yeshua said to him: 'What you must do, do quickly.'"

---

24   **Spikenard** [N] [E] Smith, William, Dr. "Entry for 'Spikenard'". "Smith's Bible Dictionary" 1901. (Heb. nerd) is mentioned twice in the Old Testament viz. in (Solomon 1:12; Song of Solomon 4:13 Song of Solomon 4:14) The ointment with which our Lord was anointed as he sat at meat in Simons house at Bethany consisted of this precious substance, the costliness of which may be inferred from the indignant surprise manifested by some of the witnesses of the transaction. See (Mark 14:3-5; John 12:3 John 12:5) (Spikenard,from which the ointment was made, was an aromatic herb of the valerian family (Nardostachys jatamansi). It was imported from an early age from Arabia, India and the Far East. The costliness of Marys offering (300 pence=$45) may beat be seen from the fact that a penny (denarius, 15 to 17 cents) was in those days the day-wages of a laborer. (Matthew 20:2) In our day this would equal at least $300 or $400.-ED.)
[N] indicates this entry was also found in Nave's Topical Bible
[E] indicates this entry was also found in Easton's Bible Dictionary

25   Definition of **rabboni:** MASTER, TEACHER—used as a Jewish title of respect applied especially to spiritual instructors and learned persons; Merriam Webster (since 1928)

We know from historical record that after the burial of Yeshua (Jesus) by Yosef of Arimathaea, when Miryam went to the tomb, found it-empty, and experienced seeing her risen Lord in transformative state, she rushed to the place where Martha and Eleazar (her sister and brother whom Yeshua (Jesus) had restored to life), Miriam—the mother of Ya'akov, Yosef, Salome, Toma, Yosef of Arimathaea, Nicodemus (who brought spices for his burial), Levi (Mattithyahu or Matthew), and Joanna were gathered.

Miryam (Mary) told them she had seen Yeshua and spoke the words he had said to her. Then they sent word to the others of what the Migdalah had witnessed, but it was many days before they returned, as all had fled Bethany in fear of the priests and Pharisees, each returning to his own home.

This fulfilled Yeshua's spoken prophecy that they would be scattered, everyone onto his own, and they would leave him all alone, but for one. And to that one... Miryam of Migdalah... he appeared and spoke a message to be given to his other disciples.

When they all came together, the Migdalah spoke to the group.

"I tell you, do not weep and do not grieve, for his grace and that of the one who sent him will be with us and will protect us. Let us praise his greatness, for he
has prepared us and made us truly human. What you think is hidden from you, I

will tell to you. My Master spoke thus to me. He said [SDU]

'Miryam, blessed are you who came and whose eyes are set upon the kingdom, who from the beginning has understood and followed my teachings. [SDU]

'I tell you in truth, you are as a tower among the people with many windows. Whosoever listens to my words will not taste death, but know the truth of eternal life. Remember this well.'"

"[SDU] Then he showed me a vision of a great tower that seemed to reach unto the stars. I saw the first window that showed the light of love and compassion, and I knew that to bathe in that light, we must be free of all judgment and wrath.

"The next showed forth wisdom and understanding. To partake of its blessing, you must be free of all ignorance and intolerance. [SDU]

"Then my master showed me a third window of honor and humility. Only when the heart is free of all duplicity and arrogance may we [SDU] in the light it sheds.

"Then came the fourth, shining with strength and courage. I heard him tell me that [SDU] must be freed from the weakness of the flesh and confront your fears, can you feel the strength from its glow.

"To look through the fifth window of clarity and knowing yourself for the first time, you must accept and understand [SDU] that you are a child of the living spirit. As my soul floated upward, I realized that I could no longer hear the voice of the world, as all had become silent.

"Then in the light above [SDU], I saw the sixth window of power and healing. My master told me that to be worthy of power and healing, we must truly have clarity and know the truth of ourselves.

"My master told me to make ready to rise to the seventh window where my soul would be filled by light and goodness, And I felt my soul, free of all darkness, [SDU] to be filled with the light and goodness that is the spirit. And I was filled with a joy beyond joy. My master pointed to the eighth and final window of the tower from which burned [SDU] the grace and beauty of the spirit. Then I heard the voice of my master call out to me. 'Miryam, whom I have called the Migdalah, now you have seen all [SDU] and have learned the truth of yourself. Now you have truly become the tower for the people and are complete. Blessed are you.'"

"And then my vision ended. This is what my master has told and shown me. I have revealed to you what is true."

Initially, many of the disciples did not understand what she had said and grumbled against her among themselves, wondering if Yeshua had indeed spoken to her privately... a woman... and not spoken openly with them. They surely pondered if Yeshua preferred her to them. When the Migdalah wept, Levi answered Shimon Kefa's doubts.

"Shimon Kefa, you have always been hot-tempered. Now you are speaking against this woman like the adversaries and Pharisees. But if our master made her worthy, who are you indeed to reject her? Surely, as his always faithful companion, Yeshua knew her better than all others. That is why he told her more than us. She was to him what we were not. Now she is that to us on behalf of the master and his words.

"Rather, let us be ashamed and do as she says. Let us put on perfect humanity and acquire it as she has done, and separate as he commanded us and preach the testimony of the Son of Humanity, not laying down any other rule or other law beyond that which he gave us."

When they heard this, they were divided and argued amongst themselves, and they began to leave separately and go forth to proclaim and to teach and preach what they understood of the words of the rabbi. And Miryam of Migdalah did the same with a joy beyond joy burning in her heart, feeling the blessing of her master, Yeshua, knowing they would one day greet each other when her journey on earth was done.

Chapter Eight
The Blue Woman – Bondage

The Romans divided slaves taken from the territories or towns under siege between personal attendants (domestic service), grounds upkeep, household, maintenance of equipment and systems, and those women assigned the gladiatorial contingent's care. Well-educated or trained slaves could work as teachers or in other professions or might engage as wet-nurses, spinners, weavers, clothes makers, entertainers, or prostitutes. There existed a wide variety of slaves in Rome and outside the city in terms of category.

Slaves belonging to one person (at least three in number) were called a *familia*, and the private slaves were classified as either the *familia urbana* (city) or *familia rustica* (country). City slaves often traveled with the master to any country villa without losing their status by departing from the town as the estate was considered an extension of the main townhouse. They were assigned to groups reflecting their specialties called *decuriae*. For instance, bakers (*pistores*) and cooks (*coqui*), as well as *ordinarii* (who ran the housekeeping) and *literati* (readers or secretaries for the household), were highly prized and above the bulk of slaves referred to as *vulgares*. Herdsmen, farmhands, or field gatherers were part of the *familia rustica*.

The victorious gladiator, Maximus, was a slave taken in a battle around 90 A. D. with one of the Teutonic tribes harassing the Roman Empire's northwestern borders. While many trading partners among such tribes existed, when the Teutones and the Cimbri struck so far south around 100 B.C. to threaten Roman armies in what would one day become France and northern Italy, a long-term threat was identified by the Romans. [The territory (that is now the area beyond the Rhine and Danube Rivers) was barbarian. Ultimately, barbarians from that area would challenge the Roman

Empire, its armies, and its civilization for many years.]

The Colosseum construction began in 72 A.D. (36-42 years after the death of Jesus Christ, whose decease is estimated between 30-36 A.D.) under the order of Emperor Vespasian, who died before its completion. During the reign of Domitian, construction was finally completed in 96 A.D., attracting crowds of up to 50,000 people for its well-organized and spectacular events. A large percentage of participants in the "games" were slaves, conquered peoples, or criminals. However, some free men from low social standing were allowed to fight for potentially immense rewards (like freedom from debt or guaranteed support of their families in the event of their inevitable death).

Warriors for the many different events depended upon skill level, experience, and previous record. Some types of gladiators were:

Thraeces – Thracians, armed with a round shield and dagger
Equites – who entered the arena on horseback
Dimachaerus – armed with two swords
Essedarii – fought from a horse-drawn chariot
Retiarius – armed with only a trident and a weighted net

While there were only three primary training schools for gladiators, it was not unusual for advocates and sponsors among the consuls or other patrician ranks with sufficiently large familia rustica to operate their own gladiator school. In a bid to best the high-quality fighters produced by Capua and the two other popular training centers, agents would roam the empire to find candidates as potential gladiators.

Once enjoined, free man or slave led a disciplined life, including being shackled and sleeping in cells, freed only for mealtimes (during which no one was allowed to speak), and training. Because their health and hygiene were considered crucial to their performance, most ate three meals a day (meat, fish, cereals, vegetables, eggs, cheese, and goat's milk) with water the only other beverage. They also received massages and hot and cold baths. While training was intense, the overall focus was on fitness, which would potentially produce a victorious fighting gladiator and justify the patrician's investment.

[Although contrary to popular belief, historians advise that most gladiators did not fight to the death, and fewer than 20% perished in the arena. Fights between two equally matched opponents could be declared stalemates, and both warriors could depart the theater if they were determined by the crowd to have fought a brave battle. Despite the preceding, the average life expectancy for an active gladiator reached only to his mid-to-late twenties.]

If a gladiator were overmatched and wounded, he could hold a finger aloft in entreaty for his life to be spared. If the audience felt he put up a good fight, they could shout in his favor. Likewise, they could cry for his death. If a gladiator had to die, his opponent dispatched the loser with his weapon, receiving money and a laurel branch, which he would afterward wave at the audience as he ran around the arena. If rewarded because of longstanding prowess and success, a gladiator had an outstanding career and was allowed to leave the school. A wooden sword (a sign that his life was no longer at risk fighting in the arena) was his award. The same was true of slaves, who were sometimes awarded their freedom after an appropriate service period and success. All gladiators were trained to fight, potentially kill, and die well.

One must place the existence of the life of a gladiator into a historical context. A twenty-year-old Roman (or indeed a member of a parallel ethnicity) knew he would probably die before he was thirty, either from disease, accident, or battle. Men of the age wanted to die with dignity and honor, as members of an uncompromising militarist society. He could witness gladiators do so in the arena, and they valued the art of killing in a way beyond modern understanding. The Roman soldier's relative success in battle was a combination of relentless and excellent training, war strategies and methods, and soldiers' innate courage in hand-to-hand combat honed and ingrained by years of broadscale mindset. The Romans, like most premodern societies, faced daunting mortality rates. An ordinary citizen's ability to singlehandedly kill was a capability upon which the entire empire depended for its continued existence. It was the symbolic issue of the ultimate and fundamental human conflict – life and death – that made gladiatorial combat captivating for the Romans (and the Greeks).

The Blue Woman was brought by a Legate visiting the familia rustica of Aquilinus Cassian Fabius on his way back to Rome after his encounter and defeat of her northern tribe.

"Aquilinus! Greetings, and thanks to you, my friend!" called Gaius Trebonius from the back of his exhausted, sweaty horse. "We force marched to arrive in time for the evening meal!" he said jovially to his host's laughter.

"Come, my friend, let me bid you a proper welcome!" Aquilinus snapped his fingers. "Prisca, see to his men and horses. Call Gallia to deal with the slaves."

"I have a thirst for some of your good wine," said the Legate. "After so well won a battle, I also promised my men hard-earned rest and much-missed Roman hospitality."

"The glory of Rome and the emperor have always been your flagstaff, Gaius! You and they are most welcome and will be well rewarded, I can assure you. Now, come with me. You need to be relieved of the stresses of battle, to say nothing of the filth and stench." The men laughed together as only longstanding comrades of rich experience can do. Before he was appointed consul, Aquilinus and Gaius fought many battles together over the years. Now retired from the dangers of physical struggle, Aquilinus mastered the art of war within Rome's political society and culture.

"There is one among the slaves taken who I am told is a healer. I would beg your permission to have her see to some of my men who sustained wounds. I brought a complement of hostages here with enough men to oversee them—the rest of the cohort I sent on to Rome with the horsemen. I can assign one of my men to guard her, but she might need your household supplies for healing. Is that a problem?"

"Nonsense, Gaius. It is no trouble at all. I will see to it that some of my staff assist her. I have no doctor in residence, but some of my slaves are good at basics. Will that do?"

"Thank you, Aquilinus; my men deserve it. They fought bravely against the barbarians, despite being outnumbered and surprised. It was a hard fight, I admit, but a good battle to win!"

The Blue Woman crouched in the courtyard, eagerly gulping a refilled cup of water. Unlocking her cuff from the chain, a soldier yanked her to her feet. "Come with me," he said, brusquely leading her down a dark hallway into the building. They arrived at an ample, open space under a broad overhang. Some of the wounded sat on the low tables; others lay on top. A group of domestics came trotting into the area bearing cloths and jugs of water. They stood before her in confused shock.

"We were told ... you were to treat these men ... and we

were to help," one of them stuttered in explanation.

The Blue Woman nodded and smiled, folding her robe's sleeves and holding her hands forward to wash. She examined the prone men first, then those who sat upright, bearing their injuries and pain. She managed to communicate to those slaves sent to help what she needed from them, but with difficulty. After a few hours, she almost fainted from exhaustion, exposure, and weakness three times. At last, she finished. None would die; all were cleaned and bandaged, if still in pain.

She looked at the men and said to the resident slaves, "White willow? Hot peppers? Ginger? Valerian? Curcumin? Aloe?" When they shook their heads in confusion, she tried to outline the plant shapes in the floor's red dust. Still, she had no success. Then one of the wounded spoke to the slaves in their tongue. He was a member of a more easterly tribe of Teutones than the Blue Woman. He had enlisted as a young man in the Roman Army and learned its language, the language of Rome, the most powerful empire in the world. The slaves understood his translation; one woman dashed away to fetch what dried plants they had from her list. When she returned, the Blue Woman explained after applying or dosing them with a liquid infusion how often they should use what she wrapped in a fresh cloth for each man, the plant and amount varying as the condition required. The Blue Woman nodded her thanks to the slaves and the soldier who had translated her words.

Looking to the Roman soldier guarding her, she motioned that she should return to her group outside the courtyard. On their way back, they encountered the Legate who had come to check on his men. The guard relayed all that had happened, including that one of their company could speak her language or, in the least, understand it well enough to help attend the wounded men. The Legate nodded to the guard.

After taking a few steps away, he stopped, turned, and said, "*Tibi gratias ago pro cura et curatio*[26]. The Blue Woman held his gaze for a few moments and then nodded. She dismissed herself by turning and continuing down the long hall to the courtyard. He watched her go, shaking his head at her prideful attitude and appearance. Those black eyes and almost every inch of her body covered in blue tattoos and scars, even her face! He shivered. Although she was reasonably attractive—if one could look beyond her disfigurement—she seemed to represent something eerie, which sent a

---

26 Thank you for your care and treatment

chill down his spine.

Returning to visit more with Aquilinus in the *tablinum*[27], Gaius said, "You are named for Cassius, the saint, are you not?"

"So, my father told me, yes. Does that interest you, my old friend? If so, why?"

"I wonder if you have any interest in any of the slaves I've brought. Since you have no doctor here, I thought the woman who treated my men might be of use. She seems to have done a fair job by all reports, and my men are as at ease as one could hope. They spoke well of her. If you want her, consider her a gift for your hospitality to my men and me., friend saint."

"That is generous of you, Gaius. I will take her with gratitude. One never knows what may befall requiring a *medicum*. Thank you. Here, have some more of this wine while we talk."

The following morning, the Blue Woman was again released from the chain of slaves in bondage to the Legate, soon to travel to Rome and an unknown destiny. She was taken to an empty cell near the wide-open space, still housing the wounded. As she passed, she noticed no one lay prone, and all were eating a hearty breakfast. They looked up as she passed; some nodded, others stood in deference. The guard gestured for her to enter. It was a darkened space with an earthen floor with a cup and a single candle on a squat wooden table next to a low bed. The clang of the cell door and the click of the lock undid her composure; she slumped onto the bed, bowing her head as tears of uncertainty and frustration flowed.

After a night and morning of separation, the noises of those departing mixed with harsh orders, horses' clatter, the clink of chains, and the crack of a whip echoed against the walls. She prayed to Father Sun (whose blessed warmth she could neither feel nor see) and Mother Earth (whose fertility had been pounded back into this red, staining, and lifeless dirt) to sustain her in all that was to come.

Before long, she heard the unlocking of cells and the movement of people into the open yard where she had treated the wounded men of the Legate's cohort. The view from her cell showed only a part of both sides of a hall. Then she saw some slaves approaching with pails and jars. They bypassed her cell and moved down the hall to turn perpendicular, presumably to the open-air space with the low tables. They returned shortly, a small slave girl stopping at

---

27   Roman men often conducted business out of their Domus from a home office known as the tablinum. It was also the room where clients would meet their patron for the salutatio, a formal renewal of their patron-client relationship.

her cell, unlocking it, and motioning her to follow. Grateful to leave that dark place, she leaped out and walked behind the girl. Shortly, they came to a wondrous place: a large, bright room with a square water pool in its center with gleaming fish. The girl pointed and said, "piscina." A moment later, the consul entered with the Roman soldier who had translated the herbal plants' names and instructions to the slaves in attendance.

"You look well, I am pleased to see," she said to him. The soldier looked at her sternly and shook his head, clearly making an apology to the consul in whispers. The consul replied softly in the strange language, and the Blue Woman was amused because he could have yelled, and it would have made no difference as she did not understand the meaning of his words.

The soldier explained that she must not speak until spoken to; that he had dispensation to stay at the *familia* rustica to assist with her acclimatization and acceptance of her new assignment as *medicum* with his help as a language translator and tutor. She would receive modest compensation for her contribution with better accommodations among the female slaves who quartered together in a large room with windows, light, and air. The consul wanted her to give most of her attention to his several gladiators-in-training to ensure their overall health and treat training wounds or mishaps. Then she was to do routine checks and treat the complaints of any staff. She would care for and attend the master and his family before others, responding when summoned, despite what she was doing. The soldier asked her if she understood, and she nodded. She had to sign a scroll, ⊕ ◉ and she drew her marks: the symbol for Father Sun and ⊕ ◉ Mother Earth's spiral. Her compliance seemed to please the consul.

A graceful, slender, fair-haired woman joined him and sat on a silk-covered chaise against the wall. The overhead sunlight poured through the ceiling of the room, making the water sparkle. The swimming fish looked like their scales were made of precious stones. The consul said something more to the soldier, Leda, who translated for her. She was to strip naked before him. The Blue Woman was not embarrassed by nakedness in any situation and readily complied, although she was uncertain about the motivation behind his request. She turned in a circle as directed. The consul stepped closer to examine her body and its blue scars and markings. There was little of her olive complexion free of applied color, and the soldier lifted her long dark hair up and away so the consul could inspect every inch of her. Satisfied, he nodded to the soldier who dropped her hair and stepped away at attention.

Again, the consul spoke, and Leda translated. She was to follow the slave girl to the baths, clean herself thoroughly, have her hair braided, and dress in the clothing and sandals provided. By the time all was completed, the gladiators would have completed their morning training and taking open-air rest in the space beneath the overhang. She was to examine them after Leda's introduction and with his help. One of the *literati* would take notes of her translated assessments under each man's name. This entry and any subsequent ones would become a part of the gladiator's permanent record.

The Blue Woman was led away by the small slave girl, followed by Leda, her permanent shadow. He asked her name. She hesitated because, for years past, she was only *Modrá Žena*[28]. Long ago, whispers of a lullaby sung by her mother played in her mind. "Zofie," she responded. It sounded strangely familiar yet distant to her. "Zofie; I am Zofie." The girl touched her arm lightly, saying, "Zofie." Then she pointed to her chest and said, "Erth, it means earth," said the small girl who could have been no older than 10 or 11 years. Ahead lay a room full of sunlight, and Zofie danced with her arms uplifted, turning round and round. The soldier called to her and explained what must be done with haste and efficiency, not to delay the master's schedule and instructions.

Zofie undressed and submerged herself into the warm bath, allowing Erth to scrub her down and wash her hair. She would have lounged there longer, but for the persistent Leda, so she rose, scraped with the strigii[29], dried off, and dressed in the offered tunic and sandals. Her skin was clean and minus the dirt of war and travel, her hair freshly braided and shining. The Blue Woman, Zofie, was as presentable as her scarred, unusually colored, and etched body could present. She obediently followed Leda to where the gladiators relaxed, just having eaten their midday meal.

The tale of her treatment of the Legate's men with expertise and gentleness circulated completely through the contingent of gladiators. Mention of her unusual appearance also spread, so while they were somewhat prepared and curious, seeing her in the flesh was shocking. No one spoke. Leda made the appropriate introduction, including that Zofie did not speak vulgar Latin, the lan-

---

28   Blue Woman
29   A flat, curved implement used to scrape the oils and dirt from the skin when bathing, similar to the commonly used "sweat scrapers" in ancient and modern horse care.

guage of Rome, and the Domus. He introduced himself as both a former member of the Legate's cohort, current translator to Zofie, and extra bodyguard to the consul.

Zofie walked among the men, checking for existing conditions or festering wounds. She found little that needed her attention as the men were in relatively good shape: physically fit, well-fed, and clean, except for the sweat and dust of their morning training session. Some would require teeth pulled out, either loosened or rotting due to arena scuffles, but there were no serious wounds, only minor scrapes, cuts, and bruises. When she asked through Leda whether anyone suffered ailments like diarrhea or indigestion, the men laughed. She explained that she could rid them of such annoyances with herbal preparations, but it was their choice if they preferred to suffer. This, too, would be noted by the *literati*. In those beginning minutes of interaction with the gladiators, Zofie established herself as entirely different from any other woman they had encountered, not only in physical appearance but also in attitude and ability.

The *lanista* ran the Ludus Gladiator training school. He scrutinized Zofie. Women in ancient Rome were second-class citizens with few rights and their value as wives directly connected to their ability to provide heirs. Men indulged in relationships with other women routinely, be they slaves or prosti-
tutes, with other men, and with children. Roman morality centered upon the male as a stable and dominant figure in all aspects of life. The lanista laughed with his men, asking if any of them cared to bed the "ugly blue woman" in their midst. A few raised their hands, one man asking if his manhood would turn blue. That resulted in more raucous laughter. While Zofie did not understand the incentive for their amusement, she knew it concerned her, intended to denigrate. For a woman whose adult life had a position of power and respect among her people, even veneration, this change of circumstance was confusing and unfamiliar to her.

"She will report this evening to me with the other women, as well as two days hence," the *lanista* informed Leda. Leda's first instinct was to object; his considered approach was to keep quiet and check with the consul if he intended his medicum to participate in the gladiators' twice-weekly sexual activities. He, therefore, did not broach the subject with Zofie.

After eating, Zofie relaxed with the other women in their quarters. They spoke quietly among themselves, only one or two making any tentative approach toward her. She had not yet had the opportunity to examine any of them. Leda returned her from time among the gladiators to the women's section of the Domus before the evening meal. Afterward, a different male servant unlocked the door to their large room. Several of the women arose and walked toward him. He motioned for Zofie to follow. She complied but did not know why she was so directed.

As they approached the gladiators' cell block, the servant unlocked each, thrusting a woman inside. Zofie was pushed into a cell as well. A gladiator whose name she recalled was "Domo," reclined on a bed against the wall. Zofie stood just inside the threshold. Domo motioned to her to approach. When she got within arm's length, he grabbed her roughly, pushing her to her knees. She cried out, which made him laugh derisively. What ensued was a combination of violation of body and spirit that included a physical beating, leaving a battered Zofie crouched by the door awaiting release, forced to listen to the snores of her attacker.

The next day, she was summoned to the gladiator area after their training had ended. One of the men had a minor but profusely bleeding head wound, and another had a dislocated shoulder that required resetting. As she approached, she heard a few sniggers and some muffled remarks. None of the men seemed disturbed by her appearance or her slow and painful gait—none, that is, except Maximus.

"Why, Domo?" he asked of his fellow gladiator.

Domo shrugged. "She knows her place now," the man shrugged. "And I'm happy to say, I did not turn blue!" The man lowered his loincloth to expose his genitals, still glistening with sweat after their training workout, to his fellows' guffaws. Leda whispered the translation in response to her squeeze of his hand.

Zofie viewed the scene through only her right eye since the bruised and swollen shut left eye matched the purple remainder of her face's left side. The bruises on her arms and legs were present and sore but barely visible because of her extensive tattooing. As she passed by the standing, still grinning Domo on her way to the man with the head wound who was at the far end, quick as a flash, she turned and grabbed Domo's genitals, delivering a sharp twist and crushing thrust. The man crumpled to his knees in the red dirt, howling. Zofie continued toward the man with the head wound, whispering to Leda. Leda replied that he didn't think he should pass on her message as it would merely lead to more trouble. Zofie gave him such a stern look that he raised his eyebrows but agreed.

As she sat down to clean the head wound, Leda said to the group, his remark directed pointedly to Domo, "The Blue Woman says to tell you: 'Now he knows his place.'" The men all looked closely at Domo to gauge his reaction. No one spoke. Maximus laughed, and the laughter became slowly contagious. Zofie continued her work, allowing a small smile to creep over her swollen mouth.

Above, on the balcony, the consul stood deep in thought, having heard the full exchange and witnessing Zofie's condition and reaction to Domo. No one but the lanista was aware of his presence.

There were several gladiator categories, but principally four: Samnites, Myrmillo, Retiarius, and Thraex. The consul's *lanista* was a notorious and previously famous Samnite, although he was sufficiently well-versed in warfare and techniques to oversee all categories. As one of the most elite, retired gladiators, he was dubbed *summa rudis*. He wore a white tunic with a purple border (*clavi*) for all formal games, serving as a technical expert to ensure all gladiators fought bravely, skillfully, and according to the game's rules. During events and during training, he carried a baton and whip to point out illegal movements. He had the authority to stop a match or combined game if a gladiator was too seriously injured to continue or compel participants to fight on in deference to his *munerarius*[30] and master's decision. Retired gladiators were called *rudiarii*. Those who achieved high levels of success in the arena also gained high respect and popularity, making the offer of a position as *lanista* difficult, if not foolish, to refuse.

Samnites were named after the great warriors defeated by Rome in the early years of the republic. They were the most heavily armed. When the Samnites became allies of the Roman Empire, the designation was dropped and changed to Secutor. Their weapons were:

Scutum: a shield made from three sheets of wood, glued together and topped with a leather or canvas coating in a large, oblong shape

Galea: a plumed helmet with small eye holes and a visor

---

30 **Munerarius:** The giver of the games, a member of the upper orders acting privately (rare after the Republic) or in his official capacity as a magistrate or priest or the emperor. Outside Rome, munerarii were generally municipal and provincial priests of the imperial cult or local governors.

Gladius: a short sword used primarily by Roman foot soldiers but also by gladiators

Manicae: A manica was a type of iron or bronze arm guard with curved and overlapping metal segments or plates, fastened to leather straps, leather elbow or wristbands

Greaves: protective leather leg armor from just below the knee to the ankle

Myrmillo (Murmillo) wore large metal helmets with a fish emblem, a *manica* of mail, metal, or leather "scales" on the left arm and on at least one leg, with a straight Greek-style sword. They were known as "fish men." The helmet covered the face completely, with small, closely spaced circles that formed a grill to provide excellent straight and peripheral vision.

Cassis crista Galea: heavy bronze helmet used to protect the entire face

Manicae: elbow or wristbands made of mail

Ocrea: shin guards

Retarius (Retiarii), referred to as "net men," usually fought with weapons fashioned on a fisherman's tools. Their legs and head were left exposed, and they wore armor only on the arm and shoulder. The Retiarii carried a short dagger, and his armor included:

Retes: a weighted net designed to entangle the opponent

Fascina: long, three-pronged trident thrown like a harpoon

Galerus: metal shoulder piece on the left upper arm

Traex or Thraces were named after another enemy of Rome and usually fought in pairs. They wore visored helmets with wide brims, *ocreae* on both shins, and carried a small rectangular or round shield. Their armor was:

Sica: a curved, scimitar-shaped dagger designed for delivering slicing attacks on an opponent

Galea: metal helmet with a wide brim

Manicae: elbow and wrist bands

Greaves: shin guards to just below the knee

Although there were other groups, they were of lesser fame and did not have the allure of being well-trained gladiators. However, they wore some armor and carried unique weapons such as nooses, lassoes, special short knives with two blades in the shape of an open pair of scissors, fists wrapped in leather and studded with spikes, and helmets without eyeholes.

Most gladiators in a training school formed a loosely bonded brotherhood. Although they trained together and spared no energy or effort to deliver blows or outmaneuver their practiced opponent, they would ultimately be matched against an outsider. Thus, their zeal in training hard was to keep the level of excellence high among the school of gladiators, able to resist and defeat all comers. Inevitably, two such men formed a bond in which each of them regarded the other as a blood brother: Domo and Maximus.

Domo was only an average-sized man in height, but stocky of build, less with flaring muscles than substantial bulk. He shaved his head and had a prickly, dark, close-cropped beard. His hands were large and powerful, and he delivered punches that caused men to fly off their feet. When he strode around the arena on his thick legs puffing his overlarge barrel chest, he radiated unstoppable force. The *non sequituri* was his high-pitched girly laugh, about which he took good-natured ragging from his comrades.

True to his name, Maximus was a large and tall man, powerfully built with well-muscled arms, legs, and lean torso. Unexpectedly for a man of his size, he was agile and could change position in the blink of an eye to deliver crushing blows. He routinely shattered their wooden practice swords, and the *lanista* jokingly threatened to take replacement costs from his pay. Maximus had a mane of flame-red wavy hair and eyes the color of the sky, making him the object for swooning female members of the audience at games.

Both fought as Secutors[31]. Individually, each man was an arena favorite; as a combined pair, they were unbeatable...so far. The consul had grand plans for each of them, separately and together.

The second time the troupe of women walked to the gladiator quarters, Zofie entered Maximus's cell. Her face was still bruised and swollen, but she did not bow her head. Instead, a fierce stare shone from one eye. Maximus stood and extended his hand, introducing himself, indicating she sit on the bed. He walked to the opposite wall of the cell.

---

31 The word secutor in English means chaser and this ancient gladiator got its name from his style of fighting literally because he chased his opponent around the arena. Very distinct in their look and style, this gladiator was recognizable by their heavy armor and sizeable rectangular shield known as a *scutum*. Their oval helmet was another critical feature which had only tiny eye holes to protect their face from the *retiarius's* attacks.

"I'm not going to hurt you," he explained in a gentle tone. Knowing Zofie did not understand Latin, he tried his native tongue, hoping that there might be some similarity to her own. Swedish Svenska is Old Norse, belonging to the North Germanic subgroup of Germanic languages. He learned that Zofie was captured during fighting with the Teutonic Tribes to the north of the Roman Empire's outermost boundaries. Therefore, he believed there might be a chance that the language she spoke bore similarities to his, purely based on geography and migrations. "Let us talk." She continued to stare at him, unreadable.

He poured some water and offered it with a strip of salt jerky. Zofie sniffed at the jerky and, deciding it wasn't poison, nibbled at the tip. She smiled at him and nodded.

"Good, now relax; I'm just going to sit down," he said, gesticulating with his palms raised.

They sat, not speaking for several minutes. Zofie talked to him, knowing he would not understand what she was saying, but trying to bridge the gap of abject silence.

"I do not like being a slave. I am a free woman, and I miss my tribe. They need me after battling the Romans." She looked down at the floor.

He tentatively took her hand in his, patting it with his other. Then he reached to place her head on his shoulder and leaned against the wall, humming. She took comfort in that gesture and his extensiveness to sit and be, as distinct to physically forcing himself on her. She had expected and dreaded another sexual encounter of an equally brutal nature. Still sore from her time with Domo, she worried about her ability to sustain another rough session without severe damage.

She looked up at him and said, "Domo," shaking her head emphatically, and began to cry softly. She leaned against him for comfort.

Maximus felt sorry for her. She was ripped away from her country and her people. She was thrust into a strange land with unfamiliar customs and language and been poorly treated only two days after being installed at the consul's *familia rustica*. She was unattractive to look at, had scars and tattoos all over her, was an unusual color as if her skin had been permanently dyed, and couldn't speak to anyone! Except for her abilities medically, she seemed to have gotten the short end of the stick.

"You have nothing to fear from me," he said genuinely. They

spent their time just relaxing together. When the servant came to the cell door to collect her, she stood and nodded to him. Just before leaving, she turned and kissed his cheek, smiling.

Time, when filled with repetitive routine, has a way of accruing rapidly. Thus, weeks that slid into months that grew into a year found Zofie acclimatized to her new life with a buried longing for freedom. She knew all the other women in their quarters by name, personality, and assignment. She knew all the gladiators' names, classifications, and styles of fighting. She also knew their bodies intimately, not exclusively from being the *medicum*. While she had learned enough Latin to engage in low-grade exchanges (albeit with grammatical and vocabulary mistakes), she could make herself understood. However, she relied on Leda to deliver instructions in the interests of accuracy and always be present when she attended the consul or a member of his family.

Zofie and Maximus had developed a deep fondness for each other that had grown into intimate expression. Their physical time together was the only such relationship she enjoyed. Sometimes it was playful; other times, desperately passionate; always, full of genuine emotion. Over time, she learned about Maximus' past, which was not dissimilar to hers in terms of capture. He lost his entire family in the unexpected skirmish for which his tribesmen were ill-prepared. For the last six years of his life, he lived in the *Ludus*. He told Zofie that the consul was, on balance, a good master with fair standards if one could ignore his participation in slavery and having a unanimous decision over whether one lived or died. Still, Maximus was defensive of the consul who had promised him his freedom in exchange for individual successes as one of his prized gladiators.

"I worry when you fight," Zofie admitted to him as they sat in his cell.

"Do not worry. I know how to fight, and the gods watch over me."

"Still, you push and push. One day, you will use up all that strength," she said, stroking his shoulders and fingering some of the scars on his torso.

"You must not say such things. It is bad luck," Maximus countered, pulling her onto his lap. "I prefer that you pray to your gods for me to be victorious!"

"That I shall do, as I always have. Is it to be soon?" Zofie asked tearfully.

He explained that a prominent man from Rome arrived at week's end with a bevy of gladiators, all of whom he had purchased from other schools, two of them from the famous Capua. They had been in contests throughout the empire in other great houses like the consul's, and had earned a reputation for being fearless, well-trained, successful fighters. Maximus and the others were scheduled for matches against them in various "games," with Domo and Maximus to meet their champions in single combat.

Before she could ask anything more, Maximus' cell lock clicked, and the door opened. She barely had time to touch his face before the *lanista* barked at her to leave.

On the day of the games, every slave within the Domus was busy preparing and arranging the banquet, seating, or any details related to the competition.

The consul had ordered that his *medicum* view the games from his balcony to see the circumstances of any potential injury before she treated the unfortunate man requiring her skills. She was to leave only if she believed the damage to be severe or life-threatening and only with the consul's permission. So it was that the Blue Woman, despite the scrutiny of the consul's guests, sat in the corner of the balcony on a wooden stool at the front rail, the ever-present Leda just behind.

The consul's competitor guest was a seedy-looking fellow, thought Zofie. He was thin, dark, and had the eyes of a predator. That his wife was frail, blonde, and young surprised her, not in the least. The poor young woman looked miserably unhappy and about to faint, despite being seated in the awning's shade and fanned by slaves. If she fell, fainted, or screamed, Zofie was convinced that her husband would be unaware, as he showed no attention, concern, or recognition of her in the least. Zofie entreated Leda to whisper to the consul about suggesting the woman be allowed to retire, as she was unsettled and might be unwell. Leda hesitated, but Zofie pressed him, arguing that it would be worse if she took ill during the games and interrupted the men's attention. Leda was convinced enough to quietly speak to the consul, who had a word with the man after glancing at his guest's wife. The senator looked at his wife, dispensed a sharp word to her, and dismissed the consul's concern with a flick of his hand. The consul glanced at Zofie briefly, raised his eyebrows, and shook his head, turning again to the parade unfolding below.

The day wore on; several of the senator's men won their

matches against the lesser of the consul's gladiators who escaped without significant injury. The consul's group match against the senator's men was declared a win for the consul's men, which balanced the scores. The wagers got more substantial as the anticipated individual events approached. Wine flowed, servants dashed about in service of refreshing delicacies and bowls of cool water and cloths to refresh perspiring bodies. Then the drums boomed the entrance of four gladiators who presented themselves before the balcony.

Domo and Maximus kneeled before their consul, their armor and weapons gleaming; two brutes for the senator--one with red plumes in his helmet, the other with black, both with armor and weapons of the most exceptional caliber-- merely bowed. Comrades at the sidelines cheered their respective champions. Taking the assumed positions in the arena, they awaited the consul's signal to the *lanista*, who cracked his whip for the match to begin.

Each pair seemed evenly matched at the beginning, with blows raining equally on opponents. After about ten minutes of constant exertion, Domo's opponent showed signs of tiring, and the blocky Domo sensed victory. His anticipation got the better of his judgment, and he rushed forward, only to be tripped by the rolling gladiator who reassumed his feet and delivered a resounding blow to Domo's lower back. Domo's bellow echoed from the sides of the stone and stucco Domus as he staggered a few steps forward. Realizing that his opponent's feint was used to make him lose focus, Domo wheeled in rage and drove back the senator's fighter with killing blow after killing blow, the clang of metal against metal ringing throughout the arena. Zofie could only imagine the reverberation each of Domo's strokes sent up the man's arm. Domo's opponent was strictly on the defensive now and tiring fast.

Meanwhile, Maximus had the fight of his life against the tall black man with muscles of steel. For every parry, his opponent had a switchback; for every blow sustained, one came in return with equal force. One blow to the head knocked off Maximus' helmet, and for a moment, his head reeled. Just in time, his natural agility saved him from what would have been a follow-up (and illegal) sword blow to the head. He leaped out of the way and, using the momentum of the man's swing, deflected his sword and sent it flying into the air. His opponent reached for his dagger. Maximus, a man of fair play, stabbed his sword into the ground, drawing his blade to ultimately make the contest fair. It was not a legal requirement of the rules but a gesture that attracted the admiration of all watching, particularly his consul, who had come to regard Maximus with affection and respect. Maximus' hair had escaped its leather tie, and his mane flew wildly about his head with the activity of combat.

"Finish him!" the senator shouted as he rose to his feet, shaking his fist.

The consul was aghast, as were his other guests, except for the senator's guests who had come to know his thirst for blood, winning, and having the upper hand in all situations.

Then, the unthinkable happened: From the sidelines, four of the senator's viewing gladiators (who had competed in the group match) dashed into the ring, two each joining their man against Domo and Maximus. Domo and Maximus now faced three opponents apiece. The *lanista* cracked his whip, but no one paid attention, nor was it heard above the din of shouts and cheers.

Domo and Maximus parried and struck and danced. They ended close to each other as they fought. Without losing focus or conviction, Maximus yelled, *"Fratrum!"* (Brotherhood!)

Domo responded with shouts emphasizing each word as he unleashed sword blow after sword blow against his opponents, downing one with a slash to the leg which took him out of the fray, *"Fratres... ad mortem."* (Brotherhood to the death!)

Domo was now battling two of the senator's men.

Maximus downed one opponent with a severe cut to his sword arm. One of his opponents threw his weighted net in an attempt to trip Maximus as he fought the indefatigable black gladiator with black plumes who had just signaled his partner. Maximus caught the gesture and jumped into the air as the net snaked in a semicircle beneath him. As Maximus was airborne, he plunged his sword into the black-plumed adversary where the top of his breastplate ended, and as he landed, he spun on the balls of his feet with his dagger extended and slit the throat of the unsuspecting net man. Maximus ran to Domo's side, and the two men faced one opponent each.

The *lanista* gave up trying to stop the match once he saw his consul's signal to let things proceed. His master was risking everything—money, reputation, and lives—on the outcome. Fighting, fueled by their anger at the opponent team's dishonor, the potency of their brotherhood, the force of their training, and the intensity of their loyalty to their consul and *lanista*, Maximus and Domo fought on with ruthlessness and power they did not know they possessed. All of the men were tired and dripping in sweat, but still, they traded blows until the senator's red-plumed gladiator stabbed the ground with his sword, nodding to his partner, who did the same. They raised their fingers to their opponents and the balcony of onlookers.

"Mors! Mors!"[32] screamed the senator. Domo and Maximus looked at each other, panting, and then at the consul. "Mors!" cried the senator again, spitting as he pronounced the word in his fierce invective. The consul gave his *lanista* the signal to end the combat and spare the challengers. Breathing hard, Maximus and Domo walked arms over shoulders from the arena, but not before Maximus cast a glance to the quivering Zofie, still in the corner of the balcony. She felt frozen in place, having witnessed the life-threatening combat, and realizing that she genuinely loved Maximus. Leda had to shake her to get her attention, pulling her away to treat the several wounded men.

Just as they approached the descending stairs, the consul called out, "Zofie!" She stopped dead, turning slowly. *"Primus nostrum,"* he added softly.

Zofie nodded and gave him a slight smile, repeating, "Ours first," so he knew she understood. As she and Leda descended, she overheard the senator cry out, "I am ruined!"

'Good!' she thought vehemently. 'And may you come down with the pox, but not until you leave our Domus!'

Several months and many successful matches later, Maximus greeted her with smiles when she made her routine examination of his company. She passed him the infusion to help with the aches from his many injuries, some old and some new. She marveled at the difference in the gladiators' reaction to her compared to her first few days and weeks. They were welcoming to her, some even teasing at times. In particular, Domo always treated her with respect, if couching it in humor to save face among the others.

"I have good news, no, I have the best news!" Maximus smiled. "I have won my freedom!"

"That is wonderful! That which you wanted most in this world is finally yours," she said, clasping her hands to her chest. "I am so glad for you, Maximus! Truly, I am," she said sincerely.

Domo jumped to her side. "I, too, my little blue Zofie, am freed! And we are allowed to celebrate with everyone this evening!

---

32 Death! Death!

You must come, but first, have you anything to relieve this pain in my back, little blue Zofie?" he said in a wheedling voice.

Shaking her head, she prepared a cup of water with one of her powders and gave it to him. "Take three pinches in water every morning. It will help. But no more, or you will be dizzy and pee yourself!" she said, handing him a cloth with more powder. Domo downed the cup and planted a kiss on her left cheek, the one he had slapped into several shades of purple years ago.

During the evening's celebration, Maximus had a private word with the consul. Afterward, he asked Zofie to accompany him outside in the moonlight, where they sat on a bench in front of the arena's edge wall, overlooking the hillside.

"I will miss you," she said levelly, repressing tears. They both knew that Maximus would not receive an offer for the *lanista's* position, as the man had several good years left in him.

"I will miss you," he said, smoothing her hair. "But I have good news for you. I spoke to the consul, and he will accept me for ten years' military service in exchange for giving you freedom... my freedom. I give it to you, *Modrá Žena*, my Zofie." He kissed her hands.

She was speechless for several moments. Then, when her wits returned, she said, "No, no, Maximus, you must not. You have earned this day with your heart and your blood. I cannot accept this sacrifice. I do not deserve it," she wept against his shoulder.

"For all you are, and for all you have done, my love, you deserve this. You leave on the morrow by order of the consul. You will go with an escort to the northern border of Roman lands, where one of the consul's trading partners will give you food and rest. Then you must find your people. That is the best he and I can do for you. You are to go and see him now, and then we will have tonight together for our goodbyes." Maximus stood and took her hand, directing her to the archway of the gladiator area where the consul stood waiting.

"Meet me in your cell," she whispered. "I hope this does not take long. I wish to be with you for as long as possible." She walked away from him, understanding that each step brought her closer to her destiny, leaving the *familia rustica* Domus and the love of her life.

Chapter Nine
The Blue Woman - Anew

The fire crackled, sending a steady but small stream of sparks to fly upward into the black sky. Vila poked at the coals, then lay down to enter her vision world in sleep. Her mother, reclining on the rocks by their cave entrance, looked at her daughter, no longer a child. The owl on her shoulder twisted its head, surveying the night sky and the hillside below, shuffling to settle on its perch.

"It will soon be time, Múdry, Wise One. She is almost ready, and I am tired." Modrá Žena, the Blue Woman, stroked the owl's breast with light fingers, closing her eyes to ask Father Sky and Mother Earth for guidance.

In the morning, Víla fixed their tea and warm ed the berry cakes. Her mother, who awakened before her, was still meditating. As if she knew the water had reached the proper temperature, she rose and walked to the fire, accepting the cup of herbal tea her daughter offered.

"Will we go to the village today?" the young woman asked.

"Not unless summoned. Today will be your day to listen and accept." The Blue Woman sipped at the tea, placed her cup on a flat rock, and walked into the cave. She came out in a few moments with some of her leather sacks. She sat by the fire with her daughter sipping tea and munching on the berry cakes.

"Have I displeased you?" the young woman asked her mother.

"Why would you think that, Víla? No, you have not displeased me. I am quiet because I do not take lightly the steps we must walk together on this day. I must make you ready. But first, I must give you my sign." Reaching into one of her bags, she withdrew a handful of dried dark berries that she placed into a bowl and ground to a powder. She added a little water, made a paste, the dark blue color of the berries coloring it. She placed her fine blade into the fire, resting on a rock, only 2 cm of the fine tip touching the flames.

"I bear the signs of Father Sky and Mother Earth, here and here," she said, pointing with a delicate finger. "These berries Mother Earth gives to us to feed us and give beauty. We show our connection to Father Sky by making our marks blue from Mother Earth's berries with the sacred dye within them. Only the *Modrá Žena* of the tribe may bear such signs. It is time for me to give you your signs, my daughter."

"But you have told me that I will be marked only when you must leave. I don't want you to leave me, mother," the young woman cried, holding her mother's hand to her breast.

"I must go to Father Sky and Mother Earth, Víla. When the moon changes, it will be time. Then your life as *Modrá Žena* for the people will begin. Do not be afraid or sad, daughter. It is the way of life; it is the way of the people; it is your destiny.

"You will care for them as I have done these many cycles in the ways that I have taught you. One day, you will pass on all the sacred knowledge to your daughter, and she will do likewise, and on and on until the end of days. You will bear all the sins of the people and protect them. You will heal them. You will help them in times of need. You will teach them. It is a great honor and a sacred trust, Víla, as I have taught you.

"There is no fear when you walk with the spirits of Father Sky and Mother Earth. You will not fear what is to come, just as I do not fear what is to come. Now lie down here, next to me, my daughter, and I will give you the sacred signs. I love you, my daughter."

The Solar cross is probably the oldest religious symbol globally, appearing in Asian, American, European, and Indian religious art from the dawn of history. Composed of an equal-armed cross within a circle, it represents the solar calendar- the sun's movements, marked by the solstices. Sometimes the equinoxes are marked as well, giving an eight-armed wheel. [A swastika is also a form of Solar cross.]

(The sun cross in its most simplified form is known in Northern Europe as Odin's cross, after the Norse pantheon's Chief God. It is often used as an emblem by Asatruar, followers of the Norse religion. The word "cross" itself comes from the Old Norse word for this symbol: kros.)

With the hot tip of her blade, she lightly incised Father Sky's symbol onto her daughter's forehead. She blotted the blood and daubed the motif with the blue paste with the end of an owl feather. When the raised image healed, the skin outlining the symbol would be blue. She continued and scribed Mother Earth's mark to Víla's upper chest, just above her daughter's breasts. Again, she brushed the skin with the blue paste. Throughout, Víla did not cry but repeated the chant her mother uttered. When she finished, the *Modrá Žena* bent to kiss her daughter tenderly and smiled.

(A triple spiral motif found on Celtic tombs is drawn unicursally (in one continuous line), suggesting a rebirth or resurrection cycle. (This hypothesis is encouraged by the fact that these appear to be deliberately placed where they catch the sun's first rays on the solstice). The sun, dying and rising every day, is a natural symbol of rebirth. The triple spiral gives an apparent connection between the solar symbolism and the nine months of human gestation. In modern times, the spiral is still spiritually significant and symbolizes Wicca's spirit, an emblem of the Goddess.)

"I am proud of you, Víla. You have proven yourself to be strong, to be ready. Now, we will share one last cup of tea. In a few days, you will be healed. Then you must gather your things and walk to the village. Present yourself to the elder mothers. They will take you to your hut and stay with you, telling you all you must do.

"The ceremony to make you the people's *Modrá Žena* will begin when you see the blue smoke rising from my fire here on the mountain into the night sky. Then you will know that I have gone to Father Sky and Mother Earth. That is when your true-life journey will begin.

"Mother, must it be so? It is too soon," Vila whispered tearfully.

"Be brave in all things, my daughter. We will see each other again, for I will be with you in every raindrop, in every ray of sunlight that Father Sun sends to kiss Mother Earth, in every river and lake, every tree and stone, in every budding plant the Mother gives to bless the people. You will hear my voice in the song of the wind, and you will feel my strength in the warmth of the fire with its colors. I will be with you through and in all things, my daughter.

"Until we meet again, I bless you. We will not see each other again in this life. Now is the separating time for each of us to meditate and listen to Father Sun and Mother Earth. They will prepare each of us for the transformation: the new living from the old; the old living in the new." The reigning *Modrá Žena* embraced her daughter, Víla, for the last time.

Days later, as Víla walked down the mountain suppressing her tears, she reviewed her life as a happy child playing on the mountain, in the meadows, the river, and the lake. Her mother had protected and loved her, lavishing her with lessons about the earth, plants, animals, birds, and even fishes. She knew the stars by name and the phases of the moon. She knew which plants healed and which plants poisoned. She had never concentrated on the stories her mother told her that spoke to the time when they must part. Her mother was her world, and she had grown to a young woman, cherished and safe in her mother's arms and care. Now the time had come to live in another world ... the world of her people ... a society that needed her ... a world for which she had been born to serve and love.

After a year among the people, she would be allowed to return to the mountain cave that had been home to all *Modrá Ženas* from the beginning of time. She would go to the village regularly to visit with the people, treat their ailments, birth their babies, ease the old ones' pain, teach their young men to be mates and fathers, and the young women to be mates and mothers. She would go to the Summer Meeting with her tribe. She would join all the other tribes in thanks and celebration for the past year and ask blessings for the new one.

She knew what she had to do and how to do it. That which was to come, the elder mothers would tell her. These were the first steps in her destiny for which she had been preparing her whole life. She looked to Father Sky and took a handful of Mother Earth. Smiling, she yelled to the mountains and the waters and the birds, animals, and living things: "I am Víla, and I accept!"

She reached the village by late morning. The symbols on her forehead and breast had knitted, the raised outlines showing a deep blue. Her mother had braided her hair in preparation, tying the various braids together so that her hair framed her head in a reddish-gold crown. She wore the plain, homespun shift appropriate for the novitiate, carrying her cape and long tunic in her sack with her sandals. During the year among them, the people would make her clothing, bring her food, welcome her into their huts, and treat her with the dignity and honor her position warranted.

She would loosen her hair and don her other clothing once the second ceremony had concluded, signaling that she had spent the appropriate time among the people in her hut at their constant disposal. When she returned to her mountain, garbed in her blue cape and white tunic with feathers and stones sewn into its edges, her flame-red hair unbraided and shining in the sun, she would resemble their image of a goddess.

These things passed through Víla's mind as she entered the village of her people.

Children ran to her, dancing in a circle, reaching out to touch her. Men and women came out of their huts to stand and watch, the men pounding their lances and the women chanting. The noise alerted the old ones whose shelter was at the foot of the village by the river. Slowly, they made their way to the center to greet her. Everyone was smiling and nodding. The elder mothers explained that all would partake in a welcome feast that evening, and they would show her to the hut prepared for her so she could rest.

As she looked at what would be her new home for the next year, Víla nodded and bowed to the elder mothers to show her thanks and honor for their thoughtfulness and provision. The hut had a dirt floor scraped hard to a gleam, covered in the most used areas surrounding the sleeping mat and cook fire by interwoven reeds and their flat leaves. Kindling lay in a small stone circle beneath a hole in the hut roof, a dried wood stack nearby. In one corner along the wall lay a stuffed mattress covered by a handwoven quilt with beautiful embroidery of flowers, trees, and animals, along with folded spare tunics at the foot of the bed. Next to it was a low table with items for personal toiletry and grooming. Another wooden table was in the opposite corner, which held writing and drawing materials with an oil lamp made of stone, charcoal, and moss. A cape was neatly folded on its stool with sandals and soft leather boots on top.

The two south-facing windows had reed shades rolled and tied at the top with a narrow leather strip; at the bottom of each tie dangled a rabbit's foot. In front of each window hung an intricately woven dream catcher with shells and dried medicinal herbs. The hut's opposite side had a wooden bench beneath shelves containing now empty pots and leather bags (which she would fill), cutting and grinding implements, vessels to hold liquids, pots for cooking, bone, and metal knives of varied sizes, and utensils.

"I am honored, elder mothers, by your kindness. I promise I

will do my best for you, and I welcome your guidance in all things." Víla said meekly with a bowed head. She prostrated herself before the older women, all of whom nodded in approval and smiled at each other.

Víla had to stay within the hut for a week preceding integration with the tribe in any way. She was allowed to take walks accompanied by two elder mothers to collect herbs and healing plants and berries. She and they took their meals in the hut each day, conversing in quiet tones about the people, the ceremony to come, protocols, and other items about which Víla had to learn before assuming her place within the tribe. In the second week, she was chaperoned but allowed to meet the tribe leader and elderly males. At the end of the week, she got introduced to many families, also with chaperones. Wherever Víla went, and to whomever she spoke, she was attended by at least two elder mother chaperones. She did not speak until spoken to or received a nod from one of them. She especially enjoyed the short time spent with the tribe's children, who looked hale and hearty for the most part. She inspected the animals from horses to livestock, repressing her desire to jump onto a horse's back and gallop through the fields beyond the settlement.

In the third week, she was startled by the sound of wailing. At first, Víla thought it was a call for help, but when the wailing grew in pitch, numbers, and volume, she became alarmed. One of the elder mothers came to Víla's hut to summon her outside. Darkness would soon fall, and as she glanced at the mountain and saw a narrow trail of blue smoke rising into the fading sky, her heart wrenched. 'Mother,' she thought. She prostrated herself on the ground before her tent. After a suitable time, the elder mothers gathered and escorted her back into her hut.

The tribe readied themselves for the final ceremony. Torches were lit in two rows from the village's head to its foot, ending at the river where the elder mothers' huts stood. Two of them stationed themselves at the river end of the path, two of them at the top end, and all of them beat a small drum contrapuntally.

When Víla exited her hut, she walked to the top of the torch-lit path and stood before the two elder mothers. She knelt, and an elder mother placed a wreath on her loose red-gold hair. The braids her mother had so carefully arranged were a thing of childhood. She stood now as a woman, facing the path lined with all of the tribe's members, including the children. She let her cape fall to the ground and stood naked before them. The wailing began; the drums beat more intensely; she walked forward intrepidly yet determined to fulfill her destiny, however frightening. As she walked ever more slowly, pausing between steps as instructed, the people lashed out with switches and branches, twigs, and short sticks, to thrash her, drawing blood with each repeated stroke. It was a long, slow, and painful walk. It was a walk of faith. It was a walk of earned trust. It was a walk that allowed the people to divest themselves of evil, woe, wrongdoing, mistakes, regrets, sadness, bad luck, and anything negative that had befallen them. Víla willingly accepted the sin, pain, and sadness of the tribe.

Bleeding and weak by the time she reached the river and the two elder mothers awaiting her, she stood still, her heart pounding, blood streaming down her face and all over her body—front and back. She didn't know if her blurred vision was from tears, blood, or faintness. The drumming stopped, the mothers put their drums on the ground, and eerie humming began. Víla drank from the cup they offered, the bitter liquid searing her throat. Now she stung from the inside out!

They took her arms and walked with her into the river, she thought to halt the bleeding. At first, the cold water relieved the incredible stinging all over her body, but shortly, its cold penetrated to her core. She felt even fainter. One of the mothers pushed her left shoulder under the water's surface, and the other mother moved on her right side. Víla quickly lost her balance, and her head plunged beneath the surface. They held her head beneath the surface, and she did not have the strength to oppose them, despite that she was desperate for air. Her eyes saw nothing but black water. Then her mind, which tried frantically to concentrate on the stars in the heavens, began to turn black with the lights blinking out one by one. A calm settled over her as she believed she was dying, drowning, soon to be with her mother, Father Sky and Mother Earth. She stopped struggling. She floated in an abyss. She felt nothing.

The elder mothers raised Víla's head from the water, signaling to the waiting men to carry her to the river's edge. Two mothers who had been at the top of the path were waiting to revive her and cleared water from her lungs and mouth, rubbing her with rough hands to stimulate circulation, wrapping her in warmed blankets and skins taken from the fireside. This part of the ceremony was critical, as not all candidates for the tribe's *Modrá Žena* survived the rigorous test. The watching people waited, some speaking only in hushed whispers. If Father Sky and Mother Earth deemed her worthy, she would survive, like her mother before her.

Víla coughed and vomited again and again. Then she began to moan. The people clapped and began to sing and chant. The men carried Víla to her hut, accompanied by the elder mothers. The tribe—joyful to have a new *Modrá Žena*—indulged in the prepared feast, free of all the burdens they had carried before the ceremony.

Over the next few hours, the elder mothers carefully applied the blue paste to Víla's body. All of her scars would heal bearing a blue color, the pattern of her body a mosaic in testimony to the people's hopes as they passed their pain and burdens to her in trust that she would survive the test of their gods. The mothers administered healing herbs and an infusion for pain. At first, Víla rejected the liquid. It subconsciously reminded her of drowning, but exhausted as she was, she swallowed the relieving liquid. She slept for two days straight. When she awoke, she was weak but famished. Eating slowly and drinking some of the infusion, she looked at her body. Although welts seemed to be everywhere, each angry red welt had a center and outline of blue. The mothers continued to apply salves to ease the cuts and promote healing, which also helped Víla feel less stiff as scabs began to form. After a few days, an almost unbearable itching started, and it took fortitude not to scratch herself raw. Wryly, she thought, 'Mothers, you didn't warn me about this part!' As time passed, she began to feel more herself, grateful for the elders' attentiveness for her every need and want.

When she fully healed, she inspected herself more closely. Her body bore swirls; straight lines; long, curved slashes she presumed were from the many switches; circular and irregular roundish outlines (likely from the ends of the sticks twisted into her flesh or stones thrown with enough force to split the flesh); and other marks and symbols applied by the elder mothers during her time of semi-consciousness. She donned a clean tunic and exited her hut to stand at the village's top between the flower-adorned posts. She waited until the people gathered in the center.

Víla stood before them, arms raised, and shouted, "I am Víla! I accept! I am *Modrá Žena!*" In the days to come, Vila's body would bear a tattoo representing each of the persons to whom she ministered in her life as the tribe's *Modrá Žena*, eventually covering every space on her body, front to back, head to toe.

The Centurion left most of his hundred men in camp, taking only twelve with him as he rode to the meeting place arranged by his trackers with the barbarian scouts. As they trotted into the valley, hills rising on either side, his friend and next in command expressed concern.

"I know, Quintillius, it looks perfect for an ambush. But we must make a show of goodwill and honor by trusting that they accept we come in peace. They already know of our force, which is why I left our men behind, as a deterrent." Maximus calmly proceeded into the valley, stopping in the center by an implanted lance. His men formed a semicircle around him.

As if they were wraiths, men appeared from behind stones and trees, previously invisible. The Romans' horses nickered, blew, and stomped at the strange smell and sight of the encroaching men coming at them from all sides. One man covered in a fur cape with long, dark hair and eyes like coal approached Maximus. He was armed with a sword and an ax.

"You are the leader?" he questioned.

"I am," Maximus answered. Leda, the soldier who had translated for Zofie, spoke Maximus' words in the Teutonic language.

"What do you want in our lands?" the man said with not a little ferocity.

"I seek the Blue Woman. I am told she is with your tribe. We have come a long way to seek her help on behalf of our consul. She knows him from past years."

"Why should she see you? You took her from us." The man spat.

"I did not; I was a slave when she arrived. The consul was good to her. She will tell you if you do not believe me. Why would I come all this way and risk myself and my men for a lie? I am telling you the truth, on my honor as a fellow soldier." Maximus spoke with genuineness and simplicity.

"Your words ring true. We were told of your journey long before you arrived and what you seek. We give you permission to follow... without your men or your arms. They will stay with some of my men until you return." The man called out orders to his contingent, and Maximus turned to Quintillius and bade him remain with the nine men.

"If there is trouble, the men will need you to give orders and establish calm. I trust no one else. You may need to take emergency action. The horn is the signal for the camp to muster to arms at the ready with one blast. Use it, but only if you fear you cannot hold. All you must do is maintain your shield circle after three blasts until our force reaches you at a gallop. I know you can do that, my friend." Maximus grasped Quintillius' arm. "I take only Leda with me."

Maximus and Leda untied their swords and removed helmets, placing them on their shields on the ground. They remounted and followed two of the fully armed barbarians into the hills, two more barbarians at their rear with arrows nocked in bows.

After about only 500 yards on a circuitous and narrow trail, the head barbarian held up his arm and turned to the two Roman soldiers. "Leave your horses here." Maximus and Leda dismounted and followed the man on foot.

"Be ready, Leda, in case our friend changes his mind," Maximus warned. Both had daggers in their greaves and in a slot behind their breastplates.

Again, the man stopped. "There," he pointed. A U-shaped clearing with a flat rock in the center was barely visible through the mist to the left side.

Maximus entered the clearing with Leda close on his heels. As Maximus approached the stone, he cautioned Leda to stay several feet back. He sat on the rock and waited. After a few minutes, an apparition appeared from behind one of the boulders. It stood still as if waiting.

"Are you the Blue Woman?" Maximus asked. Silence. Stillness. Maximus turned and nodded to Leda, who repeated Maximus' question in the Teutonic language. The figure, fully covered by cape and hood, nodded.

Maximus struggled to make sense of this meeting. Had he contacted the wrong woman? He was never told there was more than one Blue Woman. Had Zofie forgotten what Latin she had learned with the consistent inundation of her tribal language? Had she deliberately erased that period from her memory because it was too painful? Why was she not more responsive?

"Zofie, it is Maximus. Have you forgotten? I have not. I have remembered every moment these past years." Maximus remained still, waiting for some sign of recognition.

"She said you would come," the figure said.

"What?" asked Maximus in surprise. "What did you say?"

"She said you would come."

"Who? Zofie?"

"*Modrá Žena.*"

Maximus was confused. "Yes, *Modrá Žena*, Zofie. That is who I seek."

"Every moon, she told me you would come, but you did not."

"Who are you?" asked Maximus, still trying to piece things together.

The figure stepped closer. "I am *Modrá Žena.*" The woman moved closer still, the mists parting to reveal she was clothed in a dark blue cape, her face hidden within its hood. She threw back the hood and cape to reveal herself: a woman of fair skin covered in blue scars and tattoos, with eyes the color of the sky, and a mane of red-gold waves almost reaching her elbows.

"You came too late. She is with Father Sky and Mother Earth. I am *Modrá Žena*. I am Víla. I am your daughter."

They walked the path back to Quintillius and his men. Víla explained the past, how she was raised by Zofie, as *Modrá Žena* for the tribe, alone on the mountain, how Víla had assumed the position after a lifetime of preparation, teaching, and the ultimate test. Her destiny was with her tribe, and she had been their *Modrá Žena* for the last two years, replacing her mother after she accepted waiting death, leaping from the mountain into Father Sky's arms and Mother Earth's bosom. Likewise, Maximus explained his past: from the time he gave her mother "his" freedom to reunite with her tribe, to the years of service and promotion to Centurion, to this final mission in search of the Blue Woman on behalf of the consul.

"He is much older now but still strong. This is his second wife, and she has lost many children. Her time approaches, and the consul is desperate for an heir. He trusted Zofie, your mother, as a *medicum*, a healer. He sent me to find her to beg her help for his wife. I know it is much to ask of you, but will you come?"

There were long pauses between exchanges, as Leda translated. Despite their conversation's uncertainties and awkwardness, Víla could sense the truth and sincerity of Maximus' words.

"My mother said she loved you. She spoke of you often. She taught me your tongue. She said your hair reminded her of Father Sun and your eyes of His sky. She was happy that I looked like you because she said it made her heart less sad. Seeing you in me, she was able to bear losing you. She also spoke often of you, Leda." Víla sighed.

Maximus said honestly, "She never told me she was with child. She must have known when she left. She never sent word." Maximus shook his head, reliving those last days, wondering if he had known whether he would have had the courage to send Zofie back to her tribe.

"No, she never did. She said it was best because you lived worlds apart. But she always said that one day you would come, and you have, but two cycles too late." When Leda finished these words on Víla and Zofie's behalf, he wiped at his eyes, emitting a sob. "I'm sorry; please excuse me," he said in both languages to father and daughter.

Víla looked at the two Roman soldiers. They had reached the place where Quintillius waited with the nine soldiers. "Return to your camp. I will come to you in two days, and you may take me to the consul's woman. I will do what I can. Mother would go, so I will go."

"Thank you, Víla," Maximus said, bending to one knee and bowing his head. She placed a hand on his mop of soft, wavy red-gold hair, beginning to show white strands.

"You may call me *Modrá Žena*. I am no longer Víla." She smiled at Leda and touched his face, still wet with tears. She reached for her father's hand and held it for a long moment to her cheek as she gazed into his eyes. "Two days," she said, "one day for each cycle." She turned and left, her blue cape flaring in her wake.

The consul brought his wife to a suitable patrician's house close to the border, as he feared Maximus' journey back to the *familia rustica* Domus would take too long, deeming it more advantageous to meet in the middle. His friend in Rome gladly offered his home for as long as Aquilinus and his retinue required it.

The consul had received word previously from a Century rider that Maximus had found the Blue Woman and would shortly return with her. Aquilinus immediately dispatched another rider with two horses to notify Maximus of the changed meeting location.

When Maximus and his Century arrived with the Blue Woman, the consul was shocked when she removed her hooded cape. He beheld a young woman with red-gold hair and eyes the color of the sky.

"She looks like you," he said, amazed, "but how?" Maximus explained, and the consul collapsed into a chair, mulling the news. "All is lost, my friend. When I heard you had found her, I had renewed hope. But, you tell me, Zofie is dead?"

"Yes, sire, she is. But Víla, as her daughter, was taught by her and is now *Modrá Žena*. She knows all that Zofie knew and acted as her assistant in all things, including childbirth, for years. I believe you can trust her." Maximus stood next to his consul, passing him a goblet of wine, genuine concern etched on his face. "How does your wife fare?"

"Not well. I fear for her and the child, my friend. Take the Blue Woman to see her and report back to me at once, if there is any hope." The consul stared at the landscape in despair.

They could hear her moans before entering the room where the consul's wife lay on a bed, attended by women holding her hands and wiping her brow. The Blue Woman gave them all a fright, and Maximus again explained her position and origins. The consul's wife, Livilla, reached a hand to the Blue Woman.

"Thank you for coming to my aid. If you can help, I beg you to save my child for my lord," the woman said rapidly, ending with a moan as another pain overtook her.

Víla quickly removed her travel clothes and washed her hands and arms. Through Leda, she gave the attending women orders for what she needed and told Maximus to have four men standing at the ready should she need them. He was mystified by this request but trusted her and ran to make the arrangements. She thoroughly examined the woman and explained to her via Leda's translations what she was doing, what she was planning, and what the woman could expect. Leda sat on a stool near the woman's head, with his back to Livilla to avail the woman some privacy and protect her dignity.

"We must be partners, you and I, if we are to save your child. I will not lie to you. But I need you to try your best to do as I say. Will you do that for me?" Livilla nodded, breathing heavily. "The child is the wrong way around, so you must do what I say when I say it. Do not push even though you feel that you must." Again, Livilla nodded her agreement. "I will try to move the child now, but I cannot promise it will work. Stay with me; do not push; try to relax and breathe."

The women arrived with the fresh cloths, two slaves carrying a low-sided tub, and several more with jugs of warm water to empty into the tub. Livilla's screams resounded through the villa and drove the consul to tears. Maximus ordered his attendant to keep his wine goblet full and returned to the hall outside the room where Livilla lay, and Víla worked to help her. They waited, and they waited, and Livilla screamed and screamed.

"Bring the men!" Víla called out.

They rushed into the room and stood as Víla instructed: two men kneeling making a cradle with their arms, two men standing behind them ready to support Livilla. Maximus carried Livilla from the bed to the tub, gently placing her in the filled tub, the standing men's arms holding her under the arms and around her back. She clung to Maximus' hand, looking frantic. She had never seen or heard of anything like this before! Except for slaves and perhaps peasants, women always birthed babies in a bed or a birthing chair (when available), not standing! Her legs shook from weakness, and her body arched with the pain of final labor. She screamed pitifully, causing the men to close their eyes and grimace.

Víla calmly explained to Livilla that they were going to let Mother Earth help her. "You must use all your strength to stay upright, Livilla. The baby will find its way out if it is drawn from you by Mother Earth. I will let it swim in Her waters just like it is swimming in your waters. It is the best chance we have. I will tell you to push when I help your child into the world. Just a few moments more. I can feel the feet, now Livilla, push, push, push!"

Livilla screamed over and over, her nails cutting into Maximus' hand, the men straining to support and hold her. She was shaking with the effort and panting hard between screams.

"More, Livilla. Give me more. Your child wants to live! Push him out to me! That's it, push! Don't stop, don't let up, push!" Víla kept a running dialogue of encouragement to the woman who stared at her as if she were a lifeline.

Víla eased the infant out of the mother into the warm bath, swishing it around a few times before tying and cutting the cord, and then scooped it out and turned it upside down, shaking it firmly. She ordered the men holding her arms to place Livilla into the arm-cradle formed by the other men, submerging her body into the tub with her legs resting against the sides.

She put her fingers in the infant's mouth to hold down its tongue while gently pinching its nose, rolling the babe onto its side on the soft stack of toweling to allow any liquid to flow out. She gently and rhythmically pressed its abdomen and thumped its chest with her fingers. Then she placed her mouth over its mouth and breathed life into the child. It squalled! What a beautiful sound for all to hear at that moment! Víla let the baby scream and strain for a few moments, then wrapped it in clean swaddling cloth and gave it to Livilla.

"There you are, there is your son! You did well! Now the rest will seem easy. I will need you to do a little more for me. Look at your son, see how he wants his mother's comfort! Now, Livilla, listen to me and hold your son close," Víla said as she talked the woman through passing the afterbirth slowly. Víla crouched on the floor next to the tub reaching under Livilla's shift to collect the afterbirth into a cloth and pass to the slaves for removal. She gently probed Livilla's genital area to determine if there was any tearing. Relieved that there was not, she exhaled in relief. Both mother and child would survive, she was reasonably sure.

Instructing the slaves to lift Livilla from the tub and dress her in a clean shift, she sat on the side of the bed to help the woman nurse her child. Like most new mothers, she was awkward initially, but her son managed to latch on almost by himself, pinching her small breasts with his strong fingers. The baby fell asleep in a short time, and Víla encouraged Livilla to rest while she could. The woman was so spent that she sank almost immediately to sleep. Leaving Livilla in the care of her maidservants, Víla left the room.

She heard voices from the outside and walked toward them. Maximus, the four men, Leda, and the consul were seated on the balcony under an awning. All had goblets of wine.

"May I have some too?" Víla asked. "You have a fine, strong son, consul, and a courageous wife who will need much rest. It was a long and exhausting birth."

Aquilinus rose to greet her, taking her hands, thanking her profusely over and over. There was a significant difference in the ages between husband and wife, which was not particularly unusual when no heirs were previously born. Men often divorced their wives and married younger women, hoping to provide an heir or more children. Still, the consul was a healthy man who radiated strength and vitality even at his age. Few lived to 40 moons or better, but he looked as if he would well surpass statistics.

"Your wife is exhausted from so many days with pain, as well as the hours spent since we arrived. It was not an easy birth, as I think you know. No activity for several days, and then only a bit each day until she is strong enough to feel herself."

"I suspect that the children she lost previously were because they were the wrong way around like this one. They were probably stillborn?"

"Two, yes. Three others Livilla miscarried partway through," explained the consul, "and it was extremely hard on her. She gets with child easily enough, but she cannot always hold the child, so I am grateful to you."

"Be grateful to your Centurion, who was merciless in getting us here. I am glad he was because if she went more days, the child would not have survived, I think. And I do not know about your wife. Poisons spread quickly from these kinds of things. Before I leave tomorrow, I will give you some things to help her feel better and stronger. I will explain it all to you or your scribe. Now, I must ask you for a place to bathe properly and a clean shift. I would also like some food."

Her straightforward manner, devoid of all the accustomed protocol, made the consul laugh heartily. "Oh, how you remind me of your mother!" he exclaimed. "She had such a strong spirit! You are much like her, even if you look like your father!" Maximus laughed with everyone else and then broke down in tears, turning away from the group to feign looking at the hills beyond the villa.

"You, Roman men!" scoffed the Blue Woman. "You have not learned that to show feelings is not weakness, but strength in the knowledge of life, pain, and love. My mother told me about you." Chuckling, she held out her goblet for a refill lifting her eyebrows, sitting down and put her feet on a stool.

Shaking his head but still smiling, the consul snapped his fingers for the attending slaves to bring more wine and food.

After advising the consul's literati about the care of wife and child, including medications, Víla sat with him and his entourage members over the midday meal.

"Must you leave us so soon?" Aquilinus inquired. "I would be pleased to have your company a bit longer."

"My people need me. It will take me the better part of today to reach the border and the following morning to reach my tribe's village. The days to travel both ways with the time I have been here are much to be away."

"Your mother was of great value to me. You, too, are of great value. But you are so far away, Víla. Is there no way I can get you to visit for longer here or at my familia rustica? We need your talents. Our *medicum* is not the same as you or your mother. I don't know why we cannot produce one with your abilities. But, I tell you truly, when your mother was taking care of everyone, we were very well. I want that again. How can we arrange something?"

"We cannot. I need to be with my tribe, and I travel to other tribes too. Those are my people. You are not my people. I take care of my people first. That is the way of life." Víla was matter of fact about the way she saw things.

"Do you not teach others to heal in other tribes?" asked the consul.

"Of course! The tribes send me their young ones, and I show them the things my mother showed me. They must stay with me for at least two years before they are adept enough to return to their tribe as beginning healers. If the tribe has serious problems beyond their healer's abilities, they send for me. I go where I am needed when I am needed. That is the way of my destiny."

"What if I sent you candidates to teach in your village? Would you accept them?" the consul asked, warming to a germ of an idea.

"You do not speak our language, and I do not speak yours well enough to teach all the things which must be learned. It is impossible!"

"Yes, but what if I were able to teach them your language? Would you accept them then?" The consul believed he had figured out a way to enlarge and improve medical care for the empire's rural areas.

"Leda cannot be everywhere, consul. But if you can solve the language problem, I can teach. But who you send must be strong. Our life is different and much more demanding, with less of the comforts you have all around you. I cannot tolerate someone soft. They must be able to survive and work hard!" Víla was adamant.

"Leave it with me, please, Víla. It will take some time to work out all the details, but I will send word to you. When we meet again, I will come to you and explain what I have been able to do. But I promise you; I believe your healing talents must be shared with the wider world. If you are willing, we will do just that. You will teach and heal, and I will make it possible for you to do both. How does that sound?" Aquilinus was pleased with himself.

"I will ask Father Sky and Mother Earth. If they want it to be so, it will be so. Blessings be upon your house, consul. I must now leave." She rose, smiling at him.

"Maximus, your daughter is ready to leave us!" the consul called to his Centurion. "Do you wish to ride a bit with her?"

A grinning Maximus appeared with Víla's blue cape on his arm. "Your horse awaits, daughter," he said, bowing. The two walked together, descending the stairs to the courtyard where Víla's escort was mounted, awaiting her arrival.

The consul mused to himself, 'They are like mirror images, father and daughter. Hmm, I wonder,' he thought. Out loud, he said to the attending slave, "I think it's time I met my son! Do you think he'll look like me, Plato? We shall see, yes, we shall see!"

Chapter Ten
15th – 16th Century France – Maiden Wife

Her sisters whispered among themselves; her mother dabbed at her eyes; her brother slurped his soup; her father glared at her, holding his goblet out for refilling. "You will do as I say, girl. You have a duty to this family, and that will be the end of it!"

"But, Papa, he is older than you! And he is mean and smelly! My friend, Michelle, has a maid who left his service, and she said..." she protested.

"Silence! It is arranged."

"But don't I get any say? It's just not fair!"

"Hush, child," said her mother, "you know you do not. It would be best if you did what your father says. He knows what is right for you." Her compliant mother refilled her father's goblet and scurried to fetch a platter of cheeses and bread.

Melisinde was horrified at her father's pronouncement that he decided to wed her to a widower from a nearby manor house. She was to report to Madame De Marigny in Paris for tuition before being presented at Court. Following the usual six weeks' lessons, she would be introduced formally, engage in conversation and pastime socials, and become thoroughly familiarized with life at Court while residing with Madame De Marigny. Depending upon her progress, after a suitable time, she would meet her intended husband. Melisinde was thirteen years of age.

Lord Brienne (seigneur), Melisinde's father, owned a combination of real estate and entitlements over people from whom he collected rents and fees, with the ability to impose certain obligations on them. [1789 abolished feudalism, and all lordships disappeared.] Melisinde was to wed to Viscomte (Viscount) Albret. The transmission of nobility passed by heredity: Limoges (Limousin) to the Comborn family in the 12th c.; the dukes of Brittany in 1301, to the Châtillon-Blois family in 1384; and to Albret in 1481. (This fief would later become united to the Crown in 1589.) A nobleman marrying a commoner did not lose his nobility, but a noblewoman who married a commoner lost her supremacy for as long as she remained married. Nobility was usually hereditary passing from the father.

[French nobility was quite different from English aristocracy, for which only a peerage conferred nobility on the possessor. In France, nobility was a legal concept precisely because of the responsibilities, rights, and privileges. Likewise, French nobility was not the same as the English gentry because gentry has no legal designation or rank. Many offices and positions in civil and military administrations were assigned and reserved exclusively for nobles, all commissioned as military officers. French nobles were usually exempted from paying taxes because of their help by fighting for their sovereign. (This practice survived until 1789 with the end of feudalism when nobility had no military activity expected.) Of course, the King could always ennoble whomever he liked whenever he wished to do so by royal grant. In the last third of the 13th c., when under financial duress, the King sold letters of nobility to fill the royal coffers.

In the 14th c., there existed 365 nobility of knightly origin. In the 15th c., 434 nobles of ancient origin; and in the 16th c., 801 nobles of origin. Those numbers increased to 3494 total nobility of pre-1789 birth via achieved supremacy because of fiscal or judicial offices, military commissions reaching the rank of General or royal grant letters. Many of these disappeared during the Revolution. Some emigrated, but almost all of these returned. Whatever numbers were left were always attached to specific land parcels, whether the nobility's status was inherited or acquired.

During this period, Burgundy's dukes had an influential presence in French politics, and by the mid-15th century, they possessed much of the Netherlands and the duchy of Luxembourg. With the Hundred Years' War and the English expulsion from French soil, King Charles VII was crowned in Reims in 1429. Following Joan of Arc (taken prisoner and burned at stake by the English in 1431), Charles reconciled with Burgundy's dukes, which fostered his gradual reconquest of towns and territories in northern France.]

Against the backdrop of uncertainty and unrest in the late 15th c. and the 16th c., (in Europe, seen as the bridge between the Late Middle Ages, the Early Renaissance, and the Early modern period), the aging Viscomte Albret was desperate for an heir to maintain title to his lands and nobility through male primogeniture. His first wife was barren, and he divorced her; his childless second wife died of fever associated with pneumonia; his third wife, the young Melisinde, was the candidate upon whom all his hopes would lie. At least, she was the daughter of a lord who held an administrative office, distinct from being a commoner.

"Mademoiselle, here you are!" A slender, immaculately dressed mature woman in green silk rose as they entered the sitting room (announced by the butler), extending her arms. Melisinde curtsied, and the woman kissed her on both cheeks. Melisinde's father completed the introductions, and they all took a seat at the woman's direction. Madame pointed Melisinde to a chair between two opposite settees. She sat nervously erect, her hands folded in her lap, unsure of what to expect. Instructing her maid to serve tea, Madame De Marigny explained her service to King Charles VII and the parents of candidates for her "finishing school."

"The King supports the interests of a strong France, of course; some of those interests lie in preserving its culture, society, politics, and nobility. Suitable marriages of young nobles, or indeed remarriages of mature nobles, require women of equally suitable breeding to meet her lord's needs, whether at home or at Court. I provide such candidates with recommendations to the King while providing families the knowledge that their children are safe and secure for the time before intended matrimony."

Addressing the following remark to Melisinde, she said gently, "My dear, your ability to learn and achieve during your time here will determine if you become one of those candidates. Indeed, you are suggested as a possible match for Viscomte Albret, as your father has proposed."

"Pardon, Madame De Marigny, but I thought the matter was settled," her father interceded.

"Lord Brienne, the matter is not settled until the King says it is decided. That you proposed such an alliance to the Viscount means only that the suggestion is brought before His Majesty at a forward time. One must complete the process as determined appropriate by the King.

"Your daughter must be qualified as a suitable wife for Viscomte Albret before the matter proceeds further. I am sure she will be so after her brief training with me here, but there is always the possibility that she might be more suitable for another match. All will be established with time. It would be best if you trust me: I have a record of success in these matters and have the King's confidence. I will keep you apprised."

After discussing the arrangement's business side, the genteel Madame De Marigny rang the bell for her maid, signaling the audience finished. Smiling at Melisinde, Madame De Marigny said, "Bid your father adieu, child. You are about to take steps into a bright future." So, began Melisinde's journey into a complex world that would change her forever.

The three young women fidgeted in their seats, awaiting the imposing Madame De Marigny: Bietriz Girard was from Cluny in the Bourgogne, dark-haired and pleasantly plump; the petite Poubelle Laval from Beaune, Burgundy; and Melisinde Brienne, physically unremarkable from just outside Paris in Auvers-Sur-Oise near Giverny.

The sound of swishing silk accompanied, "Good morning, *mes petites femme*, I trust you are ready to learn! We have much to accomplish in a short time to prepare you for Court, so please pay close attention.

"A few rules for success: Do not interrupt me; wait until I say you may put questions to me. I will never lie to you; you must never lie to me on the punishment of immediate dismissal. Expulsion does not bode well for a secure future. Understand that your destiny is not entirely in your hands and accept that fact. I will teach you how to make the most of your circumstances; you will determine your success or failure."

Probably from the stress, perhaps from fear or pure excitement, Poubelle began to cry and then wail. Melisinde placed a hand on her arm, looking worriedly toward their instructress, whose face was a composed mask of calm. Melisinde presumed she had witnessed this reaction before. Bietriz smiled nervously and shifted in her chair, fussing with the folds of her dress. Eventually, the room became quiet save for an occasional sniffle from Poubelle.

"You young women are all from good families, and therefore we shall dispense with elementary manners. What you shall need to know is Court Etiquette. Etiquette is the 'language of manners,' and Court Etiquette has specific patterns. Manners may tell us what is appropriate, but etiquette tells us how to be suitable on all occasions and events.

"You shall become comfortable with the social conversation on relevant subjects as addressed 'at Court,' as well as foods different from your typical fare and the proper way to eat them. You shall learn the appropriate dances, and--if you do not already know them—the most popular card games. You will enlarge your appreciation of music, dancing, literature, and the art of entertaining, always appearing feminine with a calm elegance and grace.

"My job is not to remake you; it is to fine-tune your natural abilities and education, familiarize you with what is expected of you, and help you to thrive in your new environment so that you will successfully partner with a noble.

"Now, let us begin," Madame De Marigny said, "with a story that will demonstrate how important one's background and demeanor are to one's life."

She began by explaining that the capitalization of the "De" in her surname was in recognition of her ancient noble family, the most recently notorious of which was a powerful chamberlain to King Philip IV the Fair. The King heavily depended on his chamberlain's advice on foreign policy and relations between King and Church. He was born in Normandy in the mid-1200s and, at first, was a courtier. Shortly after the turn of the century, he rose rapidly. The King promoted him to Count de Longueville, grand chamberlain to the King, captain of the Louvre, and superintendent of finances and buildings. By 1314, he was in charge of the royal treasury. Toward the end of Philip's reign, he was charged with corruption in his financial administration by the King's brother, with whom he had become unpopular because of his oppressive taxation policy to keep the ailing royal coffers stable.

"He was cleared but imprisoned, as so often happens in political circles. Louis X was the new King at the time, and he was inclined to banish Marigny. Still, his staunch enemy—Charles of Valois—accused Marigny further of sorcery and demanded his immediate execution. My ancestor was famous and accomplished, yes, but he also fell into disfavor with powerful people and, although innocent of the charges leveled against him, was executed. Now, what is the point to my story, *mes doux*?"

"That no matter who you are, or how well you do, you can end up dead?" asked Bietriz.

"That politics is dangerous, and one should avoid it?" suggested Poubelle.

"That matters of Court and the King's favor have limits and are changeable according to influence?" offered Melisinde.

Smiling in approval, Madame De Marigny nodded her head. "You are all correct. Bietriz, we all die eventually, but we must always take care not to hasten our death by displeasing the powerful. Poubelle, politics are dangerous but also an ever-present power one cannot escape. It is important to understand it as best we can, but not to meddle with it or interfere with those involved. And Melisinde, you are also correct in that it is critical to always bear in mind that 'favor' at Court changes like the wind. To survive, you must each be acknowledged and viewed as graceful, supportive French subjects who present no threat but promote a sense of decency, calm, obedience, and well-being. Those qualities will ensure your survival both at Court and in the home.

"Now, let us address Court conversation and topics with which you must become comfortably familiar," the gentlewoman continued. "Subjects vary from philosophy to military affairs, and most will try to show their knowledge of classical literature, current events, or the latest fashion rage. Proficiency in these will help you to appear interesting, but you must not be overly expressive of your opinion—whether you have one or not. Always redirect the conversation to another person once the subject is broached. Here are some ways to do that: pay close attention."

"I like the estampe and farandole the best," chirped Poubelle.

"They're nice, but the more avant-garde style of the Provence is my favorite. I reckon the dances from there are more innovative because they are influenced by proximity to Italy, and everyone knows Italy is the leader in dance!" Melisinde twirled round and round, her hands on her hips and her feet barely touching the floor as she was light-footed and lithe.

Bietriz looked miserable. "I can never remember all the

steps, I have trouble keeping time, and I run out of breath. Just look at me: I'm sweating again!" The depressed girl burst into tears. "I know Madame De Marigny will tell me I'm not suitable! Then what shall I do? I'll end up wed to a poor farmer, become a spinster, or end up in a brothel!"

"Now, Bietriz, let's go over the Bassedanse from the Burgundian Court. The sequence is just like a processional, and since it's in triple time, it is harder to notice if you are in perfect beat, yes? Come on, try it with me; you'll see!" Melisinde held out her hand to the glum girl.

"Oh, thank you, Melisinde! You help me with dance, and I shall help you with food, yes?" The girl had resumed her usual good-natured demeanor, and Melisinde responded by nodding agreement, as she had no interest or ability with foodstuffs or much else connected to running a household.

"Yes, Melisinde, remember Madame told us that we must know those things. And it occurred to me that if the Black Death comes again, we must know how to survive. If all the maids, cooks, and valets perish, how would we eat and dress?" Poubelle questioned.

"You shall both come to me," Bietriz announced. "I can make a tasty meal from almost nothing, I know how-to put-up food, so it keeps well, and I am a good cook! Mama taught me. It's one of the benefits of growing up in the country. I also know how to pluck a pheasant, do you?" Bietriz giggled as her companions made faces and gasped.

Mademoiselle Aalis, Madame De Marigny's trusted assistant, spoke with the young women as they sipped tea following their midday meal. "I shall be overseeing the more personal aspects of your training, like hygiene and personal toilettes.

"Ysole, one of the maids under my supervision, will do your coiffures and teach you styles you can manage on your own.

"Emilde is an excellent seamstress and will measure you for Court garb and advise each of you regarding style, color, and fabric.

"You will spend time with Mabile, the cook, to watch and learn. Only one of you has shown ability in this area; I suggest the other two of you take this part of your instruction more seriously.

"Before you begin any of this training, you will submit to an examination by me. You will have an opportunity to disclose any misadventures to me privately beforehand. Following the examination, assuming you are all still maidens, I will explain certain things you must know before you go to Court."

"You mean like men trying to kiss you?" an excited Bietriz interrupted with an enthused grin followed by a chuckle. "Tell us about that, Mademoiselle!"

"Yes," the stern-faced Mademoiselle Aalis answered, "among other things you may experience."

"How exciting!" the ingenue Poubelle exclaimed.

"It is not exciting, Mademoiselle Poubelle, I can assure you. There are signs and situations you must be able to overcome to avoid detrimental positions or harm. I will teach you; you must take this seriously, as it is not a game, but something which could destroy your future.

"On a brighter note, I will also teach you the art of being a wife in the bedroom. Now collect your notebooks and retire to your sleeping room, remove your day clothes, and strip down to your shift. I will call for each of you in turn. Gilia or Osana will come for you." Mademoiselle Aalis turned and walked briskly from the dining room. The girls looked at each other and burst into fits of giggles.

As they reached their room, Melisinde whispered, "If my Papa knew about all of this, he would be storming around the room! He seems to think girls are useful for little but cleaning, cooking, and making babies. I don't know what Mademoiselle Aalis is going to tell us, but I'm sure Papa would disapprove of me knowing, thinking, or being able to do anything but cook, clean, and make babies with my mouth shut!"

"But surely he knows how babies are made. He is your father and that of your siblings, after all!" Poubelle looked confused. "Why, everyone has seen dogs' mate, haven't they? I don't see why all the fuss. You do it, and then you have a baby in your belly, right? That fulfills your duty as a wife—to provide an heir. And we'll probably all have maids and cooks, so the rest we will likely never have to remember how to do, unless all the maids, cooks, and valets perish with the Black Death, if it returns."

"Be quiet about that scourge, Poubelle! It's not coming back—enough people died, and more had their lives ruined. I don't understand why you keep dwelling on it." Bietriz complained.

"Because we…" Poubelle began to retort when Melisinde cut her short.

"Enough! None of us knows anything about that, and we're not supposed to talk about things we don't know, remember? Say a prayer, Poubelle, and God will take the worry from your mind. Meantime, I'm all for hearing what Mademoiselle Aalis has to say. I'll bet Father Etienne would call it 'censored information,' what do you think? I, for one, am nervous about a wedding night and all that follows."

"Not me!" the jolly Bietriz replied. "Have you ever seen a naked man? I have! My friends and I were picnicking by the lake, and we heard noises, so we crept closer to see what caused it. One of the boys from our village was humping a bad girl. After a bit, he stood up and stretched. And there it was! All right there in the bright sunlight! My friend made a noise, and we had to run away because he turned when he heard us, but we got a good look then!"

"Did the girl want a baby?" Poubelle asked.

"How should I know that?" Bietriz shook her head in annoyance. "Have you been living in a convent?"

"No, of course not, you know I haven't! I just don't understand why they would be 'doing it' if they didn't want a baby, that's all." Poubelle was blushing.

"Because you don't do it only once, you blockhead!" the frustrated Bietriz said.

"What? I thought..." Poubelle was confused.

"You would do well to pay attention to Mademoiselle Aalis, Poubelle. There is a lot you need to learn. There is a lot we all need to know! It's scary, but it is also thrilling, don't you think?"

Melisinde said with a smirk. "I've got goosebumps!"

There was a knock at the door, and Osana entered. "Mademoiselle Aalis will see you now, Mademoiselle Poubelle. Please follow me."

Bietriz gave Poubelle a "thumbs up," and Melisinde blew her a kiss. Poubelle walked out slowly, looking back at them uncertainly as she crossed the threshold.

"She looks scared. Are you scared?" Melisinde asked Bietriz.

"Yes, I am, all of a sudden." Bietriz reached for Melisinde's hand. The two waited in silence.

After a short while, Poubelle returned, her head down, her steps slow. Gilia accompanied her, announcing, "Mademoiselle Melisinde, you are next."

Melisinde looked at Poubelle, saying, "Well? Tell us!"

Poubelle raised her head, and both girls could see her

tearstained face. She walked to her bed and lay down, covering her head with the quilt.

Gilia said, "Mademoiselle Melisinde, now, please." Melisinde followed meekly and intrepidly. She looked back at Bietriz as Poubelle had done shortly before. Bietriz sat stunned, her eyes wide.

The room where Mademoiselle Aalis awaited her looked like an ordinary spare bedroom. Mademoiselle Aalis told her to lie down on the bed. She removed her slippers and complied. With a pinched expression, the woman approached the bedside with a linen cloth slung over her arm.

"Do you have anything to say to me?" she asked Melisinde.

"About what?"

Mademoiselle Aalis inhaled with annoyance. "Have you been with a man?"

"Only my father and brother, except we did visit my uncle a couple of years ago, and I played with my cousins. They're boys."

Mademoiselle Aalis huffed. "Have you ever been intimate with a boy or a man? Have they touched you with their hands or another part of their body under your shift?"

"What? No!" Melisinde protested with disgust and insult.

"Raise your knees and let your legs relax apart," Aalis instructed. "This won't take long."

Melisinde's eyes opened wide, then shut tight, and she heard her throat emit a gurgling sound. She breathed rapidly. "Stop! What are you doing?" she said, too late.

"Relax, now, girl. You are still a maiden. You passed." Mademoiselle Aalis wiped her hands with the towel and rang the bell on the nightstand. Osana entered and waited by the door. Melisinde looked at Mademoiselle Aalis as she redonned her slippers. "Why did you do that to me? How dare you! It was terrible. I think I'm going to be sick, argghh."

Calmly, Mademoiselle Aalis handed her a bowl, also on the nightstand at the ready, showing signs of a fresh rinse. Poor Melisinde lost her lunch. Mademoiselle Aalis nodded to Osana, who approached, gently taking Melisinde's arm to steady her as they walked from the room. On re-entering their shared bedroom, Melisinde saw that Poubelle remained buried under the quilt, and Bietriz sat white-faced and wide-eyed, waiting. Melisinde had no words and meekly walked to her bed, nodding her thanks to Osana, who said, "Mademoiselle Bietriz, come with me, please."

Afterward, all three girls lay silent. A knock at the door produced Gilia's and Osana's entry bearing trays of food and drink. On one of them, a large bowl steamed.

"There are hot, wet towels for each of you to refresh yourselves," Gilia said gently. "There is nothing more for you today. I bid you a good evening and a restorative sleep, Mademoiselles."

Poubelle started crying again; Bietriz was silent; Melisinde angrily punched one of her pillows, thinking how much she detested being born female.

Over the next few days, the girls tentatively shared their experiences, reactions, and thoughts. After the shock and embarrassment of the examination wore off, they agreed not to harbor bad feelings against Mademoiselle Aalis, who was only doing her job. They had all realized that their husbands would similarly violate their bodies. None were excited at the prospect.

Madame De Marigny continued with their tuition, never raising the subject until it was time for them to be assigned once again to Mademoiselle Aalis.

"I refuse to go through that again!" Melisinde said emphatically. The two others nodded their agreement.

"You do not have to do anything of the sort, *chérie*," said Madame de Marigny. "Mademoiselle Aalis will teach you other things to help you protect yourself, things you need to know. It will not be trying for any of you, but it may seem complicated. I realize the inspection was a shock for you, but it was necessary because, as brides, you must also be virgins. We had to verify that.

"Consider, is it not better for Mademoiselle Aalis to have examined you than a priest or physician as is more usually done? That is one benefit you garner being in my care. The King accepts our word because he trusts me. You are an unknown to all of us, so your word is also not enough. Try to understand. No one wished to hurt you but to help you on this path." She patted Melisinde's hand and went to each of the girls, in turn, to dispense an affectionate gesture before leaving the room.

She stopped in the doorway to say, "I have arranged for you to take dinner on the terrace by the fountain. Tonight promises to be mild and lovely. You shall have wine to celebrate your status as you have all done well and are close to the finish line. Enjoy your evening; *bonne après-midi*."

The next day after reviewing personal hygiene, which included tips on treating common ailments, Mademoiselle Aalis gave each girl a glass bottle. "This is a scent made by the nuns at the convent. It is a combination of rose petals and hips for sweetness and lavender for health and well-being. Apply it here, here, and here. Just a dab, no more."

Mademoiselle Aalis watched as they followed her instruction. "I am so proud of all of you." All three were shocked to see the Mademoiselle wipe her eyes. She had always seemed so detached and emotionless.

She explained many things: possibilities that might happen at events or casual socials; hostile reactions from some at Court designed to embarrass them; deliberate provocations; disputing their right to be part of Court company; and many other situations they potentially might encounter. For each, she had a recommended action.

Before she finished, she addressed a touchy subject by explaining that while courtiers had a code of ethics to follow, they were men and subject to weaknesses of the flesh and attractions. She further explained how a seemingly innocent suggestion (like an afternoon walk in the maze with a charming man) could turn into a distressing and isolated situation.

Such might find them fighting off unwanted, urgent, and forceful attentions or being overcome and succumbing-- the latter guaranteeing complete ruin and subsequent scandal.

"Word gets around like wildfire at Court. There is no coming back from a tarnished reputation. Men have a habit of sharing their conquests with others to make themselves seem more of a man than they are. It is the way of things. You must politely decline all those invitations. Go nowhere alone, never be unattended, politely suggest an alternate plan that provides protection, or simply say that you do not believe it would be appropriate, despite being flattered at the invitation. In these ways, you will not offend but appear proper and obedient. Remember, girls, it is your future that is at stake. Fight for it to remain pure! You are chaste and need to remain so."

Bietriz, the most forward among them, posed a question. "We were verified as virgins, yes, Mademoiselle. I understand why it is important and that our future lords demand only maidens. But if something beyond our control happens to us, who would know? I mean, except for the one who did it to us--and maybe he wouldn't brag about it if he were nice or cared about us—but who would know since we have already been examined? Besides, it wouldn't be our fault, would it? So, we would not be guilty of poor behavior, unless..."

"Have you heard of the bedding ceremony?" Mademoiselle Aalis asked quietly.

"What?" questioned Poubelle.

"It is not always done, but many of the nobles take part in a bedding ceremony. After you retire from the celebrations, the master and some of his best friends enter the wedding chamber on your wedding night. There is usually an experienced maid on hand as well, and while they wait for you to present yourself, the maid serves them wine.

"Remember, everyone has been celebrating all evening, so they are a bit unsteady, and at least some are drunk. Caution and manners are thrown to the winds on those occasions, trust me. Remember, it is acceptable for men to frequent brothels, even though the Church frowns officially. There is no propriety and gentility in a brothel, and it is not uncommon for people to couple in full view or share partners or other unsavory things.

"But in the chamber awaiting the bride, there is usually a lot of laughter and bawdy remarks. When the bride enters with her handmaid, the master greets her in whatever fashion is his habit or desire. He may be kind and soft-spoken or rough and insensitive.

"I have seen grooms tear nightclothes from their wife's body and throw her down on the bed or make her stand naked or walk around the room in front of his friends. Those are the awful cases. But the point is, the groom's choice determines everything done in that room, and he takes his wife in full view of the onlookers."

All the girls gasped.

"Afterward, the sheets are checked for a bloodstain. Some or all of the others in the room corroborate the presence of virgin blood. They witness both the consummation of the marriage and the proof that the woman was a virgin. All of this bodes well for the union, the production of an heir, and the bloodline's pure preservation.

"Of course, it is up to the master whether a bedding ceremony will occur. The bride has no say in it whatsoever. I thought you should know. I don't know if it is possible to learn what you will face beforehand. At the moment, we don't even know who you will wed you for certain. Whatever the case, the wedding chamber is the last step to take before becoming the Lady of the House. I hope each of you will be spared the bedding experience, but we cannot know. What I do know is that you can and will live through it with God's help if it becomes necessary. I have faith in each of you."

Mademoiselle Aalis turned to go. "I have given instructions, and a bath awaits you. The maids will be in presently. I give you all my blessings. Rest well, *mes doux.*"

When Melisinde and her friends were presented at Court, she was six months shy of her fourteenth birthday. Their time with Madame De Marigny, Mademoiselle Aalis, and the others had given them a foundation in preparation for their time at Court and their roles as future wives of noblemen. Six weeks' tuition, while better than nothing, was woefully inadequate, and the girls were falsely confident in their ability to handle whatever circumstance might befall them.

Initially, they were regarded with curiosity or indifference by the males and haughty suspicion by the females. In more than one instance, one of the more popular ladies of the Court successfully maneuvered the conversation to embarrass one or all of them.

Poor Bietriz was deliberately set off balance and tripped on one occasion to find herself careening into a card table and scattering everyone's tabled cards. Despite profuse apologies, Bietriz was humiliated by comments of cumbersome clumsiness and her physical constitution being more *apropos* to an ungainly milkmaid than a lady of the Court. The unkind titters evoked by this occurrence drove Bietriz from the room in tears.

The petite Poubelle was a favored partner, and her dance card was usually full. After an evening of nonstop dancing, poor Poubelle was dizzy with excitement and wine. She temporarily lost her sense, allowing herself to be whisked away to the balcony by a man, only to find herself in the company of three at once. They took great pleasure in passing her around, whirling and whirling, until she was close to fainting. Inappropriately grabbing her tightly and leaning her against the balcony rail, one of the men pulled her bodice away from her body, remarking to his friends that they should all take a look and feel of 'budding roses.' They were laughing rowdily when Bietriz and Melisinde appeared, scurrying to Poubelle's rescue. The dizzied Poubelle was fully compliant to Bietriz's grasp, bustling her away.

To distract them, Melisinde said, "Monsieurs, naughty, naughty!" with a becoming, coquettish smile. "Surely, such handsome, powerful men as you have little need of a mere girl. I have seen the ladies of Court sending admiring glances in your direction. You can choose among them with success, allowing this poor girl to grow in dignity as befits your attentions! Good evening," she beamed with a quick curtsy, dashing to catch up to Bietriz and the weakened Poubelle.

When Melisinde was introduced to Viscount Albret, she nearly fainted and was overcome with nausea. He was presented by Madame De Marigny, who blessedly remained at Melisinde's side during the brief encounter. The man was elderly, and while elegantly outfitted, was indeed smelly with greasy hair, wrinkled face, ogling eyes, and missing teeth. Melisinde could not help herself from imagining sharing a marital bed with him to her disgust.

The two nephews who attended with their uncle were as different as chalk and cheese. Gidie (Giles) was stocky, of medium height with an unruly mop of black, curly hair, and dark stubble indicating a heavy beard; Piers (Peter) was tall and fair, of slender build with beautiful hands. Both greeted Melisinde with obvious delight and charming politeness. They were brothers by the same father and different mothers and lived with their uncle following their parents' deaths.

When the Viscount invited Melisinde to dance, she was speechless, trying in vain to produce an excuse. Fortunately, as the man explained, he was no longer up to dancing because of an old leg injury received in the King's service. The Viscount suggested that she dance with one of his nephews. He would content himself with viewing her form from afar. He gestured to Gidie.

"Thank you, sweet God," Melisinde whispered.

"What did you say?" asked Gidie.

Briefly stymied for an answer, Melisinde replied, "With pleasure, my lord, but I should have said it louder, as with all the music, my lord could not hear me." She took a deep breath and accepted his arm, walking to the dance floor.

A portion of the evening alternated between dances with each of the nephews. She found Piers to be on the shy side, and while perfectly polite, they conversed little and only shallowly. Gidie, on the other hand, was pleasant and amusing company, making her laugh and putting her at ease with his dissection of other members at Court, which she found at once hilarious and informative. At last, Madame De Marigny reappeared, announcing that Melisinde must circulate among the other guests, and she took her leave of the Albrets.

When they were seated alone, Madame De Marigny questioned Melisinde about her impressions. The two nephews were, at present, the only heirs to the Viscount's estate and holdings, barring the Viscount's ability to produce a child, preferably a male son and heir who would also be titled. "Do you have a preference between the young men?" asked Madame.

"They are both very polite and charming, each in his way," answered Melisinde carefully. "I am sure they are of great help to Viscomte Albret, as he appears somewhat doddering and not in the best of health or condition."

"Astute, *mon petit*, well done!" Madame De Marigny seemed pleased with Melisinde's assessment. "Now, there are some others to whom I would introduce you before the evening's end. Come." The women rose, and Madame led Melisinde to a group of mature, imposing, wigged gentlemen in the far corner of the room. Mademoiselle Foix was at their center, holding a "court" of her own. Her eyes flashed warning when she saw Melisinde and Madame De Marigny's approach, despite her fawning attitude of greeting Madame Marigny. The ensuing conversation became a duel of wits and demeanor between Melisinde and Mademoiselle Foix.

When they took their leave, Madame De Marigny said quietly, "I would characterize that as a draw, Mademoiselle. You acquitted yourself well, particularly as Mademoiselle Foix is a well-experienced woman at Court."

"Thank you, Madame. But why is she not married to one of the noblemen? She is indeed a beauty and well-versed in Court life."

Looking kindly at Melisinde, Madame De Marigny said, "Why, my dear, she is the King's mistress... or should I say, the King's mistress 'at the moment,'" the wise and wily Madame De Marigny responded. "By the time the King tires of her, she will have fine jewels, coin, and land to support herself and take a man of her choosing. Taking the King's leftovers is a coveted position among the nobles and confers unique status. I know not one of them who would refuse that distinction. In the meantime, they pander to Mademoiselle Foix, hoping that she will curry the King's favor according to what they whisper in her ear. Beware Mademoiselle Foix, Melisinde. She is from a powerful noble family and well-versed in the politics of Court."

"My father taught me, 'Never pick a fight you can't win; it only strengthens your enemy.'"

"That guidance will hold you in good stead at Court and in life, my dear," assured Madame De Marigny.

An enlightened Melisinde nodded her head and remained quiet. Between what Gidie told her, the bits and pieces she overheard from other conversations, and this revelation from Madame De Marigny, Melisinde took another step forward in education, understanding, and maturity.

In due course, she survived the months at Court, Madame deemed her successful, and the King approved the petition for Viscomte Albret to wed Mademoiselle Melisinde Brienne. Madame De Marigny presided over the financial and official arrangements, including both a bride price and an additional posting for Melisinde's father, thereby ensuring her family's security. Her parents were responsible for her dowry. Melisinde's only responsibilities were to remain chaste, be charming, and accept all others' decisions concerning her life. Inwardly, she fumed at what she perceived as the unfairness of her situation. Outwardly, her demeanor was perfect. She dreaded the thought of her nuptials, which were scheduled a scant three weeks away.

When she and Poubelle were granted permission to visit Bietriz (who had already been wed to a middle-aged widower with two small children from a large country estate outside Paris to the south), they reveled in the upcoming weekend of freedom during the carriage ride.

"Who would think that Bietriz would be the first bride!" the amazed Poubelle remarked. "I wonder if she is happy. Do you think we will all be satisfied, Melisinde? Did I tell you that I am to meet my intended on Wednesday next? I am so excited. He is the son of a nobleman who is a master of the Grande Boucherie. Did you know that Parliament must consider any appeal of a ruling from their judicial counsel? That makes them especially important—the Grande Boucherie, I mean, and my father-in-law-to-be is the master! Of course, they have a counsel in Parliament and one at the Châtelet who are in their pay. That makes them even more powerful!

"The family is rich. His father is the proprietor of three Paris stalls. Jacquet's father, Gilles de Souvré, belongs to an old family of the Perche. Imagine! He holds three titles: Marquis de Courtan-vaux, Baron de Lezines, and marshal of France! Someday, Jacquet will be titled and famous too, and I will be a viscountess, maybe, of their lands in the southwest of France, with the Pyrenees Mountains, Soule, Lower Navarre, Labourd, and small bits of Gascony at my feet. I can hardly believe my luck! Melisinde, are you listening to me? Does that not sound like a dream come true?"

Poubelle had been prattling on, and Melisinde shook herself from thoughts of her future. "I heard every word, my dear Poubelle. You richly deserve the fulfillment of your dreams. I am so incredibly happy for you. What do you know of Jacquet?" she asked, genuinely interested in Poubelle's prospects.

"Umm, not very much. There is a slight complication, *mon chèr ami*. He is five years younger than me, but I can wait for him to grow! The plan is to have an overlong engagement, perhaps a year, and then the wedding ceremony. Of course, by then, he'll be only nine years, but I think that by 14 years, he can sire a child. What do you think? In the meantime, I will, of course, live in one of the family homes. They have a family house in Paris and four country houses. I heard gossip that his father spent 3,000 florins [33] rebuilding his Paris house alone. And they say that his wife's jewels, belts, and purses are valued at upwards of 1,000 gold francs."

"Poubelle, you realize that you will be about 19 years when you finally consummate your marriage? That is if he can... consummate, I mean. I don't know when boys... I mean, you will already be a grown woman with a young boy as a husband! Are you sure this is what you want? Jewels and money are not everything, and much can happen in six years' waiting." Melisinde reached to grasp her friend's hands.

"It is the best deal for my future from among those offered, Melisinde. It will be fine, and in the meantime, I shall have a wonderful life and plenty of time to get to know my intended husband. You shall see!" Poubelle said firmly, but Melisinde wondered if she was trying to convince Melisinde or herself.

"Now, tell me what you think of Bietriz and her new life. Two children to raise! Ugh!" Poubelle had closed the subject of her arrangement, and the two girls chatted about Bietriz and their

---

33   The florin at the time was worth 12 francs; thus, the cost of the Paris house rebuild was approximately 36,000 francs in the currency value of the mid-century, a vast amount by any measure of time.

imminent visit convivially.

The weeks flew by, and with them, the date of Melisinde's marriage drew ever closer.

Madame De Marigny's health took a turn for the worse, and she shared with Melisinde that, although she would do her best to shepherd Melisinde through her responsibilities regarding her nuptials, she was not going to continue operating her "finishing school." The loyal Mademoiselle Aalis and several of the maids and other servants decided to remain with the Madame for as long as she required their services.

"*Mon amour*, I have secured permission and arranged for Mademoiselle Aalis and two of my maids that you know well to attend you throughout the events surrounding your wedding and on the night. Have no fear. All will go well for you inasmuch as we can help you make it so."

"Oh, Madame, I do worry for you. Thank you so much for all you have done for me. I can think of no way to properly thank you. May I do anything for you? Anything, Madame, anything— you have only to name it," a tearful Melisinde said to her mentor.

"Remember what I have taught you, sweet Melisinde. That will be thanks enough. Now I must rest, my dear. Come to me tomorrow afternoon for tea." Having been dismissed, Melisinde ambled to the central hall where Mademoiselle Aalis awaited her.

"She looks so wan and pale, Mademoiselle. I worry for her," Melisinde said.

With downcast eyes, Aalis confided. "She is very unwell, Melisinde. Madame is also aged, although she masquerades it well, even now when she is indisposed. Come, let us walk in the garden and I will explain the plans made for you. There is much to discuss."

Fingering her headdress, Melisinde shook uncontrollably. She was about to wed an older man whose countenance repulsed her, much less could she contemplate the proximity to him over hours of a wedding celebration and the intimacy expected afterward. She considered that life in a convent might be preferable, but now, it was too late for even that. She knew that spinsterhood was not an option insofar as her father's opinions were concerned. That left only life in a brothel, which was equally horrifying, except that in a marriage, one had to contend with only one man, not the multiples of a brothel, many of which might be as disgusting as her husband-to-be.

"*Ma douce*, I cannot stand what I have learned will happen to you in a short time," Mademoiselle Aalis frantically whispered to Melisinde, seated at the dais looking faint. Her husband was in the company of a group of men at the side of the large hall indulging in drinking and laughter, casting her frequent lecherous glances.

"What is it, Mademoiselle? Surely, nothing can be worse than having that man make me his wife," Melisinde said. "I almost said no when the Cardinal asked me to recite my vows."

"He plans a bedding ceremony in the wedding chamber!" Mademoiselle Aalis whispered desperately. "He is depraved and not worthy of jewel like you!"

Melisinde felt hopeless. "Is there no potion I can take to make me forget this night?"

"None that I know of, *mon amour*, but I have a plan. One of the maids is of your build and coloring. She could pass for you if you let your braids loose, hold your head down, and let your hair cover your face. When I take you behind the screen to change from your gown to your bridal nightclothes, we will make the switch! She will be waiting behind the screen. The girl will re-enter the bridal chamber through the same archway we use to take you away behind the dressing screen."

"Can it work?" Melisinde said with a glimmer of hope evident in her voice. "But who is this girl who is willing to stand in for me?"

"She is a sister to one of the maids you know: Osana. She comes to us from a brothel frequented by noblemen, eager to escape that life for one of a maid-in-service. She can endure the Viscount's attention, I assure you. She has experience. Are you willing?" Mademoiselle's eyes were full of tears for the girl she had come to care for so deeply.

"You put yourself at great risk on my behalf, Mademoiselle, if we are discovered."

"I know, but I think we can manage it. I simply cannot bear the thought of the indignity you would have to suffer. It is the height of debasement and cruelty!" the woman sobbed.

"We shall try, all of us together. Although it is only a postponement of the inevitable, I thank you for saving me the trial of the bedding ceremony," Melisinde whispered as she kissed Aalis's hand. "Go now, make things ready. And tell Osana's sister that she shall be well rewarded for her role and her silence. Go." Mademoiselle Aalis drifted away, fading into the background as if she were never there.

A half-hour passed, and then another. Piers came to her side, looking worried.

"Join me, Piers. What is wrong?" Melisinde indicated the empty chair at her side.

"It is time," he said softly, looking at her with sadness in his eyes. "I am to escort you."

Melisinde's stomach fell, and she began to breathe rapidly. Slowly, she raised her wine goblet to her lips, looking at Piers while she drank. "Will you hold my hand as we walk to give me courage?" she asked forlornly. He nodded his assent, stood, and took her hand.

When they reached her private rooms, loud voices and laughter assaulted Melisinde's ears from the bedchamber through the archway. Entering, she saw a group of men scattered throughout the room, drinking wine and worrying the two serving maids with remarks and slaps on the bottom. Melisinde could not see Mademoiselle Aalis anywhere. Piers walked with her into the room and approached his uncle, extending Melisinde's hand to him.

"Uncle, your bride." As he said those words, his voice choked with emotion.

"See how my nephew loves me, my dear! He is overcome with happiness for us!" he croaked into Melisinde's ear. The old man called out to his friends, "What do you think, my good friends, will this one give me an heir?"

Various ribald responses made Melisinde blush.

"Let's take a look at you, then," the old man rasped, reaching for her.

Melisinde said, "Wait, my lord, please. I must retire for a few moments to change from my wedding garb." As she said this, she turned toward the archway with the dressing screen just beyond and spotted Mademoiselle Aalis standing to its side in the adjacent room. Aalis nodded slightly, and Melisinde allowed herself to smile and breathe in relief.

She felt a rough hand spin her around. "Nonsense, girl. There's no need for bedclothes, is there, my friends?" her husband said with a leer. Spittle drizzled down his chin, reminding her of a dog slathering over a piece of meat. Before she knew what was happening, the Viscount grabbed the front of her wedding dress and tore it open. Melisinde screamed. The Viscount snapped his fingers, and strong arms held her arms from the back.

"Feast your eyes, my noble friends. Fresh, young, and untouched!" the disgusting man said, his lascivious laughter followed by a coughing fit.

"Please, my lord," Melisinde managed to utter through her tears.

"She begs for you, my lord," called out one of the men with a lewd grin.

As the Viscount moved closer to her, kneading her small breasts, he whispered, "Take everything off, my dear. I want to see all of what I've paid for." Melisinde thought she would faint at the smell of him. Even the traces of wine on his breath could not cover his foul stench.

"No, I will not!" she said, struggling in vain to free herself from the man behind.

"Hmm? Spirited, eh? Well, we shall cure you of that, *mon animal de compagnie.*" Wheeling around, he called out, "Nephews! Disrobe her!" He turned to recline on a chaise, accepting a full goblet of wine while the onlookers jeered and egged two young men on, who had hesitated in completing their ordered task.

"To show how much I love you, nephews, you may have the first good feel, as mine was only brief!" their uncle said to the guffaws of others present.

Melisinde stood naked, surrounded by strangers, mortified, and afraid. When she opened her eyes, her husband stood before her in only his tunic, supported by two of his friends. He rubbed himself with one hand and her with the other. Gesticulating to his friends, Melisinde was marched toward the bed and thrown onto it. Mademoiselle Aalis had joined the other servants in the room, and Melisande glimpsed Mademoiselle Aalis crying uncontrollably as she fell to the mattress.

"Turn her," the man rasped and coughed, "I want to waste none of my seed!"

In moments, she was aware of his insinuating body and smell, a searing pain accompanying the vile feel of him, her sobs punctuating each thrust. Shortly, it was over. The assemblage cheered and laughed, except for the Viscount's nephews and the servants.

She felt Mademoiselle Aalis' protective arms gathering her

into a robe and leading her out of the room, her rubbery legs just able to navigate slow steps.

"Come, *mon petit*, I have a bath drawn. I am so sorry. We did not have a chance to put our plan into play. Cry, now, *mon amour*, let it all go. It is over. There, there," the woman said.

But it was not over as Melisinde well knew. There would be other times of having to suffer her husband's urges. She asked God to forgive her, but she wished him ill health to be unable to demand his conjugal rights. As the gentle Mademoiselle Aalis bathed her, she thought of her friends. She thought of Madame De Marigny. She thought of her family.

With bitterness, she thought of her father. 'I will never forgive you, never!'

Fig. 541. Anne, Duchess of Bedford[?]

Chapter Eleven
The Path to Viscountess

With some tips from Osana's sister, Melisinde endured those occasions when she performed as a wife in the bedchamber. Because of his age and poor health, she hastened the conclusion of those few occurrences using the methods Tiece shared, with nature's help. When she was confirmed "with child" and constantly nauseous, the foul man still insisted on her compliance.

"My lord, I am truly unwell, and I get sick with too much activity or when I take all but the simplest of foods," she explained to him when he remarked that she had lost her bloom and appeal. "I am trying to protect your child by taking great care." He merely scoffed and ordered her to the bedroom. On one such occasion, she vomited all over him. While her regurgitation compounded the dreadful episode, there was an upside: he was sufficiently discouraged from demanding her participation any further for the remainder of her pregnancy.

As often happens, once she passed the first trimester, she felt better and better, nausea departing. However, she was careful to promote the rumor that she was still unwell to stave off the Viscount's attentions. Instead, she made friends with his nephews, Piers and Gidie.

Piers was in charge of his uncle's businesses and estate's financial end, completing all negotiations, ordering, and all the associated and official paperwork. Gidie was a "hands-on" type, liaising with the farmers, checking the produce, collecting rents, overseeing all aspects of production and marketing. Between the two, Viscount Albret's interests increased, and his businesses and net worth flourished. Because of her aptitude and Mademoiselle Aalis' assistance, Melisinde began to take charge of the household from operation to ordering to staff supervision. While hers was the smallest responsibility of the three, it functioned flawlessly and more economically than previously.

"How are you feeling, Melisinde? It has been several months now, but you barely show your child. Are you sure the household is not too much for you? I must say, your records are impeccable, and you have done a good job supervising the staff. Everyone is fond of you." Piers patted her hand as they walked through the garden arm in arm.

"I feel much better than I did in the early stages. I confess I was sick many times each day. No one told me it could get so bad, and it frightened me. I thought I was losing the child, perhaps because I was so young when I was blessed with a child. Then an old herbalist came to the chateau hawking her wares for our lord's coughing sickness. I happened to mention it to her, and she assured me it was normal. Some women get sick for the first months, and then it abates, but others continue with nausea throughout their time. I thank God I am not one of those. Now, but for an occasional backache, I can do other things and be useful."

"Well, I must compliment you, as even our grumpy gardener has given his best and seems to adore you. Just look at these roses!" Piers bent and snapped off a lovely bloom, giving it to her. "A beautiful rose for a beautiful lady," he said with embarrassment.

"You are kind to me, Piers, but we both know I am far from beautiful, particularly now."

"I disagree; you are blooming, just as these bushes bloom."

"As concerns the household, I am glad you are pleased. It was not too difficult to rally the servants once they realized their role was appreciated and valued. I think perhaps our lord was too brusque and unfeeling with them. Forgive me, Piers, perhaps I speak out of turn beyond my station," Melisinde lowered her eyes, the last phrase falling to a whisper.

"No, no, my Lady speaks the truth of it. Uncle is, at best, a harsh and demanding man. I am told he was not always so; that is, he is said to have been different in the early days before my brother and I came to him. Perhaps sadness and disappointments have made him thus. I admit he is failing and has all but withdrawn entirely from all estate and business matters, staying in his suite all day long. His valet says he barely sleeps as the cough is worse at night." Piers looked genuinely concerned.

"Piers, I want you to take comfort in the knowledge that whatever happens to our lord, for better or worse, I have no intention of asking you and Gidie to relinquish your positions or leave the chateau. We would all be lost without you, and you have both proven yourselves times over. I think we three make a good partnership, what say you?" Melisinde playfully punched his arm, smiling up at him. "Ooh," she said suddenly, bending over.

"Melisinde, are you all right?" The concerned Piers placed an arm around her waist, supporting her arm with his other. He looked around for a bench, a wall, or the gardener. No one and nothing was in sight. "I should spend less time with my books and papers and get out more," he mumbled. "I have no idea where a bench might be or the pergola we paid to have built, or....."

Melisinde laughed. "Oh, Piers, do not worry. It was just a pain, and now it is gone. But I agree: you must take the air more than you do. Everyone needs a share of fresh air and sunshine. Promise me that you shall try in the future?"

As the three friends supped together—as had been their habit for the last seven months—she recognized the strong three-way compatibility between them. Each had his and her role; each was good at what they did; each part complemented the others. Gidie's good nature and hands-on methods encouraged solid production, which filled the coffers Piers controlled. He managed all the expenses, prudently setting aside funds for repairs and improvements while still increasing the family's savings. Melisinde had the household and grounds running like a top, kept bright, clean, scrubbed, and productive, with happy workers and healthy food for all. Everyone benefitted from each other's role, which is the way things should work ideally. In all of this, the Viscount had no operative part. Undeniably, however, his previous decisions and ownership of all the businesses and considerable landholdings had allowed them all to find their place in life.

"To our lord," said Gidie raising his goblet. They toasted the Viscount, as they did each evening. However, Melisinde sipped only apple juice during her pregnancy, as wine upset her digestion.

"I was thinking, gentlemen, if I may have your attention," Melisinde said coyly. "Shortly, my child will make us 'four.' But it has nowhere to sleep. Could we procure a cradle, do you think? Or, perhaps, a crib?"

"Ah, yes, of course," laughed Gidie. "We should have thought of that, right Piers?"

"Indeed, we should have. Forgive us, Melisinde. And please forgive me," Piers said gently, "for correcting you: it is 'five,' not 'four, including the baby and not forgetting our uncle."

Chagrinned, Melisinde said, "Of course, forgive me, both of you. It was an innocent error."
For a moment, they all felt discomfort. Then Gidie—as was so often the case—relieved the tension by asking, "When does a child start walking and climbing? How old and how big do they have to be?"

"I believe they walk at about two years and climb from 2 ½ to 3 years and upwards of that age, at least based on my friend's children that seems to be the time," Melisinde offered, remembering Bietriz and her brood.

"Well, I could make the child a bed that would suit from infancy through babyhood until it moved to a normal bed! What say you both? If I scale it down enough, it could work. I could check with some of the farm families to get an idea of the size the children are at certain ages."

Piers added, "I think it's a splendid idea, Gidie. You might wish to add some carvings too." Addressing this remark to Melisinde, he said, "Gidie was always carving animals from wood for our toys when we were young; he is quite good at it. I'm embarrassed to say that our childhood was so isolated that we never played with anyone but each other. We're a bit lacking insofar as knowing about other children, what they need, how big they get, and the like. We just grew up together and never had to pay any attention to those sorts of things as we always lived with only adults. Our exposure to other children was nil."

"Our exposure to anyone was pretty much nil, Piers. It wasn't until we were sent away to boarding school and then to university that we interfaced with others our own age. It was always servants and tutors with an occasional five or ten minutes getting introduced to visitors, and then banishment."

"Melisinde, perhaps Gidie's apt description will help you to understand why he and I are so close, despite that we are so different!" Piers explained, lifting his goblet to toast his brother.

"To my brother: my dearest friend and the best man I am privileged to know!"

To her surprise, Gidie's eyes streamed. He was without a response and merely sipped his wine. Melisinde said, "And to my dear friends, related by marriage, but to both of whom I owe my survival, friends of my heart!" As she sipped her apple juice, Melisinde could not help but notice that each man was staring at her, unashamedly allowing tears to fall to their cheeks.

'Somehow, I think these two have never received love or praise from anyone except each other,' she thought. 'All children should experience the security and joy of being loved and valued.' Melisinde made a private vow to keep her child close, instilling in it the knowledge that it was loved and treasured. She looked forward to sharing the joys of her child's development with these two wonderful men who would also be good role models for the child's future.

～

Mademoiselle Aalis appeared to announce the Doctor's arrival for the Viscount. Piers and Gidie rose immediately, took their leave of Melisinde, and went to the reception hall to greet the physician. Melisinde advised Mademoiselle Aalis that she needed her help to mount the staircase to the Viscount's quarters to attend the doctoral visit.

[On Madame De Marigny's death, Mademoiselle Aalis accepted Melisinde's invitation to be her personal assistant in the running of the chateau and to be her companion through the pregnancy and birth of her child. Along with Madame's maids, she, Osana, and Osana's sister, Tiece, and Madame's cook, Mabile, joined Melisinde's household staff. The existing cook was terrible and was dismissed with a sizable purse. The maid—Perrete—was only too glad to have two additional women to help. Perrin, the gardener, appreciated Melisinde's interest in plants and trees such that she breathed new life into his work, which showed in the state of the chateau's beautiful gardens. More importantly, he felt appreciated for his knowledge and work and looked forward to their daily strolls and discussions.]

The Viscount reclined on a chaise by the windows, his complexion looking grayer than previously. Melisinde respectfully greeted him, motioning to Mademoiselle Aalis to place the vase of roses on his side table. On their heels, Gidie, Piers, and the Doctor appeared.

"See what beautiful roses Perrin has grown for you, my lord. Their perfume and color are like no other flower, and I hope they bring you pleasure," a respectful Melisinde said.

"Haven't you birthed that baby yet?" the cranky man snapped, coughing repeatedly.

"Not yet, my lord, but soon I trust. May I get anything for you?"

"Send me someone young and pretty to sit on my lap and take that lumbering body of yours from my sight," the disagreeable man ordered.

"That will have to wait, my lord. The Doctor is here to see you," Melisinde answered.

"Doctor? Doctor? Who sent for that quack? Why didn't you say so at once instead of wasting my time with idle chatter, woman?! Bring him to me."

Melisinde curtsied and motioned to the Doctor. "His eyesight fails as well, sir. Please excuse him. These days of feeling increasingly unwell put him in a temper."

Bowing slightly, the Doctor inclined his head toward Melisinde, whispering, "And you, my dear, are an angel Heaven sent." Melisinde smiled, tilting her head, and withdrawing.

Madame De Marigny's words rang in her memory: 'To survive, you must each be acknowledged and viewed as graceful, supportive French subjects who present no threat, but promote a sense of propriety, calm, obedience, and well-being. Those qualities will ensure your survival both at Court and in the home.' For not the first time, Melisinde was grateful for all Madame De Marigny and Mademoiselle Aalis had taught her.

"What have you got to say for yourself, Monsieur Doctor? That foul tonic has done me no good; no good at all!" the perturbed Viscount spat.

"Ah, my lord, I am sorry to hear that. I have brought another concoction, and..."

Throughout the examination, the exchange went on until the Doctor, red-faced from enduring insult after insult, bade everyone goodbye, handing written instructions to Melisinde.

"I fear there is no cure for consumption, my Lady. I cannot say how long this will continue, but I can say he will never improve. You have my best wishes for what will be a difficult time, all things considered," the Doctor said, looking back at the noisily snoring Viscount and nodding at her protruding belly. "*Courage, mon cher. Adieu.*"

On a late morning, Melisinde buckled over during her walk with the gardener. She asked that he summon Mademoiselle Aalis as she collapsed onto a garden bench. In a few moments, Aalis came running to her, accompanied by Piers.

"I believe the child is finally coming," a breathless Melisinde advised.

Piers lifted her with ease, carrying her into the house and up the stairs to her rooms. Aalis mobilized the staff, directing the gardener to fetch the Doctor. When all was in readiness, surrounded by her faithful assistant and maids, Melisinde walked in the steps of hundreds, thousands, and millions of women before her as she labored for hours to bring her child into the world. Piers and Gidie paced outside her room. They had informed their uncle of Melisinde's condition. He remained in his room, directing them to notify him when the birth occurred and to bring the child to him for inspection.

Melisinde was still a teenager, so the birth was not an easy one. Still, she produced a healthy, bawling baby. Drenched in sweat and weak, she cuddled her newborn swaddled child. Looking with questions toward Mademoiselle Aalis, she cried at the news her child was a girl. After a few moments, her tears subsided, and she said, "I name you Jeanne, and I promise you shall never have to endure the travails of your mother. You shall be loved and encouraged. I shall always listen to your dreams and try to fulfill your needs. I shall teach you to have the courage to be all that you can be and reach to become all that you want to be. I vow this in the name of God the Father, God the Son, and God, the Holy Spirit."

Melisinde's baby girl, Jeanne, looked up at her mother and smiled. Although she nor the others in attendance realized at that time in history that the child did not have full sight at birth, the smile from the baby seemed a good omen and bond between mother and child.

Piers and Gidie crept into the bedchamber to pay their respects. Their first concern was for Melisinde, who, although smiling, was clearly exhausted and pale. The look of joy and wonder on their faces as they beheld the family's newest member touched Melisinde's heart.

After a few moments of conversation, Gidie said, "Uncle wishes to see the child, Melisinde. Would you entrust her to me?"

Melisinde sat up with not a little discomfort, cradling her baby close to her. "Why? He has not had a kind word for me throughout my waiting time. Can you not simply tell him that the child is a girl? I fear for his reaction and disappointment that she is not the son he needs[34]."

---

34 **Jeanne d'Albret** (Basque: Joana Albretekoa; Occitan:Joana de Labrit; 16 November 1528 – 9 June 1572), also known as **Jeanne III,** was the queen regnant of Navarre from 1555 to 1572. She married Antoine de Bourbon, Duke of Vendôme, becoming the Duchess of Vendôme, and was the

Piers said, "I will be with Gidie. I promise you; no harm will come to Jeanne while we live and breathe, Melisinde."

Reluctantly, she agreed and passed the bundled baby to Gidie, instructing Mademoiselle Aalis to accompany them. "Osana and Tiece can help me bathe and change while you are gone, but I beg you to return her as soon as possible. I put my trust in you both."

Piers knocked on the door, and the Viscount's valet answered. "He has just awoken in a foul temper, I am afraid, my lords. Tread carefully." The valet nodded to Aalis, who trailed behind with trepidation.

"Uncle!" a cheerful Gidie called as they walked toward the chaise by the windows. "May I present your child, Jeanne." Gidie stood next to his uncle, bending slightly so the man could see the baby's face.

"*Mon Dieu*! A girl is it?" He scoffed, then coughed. "She couldn't even give me a son! What use is she? Take her away," the horrid man said. "I am cursed. Tell that useless wife of mine I shall expect her attendance tomorrow evening in my chamber. We must get on with getting me a son! Do you hear? A son, *par Dieu!*" The effort of the exchange brought on another fit of coughing.

"With respect, Uncle, your wife has only just given birth. She is in no condition to... uh..." said Piers worriedly. "She will need a few weeks at least to heal. She is still not well enough..."

"You will deliver my message, and she will do as she is told! Sick, sick, that is all I ever hear! She's sick, I'm sick, who else in this infernal house is sick? Get out of my sight with all your pandering and take that brat with you! Jehan! Bring me some brandy!"

With all the harsh sounds and loud voices, the baby had begun to squawl. Gidie handed it to Mademoiselle Aalis, who quickly left the room with Piers and Gidie on her heels once they had taken leave of their uncle.

"We must keep most of this from Melisinde. Hear me, Mademoiselle Aalis! She will only become distressed," Piers suggested to Gidie and Aalis.

"What shall we say when she asks us about Uncle's reaction—and you know she will." Gidie paced outside the closed door

mother of Henri de Bourbon. The latter became King Henry III of Navarre and IV of France, the first Bourbon king of France. Jeanne was the acknowledged spiritual and political leader of the French Huguenot movement. Strage, Mark (1976). *Women of Power: The Life and Times of Catherine de' Medici*. New York and London: Harcourt Brace Jovanovich. ISBN 0-15-198370-4; Robin, Diana Maury; Larsen, Anne R.; Levin, Carole (2007). *Encyclopedia of women in the Renaissance: Italy, France, and England*. ABC-CLIO, Inc.

while Aalis rocked and tried to quiet the baby.

"If I may, gentlemen," interrupted Mademoiselle Aalis, "keep as close to the truth as possible. She is an intelligent young woman and will sense if you are lying to her. Tell her the master was disappointed that she bore him a daughter and not a son. Explain that he was in a coarse mood and therefore had no interest in inspecting the child, as is typical for a father to want to do. Tell her that he expressed that he still wanted the two of them to produce a son and heir. That will give her reassurance of her position as his wife.

"Just leave out the beckoning for tomorrow night. Leave that part to me; I will think of something. That part is women's business." Mademoiselle Aalis looked to both men for their agreement. Receiving confirmation, she made her way to Melisinde's rooms.

"Let us try to make little of this, brother. We can get the crib you made and carry it to Melisinde's room. Surely, that will help to distract her and perhaps assuage her worry." Piers clapped Gidie's back, and the two hurried down the winding staircase to fulfill their task.

Melisinde was just returning to her bed when Aalis walked through the door with the baby. She held out her arms, cooing to it, stroking Jeanne's mop of dark brown hair. Looking to Mademoiselle Aalis, who poured a glass of water, Melisinde queried, "Well? How awful was it?"

Aalis extended the water to Melisinde. "You must drink, my Lady, to ensure your milk will flow. Several glasses a day if you please. Give me the child, and I shall wrap it in fresh cloths and blanket. We have barely had time to go through our normal after birth procedures! I will bring her back presently, all fresh and ready to suckle." Melisinde surrendered Jeanne to Mademoiselle Aalis. She would have limited time to nurse her child, as it was the habit for wet nurses to be employed by noblewomen to ensure that the Lady of the house remained young-looking, shapely, and alluring.

Piers and Gidie knocked at the door, slowly opening it partially. Piers asking if they could enter.

"Of course, you may. I am clean, my hair is brushed, and I feel much more inclined for company. Tell me of your visit to my lord," she said with a slight touch of imperiousness in tone.

As they entered, each man at the end of a richly carved wooden crib of immense proportion, Melisinde's eyes widened in surprise and delight.

"Oh, Gidie, it is so beautiful! The images in the carvings are amazing!"

"I contributed the staining," said Piers. "That is not so much, I realize, but Gidie let me take part in the surprise. And I helped support it while he put it all together." Piers grinned.

"You have both given Jeanne and me a wonderful gift, and I thank you! It is far grander than I could imagine. Your idea, Gidie, will carry us through nursery years for sure until she has a full-sized bed of her own. When Mademoiselle Aalis returns her, I will place her in it after her feeding. The day of her birth will be the first day she sleeps in her new crib, the first day in the Albret heir's life. With her birth, I know we must discuss some things.

"Jeanne can inherit the estate and landholdings, just not the noble title. So, she is an 'untitled noble,' as things stand. If the Viscount and I have a son, the Viscount will have an heir to which his titles will be transferred, plus the estate and landholdings. Only God knows what will happen. I do not wish to think about any of it now, as it would only sully my joy and gratitude for the blessing of Jeanne.

"Whatever happens, you will both remain here as it is your home. When the Viscount passes, as he undoubtedly will with time, we will discuss the overall matter in detail. In the meantime, Piers, I suggest you quietly research the law. I wish you and Gidie to have security and comfort, and we need to know your full entitlements. I have also been thinking about my future and my place. I have a matter I wish to discuss with both of you. It is a bold initiative, but one for which I believe I may successfully gain permission and support from the King, given past and current circumstances. We will speak of this much, much later. There are many details I must work out.

"In the meantime, dear hearts, thank you for your love and support. I wish to assure you that you have mine as well. Now I must feed Jeanne and then rest. You may stay or go, as is your preference. Now that I think things through, it would please me for the two of you to place Jeanne into her crib for the first time if you are of a mind to do that."

Both men agreed, and Mademoiselle Aalis poured them goblets of wine, ordering a tray of cheeses to occupy them during the wait. The three friends relaxed in each other's company, delighted to celebrate together without any taint of unpleasantness.

"Welcome to our world, Jeanne," toasted Piers, joined by a

smiling Gidie.

After a short while at the Lady of the house's direct permission, each staff member paid their respects to mother and child, receiving 5 deniers apiece in coin as a celebration gratuity. [This was enough to buy a bottle of wine.]

"Thank you for your cooperative service," their caring and genteel mistress said to each with a genuine smile. Rarely receiving a kind word in their employment, each was imbued with a sense of loyalty to Melisinde, their "Lady."

As she knew it would, the time came for her to accede to her husband's constant, vociferous demands for her attention. He was uncontrollably strident with every servant, including his faithful valet, Jehan, whom Melisinde supposed was the most patient man she knew.

She entered his rooms, hoping against hope that he would be sleeping. He was not. Eyeing her with a malicious smirk, he said, "So, you finally respond to your lord's command, you ungrateful girl! I should send you to the brothel to learn your place and how to treat a man!"

"I beg my lord's pardon. The birth of your child took a great toll on me. I am only recently well enough to attend, my lord," Melisinde said sweetly, the words sticking in her throat.

"Hmm, yes, I know you produced a girl. Couldn't even get that right, could you?" he snapped unpleasantly. "Come closer and pour me some fresh wine. Jehan, leave us unless you wish to watch," the sneer apparent in his tone.

"Thank you, my lord, but I have much work awaiting me," said his valet, bowing and departing with haste.

"Well, get to it, girl!"

Melisinde poured the wine slowly, if a bit unsteadily. The Viscount grabbed her dress and pulled her to him, shoving a hand between her legs beneath the hem. He laughed.

"Nice and warm, you are, my dear. Bend over before your lord and master!"

Pulling himself to a standing position by grabbing the back of her dress, he pushed her chest and head onto the table, upsetting the pitcher of wine. "I shall make you pay for that waste," he said, exposing her bottom. He had difficulty entering but managed it eventually to her regret. His grunts and moans sickened her; his harshness hurt her still tender body, yet he seemed nowhere close to finishing. Tentatively, she reached behind her to gently squeeze him as Tiece had instructed. The Viscount yelled aloud, collapsing on her, culminating in not only his release but a fit of liquid-sounding coughs. Melisinde felt faint and nauseous but controlled both urges to escape the hostile scene and the repulsive Viscount. She managed to disengage him with a twist of her body and push him back onto his chaise. She fled his rooms in a limping gait. The valet was waiting in the corridor.

"Are you all right, Madame?" he inquired gently.

Melisinde was close to losing complete control and slumped against him while she caught her breath. "S'il *vous plaît excusez-moi,* Jehan, I shall be fine in a moment or so." Regaining her composure, she said, "Your lord needs your attention and his toilette. *Allez, allez, s'il vous plait.*"

Feeling the same violation as on previous occasions and longing for a bath, Melisinde made her way slowly to her rooms, ringing the bell for Mademoiselle Aalis after she locked the door leading to the central upper hall. She crumpled onto the floor in tears.

'I shall do all in my power to save you from this, *mon petit* Jeanne,' she vowed.

Fortunately for Melisinde, there occurred only five additional episodes with the Viscount. Following those five occasions, his health deteriorated rapidly. Despite his continuing wishes to undertake conjugal privileges, his body no longer cooperated, and he was not strong enough to do so. A young and fertile female, Melisinde became pregnant with her second child. She prayed each night for the child to be a male.

News of her pregnancy spread throughout the chateau. Although she was concerned that she was with child so soon after giving birth, both the Doctor and Mademoiselle Aalis assured her that such sometimes happens. Still, she and the child would be all right with the pregnancy progressing normally with care and rest.

Mademoiselle Aalis marshaled Tiece to visit the Viscount once a week to manually satisfy his needs and hopefully forestall his demands on Melisinde, particularly in her current condition. Such ministrations exhausted him for a few to several days, making the scheduled visits farther and farther apart to everyone's satisfaction, except perhaps for the Viscount.

After an incredibly long session, the waiting valet heard the Viscount roar. He assumed that it was an expression of pleasured release and rushed to the laundry for fresh toweling and a clean nightshirt. The hassled Tiece took her leave, hurrying down the back stairs to the servants' hall. When the valet returned to the Viscount's rooms, he found his master gasping for air and clutching his chest. In a few moments, the Viscount's arm fell away, his face in death rictus; his tunic soiled and in disarray; his hair oily and sweaty; his body splayed on the chaise.

Looking through the open windows toward the meadows, the valet said, "May you finally find peace, my lord." The faithful Jehan cleaned and dressed his lord's body, carrying him to his bed. He arranged the coverlets and placed a clean bed cap on the Viscount, hiding most of the oily gray hair beneath. He put a Bible in his master's folded hands and moved the small vase of flowers to his bedside table. The Viscount's sweet wife picked flowers for him each day, asking Jehan to deliver them with her regards.

He stood quietly for a few moments, said a quick prayer begging God's mercy for the Viscount's troubled soul, lit the candles, and adjusted the windows to help with the inevitable smell. Checking the room to ensure all was in order, Jehan left the Viscount's rooms, slowly descending the back staircase to the servant's hall to notify the cook that there would be one less for dinner with no need to prepare a tray for the Viscount. Then he told Osana to fetch the brandy decanter. He sat for several minutes, savoring his cup before mounting the staircase to request an audience with the sweet Lady Melisinde.

Chapter Twelve
The Matchmaker

Melisinde was to appear at Court in two weeks, an audience with the King granted and scheduled. Gidie and Piers would accompany her to Paris. The three discussed Melisinde's proposition to ensure it was concise and airtight, knowing the King's propensity toward impatience. As they partook of their meal on the balcony, the men suggested that Melisinde engage a seamstress.

"My dear, you no longer fit into your gowns and day dresses. For such an auspicious occasion, you must be suitably garbed. As it is, some of the ladies at Court will challenge you as lacking grace for being seen in public in your condition, much less for attending Court, and worse, for seeking an audience with the King!" fretted Piers.

"Are you certain you do not wish to postpone this until after the child arrives?" asked Gidie. "It is not that much longer until the baby comes, and I worry about the trip to Paris. It will be at least a two hours' carriage ride, slower if the roads are very bumpy."

"I shall be fine, monsieurs, but I thank you for your concern. No, we shall go ahead. Once the King grants an audience, one must comply with only plague or death preventing attendance. We must strike while the iron is hot! Still, I will pray that the baby waits until after our audience to come!" Giggling, she said, "Could you imagine having to beg the King's pardon, asking him to hurry with his deliberations because I was about to give birth in his throne room?"

"For shame, Lady, having such wicked thoughts!" said Gidie laughing.

"Oh, my dear, could that happen, do you think?" a worried Piers asked.

Gidie and Melisinde laughed all the harder. "You are so serious, Piers! I was just teasing!"

"Thank the good Lord. I mean, what would we do? I do not know how to deliver a baby, and neither does Gidie. What if something happens during the ride there or back?" Piers had gotten himself into a state.

"I shall have Mademoiselle Aalis in attendance with Osana, as well. All will be well, dear Piers, but that does mean two carriages and an additional room for the servants. I trust you with all the arrangements," Melisinde said calmly, soothing his worry by giving him a job to do.

⁓

"Your Majesty has favored me, and I bless His grace and kindness," Melisinde said meekly, bowing as low as her condition allowed.

"Rise, Viscountess Albret. You are, I believe, one of my dear departed Madame De Marigny's last pupils and her favorite protégé, are you not? And recently widowed as well? I see you are with child. Such a pity, the Viscount did not live to see his second child. No matter, but these five circumstances are what inclined me to give you the audience, as well as curiosity. I will hear you now," the King said, folding his hands and staring hard at this young woman who so insistently petitioned for an audience with her King.

Melisinde inhaled deeply and held her breath so that rising from her low curtsy would be graceful and seem effortless. "Your Majesty is most generous," she said.

"The great Madame De Marigny, your faithful servant, instilled in me the responsibility to place service to my King first and foremost," she began. Melisinde then continued to outline her proposal, covering all the benefits to the Crown, Court, nobility, and France's future culture.

"My circumstances allow me to guarantee His Majesty the continuance of contribution from my late husband's estate, landholdings, and businesses, thanks to the constant, faithful support of his nephews. I beg Your Majesty to make their positions perpetual with suitable titles and entitlements as part of this noble family, should Your Majesty grant my petition for this initiative.

"No one can ever replace Madame De Marigny. I wish to honor her memory and service to His Majesty with my expanded idea, which also guarantees the Crown a percentage of my additional income while protecting nobles from the threat of disease from brothels. Of course, if their preference is to continue frequency at brothels, they can transmit undesirable infections to their noble wives, which hinders producing subsequent healthy noble heirs. A controlled environment satisfies particular needs while averting a potential disaster. A quiet word of His Majesty's preference would be most welcome and would not... could not be summarily ignored by his retinue of faithful nobles." The attending Cardinal coughed; the King smiled, nodding for her to continue.

"Further, while the instruction of candidates to familiar-ize them with the necessities required for a satisfying life for their lords can only cement the stability of the noble families of France, it should also minimize brothel attendance by noblemen, except for those unattached or unsuitably matched in existing marriages. This likelihood should be viewed with favor by His Grace, the Cardinal, as it promotes the aims of the Church.

"There will always be a business for brothels, my lords. My concept provides a safe, monitored alternative, the choice being up to noblemen. No one with an existing condition will be allowed to partake in the get-togethers or parties for safety reasons. Your physician's advice and cooperation in this regard will be invaluable, and I am confident he, too, will look upon this with favor for His Majesty's noble families.

"By definition, young maidens have no idea of the true breadth of wifely duties, and many if not most of them are fright-ened when faced with the obligations of the marital bed, and inept at fulfilling the satisfaction of their lords. My plan provides gentle familiarity for candidates immediately before their wedding cere-mony to diffuse their fright or unwillingness and augment the no-bleman's wedding experience and beyond. I am sure confidential conversations ordered by His Majesty will confirm that many no-bles simply impregnate their wives to secure an heir but do not enjoy a genuinely fulfilling marital relationship. Hence, their weekly visits to brothels with the associated, outlined risks.

"Last, this proposition does not in any way challenge the exis-tence and value of His Majesty's Court. Candidates will continue to be presented at Court for the final phase of their clearance as 'suitable,' learning by personal observation from the ladies at Court the finer arts from those with experience. Unmatched candidates will remain at Court, adding to the female complement, until His Majesty deems another potential match is possible or likely. In this way, His Majesty's Court enjoys both continuity and the injection of new life, if you will, thereby underwriting the superiority and seniority of current ladies at Court.

"Think of 'Court' like a rose garden: the mature shrubs produce fragrant, lovely blossoms to enjoy; the newly planted shrubs, only immature buds with no fragrance or bloom because they need time. Together, they present a healthy, everlasting garden.

"I respectfully ask my King's permission and underwriting for this concept I propose for the good of Crown and country. With His Majesty's blessing and support, I believe it will enjoy success for the good of all. Thank you, Your Majesty," Melisinde said as she briefly curtsied, remaining standing at attention with her eyes and head lowered.

"You are, by all accounts, Viscountess, an unusual woman," the King said as he stood and descended the stairs from his throne. He extended his hand to Melisinde. Surprised, Melisinde accepted his hand, kissed it, and looked him in the eye.

"I need no additional time to consider this proposal nor conversation with my advisors. May I say you do honor to the departed Madame De Marigny, who was very dear to me? She was not at all wrong about you. In one audience, you move from a young, pregnant widow to Madame and Matchmaker! I grant all that you wish and will order the appropriate papers to be drawn and executed.

"By way of interest, Viscountess, are you aware you are the first woman to appear at Court in your condition, at least to my knowledge?" the King inquired with amusement.

"I am, my King," the pregnant Melisinde smiled up at her King. "I am."

The King shook his head and remounted His throne, shaking his head, motioning for the next audience to be announced.

"Thank you for mentioning us," Piers said, holding Melisinde's hand. "We didn't expect that, as it was not in our revision."

Reaching for Gidie's hand, she held both men's hands to her face. "How could I not?"

"But you went further and solidified our futures with titles and entitlements!" Gidie remarked with amazement. "We don't deserve that, Melisinde. We would have been happy with the King's approval to continue working with you."

"You deserve that, and more. But think you not that it will

be an easy road. My plans—if they are to be a success—will involve the two of you, as well. Let me explain," Melisinde told them with obvious delight.

"With His Majesty's blessing, no longer will young girls have to suffer as I did."

Piers said, "At least the ones who come to you will not, but those are only a few against the huge population in France."

"It is a start, Piers," Melisinde said with conviction, "a start that will with time enact change, and change will inspire new possibilities, and from new possibilities will grow new opportunities, and new opportunities will create new attitudes. It is the start of great things to come. I foresee a kinder, gentler France ahead of us, one which has more regard for women."

The bumpy and slow carriage ride home was filled with exchanges between the three friends, soon to become a tour de force in 16th-century French society and culture.

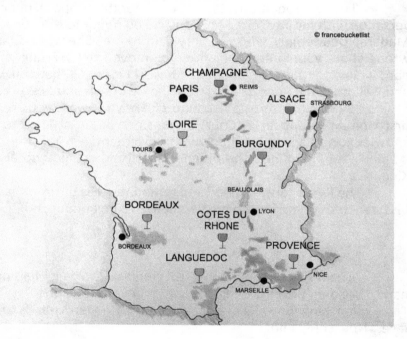

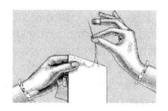

Chapter Thirteen
Griffiths Seamstress Shop

Civil War Section: Union v. Confederacy - Southern Coastal US

The rays of the afternoon sun shone through the stained-glass windows painting the sitting room with glorious hues. Lottie hummed as she dusted the tabletops and bookcases, fluffed the pillows, and placed small vases of fresh flowers throughout the room. In short order, all would be ready to receive tomorrow's customers, just as Miss Jessica liked it. Lottie prided herself on the ability to anticipate Miss Jessica's needs and preferences. She was such a kind and all-embracing woman, Lottie never hesitated to do all she could to please her as an expression of gratitude for Jessica Griffiths' acceptance of her as a free woman and employing her as an assistant.

Jessica carefully folded lengths of fabric for tomorrow's display on the large table in what was formerly the dining room. As she did so, thoughts of long-ago dinner parties for twenty filled her mind, the muted sounds of laughter, tinkling glasses, and the smells of food platters occupying her mind. Since the war, Jessica had reorganized the house to accommodate her seamstress shop to provide revenue to maintain the diminished income from her husband's family plantation. She still employed some workers to harvest rice, but the operation's scale did not come close to past years. Social, political, and economic situations were vastly different from years earlier when Jessica and the Colonel lived peacefully at Rice Lands Plantation. It was wartime; she alone had to maintain the family home until the Colonel returned, and conditions in the South made life difficult for everyone, but particularly for a woman alone.

Jessica recalled how imposing her husband looked as he blew her a departure kiss, the three stars on his uniform glinting in the morning sunshine. His horse, Titan, stomped with anticipation as Colonel Richard Griffiths took one last gaze at all he was leaving: his ancestral home, with its sweeping two-story porches, its land running parallel to the river; the lush apple orchards and gardens; his petite wife dressed in her usual white blouse and skirt, wisps of curly brown untamed hair blowing in the damp, morning breeze; and his faithful Boykin spaniel, "Mister," wagging his tail. He saluted, turned Titan, and cantered away to join his waiting regiment. That last image filled Jessica's heart and mind as she smoothed the fabric swatches for tomorrow's gathering of scheduled customers.

She received only one letter in the years the Colonel was away at war. Carefully stowed in her dressing table, she read and reread it over the long months of struggle. His closing words kept her going at the most trying of times:

I know, dear heart, that whatever befalls, you shall do your best. That is all you can ask of yourself. Stay secure in the knowledge that I shall move heaven and earth to return to you and Rice Lands, God willing. You are my life, my heart, my thought upon waking to face each day.

Pray for me as I do for you.

Eternally yours, Richard

"Lottie, we'd better get those scones done today. I feel that Leticia Willis will be early tomorrow, thinking of getting a leg up on the others. How about we sit a while on the back porch so we can keep an eye on the scones as they bake? And put these fabrics on the shelves in the backroom, please, Lottie. Make sure you cover them with sheets. It will be a while before the patterns are made. I'll be done in a few minutes, and then I'll have some tea on the porch."

"Oh, Miss Jessie, the Mayor's wife sent a runner jus' a bit ago. She say she wanna come for 'notha fittin' mebbe Thursday. Sorry, I forgot to tell ya; them boxes come, and we got to haulin' an' a'fussin' over them rolls. Her boy still waitin' 'roun' back. Should I tell him ok or to skedaddle?"

"Hmm, let's see," Jessica said, checking her work schedule. "Tell him Thursday is fine after midday meal—about 2:00 PM. Thanks, and give him a slab of cheese on bread for his troubles and warn him to finish it before he returns to Blythewood, or he'll catch it for sure!"

Laughing, Lottie chided her employer, "Y'all knows all them kids throw lots to see who git to come hyah? They know Miss Jess a soft touch for food' n' stuff."

"Just so, Lottie, but they have precious little in their poor lives to bring pleasure. I'm pleased a run over here is worth their while, even in such a small way. I'm parched and tired, Lottie, so how's the tea coming?"

"It's a'brewin', Miss Jess, it's a'brewin'. Set yo' sef down for a bit, hear? We got an even biggah day tomorra: two in the mornin' an' three in the af'noon. Y'all need to res'."

"Plenty of time for rest when I'm dead, sweet girl." She leaned back in the rocking chair, closing her eyes, and sighed with the gentle touch of the afternoon breeze. Reddish-brown tendrils danced around her face stroking her to a relaxing, brief doze.

Like many plantation homes, the rear of the house held a kitchen area with a separated cooking kitchen to ease access to the woodpile, woodstoves, and ovens. It was a separate building and was the accepted design for the older houses in the region. Average summertime temperatures were high in the South and keeping the radiant heat of cooking separate to the domicile was an accepted practice, as well as a fire preventative. One could lose the entire house should a fire erupt in the kitchen from the woodstove, ovens, or stovepipe. In contrast, people could contain a fire more readily in a small, separate building, particularly with proximity to the river. Slaves, servants, or staff carried platters of food from the "cook kitchen" to the smaller house kitchen or butler pantry for service in the dining room.

Lottie gathered her cleaning supplies, took one last look around the room with satisfaction, and hurried to the dining room-now-workroom. "Do you need me to get any mo bolts down, mam? I be along in jes a minute."

"No, dear, I think what I have will suffice. Of course, there's no accounting for picky Polly Mathers! She may not like what I've chosen, but we'll deal with that as or if it comes. Thank you for seeing to the sitting room, Lottie.

"Now, let's get those scones made so we can have our afternoon tea. I think we've earned a rest, don't you?" Jessica began the process of mixing and kneading while Lottie gathered the pans for the oven.

Later, relaxing on the porch, the lazy river's flow hypnotic, Jessica said softly, "It's moments like this when I miss the Colonel ever so much."

"Yes'm, me too. I miss the boom of his voice. All was well when da Colonel was hyah." Lottie blanched. "Not that y'all ain' done a good job, Miss Jess, I jes meant that..."

Jessica's easy laughter drew a smile from the young girl. "No, Lottie, never you mind. I feel the same way. His absence has left a gaping hole, hasn't it? Let's hope it's not for too much longer. This war is a nasty business. For that matter, all war is a nasty business, if you ask me."

"Yes'm. Y'all said it, right enough." They both sipped their tea, stealing a rare, few moments of peace.

The next morning, shortly before their customers arrived, Lottie burst into Jessica's upstairs sitting room. "Mam, Joel from town, he at the back a'lookin' mighty troubled."

"Joel? Oh dear, now is not the best of times. Run and tell him I'll be down presently." Jessica set aside her pen and paper, kicking off her slippers and bent to button her shoes.

Once downstairs, she rushed down the hall to the back door in the kitchen's storage room.

"Joel, what is it?" She took in the young man standing before her covered in a sheen of sweat, his hands wringing his hat.

"Big Janey sez to tell y'all that Clement and his family a'leavin' tomorry. She ax me to ax y'all if'n y'all kin hep. Clement's got a baby comin' an Sally, his wife, she ain't doin' good wif all what's a'goin' on. So, he, Clement, sez they gotta' go an' git! Big Janey, she sent me and sez hurry up and go ax Miss Jess. Here I is, Miss Jess! I run all the way like Big Janey sez."

Scrutinizing the young man, Jessica asked Lottie to fetch him some water and a scone. "You tell Big Janey that now is not a good time, Joel. She'll have to keep them wherever she can for the next several days until I send word. Lottie will bring her a message at the General Store when it's safe. Ok? You understand, Joel? Not now, wait for Lottie to bring Big Janey a message. Got it?"

He gulped down half the cup of water, his mouth still full of the scone, and said, "Yes' um. Thank y'all kindly." Donning his cap, Joel turned to go. Looking back, he said, "Bye, Miss Lottie." Then he ran into the orchard.

The two women looked at each other, breathing heavily. "Lord, keep us," said Lottie. They re-entered the house just as the front bell jangled. Outside stood an impatient Leticia Willis with her maid, Jonquil. Lottie opened the door and greeted them, and Jessica ushered them to the waiting sitting room.

"You may put on the tea, Lottie," she said as she offered an adjacent chair to Jonquil, who stood rigidly behind Mrs. Willis.

"She's just fine where she is, Mrs. Griffiths, thank you."

Lottie poured the tea for Mrs. Willis and looked at Jonquil questioningly. Jonquil shook her head and looked down at the floor.

"Thank you, Lottie," said Jessica. "Why don't you show Jonquil to the kitchen porch, and you two can share a glass of iced tea? I'm sure Mrs. Willis would appreciate the privacy for our discussions, yes?"

Jessica smiled delicately at Mrs. Willis. The woman inclined her head and impatiently motioned to her slave to leave the room.

"You know, Mrs. Griffiths, that darkie of yours has airs and graces beyond her station! You would do well to rein her in before something untoward happens." Mrs. Willis sniffed indignantly.

Calmly—despite her inner frustration—Jessica said, "Ah, well, thank you, Mrs. Willis, but Lottie is not "my darkie," as you put it. She is a free woman, born free, with papers to prove it. She is my employee, and a good one, at that. Now, let me show you the swatches I put aside just for you!" The bell rang, blessedly ending the conversation, and Lottie magically appeared to open the door and show the assembled ladies to the sitting room, serve tea and scones, and fade from sight in her gracious way, taking any accompanying slaves with her to join Jonquil on the back porch.

"These designs are fresh from New York, with my amendments as to fabric in consideration of our southern temperatures. I'm happy to say we can all do away with those cumbersome hoops for everyday wear. You see, I have designed a series of pleating and ruching that will give fullness while eliminating the need for the extra undergarment." Jessica passed around her drawings, illustrating the new designs. They were well received, and the ladies excitedly chattered among themselves.

"These fabrics are lighter in weight and far more suitable for us here. This group will do nicely for skirts and jackets or dresses. These are best for blouses, and these for nightdresses or tunics."

She unfolded various swatches and draped them over the

dress forms. "By ruching vertically in the waist area, and horizontally over the bust, my designs make the waist smaller, and the bosom ampler for whatever situation is desirable. Also, the gathering at the rear of skirts, for example, adds fullness without the need for a bulky, unwieldy hoop yet properly conceals the figure. The peplum on either blouses or jackets is a ruse as well, in that the peplum, while decorative, can conceal a tummy bulge that can plague the best of us! It also eliminates the absolute need for a corset, stays, and laces."

"We haven't had access to this type of work for too long," said Mrs. Mathers. "To get a dress, new suit, or gown, one has to travel to Richmond, Charleston, or Atlanta! We all know how seldomly our husbands are willing to do that!" The ladies twittered. "Given it's been a few years since I got any new clothes, I, for one, will place an order. I assume that means I get the first choice of fabrics?" The haughty woman looked around the room with her eyebrows raised in challenge.

"If you'll bear with me a moment, Mrs. Mathers, I thought these fabrics and colors would suit you very well," said Jessica, reaching for a basket with a bright blue ribbon tied to the handle. "This shade will complement your lovely eyes and pale skin. And this solid and this subtle plaid go nicely together, match the lighter blue, and is appropriate for a suit or a dress. I was thinking of the bodice with matching cuffs in the plaid, with a solid peplum to match the skirt. That would work for either a dress or a two-piece suit, whichever is appropriate to your need and choice." Jessica displayed her vision on the mannequin's torso dress form, pinning the fabric to illustrate.

As Mrs. Mathers considered the example, Jessica passed the other baskets to the ladies, each with a different colored ribbon, offering her ideas on her fashion designs in styles for each individual. After several cups of tea and depletion of the scones, Jessica ushered them all to the front hall by noon. Their respective attendants scurried out in advance to fetch their carriages. All in all, the morning hours were productive, resulting in several orders, the fees for which guaranteed sufficient funds for supporting Rice Lands' immediate future.

"Ain't it a fine thing y'all was a seamstress up North, Miss Jessica! I cain't figure how y'all woulda kep this place a'goin'." Lottie dried the cups, saucers, and plates, while Jessica prepared a light dinner for them both. "Dem gals tole me 'bout a passel of folks jes a'walkin' away, now the war's a'goin full steam ahead. They say they be free in no time. Y'all think dat so? But they tell dat a'gittin' caught happens mo likely, and dat is bad, bad, bad. Dey pay fo it, t'be sho. An guess what? The Klan burnt down the smithy shop t'utha day cuz old Massa Crump put dat high yaller, Moses, in charge ta do all da heavy work. Da Klan don' like dat, no, not one bit! Dem's scary, I say. I's glad we be outta town a bit. Don' wanna fool wif dem Klan folks. Mm mm, no, not one bit!" Lottie's eyes were big as she shook her head.

"Now, Lottie, let's not borrow trouble. Those girls were sharing gossip. There's no way to know if what they told you is accurate. Nothing much will change in the short term except that it will get harder and harder to keep our heads afloat. If the Union soldiers break through our lines and invade our towns, they'll likely ravage the countryside, the towns, and the villages. It's hard enough now to get certain foodstuffs. I dread to think what life would be like if that happens, to say nothing of the loss of life.

"You and I just have to keep believing that things will work out, keep our heads down, work hard, and pray. Thank the Lord that those orders will take a while to fulfill. We won't take any more appointments from those nosy, irritating women for a bit. That will make it safer to have those folks here in the basement storage rooms. One can never be too careful about noise and discovery.

"But tonight, my dear, we must prepare sacks for the raft captain if we are to help those people Joel spoke about earlier. The contents of the bags will pay for their raft ride across the river. How are our food stores holding up? Soon, we'll have three more mouths to feed for who knows how long. At least the blankets are washed. Let's hang out the bedrolls in the orchard tonight to air them well. We'll have to get them in before first light. Come on, now, let's eat. We've still got hours of work ahead of us."

"Yes'm, Miss Jess." Between mouthfuls, Lottie asked, "Miss Jess? Y'all ever wonder what Massa Griffiths say if'n he knew what y'all been doin'?"

Smiling, Jessica chuckled. "Yes, Lottie, I think of that all the time. He's fighting in the Confederate Army; I'm helping slaves escape. It seems like we're on opposite sides of the question, doesn't it? But the war isn't just about slavery. It's about states' rights, the industrial North versus the agricultural South, economics, differing political views, electoral seats, influences, and about as many complicated issues as you can imagine.

"So, it's not accurate to say that we favor opposite sides, Lottie. Richard's family has never owned slaves nor approved of slavery. Only a tiny percentage of Southerners own slaves, and they're mostly the big landowners. It's less about culture and more about self-determination, I think.

"The South believes it's losing the power to have a say in the government because Northern politicians and industrialists control it, many of whom are abolitionists. With the expansion of the Union moving west, that raises even more disputes over issues. The industrial North is economically more powerful than the agricultural South.

"I guess the answer to your question is that I hope my Richard would understand why I help people escape adverse circumstances. I think he would oppose those bad conditions as much as I do, but to be fair, I think he would do it differently, using his power and influence politically and socially. I can't see any other way open to me as a woman, so I do what I can with what I have. Do you understand?"

Noting the frown on Lottie's face, she said, "Well, perhaps not. I think you and I should concentrate on what we know to be true, good, and right. Let's leave it there, all right?"

"Yes, mam, I unnerstan' that. It ain't right or good to be a slave, cuz God loves all folk, don' He? An' some o the disciples n such was colored too, Pastor said so! Y'all remember dat?"

"I do remember, Lottie. He spoke about that when he told the congregation that the South had put the North to shame by arguing scriptural references supporting slavery, like St. Paul in particular. Do you remember that? No? Well, no matter. It's just another issue of dispute. That's the result of how the world was in St. Paul's time, not much different from what's happening now. You just hold fast to what Jesus said, 'Love one another as I have loved you.' Right? That's the way you and I shall continue to carry on."

Lottie smiled. "Yes'm. How come ever' body else cain't see dat?'

"I don't know, Lottie. I don't know. Maybe God is using us to show them what they seem to have forgotten. Enough now, time for bed. You shut things up, and I'll see to the wood fire. Good night, Lottie. Sleep well, and don't forget to say your prayers."

Chapter Fourteen
Brutality

When sufficient time beyond the ladies' combined visit had elapsed to ensure there existed no need for measurement or selection adjustment, Jessica deemed it safe to dispatch Lottie to the town to do some errands, including passing a message to Big Janey about Clement and his family.

Lottie relished the walk to town, which was just over two miles, much of it bordering Rice Lands' property. She hoped she might see Joel in the General Store for a few moments before or after she passed the message to Big Janey. Joel had a job at the General Store doing odd jobs, which allowed him flexibility regarding his time and whereabouts. Maybe they could share a glass of lemonade. "Pish posh, girlie. Whatcha spendin' time on foolishness like dat?" Lottie said out loud to herself. But a small part of her remembered how he had turned back to say goodbye to just her when he was last at Rice Lands. She smiled to herself and increased her stride.

On reaching the General Store, she meandered through the shelves, selecting the items Miss Jessica had requested while keeping watch for Big Janey. There she was! The corpulent woman was loading fresh tomatoes and squash into bins from a small wheelbarrow.

"Hey there, Big Janey. Them's purty tomatas, ain't they? I take six of 'em but not too ripe."

"Hyah yo is, gal, six a da bes. Y'all got somepin fer Big Janey?" The woman smiled, showing a toothy grin with missing teeth.

"Yes, mam, I kin say that the weatha' is jes fine, and by dark, it be aways cooler. Our first apples need a'pickin from da trees, and Miss Jess reckons they be picked out by Friday." Lottie smiled at the big woman. "Y'all get dat?"

"Yep, apples ready fo pickin' tonight in da cool dark but gone by Friday. Thank ya', Lottie. I'll be by." The woman turned back to her work, saying, "Y'all give Miss Jess my bes', hear?"

"Yes'm, I will. You seen Joel hereabouts?" Lottie asked coyly.

"Sho' nuff. He aroun' back. Pay up an' then have a walk 'roun, yeah?"

"I might do jes so, Big Janey. Bye." Lottie walked to the counter by the front door and placed her items on the bench with her basket. The shopkeeper greeted her and asked her to give Mrs. Griffiths his regards. He tallied her purchases, she paid, dropped the change into her purse, and left smiling. In her basket was a jar of fresh lemonade.

As she rounded the building for the side street, she saw a group of men smoking on a bench outside the blacksmith shop. Her heart pounded as she knew them to be no-good troublemakers. She walked faster, keeping her eyes to the ground.

"Well, well, if it ain't little Miss Priss! Ain't no accountin' for the folks they let into the shops these days, is there, boys? Where you a'headin', little gal? You lookin' fer Moses, the high yaller fella?"

The group burst out in guffaws, hoots, and hollers. "Mebbe, you wanna put a yaller bump in yo belly and make mo yallers? C'mere, hon, I got somepin fer ya make that bump even lighter!" He grabbed his crotch, and again the group sounded with their offensive comments, laughter, and hoots. Just as she neared the end of the building, preparing to turn the corner and walk to the rear where she hoped Joel would be, Joel rounded the building. She looked at him with relief as he extended his hand to her.

"Aw, Miss Priss, that ole boy gonna make that bump a darkie! Why he's as black as the Ace of Spades! What you thinkin', girl?"

"Don' say nuthin,' Lottie, jes come wif me an' quick," said Joel, pulling her away and into the back storeroom behind a hanging burlap doorway sheet designed to defray sunlight.

"Oh, them men, I hate 'em. They's always so mean," she said to Joel, as he brushed off a crate and gestured for her to sit. "They scare me."

"Nah, don' worry, y'all wif me, now. Is jes fine. Dey gives up in a bit now y'all gone." He smiled at her and sat beside her. They shared the lemonade and chatted about commonplace things for what seemed like a few moments or an eternity.

Finally, she said, "I bes be goin', Joel. Nice to see ya'. Stop by any time, Miss Jessica say."

Joel grinned broadly. "Dat somepin y'all would like too?" he asked the blushing Lottie.

"I say so, dint I?" Her attempt to be offhand failed. She matched Joel's smile and blew him a kiss. "Mebbe we could go on a picnic sometime? Jes you an me. I don' work Sundays; you don' neitha. I could pack us a basket an' bring a blanket. Mebbe down by da riva? S'nice n'cool there."

"Is a date. How 'bout this Sunday afta church?" Joel grinned.

She nodded and waved. When she left the storeroom, Lottie's face sported a big smile, and her head was full of speculations.

Arriving home, she told Jessica first about Big Janey, and next about the sleazy men. "I do believe in God, Miss Jess, but I don' like dem men one bit. No, not one bit. So, how's I sposed to love dem like Jesus sez?" The innocence in her eyes cut Jessica to the heart.

"Honey, I don't have a good answer, but I can tell you that nothing worthwhile comes without a lot of hard work. And trying to love them like Jesus says we should love takes a lot of hard work. I know it doesn't seem like they deserve it, but we're not the ones to judge. Only Jesus and God can do that, right?" She patted Lottie's hand and put the tomatoes into a bowl on the shelf.

After dinner, Jessica turned the kerosene lanterns in the sitting room and living room down low enough to provide only a small glow. She knew that the stained-glass windows on the front of the house would show only a multi-colored shimmer, which was the prearranged "all-clear" signal that she and Big Janey set long ago. If the interior lighting showed brightly, fully illuminating the colorful stained glass, the transfer was unsafe—only flickering color from the low light within signaled safety. Lottie was already stationed at the back door beyond the storeroom. Jessica hurried to the basement door to light the candles in the rooms the women had prepared for the family.

A slight breeze whispered through the apple trees, and Lottie listened intently for footfalls. At last, she saw them: Big Janey was carrying a sleeping child against her cushiony bosom, and a man and woman, each toting a large, burlap sack followed. Lottie moved into the moonlight from the shelter of the back-doorway roof.

"Pssst! Hyah, dis way," she called softly. Big Janey nodded, and Clement waved an acknowledgment. The wide-eyed woman cried silently.

Lottie led the small group to the basement access, slowly opening the iron gate, the hanging posts, and latch of which she judiciously kept well-greased with bacon fat. She held the gate open, gesturing and whispering, "Through hyah."

Jessica stood waiting in the aisleway, a picture of calm and welcome. She hugged Big Janey first, careful not to awaken the small child.

Turning to Clement and his wife, she said, "Welcome to a couple days' rest at Rice Lands. It's not fancy, but we've made it as comfortable as possible under the circumstances. There's food and drink on the table, the mattresses are clean, and so are the blankets.

"The stacked rice sacks will give you ample protection from the night chill. Come; I'll explain what you have to do at different times of the day. Let's put your child to bed, although I'm sure she'd prefer the soft warmth of Big Janey!" That last remark drew a relieved smile from the mother.

Blessedly, the child slept soundly and curled into the fresh-smelling mattress and blanket her mother tucked around her. As the couple quietly ate, they thanked the three women for helping them.

"Clement, it's all right," crooned Jessica. "And it will all be over in a short time, God willing. I must warn you both that you must keep your little one as quiet as possible, which I know is difficult with children full of energy."

"Is ok, Miz Griffiths, she know ta be good, know 'bout no talkin' cuz when da Massa come, no one talk but him. She seen her mama get beat n'worse, so she good wif dat; she know a'talkin' bring trouble."

A chill ran down Jessica's back. No child should ever have to witness cruelty up close, much less with her mother as a victim. "I'm so sorry, Glory," she said, reaching for the woman's hand.

"I must ask you not to light candles anywhere near the rice sacks; use only the table and leave them in the metal holders. Light the candles only at night after Lottie locks the gate and secures the doorway's light shade. That way, no one walking by the river will see any light coming from the basement, and the big padlock is secure. There are only three keys: Lottie and I share a key we keep upstairs in a tin of rice on the shelf over the sink; Big Janey has one for emergencies, and here is yours. Use it only if the house is on fire; otherwise, one of us will come for you or yell for you to use it and leave.

"Lottie and I will check on you periodically to make sure you are all right and bring you food or whatever else you need while here. There's only a big pail, I'm afraid—no chamber pot. But there's a board with a hole on top, the best we could do for a seat. One of us will collect it daily. Just use the trowel to shovel wood ashes from the pail by the door over top of the waste. It helps with the smell.

"When it's time for you to go, we'll give you plenty of warning to get ready. One of us will lead you to the river to meet up with the raft captain." Clement started to interrupt, but Jessica held up her hands. "No, no, Clement, don't worry about passage money. The Captain and I have a longstanding arrangement.

"You just give him the sack from me; we've prepared it already." She pointed to the doorway that led to the iron gate. A full sack lay propped against the open doorframe with a string threaded with a quartered apple. Clement smiled and nodded.

"All right, now, you take some rest. There are some books, cards, paper, and pencil on the shelves. Help yourselves. Remember, no noise, no matter what you hear from upstairs. Our lives have to go on as normal, and we can't foresee who might visit. You have to trust us and trust in the Lord, Clement. No noise, and keep movement to a minimum if you hear sounds from upstairs or outside, got it? Make it a game for the child; pretend you're ghosts. And in all cases, stay away from the doorway and the gate. No noise, no light, no movement, stay away from the doorway and gate. Those are the rules, ok? Unless you hear otherwise from Lottie, me, or Big Janey, that's what you have to do to keep your family safe for now."

"Yes 'um, we will. I promise." A sober faced Clement with tears spilling down his cheeks, nodded his head, mumbling, "God bless you, Miz Griffiths."

Jessica's heart wrenched for this family. She put her hand on his shoulder, smiled at Glory, glanced at the still sleeping child, and motioned for Lottie to follow up the stairs to the hallway. The women shared their usual nighttime cup of tea in silence, each a captive of their thoughts.

Jessica bade Lottie a good night as she rinsed the cups, and the young woman touched Jessica's back as she made her way to the cellar to check on their charges, lock the metal gate and cellar door, and unroll the nightshade. Jessica climbed the stairs with a feeling of trepidation that always accompanied these occasions. She would not feel relief until they were safely discharged and on their way across the river to connect with others who would shepherd them to the freedom of victorious escape.

Jessica removed her hairpins and clothing, donning her nightclothes and slippers. Walking to her desk, she sat intending to complete her letter to Richard. It was left unfinished when Joel came with his message from Big Janey about Clement and his family. She was too busy at the time before their arrival to finish writing to him. Exhausted, her nerves pushed to their limit, she tried to compose herself so that her letter would be a welcome comfort to her husband.

A crash and a scream interrupted the silence! Noises and cackling laughter from downstairs drifted upward, making Jessica's blood run cold. She hurriedly opened her wardrobe, removing a double-barreled shotgun, her hands shaking as she loaded it. Hurrying down the staircase, Jessica crept through the sitting room toward the workroom and kitchen, where the noise was loudest.

Three men were in her kitchen with soiled white hoods, passing a bottle of liquor between them. One of them held Lottie's arm as the frightened young woman struggled to free herself, crying pitifully.

"Let her go!" Jessica called to the man. Surprised at her appearance, he released Lottie, who fell back against the room's corner next to the sink. The man to Jessica's right made an advance toward her, and Jessica discharged one barrel at him, catching him in the upper arm.

"Get out! Get out of my house!" she said with venom.

"Now, now, Missus, they's no need for all that," said the third man standing at the kitchen table's head. "Why don' you jes' go on up back to bed, and pretend you ain't seen none o'this? Go on now," wheedled the man, moving around the table. His companion had crumpled to the floor, holding his arm, breathing in gasps. "We jes' come fo a bit a fun with yo little gal here… unfinished business, you might say."

"I said leave! Do it now, and you might get away before I let loose another shot!" Jessica yelled defiantly.

"Way I make it, y'all got only one left," the third man said as he rushed her, knocking the rifle from her hands, grabbing Jessica's arms. The other man on the side of the table where Lottie huddled near the sink retrieved the gun. The man Jessica shot still sat on the floor, blood streaming from his wound.

"What we gonna' do now, Flint?" rasped the man with the rifle.

"Shut it! No names, remember, dummy? See to him," he indicated to the wounded man. "I reckon it's just a flesh wound sho 'nuff. Wrap it up and give him another slug; he be fine."

Everything happened so quickly that Jessica fought to make sense of the situation and somehow manage to avert the impending disaster she felt in her bones. While the wounded man gulped a few slugs of the whiskey, the man with the rifle grabbed a linen tablecloth from the shelf and tore it into strips, poorly binding the wounded man's arm.

"Righty ho, it's gone clean through! Glad to say, mam, but y'all cain't shoot worth beans!" the man with the rifle said.

Jessica struggled and wriggled, but she could not escape the big man's iron grip. "We have no money or jewelry. What are you thinking, breaking into my house? You'll pay for this!" she spat.

"Oh yeah? Well, I don' think so, mam," the big man said, lifting her from the floor and slamming her down hard on the table. "Won' be any ev-ee-dence, now will there? Help me over here and hold her still," the big man ordered the man with the rifle. He did as he was told and stood at Jessica's head, taking her arms above her head, and holding them down against the edge of the table. The big man slapped her again and again. He punched her in the side of her abdomen, which knocked the wind out of her. Jessica struggled for air, gasping loudly.

"That took some of the fight outta ya, dint it?" The big man laughed viciously. "You an all them fancy dancy idears. Y'all has been too long without a man to show you what's what, that's what I think!" he sneered. "Well, missus, we can fix that right proper, yes, siree, right proper!"

Jessica's vision was clouded, and she tasted blood in her mouth. She was still struggling to breathe and felt a sharp pain in her chest. From what seemed like a distance, she heard Lottie's cry, "No! No, don', please!" Jessica felt the man tear her nightdress from the collar and open it wide, exposing her body. He grabbed her legs and pinned them against the edge of the table, leaning his bulk against her calves until her legs felt numb. Meanwhile, he rubbed his filthy hands all over her, as did the man who had entrapped her arms, tying them with a tablecloth strip.

"Gimme some more of them strips," the big man ordered. The wounded man got up off the floor and handed them over. The big man ordered him to hold one of Jessica's legs while he tied the other to the table leg. He then tied the other ankle to the opposite leg, so Jessica lay spread-eagled and naked, her hands bound above her head, her face swelling, and having difficulty breathing.

"Well, well, missus," said the big man stinking of whiskey, "ain't this a sight!" he said, pawing at her. "That feel good, hon? How 'bout dis?" Jessica felt like vomiting. "I got somepin real good for you, missus. Teach you not to be such a nigger lover, mebbe. Teach y'all ta love your own kind, mebbe. Here, you bitch, how's this?" The big man thrust into her roughly, again and again, dripping saliva onto her chest and breathing hard in her face. "You want more, nigger lover? We got more, right, boys? Your turn," the big man said. Squeezing her nipple cruelly, he said, "Thanks, darlin'."

The big man motioned to the man who had taken the rifle to change places with him. He began where the big man left off; next, the wounded man took his turn with a vehemence Jessica attributed as revenge for sustaining a bullet wound. She thought he would never finish and, despite her best attempts, cried and wailed at the pain and defilement.

She heard a loud pounding at the front door. The man inside her stopped pumping. The big man told the man who had put the rifle against the wall by the shelves to go and check, making sure he wasn't seen. He did, and in moments came running back, whispering to the big man. Vaguely, Jessica recalled him as "Flint." The pounding continued, now with loud voices calling out.

The men scrambled around the kitchen, making for the back door through the storage room off the kitchen. Once they were gone, Lottie got to her feet and shakily made her way to the front hall to peek through the glass. Pastor Mason and Joel! 'Thank the Lord,' she thought, as she opened the door to admit them.

The Pastor shook her to stop her crying and tell him what had happened. She bawled and could not speak, only point toward the kitchen. The Pastor yelled to Joel, "Take care of her," as he dashed through the workroom into the kitchen where Jessica lay semiconscious splayed and bloodied, bound to the table. "My good God," the Pastor exclaimed.

Running back to the parlor, he ordered Joel to fetch Dr. Simmons, assuring him that he would look after Lottie and Jessica. Joel ran for all he was worth, not thinking about anything but his mission. Ahead, just short of the doctor's house, he saw the band of three bullies laying under one of the trees in the town's central square, passing a bottle between them and silly with laughter. Joel was sure that these were the culprits responsible for the troubles at Rice Lands. Every bone in his body wanted to lunge at them and beat them to a pulp, even though he knew that even drunk, the odds of three to one stacked poorly in his favor. So did the fact that it was in the dead of night and he was a black man.

'No, not now, but I promise...' he thought as he dashed to Dr. Simmons' side door. He would make a plan; he would get back-up; he would have revenge for Lottie and Miss Jess. But now he had a more important job to do.

He saddled Dr. Simmons' horse and brought it around to the door just as the man came rushing out with shirt unbuttoned, clutching his doctor's bag and jacket. He helped the doctor mount and leaped up behind, yelling what he and the Pastor had found. In short order, they arrived at Rice Lands. After tying the doctor's horse securely, Joel rushed into the house on the doctor's heels. The Pastor was cradling a blanketed and wailing Lottie in the work-room. Jessica still lay on the table, covered with an embroidered tablecloth. Ironically, it was her most beautiful cloth, part of the Hope Chest she brought with her after marriage to the Colonel.

Joel knelt before Lottie, speaking softly to her, asking questions. Dr. Simmons blanched at seeing Jessica while the Pastor explained he didn't want to untie or move her in case she had broken bones, deciding to wait for the doctor's arrival. The doctor removed the tablecloth and gently checked Jessica's arms and legs. Bruising was apparent and would get significantly worse with time, and he explained his concerns to the Pastor as they untied her bonds. The doctor inspected her chest, neck, face, and head. Finally, he recovered her, walking briskly to the workroom where Lottie sat quietly, holding Joel's hand.

"Miss Lottie. We'll need to ask you some questions, but not until later. Can you help me now with Mrs. Griffiths? We need to wash her down and dress her so that Pastor Mason can carry her upstairs. Can you do that with me, please?"

The doctor's tone was gentle and soothing, and Lottie shook her head in affirmation. He took her arm, and they went into the kitchen, closing the door. Pastor Mason and Joel sat conversing in the workroom. Joel related how he had come to Rice Lands to deliver a surprise bouquet for Lottie. Joel thought it would please her as they both looked forward to having a picnic by the river after church. When he arrived at the house, he saw the flickering of dim light through the stained-glass windows. Assuming the lights were turned down low as a night light, and knowing a late-night caller would not be appreciated or welcome, Joel decided to leave the flowers on the porch table for Lottie to find when she opened the house in the early morning. But he had heard a scream and then seen Miss Jessica running through the house when he peered through the windows. The images were not clear because of the stained glass, but instinctively Joel knew that there was something badly amiss. Then he heard the shot and knew for certain that there was trouble.

His first thought was to help, but a black man forcing a door open into a plantation home in the dead of night was a bad idea on any occasion. Annoyed that he had wasted so much time in dithering, Joel ran for the first house at the town's edge: Pastor Mason's parsonage, which lay just before the church. It took a while before the Pastor opened the door. He told Pastor Mason there was terrible trouble at Rice Lands, and the man--who had been working late on his sermon in his upstairs study--rushed to the plantation on foot with Joel. The remainder, the Pastor knew firsthand.

Finally, Dr. Simmons opened the kitchen door and summoned both men. He requested that Pastor Mason carry Mrs. Griffiths upstairs to her room, preceded by Lottie, who would show him the way. He directed Joel to pour boiling water over the table to sterilize it and use the leftover heated water to clean the floor and cabinetry of blood spatters. Last, he directed Joel to put more water on to boil for tea. Then the doctor collapsed into a chair and scribbled some notes in his book. He felt as if he had aged ten years.

When Pastor Mason and Lottie came downstairs, he asked them to join him in the sitting room so he and the Pastor could make some sense of what had happened. Joel arrived with a tray of tea and cups. Lottie immediately moved to serve out of habit, but Joel shook his head and returned her to a chair, tucking the blanket around her protectively.

"All right, now Lottie dear, tell me about the troubles here tonight if you will. Take your time, my dear. Everything's all right now, and Miss Jessica will be all right, too, with time. But I need to know exactly what happened so I can properly deal with this situation. Do you understand, Lottie?"

Lottie nodded and began a step-by-step recounting of the episode, including one man calling the big man who seemed to be the boss, "Flint."

"Them men, dey jes wouldn' stop! Nobody listen to me! I begged n' begged, but dey kep a'goin' no matter! Oh, doc, they hurt her bad. Dey ony punches me once, but her... dey hit her n' hit her! Was dat big' un dey called 'Flint.' Called her a 'nigger lover,' an dey laugh n' laugh n' hit n' raped n' laugh mo!

"Said how'd I like watchin' what was gonna' happen t'me nex! I don' know, I couldn' do nuthin'. One of 'em had Miss Jess's gun n'he never let it go. Not till it was his turn... an... oh," she lapsed into tears again.

"Now, now, Lottie, that was very good. You couldn't have done anything to help Mrs. Griffiths. It was three strong men against one young woman who had already been punched to the floor, and they had the firearm. Put that straight out of your head, my dear. Now, let's have a look at you again. When I first examined you in the kitchen, you were only sore. Any changes? Any difficulty in taking a deep breath?" he asked as he applied his stethoscope to her back. She shook her head.

"I'll stay here for tonight, and however long we decide is prudent," said Pastor Mason. Looking at Joel, whose eyes were wide with shock and disgust, he said, "Joel, you've done well tonight. You made good decisions. Getting me first was critical, as our appearance stopped everything dead. It could have gone much worse had you not reacted so sensibly. Well done, lad." Pastor patted Joel's shoulder.

"I saw 'em," Joel admitted.

"What?" asked Dr. Simmons and Pastor Mason in unison.

"I saw 'em a'sittin' an' a laughin' in the square, passin' a bottle 'roun. One of 'em still had a hood on. A hood! The KKK!

"I coulda' kilt 'em, but I went on to the doc's like you tole me, but I coulda' hurt dem like dey hurt Lottie and Miss Jess! But I dint! I dint!" Joel sobbed.

"Now, now, Joel, my boy. You did right to get me. Don't you see? Had you jumped into the fray when you wanted retribution, you wouldn't have alerted me, and I wouldn't have been able to help anything or anyone! The Pastor was waiting here all alone, and Miss Jess, well, she needed care. No, no, my boy, you showed good judgment and did the right thing by putting your feelings aside. You are a hero!

"First, when you realized something was amiss, you ran for help in getting the Pastor. Next, you got me. Third, you've helped us here. Fourth, you unselfishly did what needed doing, despite that you wanted to pound the hell out of those thugs. No, you did right, Joel, hear me? Right!"

The doctor held his hand toward Joel. The surprised young man shook it and nodded.

"Y'all is a hero," Lottie whispered. "My hero, Joel. Thank ya. Y'all saved me." Tentatively, she reached out her hand to him. He took it and smiled.

"Well, I think we should all have a prayer together of thanksgiving," said Pastor Mason.

"Yes, and after that, one more cup of tea. Anything stronger in the house, Lottie? As a doctor, I prescribe a small dose for each of us. I know I could use something to calm my nerves!"

For the first time in hours, everyone breathed in relief; some even smiled slightly. It was a night none would forget. It was a night that foretold future troubles.

Chapter Fifteen
Effect

For what was only hours but seemed like days, Jessica lay in her bed as still as a corpse. Throughout the night, Pastor Mason sat in her room, checking her brow for fever as per Dr. Simmons' instructions. The doctor was not expected back until the day following the incident as he was certain that the sedative he had administered would give Jessica the best treatment: rest and a temporary cognitive escape from the attack.

The minister spent much of his time in prayer and reading Scripture. Lottie appeared several times during the night, and Pastor Mason ministered to her as well, knowing that the girl had also been traumatized and suffered the fear of losing the "rock" of her precarious existence and life. She genuinely loved Jessica Griffiths, who was not just a kindly employer, but the only person in Lottie's life that could equate with family.

Fortunately, Jessica had taught Lottie well and involved her in much of the daily operation of Rice Lands. The young woman feverishly followed their established routine, including the initial layout of the patterns for recent orders.

"Pastor? Any change?" Lottie inquired, placing a tray of iced tea, sandwiches, and fruit on the side table. "I sit wif her awhile. Y'all mus' wanna' clean up a bit or stretch yo' legs."

"Thank you, Lottie. No change yet, I'm afraid, but I have full confidence we shall see an improvement in a short while. Sleep has done her a world of good and allowed her freedom from pain until the doctor returns to deal with it. And yes, once I've eaten this lovely food you've prepared, I'll change places with you and wash up a bit."

"She all done in, Pastor. She looks..." Lottie choked and covered her face with her hands.

"Now, Lottie. You recall what Dr. Simmons said, don't you? The worst of the bruising has come out now, so she looks much worse than she is. Bruises eventually disappear, so does soreness, and broken ribs and cuts heal, as well. Thanks to your young man, Joel, this ugly time will become just a bad memory. We shall have Miss Jessica back with us in no time. It will be difficult for you both to put this behind you, I know that. But that is what you both must do. I'll help in any way I can. For now, just having a man around through the nights will make you feel secure and not so vulnerable. The rest, well, that remains to be seen. We won't borrow trouble, Lottie. We'll take it one step at a time, all right?"

Lottie nodded, lightly touched Jessica's hand, and whispered, "I here, Miss Jess. I ain't a'goin' nowhere. You jes come back to us, ok? Res' and come on back, hear? Everthin' is jes fine here. Res' now." She smiled at the Pastor and retreated from the room.

Shortly afterward, just as the Pastor finished his lunch, Jessica's eye flickered open. Her left eye was swollen shut amid ugly purple and blue bruising and several cuts on her cheek. The left side of her jaw was also swollen, bruised, and cut, as were her lips. As she awoke, her breathing quickened, and she moaned. The cuts on the side of her face stung from tears streaming from her right eye. "Flint" had used sufficient force to split her face from the percussive blows with the "back and forth" slapping.

"Jessica, oh Jessica," intoned the Pastor, holding her hand. "Welcome back." The Pastor leaned close and gently placed a cold cloth to her open eye and cheek absorbing the salty tears streaming freely. "I knew you would return to us with time," he said, immediately feeling angry at himself for such an ineffectual greeting. "Are you thirsty? Or hungry? Can I get you anything?"

True to form, Jessica gathered herself. "Pastor, how long have you been here? Where's Lottie? Is she all right?" She tried to sit up but collapsed back against the pillows. Her speech was slurred because of her swollen lips and jaw, but she was communicating sensibly.

"Now, now, Jessica, rest easy. Plenty of time for that, my dear. I've been here since...well, last night just after...Dr. Simmons was here as well. Lottie is fine, a bit frightened understandably, but in much better condition than her mistress. You're safe, Jessica, and the doctor says you will heal from the beating, and with a little time, all the soreness will disappear."

"How bad is it?" Jessica asked, staring at the ceiling.

"I've seen better," the Pastor said, smiling. "You've got a couple of broken ribs, Dr. Simmons thinks, some cuts and bruises, but thanks to Joel's appearance and discovery of the break-in, you're alive, and all things will be set right in no time. Oh, and he said you have a nasty bump on the back of your head, and possibly a slight concussion. So, if you feel lightheaded, that's why, but it will heal fine in a few days or less. You'll be right as rain, Jessica, but you must give it time and rest."

"Right as rain," whispered Jessica. "Hardly, Pastor. Nothing will ever be as it was. How much do you know?"

"Joel ran to fetch me when he realized you ladies were in trouble. We scared them off, but unfortunately not until after your... beating. Lottie sustained only a punch and maybe a few slaps. Joel then ran for Dr. Simmons, and I stayed with you to await his arrival. He examined and treated you both and then left sometime in the middle of the night and will return this afternoon just before the dinner hour. He did give you a sedative to ensure you remained quiet through the night. You did."

Jessica wept softly. "Then, you know all of it. You saw."

Holding her hand to his cheek, he said, "Yes. I'm so sorry, Jessica. You didn't deserve any of this. Nor did Lottie."

"No one deserves this, Pastor Mason. No one," her voice trailed off. "Please ask Lottie to come up; I need to have a few words with her."

"Of course, and you're right, no one should be treated so. What I meant is that you and Lottie of all people..."

"But men always overpower, beat, and rape women, don't they? Why do you men always do that, Pastor?" she said with vitriol. "Does it make them feel powerful and invincible, do you think? They're not, you know. And I'm going to make sure..." her voice caught, and she wept again.

"Jess, don't think of it now. Try to put it out of your mind or talk about it if you must. Whatever you say to me remains between us. I'm here to help you in any way I can if only to listen and sit with you to help you feel safe. Dr. Simmons and I will keep your confidence, I assure you. Now don't make your face more sore by too much talking. Give it a bit of time, ok?"

"Yes, thank you. Please ask Lottie to come now, Pastor. I'll need some privacy with just her. Personal things."

"Very well. I'll go down and ask Lottie to come up. Do you want her to bring anything to you?" Pastor Mason was at a loss. He had not had to deal with anything like this in the past among his parishioners. Rapes occurred, yes, he had heard disgusting tales; he had seen the results of rapes in the bellies of slaves. What he was unprepared for was the emotional devastation that followed such brutality, and how inept any attempt at comfort by caring people was to the victims. There were no appropriate words that could wash away the ugly memory. It remained a stain, a burden, an ever-present fear in the mind of the attacked woman. He was sure there were other psychological repercussions, but he had no idea how to cope or counsel except to reassure safety, extend care, and pray with them for strength in the knowledge of God's love in which they could take shelter and comfort. But was that enough?

Lottie entered Jessica's bedroom bearing a tray with a pitcher and glass, fresh cloths, herbal ointment, and some of her homemade applesauce in a small bowl. "Miss Jess, y'all wanna sip? Lemme hep ya'."

Lottie gently supported Jessica in a sitting position and rearranged the pillows. Holding the glass to Jessica's lips, she said, "I knows y'all prefer lemonade, but thas bound ta' sting, so dis iced tea be betta, yeah?"

"Thank you, Lottie. Are you all right? They didn't...you know, did they?"

"No, mam, dey was gonna' when dey done wif you, but Pastor and Joel come, so dey ran off. Oh, Miss Jess, y'all gonna be ok?"

"Yes, Lottie, I'll be fine. But what about the folks in the cellar? No one can know about them! Have you been seeing to them?"

"Yes' um. Don' worry yo' sef. They heared some noise, but Clement kep them quiet cuz he afraid to do somepin. I s'plained that some drunks broke in, but y'all chased 'em off with the gun. They ok. I fed 'em and did the pail. Nobody but nobody saw me; nobody but you, me, and Big Janey know dey wif us. Is ok, Miss Jess. An I got dem men a'workin' in da fields, jes like we allus do. I even set out the pattens fo da dresses."

"Oh, my sweet, dependable Lottie," Jessica said as she grasped the young woman's hand to her cheek. "You've done well. Now, I desperately need the chamber pot. Can you help me? I don't want to soil the bed linen, and I reckon Pastor Mason has seen altogether too much already." Jessica attempted a smile.

Jessica sponged herself down with Lottie's help to remove the leavings of the incident. Lottie gently brushed Jessica's hair and braided it, after tentatively applying ointment to her face. With Lottie's help, Jessica changed into a fresh nightdress and a bed jacket. Exhausted, the woman lay back against the pillows.

"That's so much better. Thank you, Lottie. As soon as you can, I want you to ask Big Janey to come to Rice Lands. I'll cover it with Pastor Mason and Dr. Simmons, who will speak to her boss at the store. I'll say you need help given I'm laid up for a bit. I'm sure they will talk to him, and he'll agree to let Big Janey come.

"When she comes, you bring her to me, but make sure the Pastor is nowhere up here. It would be best if he goes on home once Big Janey is here. We can get her to help with Clement and his family. We'll work out the details later. Can you do that?"

"Course I kin! Y'all jes leave it to me. Don' worry, Miss Jess. We gonna' go on jes like befo!" For the first time in many hours, Lottie smiled.

Big Janey arrived Friday morning. She lumbered up the stairs to Jessica's bedroom. The kindly woman's eyes opened wide when she saw the state of Jessica's face. "Oh, my good Lord, Miss Jess."

"I know I look a fright, Janey, but it's not all that bad. Doc says the colorful skin will disappear in several days. The swelling's almost gone, but my chest still hurts when I breathe, so I'm not much use for a bit. Any little thing I do exhausts me. But let's put that aside. Thank you for coming. You and I have to discuss Clement and how to get them safely to the raft tonight. Now come close," Jessica gestured to Big Janey as she whispered instructions.

Pastor Mason and Dr. Simmons arranged with Big Janey's boss that she was needed at Rice Lands to help Mrs. Griffiths after sustaining a brutal attack and break-in. The good man was only too willing to help and assured the men that Big Janey could stay as long as needed. There were several people available to take her place at the store and market temporarily.

Late on Friday night, Clement and his family stood ready to leave, their repacked sacks full of fresh, clean clothes supplemented by additions from Jessica's collection of spare garments. Clement shouldered the sack for the raft captain and held his child in his other arm. His wife, Glory, stood next to their bags, waiting for Lottie to open the doorway and gate. Big Janey kept a watch outside. When she was sure it was safe, Big Janey let loose a hoot that exactly sounded like a hoot owl. Lottie worked the padlock and motioned to the family. They hurried out barefoot, their boots knotted around their necks.

"Y'all walk where I walk, y' hear? No talkin', not one bit!" warned Big Janey. They trudged through the marshy ground, some-times wading through water almost up to their knees, their feet sinking in the sodden mud beneath. Each adult pushed thoughts of snakes and gators from their mind, concentrating on the dimin-ishing amount of ground to be covered before they reached the sandy soil of the muddy riverfront. Just as they cleared the marsh ground, the tip of the raft rounded the trees. Big Janey waded into the water and snatched the thrown rope to stabilize the raft's slow glide. The family scurried aboard, the Captain relieving Clement of the sack adorned with apple slices. The family huddled in the small cabin in the middle of the raft, Clement waving to Big Janey as she threw the rope onto the raft and shoved it back toward deeper water assisted by the Captain's pole. Big Janey, breathing hard more from nervousness than physical effort, threw her hand up in one last wave.

"Da good Lord be wif y'all," she whispered. She turned to retrace her steps to the house through the marsh and apple or-chard. She saw Lottie waiting expectantly by the cellar gate. They hugged each other and entered, anxious to remove all signs of habitation. With everything packed away, the women hurried to the waiting Jessica to report their success.

Over the next week, the townspeople rallied, and many dropped off dishes of prepared food, cakes, biscuits, and fresh fruit or vegetables to Rice Lands in support. When word spread that the women were attacked, some men formed a guard watch around the property for a few weeks. The matter was reviewed by a town meeting, as well. Pastor Mason counseled against vigilante action; the Mayor made a show of support by pushing through a bill that guaranteed severe consequences for anyone found guilty of this or similar crime against the townspeople (passed unan-imously); the Judge increased the paltry roster of deputies, as most of the able-bodied men enlisted in the Confederate Army. Everyone knew, but no one said aloud that members of the Ku Klux Klan were also townspeople. The war between the Union and the declared Confederacy carried with it collateral damage that touched every level of Southern life, not soon to be resolved despite the opposition of the two armies. This, too, was a known reality within the hearts of the people -- white and black.

Chapter Sixteen
Aftermath

The following Sunday, Jessica Griffiths and Lottie faced each other in the front hall. Each was in a freshly pressed outfit: Jessica in her signature garb, a skirt and high-necked blouse, Lottie in a calico print dress. Each woman donned a hat over meticulously upswept coiffure. But for the leather hip holster and pistol strapped to Jessica's hip, they were in their usual "Sunday-go-to-meeting" clothes.

When they reached the church imminently before the service began, they walked down the aisle to sit in their usual pew. Unmistakable whispers and gasps emitted from the congregation when they saw the pair and got more animated once they spotted Jessica's holster. She smiled to herself. The organist concluded the prelude to worship, and the chords of a well-known hymn blared through the small church. Everyone arose as the minister and choir filed down the central aisle, tentatively singing the opening lines "Soldiers of Christ arise, and put your armor on..."

Pastor Mason's delivery of his sermon was noticeably low key and lacking his usual fervor. He seemed distracted. Before closing prayer and the benediction, he overtly welcomed Jessica and Lottie back to the fold at the end of the service. The Pastor thanked God's mercy for sparing their lives and healing their bodies, minds, and hearts from the unspeakable episode at Rice Lands. He accused the perpetrators as the most "heinous cowards," who he was sure would be brought to justice. A few muffled sniggers could be heard, followed by quiet mumbling.

As the congregation filed out of the church, Jessica linked her arm through Lottie's, whispering to her to hold her head high and stroll slowly. They were among the last to leave the church. Pastor Mason's face alighted with a broad smile as they neared him and the elders standing at the front threshold to greet parishioners.

"Good morning, Mrs. Griffiths and Lottie. I am so pleased to see you back; everyone is. You are both looking quite well, I am happy to say."

Jessica nodded and smiled. Lottie thanked the Pastor, and the two walked forward into the sunshine. Ahead, the three men who had first accosted Lottie in the town and later broken into Rice Lands' main house to pillage, beat, and rape, were looking in Jessica's direction and whispering among themselves. Again, Jessica smiled to herself. Holding Lottie's arm tight to her side, she strode right up to them.

"Good morning," she said acidly, resting her hand on the pistol and looking straight at Flint. Slowly, she looked from Flint to each of the other men with a piercing look.

"Mornin' mam." The other two men said nothing. As she took a step to walk by, Jessica reached her right hand to the skinny man's upper arm, grasping it for all she was worth, pressing her thumb where she imagined his wound to be from memory of that wretched night. The man yelled out, then wailed. Jessica dug her nails more firmly into his arm, refusing to let go. All surrounding conversations immediately ceased. Everyone's attention concentrated on the scene unfolding before them. The man's shirt began to flower with a bloodstain. People gathered around the scene.

"Ah, Jimmy Michelson, isn't it? It seems your arm hurts, Jimmy, and oh yes, look, it's bleeding. Could it be from my shotgun?" Jessica smiled into his face. The skinny man went to his knees, and still, Jessica held her grip. Finally, she released him with a push, and he fell to his backside.

"And you there, Bert Frome! Shame on you coming to the Lord's house stinking of whiskey. I'd recognize that smell anywhere; it's a giveaway when you drink cheap hooch, Bert. Besides, you drooled some on me, remember?" The man looked at the ground and wiped his mouth with the back of his hand, taking a few steps backward while looking at Jessica's hand on her pistol.

"And last but never least: Flint!" she said viciously. "Your friend, Bert, here...remember he named you at my house? No one else in this town has that name, do they Flint? And no one's quite as big as you, except some of Lottie's friends. You know, those men you bully because they're Negroes just trying to do an honest day's work. But that's what you do, isn't it? Bully people; try to make them afraid; push them around; beat them up; burn buildings and crosses. Well, I know what else you do, Flint, don't I? I name YOU and these other two worthless friends of yours for the trouble at Rice Lands! Yes, that's right, I name YOU in front of God and these witnesses!"

The wounded man began to cry; the skinny man started to protest, stuttering over his words; Flint said nothing, just glared at her.

"I name you as the lowest of the low! Cowards! You're grown, no-account men who attack women! I'm not afraid of you, and I warn you: step one foot on my property again, and I'll shoot you for trespassing and what you've done! Only this time, Flint, I'll be aiming between your legs so you can't rape another woman. Oh, and Flint--just to let you know, I've been practicing," she smiled and patted her pistol. "Now, I never miss! " Jessica pulled Lottie along with her for a few steps while the townspeople gaped in shock. No one spoke.

On her fourth step, she released Lottie's arm and turned around to face Flint and the churchgoers. "You might turn your energies to joining with the other brave men from this town who are fighting in the war. But, no, you prefer the life of a coward and a bully, don't you?" To the townspeople, she nodded as she said, "Good morning to you."

Turning again to take Lottie's arm, she marched from the churchyard, singing loudly, "Soldiers of Christ arise and put your armor on..." Lottie was smiling as she added her voice. When they were away from the gathering, Jessica relaxed a bit. Turning to Lottie, she kissed her cheek.

"You did well, Lottie. I'm sorry I couldn't give you any warning."

"No, mam! Y'all was perfec! Did y'all see that skinny Bert fella a'shakin' in his boots? Why I never seen such a thing as y'all takin' all them on, and wif everbody a'watchin' an all! I reckon dey all be a'buzzin' fo weeks 'bout dat scene!"

"In truth, Lottie, I wore my holster to give me the courage to walk into that church after all that's happened. And I knew those men attend with their families, so I meant it to send a silent message of warning to them. I never intended to speak out like that. But that nasty Flint with his sickening smile...when he stared at me... I just couldn't help myself. Someone has to do something about their lawlessness! They have no regard for other people whatsoever. I just hope I haven't cooked my goose!"

"Cooked yer what?" queried Lottie.

"Never mind, sweet girl, it's just an expression. Now, let's get home and change out of our good clothes and spend the afternoon relaxing, shall we?" Jessica's stride quickened as they neared the pillars and gates of Rice Lands.

"Well, mam, if'n is awright wit y'all, I is havin' a picnic wif Joel by the riva, less'n y'all got somepin fer me ta do." Lottie looked at Jessica sheepishly.

"Lottie! That's wonderful! No, you and your young man enjoy the afternoon with my blessing. Be sure and take some of your delicious applesauce and some fresh apples from the trees. You have yourself some fun!" Jessica smiled, pleased that one of them could move forward out of the shadows.

Lottie had gone an hour before when the front bell tinkled. Jessica put down her embroidery and opened the locked door to see Pastor Mason standing with hat in one hand, flowers in the other.

"Pastor! Hello, come in. I suppose you're here to chastise me for the scene after church?" Jessica accepted the flowers, mumbling a soft "thank you," and led the Pastor to the sitting room.

"Jessica, no, that is I wanted to say..." he stammered.

"Would you like some lemonade? I made it fresh this morning. Or tea, I can give you hot or cold, your preference." She placed a mat on the end table beside his chair.

"Lemonade would be delicious. I don't get it much at the parsonage. Mrs. Drake, the housekeeper, makes only hot tea and wretched coffee." He smiled and loosened his tie.

"For heaven's sake, take off your jacket. It's too warm a day for formality, Pastor." She returned from the kitchen with a pitcher and two glasses. "I keep it in the icebox, so it's nice and cold. No need for ice; just waters it down," she said, smiling to ease his nervousness.

"Jess...Jessica, excuse me, but about the matter at the church. We need to talk about it. I have to say, I didn't know you were wearing that pistol holster. Not exactly appropriate church wear, would you say?" he said pointedly, raising his eyebrows.

"No, you're right, it wasn't, but I needed it for courage and protection, I thought." She wanted to look him straight in the eye but seeing him again in her house caused the memories of that night and the aftermath to come flooding back. She reddened with embarrassment. Fleetingly, she wondered if--when he looked at her--he saw her as she was now or lying exposed on the table. She shook her head to clear her concentration and push away those thoughts.

"I must say the town was a bit shocked. Everyone has heard about the troubles with the break-in, and there's been much speculation and gossip, but no one knew for certain about the beating and rape until you blurted it out. That was incredibly courageous of you, Jess. You set it all out for them. The Judge spoke to me afterward and asked me to ask you to see him for a statement. Will you do that? I could come with you."

Jessica breathed heavily. "Yes, I'll do it. I suppose I let myself in for that, didn't I? But I just couldn't let them get away with it, maybe to do it again and again! I wanted everyone to know what filth they are! Was that wrong of me, Pastor?"

"Please, Jess, after everything, please call me James. Except in public, that is, well, at least for now." He concentrated on drinking his lemonade.

"What are you saying, Pastor...uh, James?" she asked with genuine confusion.

"I'd like to court you, Jess. With your consent, of course. As you know, I'm unmarried, and Mr. Griffiths has been gone for two years or so, and I'm extremely fond of you. I feel we got to know each other fairly well with all the hours we chatted when you were, uh, indisposed."

"But I'm a married woman, James! You of all people should understand 'til death do us part' of fidelity. Richard, the Colonel, isn't dead! I've had no letter, no notice, nothing to make me think he isn't coming home.

"One of the last things I told him was that I would wait, and I always keep my word. I'm sorry, James, but I cannot. I simply cannot even entertain the thought. It would be like giving up on him! Do you understand?" She looked so earnest, believed so thoroughly that the Pastor could only nod his head.

"I'm sorry if I've offended you, Jess. That was never my intention. I hoped you had some fondness for me, something that might one day grow into love. And having a man around is always a good deterrent. You and Lottie—while you're doing a magnificent job here—well, you're vulnerable here at the end of town, all alone. I thought..." Rubbing his hands over his face, he looked at her and smiled, his composure regained.

"I should go. Can we remain friends? See each other once in a while, just to make sure you ladies are doing well? A consistent male presence couldn't hurt, particularly an irregular one." He grabbed for his jacket and looked back at her.

"Yes, James. In public, Pastor Mason!" She grinned, saying, "You can come by whenever you have a notion. We don't have fancy meals anymore with all the shortages of foods, but there's always something. I'd be happy to share it with you, and I'm sure Lottie will feel reassured by your visits."

They walked to the door, and he turned, taking her by the shoulders. "I know, Jess. I know what you do to help people, the darkies. You must know it makes you a target, puts you directly in danger. I've wanted to speak to you before all this nastiness happened, but now I feel I must counsel you to stop before something even more serious occurs."

"How did you find out?" Jessica was shocked at his admission, and her mind immediately went through the protective steps she, Lottie, and Big Janey had taken over the months. Somewhere, she had made a mistake, slipped up, or one of them had done so.

"I miss little, including absences at the church or the Negro spiritual gatherings. Didn't you know I attended them? Well, I do. Not every meeting, but when I can, I go to give support, lend a hand, offer encouragement, visit the sick...or beaten down. I've heard the whispers. I didn't know for sure, but when I questioned Joel more thoroughly, he admitted that he'd seen Lottie taking people to the river and sometimes you. You see, he's keeping watch over her because he fancies her. He isn't duplicitous, Jessica. It's love that motivates him."

"Oh, yes, well, I don't know quite what to say. It all just happened, just sort of fell into place with the property setting and the river boundary. Those poor people were so frightened and mistreated, no life, no future, all of it such a dismal existence. I simply had to help them." Jessica looked up at him, her eyes full of empathy.

"I understand, and while many of us don't own slaves and agree with you, it's a dangerous and perhaps foolhardy business for you as a woman alone, Jessica. Surely you can see that." He held her hand. "I know that intractable side of you, Jess. You displayed it at church again today. Going after those hooligans all by yourself with only two slugs in your shotgun is another example. And risking everything and your life by hiding and helping these folks is yet another sign. But I must ask you to consider giving it up. For your sake, for Lottie's sake, for my sake, even for Richard's sake and the reputation of his family—please, Jessica, stop."

Jessica shook her head and looked down at the carpet. She pulled her hands away. "James, the Lord tells us to love others as He loved us. You cannot deny that. I cannot. It's a great wrong that I must oppose in whatever way one can. This is my way, my little bit. I'm sorry. Please, keep my confidence, and I beg you never to speak of it again. If we are to have any kind of friendship, you must promise me."

The Pastor looked defeated. Gently, he stroked her cheek. "I will protect you as much as I can. You know you can always call on me, depend on me. I will not take part in those activities, but I will be here for you, Jess, if ever you need me."

"Thank you, James. Pastor Mason, I asked for your promise. Will you give it?" She looked up at him intently.

"As a man who has feelings for you, and as Pastor Mason, I give you my promise." It was with a heavy heart that Pastor James Mason walked the path from Rice Lands' front door to its gates. He steeled himself not to turn and look back.

Jessica stood in the doorway, tears dampening her face, her heart awash with emotion. She would somehow find the strength to honor her beliefs and continue to help those less fortunate; she would continue to try to keep Rice Lands functioning and afloat. She would honor her promise to wait for her beloved Richard, believing he would return until she had verifiable news to the contrary. She would try to soothe the heart of the wonderful man walking away with a caring friendship.

"I will, I will, I will...somehow..." she whispered to herself.

Slavery had many faces, but the underlying designs were the same: slaves were property, and their status enforced by either real or threatened violence, any caring or habitual relationship tempered and limited by the power imbalance under which slavery existed. Within those confines, one found connections from the compassionate to the contemptuous, but none ever approached status equality.

Although most non-slaveholding White Southerners did not benefit from slavery as an institution, they identified with it. Be they shopkeepers, yeoman farmers, poor folks, or anything in-between, the existence of slaves allowed them a sense of superiority. They might not be in the elite ranks of 25% of the Southern population who owned slaves, but they were not black, and they were not slaves.

Although cotton was the major cash crop, plantations also raised rice, tobacco, corn, vegetables, and sugarcane. Slaves planted and harvested; they cleared land, cut, and hauled wood, cared for, and butchered livestock, and repaired buildings. Slaves learned to be and functioned as blacksmiths, farmhands, mechanics, butlers and maids, drivers, carpenters, nannies, cooks, and every position required to keep a plantation business and its household running solidly. Female slaves also had the responsibility of caring for their children and the master's children, cooking, and cleaning their personal living quarters and plantation homes. Domestic house servants did not, as is commonly thought, have an easier life or job than field hands or other workers. They worked long hours at the whims of their owners, had less privacy, and were always under scrutiny. Still, it was not unusual for black and white children to play together, oblivious to the overall system to which they both would ultimately adjust.

Diets, sanitary conditions, housing, and nutrition, were inadequate to barely adequate, making slaves susceptible to diseases like pneumonia, tuberculosis, and malaria, or getting sick because of unrelenting hard work, even in bad weather. Uppermost in most of their minds was the potential threat of being sold and separated from their immediate or extended families, with the likelihood of never seeing each other again. Sexual exploitation among female slaves was a constant threat, and the abuse was widespread and did not qualify legally as "rape."

Slaves lived under "Slave Codes," which varied from state to state, and they had none of the rights common to whites. They could not retaliate and strike a white no matter the circumstances, own a firearm, make a contract, leave a plantation without permission, testify in court, or visit homes of free blacks or whites, among other things. They were punished by their masters or overseers for not working fast or hard enough, being late, defying authority, learning to read and write (forbidden by law), running away, or sundry other behaviors deemed unacceptable and beyond their entitlements. They could –depending upon their master's authoritarian severity—be whipped, beaten, mutilated, imprisoned, murdered, or sold.

Slaves comprised approximately 20% of Southern cities, with slaves and free blacks outnumbering whites in Charleston, SC, where the first shot in the Civil War was fired. Most slaves (about 90%) lived on plantations, but some lived and worked in urban areas, hired out by their masters for a day to up to several years.

These facts of her place in time swirled through Jessica's head. She was a transplant from the North because of her marriage to a Southern gentleman. While she had done her best to acclimatize herself, her life's socio-political aspects never settled into complacent acceptance but rather opposition. She realized that despite the associated danger at worst or repudiation and rejection, she could not discontinue helping slaves escape their despicable circumstances. She had to tighten up her operation, exercise more care and planning, and adopt a public *persona* free of any association to rebellion. 'I will; I can,' she thought.

In the I860's, bacteriology had yet to be discovered, and knowledge of the importance of sterile dressings and antiseptic surgery, sanitation, and hygiene was a tragic unknown. For every soldier who died in battle in the Civil War, two died of disease, particularly from typhoid, dysentery, and diarrhea, which claimed more lives than battle wounds. At least her Richard was a properly clothed officer with some tent protection from the elements and the rest of the troops. That gave him a fighting chance to survive, provided he did not suffer battle wounds and subsequent infection (septicemia was unknown).

Lack of water meant that doctors treating soldiers did not wash their hands or instruments routinely; bloody knives were used as scalpels; bloody fingers were used as probes; doctors operated in pus-and-bloodstained coats. [The antiseptic era was in the future.] Surgical fever and gangrene were constants; camp hygiene and sanitation were woefully inadequate to nonexistent; there was no knowledge of causes to disease, nor were there qualifying physical examinations. Thus, rural troops were clustered into crowded areas with larger groups and exposed to infections with no immunity. The humid regions, insects, and vermin complicated the failing condition of poorly fed and clothed troops already suffering from disease exposure. Battle wounds —some with massive injuries-- and subsequent brutal "medical treatment" decreased survival with lingering earmarks of the overall tragedy. Man killed man; brother, killed brother; a friend killed a friend. Many left home to enlist in the army they believed defended their way of life; far fewer returned, and among those who returned intact or with limbs lost, each man lost a part of himself and was forever changed.

As the war raged on, their little town suffered the plunders of supplies, buildings, livestock, horses, and all foodstuffs. Anything that could support the war machine, or the support of troops got appropriated. Jessica's out-of-the-way house escaped overrun by standard requisition and got reserved instead for officers' meetings and short-term overnight stays. Its proximity to the river meant that off-loaded supplies made for the road and camp delivery almost immediately, once the officer in charge assigned destinations for various cargo boxes. She and Lottie continued their day-to-day existence, fulfilling as many routine tasks as possible. Barter for labor was the only practical way for the rice to reach harvest, as a factor of 66.77% devalued Southern currency.

They served coffee made from browned okra seeds, roasted acorns, or wheat berries. The tea Lottie brewed from sumac berries, sassafras roots, and the leaves of raspberry, blackberry, holly, and huckleberry was quite palatable and far better than the coffee. They substituted molasses, dried ground figs, honey, and sorghum for sugar and made flour from rice, cornmeal, or rye. When they ran out of salt for seasoning, they used wood ashes. They served Hopping John and fried ham with red-eye gravy and biscuits when she had bits of the slaughtered pig left in the smokehouse, or opossum if Lottie was lucky enough to tree and capture one. They ate corn, beans, tomatoes, cucumbers, lettuce, and potatoes hoarded in the hidden and locked root cellar from wandering thieves.

Jessica had attended a town meeting at which sharecropping got discussed as a means for plantation owners to regain some of the wealth or stability lost. Many had already fled to the mountains of North Carolina to avoid the fire of Sherman's army reputed to routinely burn many plantations, setting enslaved labor free to do as they wished. Many large landholdings were left burned and desolate with large rice, cotton, or vegetable fields overgrown and flooded, burned barns and homes, and little or no labor remaining to help rebuild. This system of maintaining her rice fields and keeping up production appealed to Jessica. Little did she know that by the early 20th century, rice production in South Carolina and some of the other Southern states would all but disappear. Marshy landscapes would not support new, improved farm machinery, and instead, states like Texas, Louisiana, Arkansas, and some other appropriate Southern states, would be useful for rice production. The

Lowcountry (the area from Wilmington, NC to Jacksonville, FL, and 50 miles inland) would also experience hurricanes and an earthquake that would fill the fields with saltwater, ruining the land for cultivation. But before any of this transpired, Jessica and some others instituted sharecropping, and Rice Lands survived the Civil War.

The Civil War occurred during the Victorian Era in the reign of England's Queen Victoria. From 1861-1865, blockades prevented fabric availability, but Victorian fashion did find its way into wartime society beyond the military uniforms of the North and South. Jessica incorporated different fabrics and patterns into everyday styles as the town's dressmaker and seamstress. Wool, with very tight weaves that prevented fraying, and cotton was widely available during the Civil War and afterward. Most women's skirts and dresses were made of cotton, which adopted a shiny finish when steam ironed. Cotton jean cloth and muslin were also popular during this time and worn by both men and women, with military uniforms made of jean cloth when the Southern climate's heat made it too uncomfortable to wear woolens.

Jessica's business experienced a slight downturn between the lack of new fabrics and the customer trend to "make do" during wartime. She began to make children's clothing to subsidize lost revenues, finding that their mothers were encouraged to partake in their children's future as carrying on the family name and the town's history. With so many mature and young men involved in the war, women concentrated on what was left behind, determined to preserve it.

Jessica accepted orders for white cotton dresses that outfitted infants until about nine months. She had orders for toddler dresses with short waists and full skirts for girls until about the age of five or six, and a similar tunic style for boys until they were "breeched" (given their first pair of trousers). After breeching, Jessica had a healthy pile of orders for long pants, Knickerbockers (trousers that buckled below the knee), and various sack jackets. These sometimes had a belt as distinct to the full cut Zouave jackets (short, buttoned at the neck, with a braided trim) fashioned from the fabric used for their mothers' clothing, in the interests of economy and eliminating wastage. By ten years of age, boys looked like miniature adults, with their suits cut like their fathers' outfits. By the age of sixteen, they were considered full-grown men. The same applied to girls, with their first stage of dress reflecting shortened hemlines to reveal pantalettes or stiffened petticoats. She also had orders for paletots and capes for classic outerwear, which she taught Lottie to make. Dresses, covered with a delicate pinafore, echoed the layered skirts of their mother's fashions. By sixteen, hemlines dropped to two inches above the floor, signaling girls' passage into adulthood.

None of it was easy. There were always fears threatening to derail one's actions or plans; unexpected and random events sometimes succeeded. Determination is a difficult word to define as its complexion changes according to the challenge. Still, Jessica kept trying to maintain, preserve, rescue, help, and wait faithfully –with determination. 'This, too, shall pass,' she thought over and over again.

On her way back from making a delivery of finished clothing in town, Lottie scrounged the market for any inexpensive vegetables to supplement their meager supply. A Captain and his Corporal stayed at the house, and having to feed their bellies had depleted Jessica's carefully rationed supplies of foodstuffs. She saw Big Janey and waved. Big Janey dashed across the street to the Village Green to catch up to Lottie. Reaching behind her apron front, she fished out two sweet potatoes and two ears of corn, dropping them into Lottie's cloth sack.

"That why y'all got yo apron on inside out?" laughed Lottie.

"Sho' nuff, missy. Dat way I got me a big pocket what hides agin' my skirt! All da betta' ta nick a few dis'n' dat's when I sees 'em. Nobody knows, chile!" The corpulent woman laughed gleefully and rolled her eyes. "Y'all ax Miss Jess if'n y'all kin take two mo fokes by da weeken'. I come by ta pick apples dis Wensdy, so's y'all kin say yes or no ta me. Bye, chile!" Without giving Lottie a chance to explain that two officers stayed with them, Big Janey dashed off.

Just as Lottie was about a quarter of the way past Rice Lands' overgrown orchard of 100 trees, a hooded figure popped out into the road. Lottie squealed with surprise. "What you got there, Dotty Lottie?" the figure whined from behind her.

She recognized his voice. Lottie whirled around, saying, "Nuthin' concern y'all, Bert Frome! I kin smell y'all from here!"

The man slunk back a step or two. "I ain't drunk, Dotty Lottie, y'all gonna see! I got somepin' here for y'all," the bully said, clutching his crotch and leering. "Missed ya last time!"

"Dat so?" Lottie spat back at him, continuing her advance. "I sez y'all betta git, fore I cut off yer prick wif dis here knife and glue it to yer forehead," she said, waggling a hunting knife. "Den y'all gonna look like a limp-prick unicorn, ain't ya? Y'all not gonna be able to hurt mo' gals then! Now, git outta my way!" she yelled, swinging her sack with the potatoes and corn, which hit him in the head and knocked him down.

"I was jes foolin', Lottie, quit it!" the cowardly young man said. Lottie trotted away, reaching Rice Lands' house quickly. As she entered through the front door, Jessica noticed she was out of breath.

"Lottie! Are you all right? What's happened?" she asked with worry.

"Nuthin' much, oney dat drunk Bert Frome was lookin' to take my sack, so I brained him wit it 'stead n tole him ta git or Lottie'd cut off his prick wif dis!" she said, brandishing the knife.

Jessica erupted into laughter; in a few moments, Lottie joined her.

"I spose y'all gonna say I done a bad thing?" Lottie asked Jessica.

"No, sweet Lottie. No. You were brave, and you defended yourself, which took great courage after our awful encounter with him here. I'm just relieved you're all right." Jessica smiled and wrapped her arms around the petite young woman.

"Y'all spose God's mad at me?" Lottie asked innocently.

"Again, no," said Jessica, walking with her into the kitchen. "God doesn't judge us by the outcome of our actions. He judges us by what's in our hearts. And your heart is good, Lottie girl, your heart is good and brave! That Bert's a slow learner and a coward. He'll think twice before tangling with you or me again, I'm sure! He's just a bully, and bullies are cowards inside."

"Hmm, I guess I shoulda' called him a 'bully limp-prick unicorn' then, what y'all think, Miss Jess? Dat sounds like it fits 'em jes fine! Now I got some news from Big Janey," the young woman said, opening the sack on the kitchen table.

Chapter Seventeen
Bonjour la France

World War 1 Section

The crossing had been rough with several of the women getting seasick. On the contrary, Gertrude loved the seemingly endless ocean beckoning to her from the rail, its dark swells jostling the massive ship, a warning of the hidden power in its depths. Above, the sky was an endless blue to the limit of her sight, the only perspective provided by a few wispy cirrus clouds beyond the reach of the whipping wind.

"Nurse G, come inside. You'll catch your death out in that cold!" Sister Agnes MacPhearson held the door open with difficulty, and Gertrude carefully made her escape across the deck, her arms pinwheeling for balance.

"Thank you, mam, but isn't it glorious?" Red-faced and smiling, Gertrude breathlessly attempted to straighten her windblown hair.

"Sister" was not a nun, but a ranking official and socialite within the American Red Cross hierarchy in charge of their little group's transatlantic journey and assignment in Europe. Her preference for the term "sister" explained her commitment to the sisterhood of nurses dispatched to alleviate the suffering of the military and war-torn people of several countries during the Great War. Their posting was to be in France, the main venue for the United States' entry into the war.

Sister Agnes was indubitably in charge, dispensing orders with crisp and sharp direction to the small group of nurses in preparation for their assignment to establish a center to both treat wounded soldiers and support townspeople. Precisely *where* that center would be on the continent had not yet been shared with the little group of nurses. A socialite widow, Agnes lost her husband early in the war. She was now dedicating her life to the support of those in suffering of any description.

"Gather the girls to meet with me in C Deck Lounge in 15 minutes. Those still unwell may stay in their bunks, but they must choose one of you able to attend to take notes on their behalf. I will entertain no excuses for not knowing the content of our meeting because of a sick stomach! Off with you, now, girl."

Nodding her head and smiling to herself, Gertrude scurried below to the section where they quartered. The group of women had all become friends. They would learn from "Fearsome MacPhearson" that they were assigned to France in an area just southeast of some of the most severe battles undertaken over the last several months. Although the Allies had medics and some doctors available behind front lines, the swell of the wounded was beyond their ability to cope. Hence, small interim centers for treatment or temporary hospitals providing short-term care were dotted across the landscape to attend to the wounded. These soldiers were later evacuated to a proper facility or hospital for long-term care and/or return home. Their ship, shepherded by a warship, was under full steam, and they arrived at their destination excited if a bit strained from the long and unfamiliar crossing. She and the others intrepidly debarked, whispering among themselves, taking in the strange surroundings with wide eyes.

Clapping her hands from the dock at the bottom of the ramp, Sister MacPhearson said, "Hop to, Nurses! Claim your travel bags to the right." An Army truck with a canvas roof and sides was parked next to the porters unloading and stacking luggage, with a similar truck adjacent accepting cargo crates of supplies bearing the well-known Red Cross logo painted conspicuously on the sides. Finding their bags (they were allowed one suitcase and one handbag only), the nurses huddled standing at the rear of the truck. Slowly, the canvas rear side rolled upward, revealing a smiling soldier who kicked down the truck's tailgate, adeptly jumping to the ground. Running along each side of the interior were well-worn wooden benches.

"Private Johnson, at your service, ladies," he said with amusement, pointing into the truck while pulling a box into place for a stepstool. "Careful as you go," he said, extending a hand to each of them. The women all shared a glance, some rolling their eyes, others giggling, and boarded with not a little difficulty. So began the first day of a new adventure in fulfillment of their volunteered mission.

The nurses of WWI were a composite group of "angels" comprised of local European volunteers, military nurses, Red Cross nurses from international chapters of the organization, and a few groups of young society female volunteers. (Despite wanting to make a "significant contribution" to the war effort, this last group of privileged women lacked formal nursing training. They were overseen by Grand Dames from aristocratic circles mainly from Britain, but some from America.) Communication between the various contributing factions was meager to nonexistent. In most cases, individual regions, areas of function, supplies, and protection were under the direct supervision of the military commander for the relevant theater of operation. Most of the military nurses were posted to the hospitals or medical centers to which the wounded were transported from several front-line, interim receiving centers for more involved treatment, operations, and long-term care.

At the outbreak of WWI, the American Red Cross launched a unique appeal for funding a relief ship bound for Europe. Principles of neutrality and impartiality would govern personnel's mission onboard, which would provide medical aid to combat casualties on both sides of the war. As a result, the Hamburg-American line offered the German passenger steamship, *Hamburg*, free of charge to the Red Cross. This first ship, the SS Red Cross, known as "The Mercy Ship," was dispatched on September 12, 1914, to Europe with medical personnel (170 surgeons and nurses) and supplies aboard. Subsequent smaller voyages of personnel and supplies received funding from the ARC, the military (the country of sponsorship), or privately.

Gertrude's group was among these later dispatched groups with a mission to supplement nursing care to the already beleaguered combined complement of nurses serving in Europe. These groups responded to a call for nurses from Jane Delano, Head of the Red Cross Nursing Service. Requirements were that nurses had to be natural-born US citizens, complete a physical examination, be vaccinated against smallpox and typhoid, and agree to a six-month commitment. During the crossing, nurses attended surgeons' lectures on infectious diseases, anatomy, and field surgery. They practiced techniques, studied French and German, and kept fit through physical exercise. Many kept diaries, later to be historical sources of the initiative. While some returned home after six months, most teams stayed in place, particularly after President Woodrow Wilson officially declared war against Germany on April 6, 1917. This proclamation marked the dramatic transformation of the American Red Cross from a small organization with limited staff and insufficient funds to a massive and globally influential institution recognizable to the present day.

During and after America's entry into the Great War, the Red Cross gave women an unprecedented opportunity at home and abroad to demonstrate their patriotic spirit, stripping away preconceived notions of women in the public arena. Teams of three surgeons and 12 nurses offered emergency aid to each of the countries involved in the war, and with later additions, 16 units were provided with 350 surgeons and nurses participating. Seventeen Base Hospital Units (each supported by sixty-five Red Cross nurses) were sent to France alone, where the fighting raged the fiercest and longest.

The sites for hospital work had to be adapted and retrofitted, sometimes involving mansions, country estates, casinos, or bombed and abandoned large buildings. Despite the circumstances, nurses performed emergency work lasting many hours in poor conditions, treated infections, terrible wounds, mustard gas burns and exposure, and any number of severe war traumas. It was not only soldiers but nurses who experienced the horrors of war first-hand. Nurses not only treated casualties of war but gave their lives to save fallen soldiers on the battlefield. As the war ended in 1918, the American Red Cross faced another deadly issue: The influenza pandemic, which broke out in Europe in the final months of the Great War and spread throughout the world claiming an estimated 22 million lives globally, with approximately 500,000 in the United States.

The overall Red Cross effort in specific regard to the war effort ended after little more than a year due to insufficient funds. By the early 1920s, the American Red Cross withdrew its foreign commissions and most foreign workers from international service and closed overseas ARC chapters formed by Americans living abroad. During wartime activities, 400 ARC workers and approximately 296 nurses lost their lives from 1914-1921.

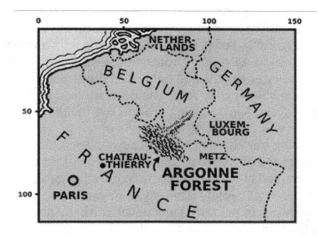

Sister MacPhearson and her team arrived at their posting in the late evening of the second day after they set foot on European soil. The town was northeast of Paris sufficiently close enough to the front to hear the infrequent distant boom of artillery and exploding shells.

Somewhat dismayed, the nurses filed out of the Army troop carrier truck, tired of travel, stiff, and rumpled. Before them towered a considerable stone, wood, and stucco mansion outside the small town, part of which crumbled from bomb damage. Incinerated vines and shrubs surrounded what once must have been a lovely setting. Three lone trees with some lingering leaves stood to the eastern side of the building where a broad expanse of overgrown lawn area, surrounded by a now burned and mostly dead but well-trimmed hedge, struggled to regenerate. What was once a large vegetable garden lay fallow on the north end of the house; a stone wall with a narrow walkway on the east end leading from the drive (obviously a delivery entry to the kitchen and back storage rooms), and the front circular drive boasted still-standing brass lanterns marking the path to the double front doors. While the women took in their destination or meandered around the structure, Fearsome MacPhearson directed the unloading of their baggage and supplies. She cast a brief but all-encompassing look at what their home and workplace would be for the duration of their stay.

"You there, Corporal or Private, whatever—we shall need to meet with your superior regarding the enlistment of some help here. I have the required paperwork and letters of introduction and authority. Please make the appropriate arrangements and send word to me tomorrow here. Dispatch a motorbike, or whatever you people do. I will have a list compiled of necessary supplies and inventory beyond what we've brought with us by tomorrow evening, so the meeting should occur no later than Wednesday at the outside. Now, you and your companion soldier may carry the bags and crates inside. Thank you very much," she said, walking around the building to gather her group together while surveying all aspects of the property.

Gathering her charges into a group on the entry path., Sister MacPhearson gazed at them for long moments before saying, "Nurses! We have arrived at what may seem a dismal place in your eyes. It is, indeed. As you will rapidly learn, I will never lie to you nor accept lies from you. More important, I will never shirk my duties nor allow any of you to do so. So, while this place looks sad and downright unaccommodating, we shall make it into a proper care center by the sweat of our brows and our commitment of spirit! Nothing is impossible to those who believe, remember that!

"I proclaim that this place shall be called "Mercy House," because that is what we shall dispense to the needy we care for and treat: mercy. Here they will find open arms with tender spirits upheld by backbones of steel. We shall immerse ourselves in the dilemmas of the time and come out the other end transported to another time and a better world. We *can* do it, and we *shall*! Never forget that! Remember, you are American Red Cross nurses!

"Now, before we enter Mercy House, I have assignments:

"Nurse G (Gertrude) and Nurse K (Katie) will go through the entire building, making a rough sketch of the existing rooms and layout, replete with the damage sustained by specific area or room. And ladies, I need measurements which will speak to repairs.

"Nurse M (Martha) and Nurse P (Paulette) will find the kitchen and related storage areas, inspect what remains and make a list of what is needed. Sort through any foodstuffs as well. I expect everything previously edible to end up as garbage. Be careful, check for rodents or other wildlife activity which should, if there is any, be most prevalent in your assigned area compared to other sectors of the house.

"Nurse B (Betty) and Nurse H (Helena) will find the utility areas and ascertain their condition—that will include if and how many lamps, light fixtures and lanterns remain, candles, kerosene, wicks, light bulbs, etc. I also want water samples taken, so locate our box of test tubes. Make a clear note of utility boxes, fuse sizes, water

pumps, and tanks, etc., and their locations with both a text description and a sketch. God may be merciful and show you a hand pump
as well—indoors or out, makes no difference.

"Nurse A (Alice) and Nurse D (Debra), inventory available furniture and list its location, condition, or repurpose value, as appropriate. This list will include any linens, towels, curtains, and the like—in
other words, anything of a fabric nature that might be usable.

"Nurse F (Felice) and Nurse C (Clare), list what remains of
cleaning implements and supplies, including such things as buckets,
ladders, and any tools. I want the attic checked as well. You shall need
to check if there are any work sheds outside. Also, note and check
the fireplaces for blockages or soot buildup. Light some paper to
check the draw, but make it small so you can stamp it out if there is
any problem.

"Nurse L (Lydia) and Nurse R (Rebecca), you are to begin the
unpacking and segregation of our supplies by category and label.
Please choose one of the first-floor rooms, not the reception hall,
even though it is of significant size. We shall need that area clear to
allow movement and placement of repair supplies, as a central holding area, and a potential workplace the spec of which has yet to be
determined.

"You all have flashlights, notebooks, and pencils. Make use
of them. Nurses G and C, we will find you something to which you
can transfer your notations on a larger scale. Leave that to me for
now. If you complete these assigned tasks, you will report to Nurses
L and R and assist with the unpacking. Are we clear? Any questions?"
MacPhearson waited for a response and, receiving none, gave the
signal to send the women about their tasks.

Sister Agnes MacPhearson sat on one of the staircase's broad
steps that connected the cavernous reception area with the sec-
ond-floor balcony, off which various rooms fed in a full "U" shape.
She bowed her head in prayer and contemplation. Then she raised
eyes burning with passion and thought to herself, 'If we lose today,
we must have faith that we will win tomorrow. God be with us!'

Chapter Eighteen
Retrofit

Wohen the going gets tough...
The tough get going.

The small complement of American Red Cross nurses reported back two by two in dribs and drabs over the next several hours. Each team presented their assessment to the group, with general discussion following. Those with specific experience or exposure garnered an appointment by Sister MacPhearson to oversee a particular area on a trial basis. MacPhearson's temporary assignments were made with a review to follow after each had some time to prove themselves appropriate for the job assumed. Initially, she identified what she considered "static" needs. These would have to be addressed in tandem with the primary role to dispense treatment and care, with only a few exceptions.

For instance, Nurse M (Martha) raised her younger siblings during her mother's ten-year illness and was proficient at stretching food ingredients and making palatable meals out of next to nothing. MacPhearson assigned her as the Cook for Mercy House.

Nurse F's (Felice) father was a building contractor. Even though female, she spent summers employed as a carpenter's assistant, learning elements of the trade, and helping with rough carpentry. Sister MacPhearson assigned her to the planning of repairs and the preliminary list of needed materials. Later, Nurse F would oversee work performed by outside help secured. Nurse F would ensure that all scrap wood would be utilized for cooking and fireplaces and continuously replenish woodpiles from all sources available. Nurses with spare capacity would help her with this last but critical, ongoing task.

Nurse H (Helena) put herself through nursing school by

working in a factory shipping department. Her large frame and personal strength were an appropriate match with her organizational skill set to oversee Mercy House's inventory, storage of boxes and crates, and replacement of overall supplies.

The petite and sweet-tempered Nurse P (Paulette) was the perfect candidate for the reception area, which required patience, calming explanations, and efficient handling of both patients and townspeople. She would make patient allocations to nurses, as well as supervise triage.

Nurse C (Clare) was an adept seamstress, learning the trade from an early age in her mother's shop. She had fashioned many of her friends' outfits at home. She was entrusted with the repurpose of any cloth, curtains, sheeting, cotton linen, and the like for use in Mercy House, either as pieced bed coverings, spare bandages or treatment material, sheeting for the nurses or patients, treatment and surgical gowns, or privacy screens, etc.. Nurse R (Rebecca) would assist Nurse C and garner whatever she could from town folk donation, large or small, for combined repurposing. This ongoing need would prove beneficial to everyone, given the ever-present need for hygiene and sterile conditions.

The fussy Nurse D (Debra) and her close friend, Nurse K (Katie), were put in charge of laundry detail, including ironing. MacPhearson believed the repetitive and thankless but necessary tasks would be made possible because of the constant chatter between the two friends, underscored by their concern with appearances.

Nurse B (Betty), whose employment history included clerical work, was designated as the secretary and bookkeeper for Mercy House in charge of all records, including patient profiles. She was a quiet woman content with her own company, close-lipped, and a consistently efficient worker. MacPhearson considered her ideal for the role, which would inevitably involve confidential information.

Mercy House would require someone to oversee general housekeeping to maintain the premises. The nurses would be involved in treatment and care once the site was operational. To manage this ongoing task and the rotation schedule of each nurse's participation, she assigned Nurses L (Lydia) and A (Alice). The later distinction between general quarters and treatment and/or operating theaters would be made with alternating obligation only once the premises were refitted and thoroughly cleaned. Since Mercy House was too large a building to be maintained by only two individuals who also had nursing duties, the women were responsible for cleaning their personal spaces. They would volunteer their free time for housekeeping through Nurses L or A.

Those responsibilities assigned, MacPhearson turned her attention to Nurse G (Gertrude). "Your father was a boat captain, and from what you told me on the boat voyage, you spent every summer and spare moment aboard with him. You are used to dealing with people from your years of contracting work for loading/unloading with the stevedores, bookings for client passage, and relationships with your father's business clients. You may have thought of those years as a lark, or perhaps just a way to help your father and the family. Still, I believe it was an invaluable experience that I intend to use in this situation. What's more, your mother, Lizzie, although a tiny woman, is reputed to be a 'force to be reckoned with,' as she was the minister's 'right hand' through these difficult times. I think some of that undauntable spirit may have rubbed off on you, Nurse G.

"Therefore, you are in charge of all relations with the military and the townspeople concerning Mercy House. That means you get them to cooperate with us in all things, from supplies to workers, spares, transportation, equipment, etc. We are to be under the general but loose supervision of the military's medical division, so we need them to support our operation, even though they are stretched thin. Our contribution will ease their position, but we must be equipped to do so, understand? Browbeat them if you have to, using me only as a last resort." Gertrude swallowed hard. This was a critical task for which she hoped she was capable. The ultimate function of Mercy House would depend on her attainment of the goals set by Sister MacPhearson.

"Insofar as the rest of you, these duties will be continuing for as long as we are here. Changes will occur as I deem necessary for suitability or lack of performance. Only Nurses F, C, and R will have spare capacity once their initial tasks are complete since Nurses C and R will not have significant repurposing sewing after the initial thrust. Nurse F will free up after construction, and repair is completed. Thus, any of you requiring assistance in your particular area should address it with me. I will get you help from one of the floaters or another department with a light load.

"Martha– Nurse M-- you may need help with potato peeling or vegetable prep, whatever, mainly as mouths to feed increases. Maybe it is only to wash and dry dishes or pots. I expect all of you nurses to offer to help others where and when you can. Nurse B will help me keep track of your individual and team progress in the short term and manage any critical requests or problems.

"However, when we are in full operation, I expect all of you to bolster Nurse M with food prep and feeding detail, and Nurses D and K with the laundry detail. Hygiene and sterile dressings will be of the utmost importance, and our soiling percentages will be high. The job is more than the two of them will be able to manage, as they have general laundry to do. You will be responsible for the launder of your personal items. Only uniforms and aprons will go to the laundry area at the back of the house. You must, therefore, either embroider or sew a handmade label onto your items for identification. Get Nurse C to advise you about this.

"Lastly, everyone will report directly to me following the weekly schedule Nurse B will compile. If there is something you deem immediately important, let Nurse B know. She will determine if I can see you without an appointment. When I am necessarily away to meet with the ARC Foreign Commission or another outpost's Director, Nurses B and G will be in charge. They will work together to ensure Mercy House runs like a top. You will continue with your duties until otherwise notified, giving primary importance to patient care and doctoral assistance as and when they begin to flow. Questions?"

The complement of nurses was dead quiet, each contemplating the various elements of their future as outlined by their Director, Sister Agnes MacPhearson, aka "Fearsome MacPhearson."

'She's well-named,' Gertrude thought to herself, wondering if the Red Cross knew what a treasure and *tour de force* they had in her.

At first, Gertrude was intrepid when meeting with various military personnel. When she realized she was given the runaround, she gritted her teeth and adopted a completely different approach. As a result of her tenacity, creativeness, and innate charm, Gertrude was introduced to a young officer assigned as liaison between Mercy House and the central medical divisional headquarters.

"Captain Edward Perry at your disposal, Miss," said a tall, dark-haired man in a crisp uniform, albeit his boots were slightly muddy indicating he was not exclusively a desk jockey.

Smiling, Gertrude nodded at the introduction, "Ah, Captain Perry. Thank you for coming so quickly. General Smythe said he would sort something out for us, but I thought I would be waiting far longer than this. But here you are!"

"Yes, Miss...?" he said, hesitating long enough for her to supply her name.

"I'm Nurse G of Mercy House. You may call me Gertrude, but not in front of the other nurses or our Director if you please. I expect we'll be working a lot together, so it seems only sensible to dispense with formality unless in that specific company. Do you agree?"

"Yes, Nurse G; understood. Now, I suggest you tell me what it is you need from us. May I suggest we do that over a cup of coffee in the Common Room? I haven't had a break all morning and could use some caffeine to fortify me for the rest of the day."

They spent the better part of two hours discussing Gertrude's list, which entailed the sketches she and Nurse Katie had drawn with measurements. They also covered the topics of Nurses Felice and Clare's spare listing of tools and the state of the fireplaces, the available furniture versus needed items (that Nurses Alice and Debra listed), and concerns over utilities like water supply and pressure, electricity, kerosene, and light bulbs (highlighted by Nurses Helena and Betty's assessment).

"I'm thinking as a first course that the right rear of the house needs to be stabilized and rebuilt in part. So, we need wood— here's the list—and workers, preferably men who know a bit about carpentry and structure. Uh, I suppose I should tell you they'd be working with one of our nurses who was a carpenter before... before she was a nurse." Smiling, the Captain nodded.

Continuing, Gertrude pointed to the next item. "The most expensive and difficult to find of the items would likely be window replacement, but I may have a solution. I spoke with the local rector of the bombed-out church, which has only a few walls standing. After the church bombing, only some of the stained-glass windows remained. Some of the glass is only in pieces, but I think we could use them for the upstairs parlor room on the east end. No lights are needed during the daytime if we replace the missing glass. The stained glass will prevent clear visibility into the room after dark, even with a lamp or two lit. Neither of us could afford to repair that wall with plate glass panels or windows, but the rector said I could have the stained glass if I did the salvage. If you can rustle up some epoxy or silicone gel tubes, I can mobilize the nurses to help me salvage the glass. Your guys who deliver the wood could go back with the flatbed to help us load the larger glass windows still standing in the church. Their frames appear stable and might require only some stabilizing. Then all we'd need is an overall framework to fit the space with some vertical support pieces. It could work!"

Captain Perry pulled a face. "It's just that it's the only place we will have to relax for a bit or have a meeting other than sitting on the staircase steps. I think it's important to make it cozy and relaxing to unwind. A solid wooden wall would make it seem like a dark cave, and that wouldn't achieve what we need it to be for our mental health. Come on, it's not that big a thing, and it would have a great positive impact," Gertrude wheedled, "to refresh the nurses and, therefore, the benefit of the soldiers they treat! I can see you agree with me, right?

"We could also use an initial workforce to carry and redistribute functional furniture. We've got some good ideas for reusing several items, which I'll show you once the pieces are moved down to the reception area and workroom.

"I shall leave it up to you whether we ask the Army to supply us with about 13 beds and mattresses or use the beds left in the eight bedrooms. Only most of them need cross planks to support the mattresses. Of course, I wouldn't refuse newer mattresses," she said, continuing when she saw his frown, "but we can figure out how to re-stuff the leftover ones, I'm sure. I think people used the wood to board up the place or for firewood in the end days. The frames are sturdy enough, and we can put two nurses in each room, with one room for the Director alone. That leaves one place for a visiting doctor or dignitary.

"I also need these water samples tested and a few purifying kits, just in case. If you have anyone familiar with electricity, we need one desperately, oh, and here's the list of light bulbs we need as starters. Candles and kerosene lanterns are good for backup but won't work long term or for treatments or emergency operations. I don't suppose you have an old sterilizing unit sitting around anywhere in storage. Of course, I'd happily take a new one, but…"

"Whoa, easy there, Gertrude. I'll do what I can, but I'm not sure I can make the whole list. Men, I've got. My group of guys are all from the Cavalry Division and chomping at the bit to do anything besides carry messages back and forth and use the horses for relocating artillery or transporting shells and other supplies. We haven't been involved in any of the real fighting, and the boys are itchy, so I can get you a good lot of them to help with whatever you need when we're freed up from routine tasks. But equipment like a sterilizer is another matter."

"Well, we'll leave that for now. We found a huge copper tub we can use in the meantime, but we need your men to build a fire-proof platform for it outside. I believe it was used for cheese-making in its former life. I'm thinking just outside the kitchen somewhere near the vegetable plots would be a good place, and they could use the stone littering the east yard for the platform. It all fell when the house caught a bomb, and it's more expedient to use wood to rebuild that corner than to get a stonemason, right?"

"On the face of it, I agree. But I'll have to see about the availability of the wood supplies needed. Are you certain this list covers the job?"

"Well, more or less it does, but I'd build in a bit extra. You could recheck it with your building guy or carpenter when you come to carry the furniture and help us clear out the place. As a suggestion, you might need a truck to carry away the refuse. We'll keep whatever we can reuse or refashion and burn some of the rest for fueling the cookstove and fireplaces for heat. But there's bound to be a pile of refuse. The place is really a mess!"

"You've got it all figured out, huh?" the Captain said with amusement.

"Listen, I've only just begun. But I think this is enough to keep you busy for a bit. I'll come by on Friday for an update. Meantime, thank you for your time and the coffee, Captain Perry. Any chance I could get a tin to take to Mercy House? We're sleeping on the floors at the moment, and there's only weak tea available. A good strong cup of coffee in the morning would go a long way to mobilize activities."

"Sure, wait here. I'll get you some," Captain Perry said affably, realizing that this group of women was living 'rough' because of the state of their posting, and in a foreign country, to boot!

"Oh, and Captain, some milk and sugar, too, yes?" she asked, showing her dimples in a lovely smile.

The nurses were excited about the promised arrival of the extra workforce Nurse G shared with them after meeting with Captain Perry. They struggled to remove debris, sweep, wash down walls, floors, and ceilings, secure open areas, and address the seemingly endless list of necessary tasks. They were generally depressed by the small progress made in turning Mercy House into a workable medical outpost, despite the constant encouragement of Sister MacPhearson. Their only refuge was with bowls of vegetable soup and cups of weak tea around the large table in the scrupulously clean kitchen kept by Nurse Martha.

"I can't figure out if my back aches from more from sleeping on the cold, hard floor or from the heavy physical work we're doing," complained Alice. "When I signed up with the American Red Cross, I didn't think it was for something like this, to be sure!"

"Well, my nana used to say, 'There's nothing a bar of Ivory soap and some hot water can't make right,'" quipped Lydia. "If only we had some good old Ivory soap!" Everyone, including Nurse A, laughed, lapsing into silence, thinking of home.

"I, for one, feel guilty that we seem ages away from providing the service we made this journey to give. All I can think about are those poor, wounded soldiers in filth and lacking proper treatment! War just doesn't make any sense to me; everyone loses, and for what? A small piece of ground? Even those lines keep changing back and forth," Rebecca opined.

"You know very well it's for more than gaining ground," countered Paulette, in her soft, Southern drawl. "It's all about freedom, a way of life, and undoing all the evil perpetrated against other countries. First, it's countries, and then it's the whole world, so it has to stop!"

"That's ripe, coming from a Confederate Southerner! It's only been a little over 50 years since the Civil War ended. That was all about 'freedom,' too. It tore our country apart, just like this war is doing—tearing the world apart." Helena argued.

"What a hateful thing to say," retorted Paulette. "Why, my people didn't have slaves and didn't believe in slavery. Not all Southerners were slavers, you know. Most of the South wasn't! We were only plain folks living under whatever system prevailed at the time. And many of our men fought against slavery by joining the Union Army. That war truly divided families. The Civil War wasn't just about slavery, but about politics, representation, and the economy, too. Get your facts straight, girl!"

"Now, now, ladies, calm down," said Sister MacPhearson. "We are all bone tired and short-tempered. Here we are in the

224

midst of a world war arguing about a fight over 50 years ago! That war took its toll on our country for around four years, yes. And it looks like this one, which began in 1914, will go at least as long. Maybe it's a cycle; I don't know. But what I do know is that war has an end for a variety of reasons. Hear me; it *ends*... eventually.

"I can remember my father, the senator, quoting Alexis De Tocqueville: 'The evil that one endures patiently because it seems inevitable becomes unbearable the moment its elimination becomes conceivable.' It is conceivable that this war and its evil will end now that America is involved in bolstering the Europeans' spirit and forces.

"We, too, shall do our part knowing that this war will end, just like all the others. But in the meantime, we will fulfill our mission and take care of the wounded, be they soldiers or townspeople in need. We must be the Red Cross angels of Mercy House. Now, I suggest we all retire to our pallets. A new day dawns tomorrow, and it will be full of promise and accomplishment. You'll see." With that encouragement, Sister MacPhearson rose and walked from the kitchen.

Temporarily mollified, the nurses cleared the table and washed up, slowly mounting the broad staircase to their rooms and a night of cold, fitful sleep.

$$+$$

The trucks arrived loaded with a contingent of men on Monday, just four days after Gertrude's visit to the military offices and her meeting with Captain Perry. Dressed for work, the soldiers leaped off the trucks carrying a variety of tools and canteens. They unloaded two wheelbarrows, cartons of canned food, coffee, sugar, flour, salt, and other edibles, as well as a stack of eight thin but newish mattresses lined up along the sides and back of the transport vehicle. In the second truck was an impressive amount of fresh lumber and stout posts; bags of cement, stone, and nails; containers of paint with a bucket stuffed with brushes; ladders; and other crates with sundry hardware, equipment, and materials that they might employ in refits of every description.

"We brought everything but the kitchen sink—anything and everything we could lay our hands on," a grinning Captain Perry announced to the gaggle of wide-eyed nurses who had gathered on the front steps and the front walk. Sister Agnes MacPhearson made her way through the nurses.

"Welcome, Captain, and thank you for fulfilling my promise to our nurses!" She turned briefly to them, saying, "I told you all that today would be full of promise and accomplishment, didn't I?" With satisfaction, she snapped her fingers for Gertrude to come to her side.

"See to these good men, Nurse G. You and Nurse F will oversee the work parties. Nurses! The rest of you do whatever you can to help and follow Nurse G's instructions to the letter, setting aside your other tasks for the moment. Nurse F choose two nurses--whomever you like-- to assist you, but first take the Captain upstairs to the East Parlor, so he knows what he's up against. The rest is up to you.

"Nurse M prepare lunch with pots and pitchers of tea. Nurse A set the table; we have guests! Then help Nurse M with lunch preparation. I'm sure these men are going to work up a thirst and an appetite! I shall be in my office if anyone needs me." A smug, happy, Fearsome MacPhearson turned on her heel and strode back into Mercy House.

After a brief word with Nurse G, Captain Perry mobilized his men to cart the supplies into the house and then joined Nurse F to assess the upstairs East Parlor, accompanied by two of his men familiar with carpentry and construction. Two others, each taking a wheelbarrow with a sack of cement, small stone in burlap sacks, bucket, and tools, walked around the house to the east to collect rubble and assess the littered stone (for possible reuse) that had fallen from the building's façade when the bomb struck. Under Nurse G's direction, two soldiers removed broken or discarded furniture to the side of the truck, loading unusable debris into its bed. While they occupied themselves with clearing out, Gertrude supervised four soldiers to lift and carry good furniture to the appropriate spaces. She instructed the men to move other pieces to the western reception rooms (a holding area for the remainder). The remaining soldier helped Nurses M and A carry the cartons of food to the kitchen. The entirety of Mercy House was a beehive of activity.

Nurse B scribbled notes in her journal as she followed Captain Perry and Nurse F, recording their comments about plans, supplies, and timing.

Nurse R took the soldier who had finished carrying food supplies with her to survey the stained glass pile the nurses had gathered from the church grounds. He claimed to be a painter by trade, an artist by desire and talent. "A man's got to eat, you know?" he said to her. She showed him what Gertrude viewed as "treasure," which lay on the floor in one of the downstairs reception rooms (later designated as a patient ward) on a sheet in a random pattern, much like a jigsaw puzzle.

"This is ancient glass, you know?" he said appreciatively. "Just look at the depth of color! Yeah, I think this will work, but is it all you've got?" he asked Rebecca.

"Oh, no, there are two more pretty big windows, just standing by themselves in what's left of a stone wall. They're in a frame, but the wood's rotten or damaged in places, and it's just a matter of time before the whole lot comes crashing down in a stiff wind or the shaking ground from shell fire. We couldn't figure out a way to safely remove them, and we have no way to transport them here."

"Jimmy to the rescue," he said. "Give me a minute, and I'll grab my buddy. You can show me where the place is," Jimmy said to Nurse R, "I've got to check with the Cap, but I'll be back in a jiff." The man ran into the house and, in a few minutes, came out accompanied by another soldier. "Ok, lead on, Nurse R," he said, helping her into the front seat of the troop carrier.

Gertrude explained to Captain Perry, whose name was Edward, what she thought could be done with some of the damaged furniture piled by the delivery truck.

"If one of your clever fellows can figure out a way to do it, I think these small side tables can be put together to make a seat... a chair with a back on a frame if you will. Then these wheels could be mounted and make it a rolling chair... a wheelchair, get it? We have no hope of getting a proper wheelchair here so we can make our own! Our seamstress could fashion a cushioned cover for it, and so long as it had a handle..."

"Why couldn't we take this bar handle off this broken serving cart and use it for the chair?" asked Captain Perry.

His fellow soldier nodded, saying, "I think there's also some casters in one of those crates we brought. They'd be a whole lot better for something the size of a chair, no?"

"That's the spirit!" beamed Gertrude. "We have to be creative! My mother always said, 'When in doubt, improvise! Use the brains the good Lord gave you.' she'd say to my brother and me when we were stumped by something. 'With the presence of mind, you can notice more, let go and use everything at any moment and in any context.'[35] I can hear her like it was yesterday. So, we've got to improvise here with everything we do. We can make it work! Now, I've got another idea: making a rolling stretcher from those wheels I mentioned and a larger table. It's inside; come with me." Gertrude's enthusiasm was infectious, witnessed by the two grinning soldiers who followed closely on her heels into Mercy House.

Everyone shared lunchtime with the men seated at the huge table. The nurses perched on the worktable and counters, a few of them standing and getting odds and ends or refills. The morning's work was amazingly productive. With the rooms cleared of broken or unusable furniture, the nurses got all of the upstairs bedrooms thoroughly cleaned the mattresses in place, and beds made. The lift they got from the promise of a comfortable night's sleep was noticeable. They cannibalized the stack of irretrievably broken furniture for usable parts; the rest the men reduced to ideal-sized firewood for the cookstove and fireplaces. Only bent or unusable items were put into the truck bed as refuse.

The power lines were intact, but there was an interruption in supply, likely from damage sustained in the town. The electricians could work with the townspeople, but the matter had to clear with their commanding officer, who would go through proper channels with town officials. In the interim, kerosene lamps and lanterns supplemented by candles would provide sufficient nighttime illumination, particularly with the extra supplies brought by the soldiers. In addition to boxes of light bulbs (for when they restored electric power), they brought some high-powered spotlights which would work satisfactorily in treatment and operating rooms.

"All we need is some electricity, the completion of the east side re-build, exam tables, a rolling stretcher, and cots for the wounded," theorized Betty, sipping her morning coffee, making a list in her notebook.

"We'll have that rolling stretcher in no time," Gert advised. "Lenny said he could make it out of that big table from the downstairs parlor using those spare wheels. He'll just have to make the legs longer on one end to account for the two smaller wheels, but the bicycle wheels will control the roll and make it easy to move and turn. He'll do it when he's here again."

"I expect you'll have to make another visit to the command-

---

35 Written by Jeff Thoren, DVM, BCC, PCC, and Trey Cutler, JD.

er, Nurse G," said Sister MacPhearson. "If they can't get us proper single beds, we can make do with cots. Surely, the Army has enough of those to spare several for us!"

"How many do you think we'll need?" inquired Sister B.

"I daresay at least 25 to start, but I'd like to have more readily available."

"I've been thinking, Sister," said Nurse G. "You know how that sliding pocket door separates the two, big, front rooms? Why couldn't we set both of those up as wards, with one closest to the treatment rooms across the reception area for the more serious cases and the other beyond the doors for recuperating, stable cases awaiting transfer? That way, they'd be close to the French Doors, and we could wheel them out to the patio for some Vitamin D and fresh air. The two wards would be separated, but available to us nurses, making care details a bit less confused."

"Good, I like that," said MacPhearson. "Make it so. But you *must* get us those cots, Nurse G. Of course, beds would be best, but beggars can't be choosers. Head Office has already refused me for them. Those boys deserve to be treated and get well in a bed; I won't have them lying on the floor!"

"I second that! Can you imagine how hard it would be to treat anyone lying on the floor?" said Nurse A. "I can just feel my back complaining about the thought of doing that!"

"They're here!" the sing-song voice of Paulette announced. "Let's go, girls. Breakfast is officially over!"

It was 7:00 AM when the roar of truck engines swept into the driveway. Most of the same men as had worked before returned to finish their respective projects. However, Captain Perry received a dispensation to include six additional men from his division. Half of these, he assigned to the rebuilding of the eastern side of the second story, the other half to chopping, sawing, and stacking wood into cords along both the east and northern sides of the house. The front reception hall was assigned for rebuilt furniture and construction of shelving units for use in the kitchen, storage, and treatment rooms. He had also requisitioned around 25 metal footlockers, which would serve well for stored items. Nurses M and H were elated. "Rodents and insects be damned!" Nurse H said with a pleased smile.

Two paint crews attacked the upstairs bedrooms—one for ceilings, the other for walls. By lunchtime, with half the bedrooms freshly painted (the remainder completed just as it turned dark), Captain Perry asked the nurses to gather on the staircase. He was almost ingratiating in his treatment of Sister MacPhearson, concerned that she would resist him taking charge of even the few small moments he planned.

"Now, ladies, first, we men would like to thank all of you for your considerable help and expertise. There's no way we could have done all that we've accomplished together without you. We've been a great team! Hip, hip…" called out the Captain, answered by a resounding "Hooray!" from all the soldiers.

"Next, we'd like to give these to Nurse M for putting up with us in her kitchen and filling our stomachs so well." A soldier dashed forward to present Nurse M with a bouquet—all wildflowers and weed greens.

"We couldn't get proper flowers, but there's some wild daisies and brown-eyed Susan's in there that I found for you," said the giant Morton, extending the bunched flowers to Nurse M. She immediately blushed, murmured a thank you, and put her nose to the bouquet, followed by a loud sneeze.

"You jerk, Morton, I told you not to put that ragweed in," chided his buddy, Joe.

"The beautiful, sunny yellow is worth a sneeze," the embarrassed Nurse M said, smiling. When everyone finished chuckling and whispering, Captain Perry went on.

"Finally, we'd like to ask Sister MacPhearson to indulge us and close her eyes." A flustered Sister Agnes complied, and Captain Perry and Corporal Jones took each of her arms to help her climb the staircase to the landing. "You can open your eyes now," said Corporal Jones.

Sister Agnes MacPhearson gasped as each soldier opened his French Door to her office and bedroom area. The room was transformed.

What once was only a large bedroom with a single-entry door was now a room with entry glass-paneled French Doors (cribbed from one of the downstairs rooms), a proper desk, chair, curtains at the three large windows, wall shelving, and a somewhat threadbare rug on the floor, but a carpet! On the opposite side of the room, a ¾ wall separated the office's sleeping space, its window curtained to match the bed quilt, and sliding curtains suspended from the wall hiding shelves and hanging space. On the wall facing the bed's foot hung a hand-hewn cross with a shelf table and candle centered beneath the cross. Sister Agnes' Bible and personal books lined the shelf. A bench made from a repurposed side table was under the window, it's cushion in a complementary fabric.

"Oh, my stars! This is wonderful! How can I ever thank you, soldiers, and nurses, alike!"

"It was the nurses' idea; we just helped make it happen. But I got to tell 'ya; Nurse G is one slave driver with ideas nonstop how to do this 'n' that, and Nurse B kept on at us all the time to keep the secret. The only thing we could get her to say was, 'Keep those lips buttoned!' Kinda' like bein' at home, you know?" Private Jimmy Burgess recounted. "But she's the one kept you outta here runnin' round to check all the work parties!"

Sister MacPhearson gave the combined group a big smile and blew kisses all around.

"Well, everyone, we've got a surprise!" Nurse M announced. "Although none of us ever thought that two full days of work would get all this done, well, mostly everything is done, we decided that we would have our celebration dinner tonight. Gert – I mean, Nurse G—got clearance from the commander, so you don't have to worry about getting back on time within reason. Nurse R got some sausages from the butcher in town, I've made rolls, and Nurses H, C, L, and K scared up onions, tomatoes, and peppers by bartering in the town. So, we've got a feast for all of us to share just like at home!"

"And our precious Nurse M made a cake, too!" said the petite Paulette, "And I made you boys my special Southern frosting or, well kind of, since we don't have *all* the ingredients!"

Everyone piled down the staircase to the kitchen, chatting amiably, laughing, rubbing elbows, and giving jibes in good-natured teasing. It was a special moment of unity and accomplishment, a happy camaraderie amid the horror of war, a memory each would cherish for the rest of their lives.

During the relative quiet after the meal, Nurse G said to the group of soldiers, "So, boys, when do you think you'll be able to come back and do that stained-glass window in the new east parlor wall? It has to be finished before cold weather, remember." Ignoring the catcalls, complaints, and groans, she said, "There's a bit of this sheet cake left. Who wants it?" Her dimpled smile smoothed away the moment, as the soldiers vied for the last squares of Nurse Martha's delicious Pennsylvania Dutch sheet cake with Paulette's icing.

"Pretty smooth move, Gert," Captain Perry whispered, accepting two plates of cake to deliver to his men. Some nurses launched into a chorus of "Pack Up Your Troubles in Your Old Kit Bag and Smile, Smile, Smile," and the men joined in.

"Oh, you think so. Well, you ain't seen nuthin' yet, Cap!"

Chapter Nineteen
Initiative

With the completion of Mercy House, the nurses prepared for an inspection from one of the U. S. Army doctors assigned to the front in their area, Paul Simons, MD. Sister MacPhearson already had discussions with him, and both believed an assessment visit was in order.

"I'm gratified that you ladies have transformed this building into a workable health and treatment center. Frankly, although some of your methods are unusual, if not unique, they will work. Anything is better than conditions at the front.

"Hygiene and sanitation are nonexistent in the midst of war. Close quarters in trenches or medical tents make it virtually impossible to sustain any high degree of antiseptic treatment. All too often, the medics must use emergency measures merely to stem a bleed out, and the wound site is not thoroughly cleaned, much less are the medic's hands sterile. But when a soldier's life is on the line, one does his utmost to save that life with the knowledge that appropriate treatment, operation, or dealing with the likelihood of infection must be set aside for another day and another medical person or team. Expediency is uppermost under poor conditions and supplies. We deal with what we have, and do the best we can. It is not enough in most cases. But the situation demands that we set aside our expectations and devote our abilities with improvisation to save as many lives as possible, easing the state of those we cannot help. It's a terrible reality to have to take those decisions based upon the overall good.

"I envision that we will send you those identified as men who have a chance to survive. Clean them up, treat them here, and --when they can sustain the trip—send them on to whatever hospital or center that can take them. Those arrangements and assessments will be up to you with some, but probably also with infrequent support from our doctors' team for others. I will arrange for one of us to make an assessment visit here as and when possible. I'll rely on your advice for scheduling one of us to come to do critical-need operations. It all depends on the activity at the front, military initiatives, and the damage the enemy inflicts on our troops. But, even a few days here to treat the men we send you will be a break for my guys and seem like a vacation if nothing more than relief from the constant noise and stink of the front. You can get messages to me through the cavalry division's dispatches, and we will use the same method for transmission to you. Questions?"

The exhausted and harried doctor left after concluding business and his thorough inspection of the premises. The nurses, filled with pride and expectation, were left feeling a mix of apprehension and disregard for their potential contribution.

"He made us sound like a half-ass 'tea stop' for the soldiers," complained Helena. "Everything here is clean and ready for our men's treatment, and we are much more than an insignificant 'stop along the way' to the hospital! Ok, we don't have a proper wheelchair, gurney, operating table, or sterilizer! But neither does he or his team at the front!'"

Her head hanging, even the cheery Paulette said, "I think he was disappointed."

Sister Agnes clapped her hands. "Enough! Whether or not Dr. Simons acknowledged our efforts enough to suit us does not matter a tinker's damn! We've done well, nurses, and we will continue to do well! Keep that thought uppermost.

"Remember, that man never gets any relief from all the trauma and death he deals with all day, every day. All of it is close to the jarring noise of warfare. I expect he's on the brink of collapse himself, emotionally, if not physically. None of us has had to deal with any of that. Our job is to accept our boys, improve their condition, treat them as best we can, and send them on as soon as possible for long-term care. Once we begin, we can expect a steady stream, I am sure. Our first arrivals should be coming by tomorrow, so ready yourselves and knock back any last-minute details. You, nurses, will be the first relief any of the wounded has seen for who knows how long. Soothe their spirits, calm their fears, be patient and encouraging. It will give them the courage to carry on. Good luck and God be with us all," said Sister MacPhearson. "Remember who you are—you are American Red Cross nurses-- 'A balm in Gilead,' as it says in the Bible!"

Halfway up the staircase to her office, Sister MacPhearson turned to Paulette's call, the shock and worry evident in her voice. "Sister, it's begun; there's a stream coming in!"

A complement of nurses dashed out the front door carrying three stretchers. A further group readied the two gurneys and wheelchair in the reception hall. The nurses assigned to treatment rooms stood at the ready in their respective doorways. Sister MacPhearson stationed herself just inside the front doors. She signed incoming paperwork and walked among those waiting in reception room chairs (former dining room chairs covered with sheeting) to ask questions, make initial assessments, and give assurances.

Paulette assisted Sister Agnes, controlled the ebb and flow from the treatment rooms, made nursing assignments, entered everything into the log, and initialized a patient form with as many details as possible. This patient profile was passed on to the patient's assigned nurse, ultimately hanging at his bed's foot in the ward for further additions and records.

In less than an hour, eight wounded soldiers in varying conditions had been unloaded, examined, bathed, received initial treatment and fresh bandages, and moved to a bed in the ward to await further treatment and assessment.

Their uniforms—depending upon condition—were wheeled to the laundry for a boiling wash, ironing, and storage (on the refurbished former drinks cart fitted with a drawstring bag beneath, tray on top to hold boots, and a basket for personal effects).

Thanks to their practiced procedures, all went like clockwork for admission and initial treatment. That was when the real work began.

Sitting together over the evening's bowl of stew, the nurses not on duty in the ward were unusually quiet. Looking around the table, Gertrude said to no one in particular, "I think we performed pretty well today. It seems like most of those who came to us have a decent chance, don't you think?"

"Yeah," answered Katie, "except for that poor guy who lost his arm. I'm not sure the doctors will be able to save that eye, either."

"I'm worried about that redheaded guy who doesn't talk. He looks like he's still in shock or some kind of a mental depressive state." Lydia remarked worriedly. "I even tried singing to him, but nothing works to break that stare."

"Maybe you ought to leave off with the singing," quipped Debra, teasing. Good-naturedly, everyone chuckled, which slightly alleviated the seriousness of the day's events.

"Thank God for those military cots! I think we'll need double the amount we have. Any chance you can get more, Gert?" Felice was scribbling in her notebook.

"All I can do is ask, Felice, all I can do is ask," Gert said, rubbing her eyes. "I'll go tomorrow if you girls can spare me. It takes a while to cycle there and back, and there's no telling how much time I'll have to wait since I don't have an appointment. Would you excuse me? I think I need to go to bed." Gert collected her bowl, spoon, and cup to put into the sink dishwater.

Once washed and undressed, she knelt at the bedside in her nightclothes. "Dear Father, you tell us in Jeremiah that 'I will restore health to you and heal you of your wounds.' Please, Lord, help the men who came to us today. Help us to help them, according to Your will. Keep us steadfast in body and spirit, and wise in our mental decisions, always remembering to do everything with love. And keep us all safe. Thank you for listening. Amen." Climbing into bed and the welcoming feel of the sheets, blanket, and quilt she wrapped around herself, Gertrude contemplated ways to improve the function of Mercy House and fell asleep.

After a tiresome day at the post, Gertrude strode toward the tent's side where she had left the bicycle. "Leaving already?" a familiar voice said.

Turning and greeting Captain Perry with a smile, she said, "Yes, I'd like to get back before it gets too dark. This pedal lamp flickers terribly and doesn't keep pace with my speed."

"May I walk with you for a bit?" he asked tentatively.

"Sure, as long as I don't get blamed for making you AWOL!" she grinned.

"No, I'm off duty, Gert. You look all in," he said, taking the bicycle from her as they walked down the access lane.

"Yesterday was our first with eight of our boys. It was pretty shocking in some ways but gratifying in others. I'm just worried we'll be able to accommodate more if there's a spike in numbers. They were in pretty rough shape, too, even though the doctor said that he'd send us men who had the best chance at survival. It makes me think of all those wounded left behind at the front... in what kind of condition are they? And what happens if the Germans push our men back and take more ground? Who's going to move the wounded, and how?"

"Gert, you have enough to worry about without getting involved in military tactics and operations, don't you think?" Edward suggested, trying to refocus her concerns.

"You're right, but I still think about it every day, particularly when one of the men asks if we know anything about a buddy or the rest of the detachment." Gert kicked at a stone. Anyway, thanks for saying 'hi,' but I've got to get going," she said with a wan smile.

As he turned the handlebars toward her, Edward leaned over and gave her a light kiss.

Gert looked up at him and stared for a moment. Then—entirely out of character—she put her hand on his neck and drew him toward her for another, longer kiss. "Goodbye, Edward."

He stood, watching her pedal away until she disappeared.

Of the twelve cots in Ward 1 just off the reception hall, eleven were occupied by soldiers with traumatic war wounds requiring frequent attention. Of the twelve cots in Ward 2 for those in static healing condition, seven were in use. Ward 2 was beyond the pocket doors at the end of Ward 1. These soldiers were awaiting transport to a medical hospital in Paris. The eighth man in the arrival group (who had lost an arm and had a damaged eye) developed an infection and suffered a debilitating fever the nurses were working frantically to reduce.

"Sister MacPhearson," Nurse B reported, "we have only one empty cot in Ward 1 and 5 in Ward 2, which means we can bed only six soldiers. On average, we receive between 8 and 10 per entry. We're short beds. I know the field doctors try to divide the wounded between all our Red Cross centers along the front lines, but we should try to plan for what seems like a certain overload for our section. Of course, that doesn't consider any potential spike incoming, such as that Nurse G raised. After all, we're really close to our lines, and the fighting is raging."

Pensive, Sister MacPhearson said, "Yes, I'm aware, Betty," and then went silent, shooshing Betty out of her office with her hand.

'She must be apprehensive,' thought Betty. 'She didn't call me Nurse B but Betty!'

The sound of engines drew Sister Agnes' attention. Hurrying down the staircase to the front door, she collided with Nurse P. "Oh my, oh my, oh my!" chirped Paulette in her sing-song voice. "Looky here what those boys brought!"

Despite the rain, smiling Privates Joe and Morton folded up the canvas truck curtain to reveal a truck bed full of cots. The giant Morton carried four at a time, his smaller companion, only two. "Just tell us where to set them up, mam," Private Morton said, scanning around for sight of Nurse M. At Sister Agnes' nod, Paulette trotted in front of them, chattering all the way.

"Praise God," whispered Sister Agnes. "just in the nick of time. 'Great is Thy faithfulness,' dear, sweet Lord. Thank you."

After four trips back and forth, the truck was empty. Sister MacPhearson invited the soldiers to a cup of tea before they headed back to the post. Off-duty nurses gathered around.

"What news have you from the front?" inquired Sister MacPhearson.

"Mixed," said Private Joe, slurping his tea. "We've taken a lot of casualties, particularly since the Germans used that mustard gas. Not everyone in the trenches has a mask. The muddy conditions have made vehicular use for heavy equipment next to impossible for any transport, so we've been kept pretty busy moving artillery and supplies. But our guys are staying strong. A lot of the wounded are just lying on the ground in the pouring rain. Some of them told me they were ankle-to-knee deep in trench water, and the place stinks to high heaven!" the little man said.

Defensively, the man continued. "You got to understand. Used to be, the Cavalry units were always at the front and leading the charge, you know? To give the men on foot a boost in courage and clearing away the first line of defense. That's also why they brought and conscripted so many horses when we got here. But this war," he said, shaking his head, "this war's changed it all. Strategy, methods, and weapons – it's all different. Horses just ain't no match for barbed wire, trenches, and gas. So, all of us do what we can, and lucky we're here 'cause the vehicles can't cope with the mud and the uneven terrain where the fighting is. So, we move men, artillery, and supplies to the front. Also, we take and deliver messages. It ain't what it used to be, but it's somethin' and still needed. We all do our part wherever we can, right?"

Nurse G interrupted, "Right you are, Joe, we all do our part wherever we can. Do you guys have any spare horses?"

"Yeah, plenty. If there's one thing we got, it's horses. A lot we brought and more got requisitioned from the locals. Guess you heard about that; it didn't make us none too popular. But we sure don't use all of them all of the time; there's lots just standin' around."

"Do you still have that flatbed wagon, or can you put your hands on one? And since you've already made the locals grumpy, how about making them even madder at you and doing something that might save our guys?" Gertrude pounded the table with that statement.

"Well, yeah, sure, I'm willing. But anything we do has to have an authorization, mam."

"Yes, I know, but there's no time, Joe! According to the weather report, this cold and rainy front will hover over us for days. By then, many more men will die! Leave it to me to deal with the commander; he's supposed to support us in emergencies. I need you and Morton to get me that flatbed and two teams of horses— four horses in all--and a hay wagon or a big hay cart, whatever you can find. Bring all of it here tomorrow; I'll let you know I got clearance and for what, but be ready just in case. I'm going to hitch a ride with you to the post, but make sure you load my bicycle in the back."

Realizing that she had just issued orders without getting permission from her supervisor, Nurse G placed her hand over her mouth. "Oh, forgive me, Sister MacPhearson! What I meant to say is if it's all right with you. It's just that these boys need to get going. But I know what I've got planned will work, and we have the extra cots, and..."

In most of her professional life, Sister Agnes MacPhearson was not noted for smiling much, if at all. Instead, she was known as dictatorial and controlling, micro-managing every element under her supervision with a no-nonsense, high-standard approach. Present for the entirety of Nurse G's speech, she stood and looked around at the assemblage.

"I believe I know what you have in mind, Nurse G. While you didn't ask before presenting it, I shall put that down to expedient enthusiasm and say, 'I approve!'"

"Oh, thank you, Sister MacPhearson. I'll cycle back as soon as I can speak to someone in authority and get the go-ahead," assured Nurse Gertrude. She paused, then said with a worried look, "What happens if I can't convince them to go with my plan?"

"Well, Nurse G, perhaps you might misunderstand, or you might misinterpret or just deliberately disobey. I cannot say what will happen. All I know is that we, here, shall be ready for you when you return with the flatbed trailer, cart, wagon, or whatever, full of our boys. You might wish to take three of the others with you if the privates have to stay on base or receive orders to do something else. Given the glut of horses with many in disuse, borrowing some is not such a serious charge, now is it?"

"What about using their flatbed, Miss MacPhearson? Don't we need permission for that, too? And what if they don't want to lend us the horses?" asked Katie.

"I cannot hear a thing over that clatter you're making in the sink, Nurse M! I cannot think about another thing just now," said Fearsome MacPhearson, turning to give the group a smile and a wink.

The women and the privates looked at each other in amazement, smiles growing on their faces. "We can make this work! Paulette, can you and Betty get things organized here? That means making all the cots and getting trauma trays... you know the drill! Now, have any of you got experience with horses?" the animated Gertrude asked.

When she saw hands raised, she said, "Great! You're conscripted! The rest of you will have to do without us for a while, but that leaves eight to do the necessaries, plus Fearsome MacPhearson! Let's get some kits together for emergency treatments and get going. We meet at the truck in ten minutes. Let's move, girls!"

The others, unaware that she hovered just outside the kitchen, had no idea they were overheard. Sister Agnes smiled at her moniker.

"What are we going to do now," asked Felice. Gertrude had indeed barged her way into the commander's office to unveil her proposition and request permission. She was denied.

"We haven't come all this far to give up!" Gertrude said, turning to re-enter the commander's office much to the objection of his assistant, Private Chase, who rose to stop her. Felice blocked his path.

Opening the door and storming over the threshold, she

pressed further. "I recognize that employing some of your soldiers might be wholly improper and outside of regulation. So, I'm asking for the loan of four horses just standing around in a stall." (While they were officially Army property whether by supply or conscription, Gertrude made a guarantee for their return or their relative value should something untoward occur. Of course, she had no authority to make such a guarantee but fueled as she was by her passionate plea, she made it anyway.)

"Please, please, let us do what we came here to do: Save lives! Those men lying in the mud and rain got wounded fighting for us... for you! We can't let them suffer any more than they've already done, and the fighting forces haven't got the time to help the wounded because every man is fighting his heart out! Come on, General Smythe, with respect, say yes!"

The commander looked at the passionate woman before him. Clothed in a drenched apron with a red cross, pantlegs peeking out beneath her tunic, her blonde hair escaping what was previously a neat top knot, and eyes the sky's color, he shook his head. "You, Miss uh Nurse, are a pain in my ass, excuse my French! Go on, get out of here. You can have the four horses and flatbed on temporary loan," he scowled, still shaking his head. As she blew him a kiss and turned to dash out of his office, he called after her, "And you'd better bring them all back in one piece, or I'll take it out of your hide... personally!"

"Ok, ladies, off we go! Let's get out of here before he changes his mind!" They had blown in like a tornado and blew out the same way. The befuddled private outside General Smythe's office sat thinking, "What just happened?"

Felice and Debra harnessed one team; Katie and Gert took the other. Hooking the flatbed trailer to Felice's team, Debra then leaped on the lead horse, and Felice took the reins, standing upright on the trailer just behind the wooden railing on its front periphery. Katie and Gert mounted their team's horses, having buckled the draft rein to the outer side of each saddle girth. They looped the coupling rein through the throat lash, ready to be buckled when the pair would be hooked to the wagon or cart. Then, they made for the town to persuade someone to trust them with a vehicle's loan, preferably a four-wheeled wagon into which they could fit many soldiers.

The clatter of hooves on the paving stone and brick driveway drew the nurses to the front doors. Gert slid off her horse while Katie steadied the horses. Behind them, Felice and Debra drove their team with the flatbed trailer. "Hurry and get me all the stretchers we have!" yelled Gert. Martha passed Gert a basket with food and water; Alice trotted to the wagon with a box of clean bandages and antiseptic; Clare brought a stack of blankets. Lydia and Rebecca got two buckets of water apiece to water the horses. Paulette strode to each horse, giving it some apple and telling each they were heroes.

"Hey, no feeding horses with bits in their mouths," chastised Felice.

"It was only half an apple each," pouted Paulette, turning on her heel to stand by the front doors, hiding the carrots in her apron's front pocket.

With the supplies loaded, Martha and Betty brought four lanterns. "Just in case you get caught short with the fading light in this weather," the thoughtful Betty said.

"Pray for us," Gertrude said, as the wagon train left the grounds headed down the dirt track for the front. All of the nurses waved and blew kisses.

"It seems an almost impossible journey," said Lydia.

"No, it's not," said the brusque Helene. "Horses can go on rough ground and through mud that fouls mechanized vehicles. Besides, they're all drafts or cross-bred draft types. They're strong and reasonably docile. And if anyone can get the job done, those four nurses can! Why don't you sing to the men we've got inside, Paulette? I promised them you would, but keep your mouth shut about what the girls are doing. We don't need them worrying." Paulette flounced away into the house, smoothing her hair after making a face at Helene.

"And here I thought Katie and Debra were fussy about their looks and appearances!" said the unfeminine, gruff Helene to the other nurses' giggles as they re-entered Mercy House. "Deb and Katie are on their way to the front where there's mud, blood, shell fire, and death. Clearly, there's more in them than meets the eye."

"It's not going to be like a fox hunt, for sure," mumbled Betty.

The nurses became more anxious as they neared the battlefield. The track had turned from wet hardpack to an increasingly muddy track. The only noise in the distance was gunfire; the artillery seemed to be eerily quiet. After they reached the outskirts of the troop tents, they turned the wagons with the horses headed back in the direction from which they came to allow more straightforward loading. Both Felice and Katie stayed with the wagon and trailer, while Gert and Debra searched for the medical tent and the doctors.

The first thing that assaulted them was the smell. The wounded and dying moans wrenched their hearts, not because they were loud, but because they were a symphony of agony. As they picked their way through the deep, slippery mud, they saw them: bodies lying on the cold, wet ground in a chaotic and irregular pattern surrounding two tents illuminated by lanterns. Intrepidly, the two nurses approached the tents. Dr. Simons came rushing out looking wan, pale, and ten years older than when they saw him last.

"My medic tells me you've come to take some of the wounded," he breathed out, clearly exhausted. "I'll get you someone to help. Wait here."

"You're welcome," said Debra nervously.

"Oh, Deb, he's completely spent. He's not thinking about politeness," Gert said sympathetically, "but I think we're going to need more like 'a bunch' than 'someone' to help us."

As it turned out, they placed all six stretchers with the worst cases in a double row down the center of the flatbed three abreast and end-to-end. Three ambulatory soldiers sat on either side and two at the end of the flatbed, their legs dangling, supporting each other, and keeping the stretchers from sliding. Those soldiers that could stand held the sides of the wagon for balance. Their comrades sat at their feet or lay prone in the center of the wagon. All in all, the four-wheeled wagon held 11 men, the flatbed trailer carried 14, for a total of 25 rescued, seriously wounded men.

Dr. Simons and the small group of men helping to move the wounded looked amazedly at the bedraggled women with their strange transport method. "Whatever works, ladies. Thanks."

"What about all these others?" Debra asked quietly.

"Most are dead, nearly dead, or can't be helped other than shots for pain. Our post-operative and treatment tents are full, and most in there wouldn't sustain the journey right now. Until this rain lets up, we have no hope of getting them to the hospital. It stinks, but it comes down to choosing the ones you can save." The doctor turned and walked away.

Gert and Debra walked back to the waiting trailer and wagon. The artillery shelling began, and the horses got jittery. Men in the wagon and trailer started to moan more loudly. Felice and Katie had treated as many as possible, blanketing the unconscious and distributing small bits of food and water among those conscious.

Her white-blond hair streaming free and wet from the light rain, Gert stood on the front of the wagon, her voice sufficiently loud to be heard by those on the flatbed trailer. "Listen up, boys. We're getting you out of here. You're going to Mercy House, where you'll get bathed, treated, fed, and have a warm, dry place to rest. Please stick with me now, it'll be a little bumpy, but we'll make it! Let's show those Jerries what Americans are made of-- you with me?"

Varying degrees of affirmative response came from the men, but some of them only smiled or nodded.

"All right then, wagons ho!" Gertrude called, raising her left arm with her hand in a fist, her right hand leading the horse team forward, Debra at the reins. Felice controlled her team, and Katie mimicked Gert. Gunfire became louder and more constant, peppered by men's muffled commands, yells, and screams. Shells exploded at the very front of the line, but some errant ones crashed to blow on the fields alongside the track over which the women led the straining horses. Foot by strenuous foot, they progressed amid the horrific and deafening sounds of war.

It took all of the women's strength to keep their teams moving forward and under relative control between the deep mud and the sounds of war. At one point, after a too close shell exploded, Katie got dragged by her team, which broke into a trot. When Gert's team realized the lead team was trotting fast, close to running, they fidgeted and jogged, threatening to join, and potentially run. Felice and Debra struggled with the reins, calling out to the teams to 'whoa,' while Gert and Katie struggled to hang on to their team's leader.

Gert could see that Katie was in danger of losing hold as her body twisted over to her back, her feet scrambling as she got dragged along. But the plucky horsewoman hung on and flipped herself. Switching her hold to her left hand, she used her right to support a running vault onto the lead horse's back. She reached forward to grab the headset of the bridle rein connected to the bit and firmly pulled until the frightened horse slowed to a walk.

Finally, the artillery barrage lessened, the gunfire again became sporadic, the sounds of war more distant. The audio changed from explosions to moaning, wailing, and crying. Gertrude couldn't decide which was more frightening. As the muddy track turned into the hardpack, she could see the outlines of the chimneys of Mercy

House. They had made it! They had done it! She always hoped they could, believed they could, but never knew they could. She only knew that they had to try. Try they did and succeed they did. By God, they would get these brave men to Mercy House, where at the least they would find care and treatment; at best, healing, and the chance for a new life.

Covering the last hundred yards, Gertrude thought of her sister Red Cross nurses. They were quite different in looks, background, and personality, each bringing something unique to their group. Corporately, they were a powerful tool for good with a unified, committed spirit of caring.

'We must all do good. If that means we suffer tomorrow, we must also trust that we'll find the way to victory tomorrow, or the day after that, or the day after that. We have to know that in God's eyes, we will be working for good, as He commanded.,'' she thought to herself as she trudged onward.

When loading the flatbed trailer and wagon to capacity (thinking only of the weight the horses had to pull through the unyielding muddy terrain), Gert had not considered where the men would be bedded at Mercy House. None of the other nurses raised the subject either because their energies focused on the tasks at hand.

As they pulled to a stop in front of Mercy House, the realization that their patients might have to sleep on pallets on the floor hit Gert head-on. 'What have I done?' she thought.

Sister Agnes ran down the path and hugged Katie, then Gert. Katie was surrounded by nurses, who took her advice about which soldiers to help off the flatbed. Gert stood rooted to the spot, tears streaming down her face, shivering. Looking at Sister MacPhearson, she said, "Now that we've brought so many of them here, I don't know where we can put them." She sobbed against Sister Agnes.

Looking into Gert's forlorn face, Sister Agnes smiled, tucking long strands of blonde hair behind her ears. "Why, we have 30 cots waiting, dear. How many men did you bring?"

Gert shook her head, not understanding. "Twenty-five," she mumbled, "but how?"

"God works in mysterious ways, Nurse G. And He uses His children in miraculous ways perfectly for that which He has planned. Come on, now, let the others unload. You need some warming up, so you won't take a chill, and I'll explain it all to you." Sister Agnes uncurled Gert's stiff fingers from the harness's bridle-rein. Gert began to object, but Sister Agnes said, "I'll have one of the others tend to the horses. Don't you worry. Come inside. Nurse K, you too, come on, Felice and Debra, fall in line and follow me." She let Sister MacPhearson lead her into Mercy House, tearful and relieved that she was home... home after being in Hell.

"Good evening, Nurse P," said a slightly embarrassed Captain Edward Perry.

"How wonderful to see you again, Captain Perry. How may I help you?" answered the coquettish Paulette.

"I wonder if it would be possible to have a word with Nurse G? I've come after dinner, hoping that I wouldn't interfere with your work schedule."

"Yes, of course. Let me just check to see where she might be. Oh, yes, here it is. She's ironing in the laundry. Please have a seat, and I'll get her for you."

Rounding the bottom of the staircase from the back of the house, Gertrude walked to reception, removing the work scarf from her head. "Edward," greeting him with a smile.

"Hello, Nurse G. I hope this isn't an inconvenient time. I hoped we could chat a bit."

"Rescuing me from a steamy ironing detail isn't ever inconvenient," she said, holding up the kerchief and laughing. "Shall we sit in the garden? I wouldn't mind some cool air."

What was once an overgrown area littered with stones blasted from the upper story and a burned, crispy hedgerow was a manicured, welcoming cloister with small groups of blooms in a tidy enclosing flowerbed. Even the hedge showed a few spots of green in response to its pruning. "We can sit here now that it's stopped raining. Can I get you anything?"

Shaking his head, he began, "Part of this is official; part of it is personal."

"Uh oh., what have I done now?" she asked him, rolling her eyes.

"No, nothing like that. The commander received a report from the doctors at the front. They were extremely impressed by what you Red Cross ladies...uh ... nurses did and the speed with which you got it accomplished under less-than-ideal circumstances, I might add." He mocked a salute.

"Oh!" Surprised and pleased, Gertrude sat taller. "I'll tell the others. They'll be pleased."

"So, they should be, although the compliment was well-earned. The fact that you did it without our help—without Army personnel involved, except those guys who helped you load the wagons at the front—well, that makes it even more impressive as regards you ladies and a bit of a black eye for us," the uneasy Captain Perry explained.

"Wagon and trailer," clarified Gert.

"What?" Edward asked frowning.

"Wagon and trailer. We didn't have two wagons. We borrowed one large wagon from the town and the flatbed trailer and the horses from the military. Just trying to keep things accurate, Edward." Gert leaned forward and gently patted his hands, white-knuckled from holding his hat so tightly. "Go on," she said encouragingly.

"Yes, sorry. The commander wants you to know that your performance was admirable. Because of its success and the medical staff's relief on the front—to say nothing of the soldiers themselves—he has given my cavalry division the job of continuing the initiative. As you know, what vehicles we have aren't of much use in certain conditions. Your good example has given my guys a real job, something of use. I'd like to thank you for that, and so would they.

"And I guess the guys transported from here to hospital keep going on about it to anyone who will listen. War stories are shared a lot, you know. So, you ladies have become quite the subject. Word spreads quickly among the troops from the ranks to the officers in charge. Personally, I think the general was a bit embarrassed he didn't launch the idea himself.

"Everyone is grateful to all of you, and the general wants me to assure you that your group will have his full support in the future. He sent me to tell you because my division was the one dispatched to help you fix the place and get settled in the beginning. He figured since my guys know you and we'll be the ones to continue the transport work since horses are of no use in trenches, that I should be the one to come and tell you."

"Well! That is a surprise and a welcome one!" Gertrude clapped her hands lightly in distinct pleasure. "And we kept my promise by returning the horses undamaged; the trailer, too," she reminded him. "I think he said 'yes' only to get rid of me because I'd been such a nuisance. But I'm glad he did agree, Edward. We got

25 men; did you know?"

"I heard afterward during the dressing down we all got for not having come up with the idea ourselves." Edward blanched.

"I see; I'm sorry, Edward. I would have shared my plan with you, but everything happened quickly, and we just forged ahead, knowing how long, and involved approval for anything takes. The weather was so bad, and we saw that the men were just lying in the mud, and…"

"No apologies necessary, Gert. General Smythe was right to criticize me. I should have thought of a better deployment for my men, but as the general said, '… a bunch of Red Cross nurses had to show you how…' which, frankly, while accurate, doesn't sit well." Edward hung his head, embarrassed.

They sat quietly for several moments. Then Gert said, "I've got another idea, Edward."

Looking at her in a combination of dread and amazement, Edward asked her to explain.

"We have triage set up here, for reasons of efficiency in treatment. There aren't enough personnel at the front to manage the flow of wounded. We found dead soldiers lying in the cold mud along with living wounded. Some soldiers treated were in an over-crowded tent. Who knows how long they laid there before being checked and attended. The inflow threatens to drown the medical teams. I'm sure they do their level best, but it's a numbers game. Do you see?"

Edward shook his head, frowning. "We don't have any more medics or doctors to send, Gert."

"No, I know that from Dr. Simons. I'm saying that when they are deluged with wounded, which seems to be all the time, one must take treatment or operating time out to walk among the wounded, identifying who needs help most quickly to save lives. In-evitably, just because of time and numbers, some men get left out.

"A not severe head wound can bleed like crazy and draw at-tention and valuable time in cleaning and dressing merely to stave a blood flow, but precious minutes get wasted when perhaps anoth-er who has lost an arm and is bleeding out is only six prone bodies away! They need two triage tents and nurses to oversee them. The men needing immediate attention could be segregated and more rapidly get to the operating and treatment shelters. The doctors could do one serious case after another, or several at a time. Mean-time, nurses could address lesser injuries and then move men to the tents awaiting removal to care centers.

"It would be so much more efficient and helpful. I suspect the doctors assigned to the front have never had a spare moment and had to set up for work on an immediate basis. They just did the best they could under terrible circumstances. They're overburdened with a mixed jumble of wounded men. Do you understand? They didn't and still don't have enough personnel, but we're here now. We could help with that!" Gertrude's face was alight with passion.

"When you get all fired up about something, you are beautiful!" Edward said to her, bending toward her to kiss her for the second time.

"Edward! Now is not the time for this!" she complained.

"I know, and I apologize. I see what you're saying, and it seems an impressive idea on the face of it, but I'm not sure how it will fly with the general... or Sister MacPhearson, for that matter. Have you run it by her?"

Gertrude shook her head and slumped her shoulders. "No, I just thought of it as we were talking, and I'm sure she won't be thrilled with me if I ask because it would leave us shorthanded here. It's just that with your division moving men from the front to get settled in the care centers and then hospitals, combined with two triage units to allow the doctors to address the more severe injuries efficiently, we could promote a flow-through that would work hand in glove for the benefit of all the wounded!

"There wouldn't be so many just looked at and left lying and thinking they are left to die. The reality, Edward, is many of them are left just like that. I saw it. Then they die, and the bodies are left in the field right next to the living wounded. It's a horrible reward for serving your country because you were unlucky enough to get injured and there's not enough staff to cope! We have to do something about it!"

"Do you want me to request another meeting with the general when I give my report of this visit?" he asked the upset Gertrude. "I'll do whatever I can to help, but I warn you, I must follow orders. There's no latitude there."

Smiling, Gert said, "Oh, I know, Edward. You've been lovely to come and give me this good news. I'm sorry if I turned it into another problem and took the wind out of your sails."

"Spoken like a ship captain's daughter," he smiled. "I'd better go, and you're cold."

They said goodbye in the garden, Edward holding her hands and promising that he'd present her proposal in his report to the general to save time and prevent taking her from her job in caring for the soldiers in residence. She shared that she would work on Fearsome MacPhearson in the interim.

Edward squeezed her hands and donned his cap. "Like the song says, 'Let me call you sweetheart...'"

A day turned into a week and a week into two weeks. Mercy House was never without patients, never without tasks to complete, never shy of willing hands and hearts mobilized by the ever-capable management and driving force known as Fearsome MacPhearson.

Pleased that their little American Red Cross center was able to help and partially heal so many, transferring a significant amount to hospitals in Paris or the surrounding area (to undertake the long road to further treatment and recovery sufficient to be sent home), Sister MacPhearson made her rounds with all-encompassing eyes.

The official compliment received by the daring escapade mounted by Gertrude and the others won them continued local and military support if a little criticism from the central ARC commission. Still, they had begun a cycle of change that benefited the very soldiers they were in Europe to treat and support. Likewise, the town folk had a more benevolent attitude toward the health center and appreciated the nurses' address of their needs, tuition regarding hygiene, nutrition for their children, and general healthcare dispensed. All in all, the ARC Mercy House had lived up to its name. She was proud of all of her nurses who arrived as tender buds from a comparatively protected environment and were now full blossoms thriving despite threatening wartime conditions. 'Great is Thy faithfulness,' she thought again, the promise of those words carrying her ever forward.

When Nurse G made her passionate presentation to Sister MacPhearson about the triage units at the front, her response was brief and swift to Gertrude's surprise. "Provided we get clearance from Commission Central, and the general also approves, we shall do it! Leave it with me." Gert almost fainted from shock.

Subsequently, the nurses worked out a rotating schedule with Betty, allowing those best suited and most needed at Mercy House to remain there. The balance relieved their sister nurses staffing the triage units at the front. Some nurses could not emotionally manage the field assignment and reassumed duties at Mercy House, making the field rotation for assigned nurses more frequent. However, combined with the cavalry division's movement of wounded troops from the front to centers like Mercy House dotted over the landscape along the winding front line on France's northern border, many soldiers' lives got saved. Although the historical record would not document to any noteworthy extent the substantial effect these small but significant changes and acts of heroism made to the troops' survival rate, their dedication would be kept alive among those who were helped and lived to tell the stories.

Chapter Twenty
Potential

"Nana, you're going to get me into trouble, putting so much butter on your toast! I'm supposed to be looking after you." Gertrude chided the tiny white-haired figure sitting in the corner chair of the kitchen table.

"Never you mind, child, it's one of the dwindling pleasures of my life," the old woman responded, peering down the galley kitchen to see if her daughter had heard the conversation.

Lizzie Lloyd, Gert's mother, was busy deboning a chicken for the fricassee with dumplings that would be their supper. "Oh, dear, my hands are all messy. Get that door, will you, Gert?" The incessant ringing of the buzzer exacerbated her headache, as did the imminence of her husband's return. She wanted everything perfect for this evening. When Lizzie Lloyd wanted something to go a certain way, it usually did. Claude, Gertrude's brother, had been gone a month aboard the "Lizzie Celeste" with their father, William. They were still at sea when Gert returned home from Europe.

Gert opened the door to a huge bouquet, the gladiolas towering above the short delivery boy. "Miss Gertrude Lloyd?" asked the boy, craning his neck around the side of the wobbling armful.

"My goodness, who sent those?" asked Lizzie. "Get Nana's big vase from the corner cupboard base," she instructed when Gert brought the flowers to the kitchen.

"Oh!" exclaimed Gert, reading the notecard. "They're from a soldier I met in France: Captain Edward Perry!"

Her mother looked sharply at her daughter. "Was it serious?"

Receiving no answer, she washed and dried her hands, poured three cups of tea, and sat at the kitchen table opposite her mother, indicating that Gertrude should join them. "Well?"

Gertrude blushed, saying, "Not really, but I do like him. There wasn't a whole lot of time for that kind of thing, Mother. The wartime life of a Red Cross nurse barely provides time for a hot cup of tea with one's feet up!" Gertrude unwrapped the bouquet and spread the flowers out on the porcelain washtub's cover.

"What does the card say?" Lizzie asked.

"He says he wants to meet up now that he's found me again. He wants to come here tomorrow at 7:00 PM and walk down to the harbor. He says he has another surprise."

"Humph! No daughter of mine is going to be wandering around the harbor in the evening unaccompanied!" Lizzie said emphatically.

"I wouldn't be unaccompanied, Mother; Captain Perry would be with me," Gert said softly. Her Nana cackled from the corner. "You all right, Nana?" Gert asked.

"Just fine, child. I just remembered a similar conversation I had with your mother, that's all. She was defensive when a ship's young boatswain came a-courting, and her father didn't think he was an appropriate suitor. Look how that turned out!" Nana giggled again.

"Very funny, Mom, but this is different. Your brother, Claude, will accompany you, Gert. No one is going to mess with you if Claude is along. They wouldn't dare!" the tiny Lizzie said with pride. Claude was a well-muscled, swarthy, and tall man topping 6'5". He had his father's build and favored his mother in looks with quiet seriousness, and soft, dark eyes and hair.

In contrast, Gertrude's coloring and features mimicked her father's fair skin, white-blond hair, and angular English features. Neither child had a petite stature like their mother and grandmother. Gert was tall and slender; Claude was very tall and solidly built. However, both adored and kowtowed to their tiny mother, as did her powerfully built but gentle husband.

When Captain Edward Perry rang the doorbell, he did so only once. Lizzie waited, making Captain Perry wait as well. When the bell did not ring a second time, she smiled. Nothing annoyed her like a repetitive ringing doorbell. Opening the front door, Lizzie looked at the young man from head to toe. "Come in, Mr. Perry." He entered and presented Lizzie with a small box of chocolates, standing rooted to the spot at stiff attention.

Gertrude left the sofa in the parlor, where they were listening to her father's daily poetry reading, and greeted the stiff Edward. "Hello! I see you found us. Not too much difficulty?"

He smiled at her, shaking his head.

"Come on in and meet the family," she said.

William and Claude arose to shake hands with Edward. Although Edward was not a short man—a little taller than Gert-- at 5'11" and slender, he seemed diminished by Lizzie's father and brother's height and breadth. After introductions, the men shook hands.

"Understand you ride horses," William offered in conversation. "What kind?"

"All kinds, sir. In the Army, the Cavalry rides whatever is available; you don't get to choose breed or type. But at home, I ride Thoroughbreds mostly."

"Gertie tell you she rides, too? She was horse mad as a little girl. Between horses and my boat, she never had time to play with dolls or do knitting like other girls." William sat down in "his" comfortable chair.

"Now, Papa, don't go giving away all my secrets," teased Gertrude.

"Ready to go?" asked Claude.

"Uh, yes, sure," said Edward with a quizzical glance at Gertrude.

Lizzie said, entering the room with two glasses of Port, "Claude will be accompanying you, Mr. Perry." Handing one glass to her husband, she seated herself next to him, reopening the book of poetry to the marked page and giving it to him. "Go on, Gertrude dear, have a nice walk."

Claude opened the front door, and Lizzie went out, followed by Edward, who stopped momentarily to collect a basket he'd left on the front stoop. Claude followed, explaining his presence to Edward as he walked behind them. Their mother considered it improper and unsafe for her daughter to be walking around the harbor where dock workers might be lingering.

Speaking to the air in front of him, Edward said, "Understood. Thank you, Claude, but I'm a soldier, and I think I could care for Gert. Still, it's a sensible plan. Two are better than one."

"Three," said Gertrude. "I'm pretty good at taking care of myself."

"That you are, Gert, that you are," agreed Edward.

Claude sensitively walked several paces behind them. The

Lloyd home was on a block parallel and a block vertically away from the sea. The summertime evening was lovely with blue sea and sky littered only with far away cirrus clouds. Arriving at benches along the waterfront, Edward spread a small, light blanket on the seat, indicating that Gertrude should sit down. Claude chose a nearby place approximately a dozen feet beyond.

In his basket, Edward had a thermos of white wine and two small cups, a punnet of strawberries, and a cupcake for each of them—one vanilla, one chocolate. He offered Gertrude her preference. At first, they were quiet with each other, munching and sipping. Then, as they relaxed, they revisited some of their times and experiences abroad. It was comfortable between them, and they quickly reassumed the ease they had felt in each other's company in France.

"You know, I started looking for you as soon as I got home. You never gave me your address before you left. I don't know what I was thinking to let that happen," Edward admitted.

"Honestly, one day, we were in full operation, and it seemed like overnight—even though it was months--they decided to send us back home. It was crazy trying to shut things down and pack everything up. I truly never thought of it. And anyway, I didn't know for sure that... "

"That I wanted to see you again? Of course, I did! I thought I made it clear, but maybe I didn't. Remember when I told you about the song? You know, 'Let Me Call You Sweetheart'? Well, the next lines are 'I'm in love with you... let me hear you whisper that you love me, too.'"

Gertrude put her head down, blushing. "I remember, Edward."

"Well, I've found you again, and this time, I'm not going to let you go, Gert." Edward reached into his basket and plucked out a small drawstring bag, giving it to her. "It was my grandmother's;" he said, "it's a promise ring."

"Oh, it's lovely," Gert replied, smiling as she slipped the sapphire ring on the ring finger of her right hand. "Thank you, Edward."

"When can I see you again? We have to figure this out, with the distance and all. Our farm in Virginia is a few hours away, but you could visit and meet my family. I'd like that, and so would they. For a few days or a week, perhaps?" he said hopefully.

"I'll have to check with my family. Let's keep in touch by letter, and I'll let you know. It's been very nice seeing you again,

Edward. Now we get to know each other all over again in a different setting with vastly different circumstances."

"Yes, that's true, but none of it will make me change my mind," he said, kissing her hand.

Claude's deep voice boomed out, "Gert, we'd better get back. It's been over two hours, and it's getting dark."

"Ok, be right there," Gert said, leaning to Edward to kiss his cheek. "Thank you for coming, for a lovely evening, and this," she said, holding her hand aloft. Just as he was about to kiss her back on the lips, she jumped up and ran over to the waiting Claude, who offered her his arm and saluted Edward.

Watching them walk away, Edward thought, 'When they turn the corner, if she looks back at me, she'll one day be my wife!'

As Claude and Gertrude turned the corner to walk up the slight hill from the sea toward home, Gertrude turned her head to look at him and blew him a kiss. He couldn't stop smiling as he repacked the basket.

[Dedicated to Nurse Gertrude Lloyd (Hinman), my maternal grand-mother and Captain Edward Perry Hinman, my maternal grandfa-ther.]

Chapter Twenty-one
Annaliese

World War II Section
Dedicated to Maya Manley

Edelweiss [Edelweiß]

Music by Richard Rogers
English Lyrics by Oscar Hammerstein II

***

Edelweiss, Edelweiss
Every morning you greet me,
Small and white, clean and bright,
You look happy to meet me.
Blossom of snow, may you bloom and grow
Bloom and grow forever.
Edelweiss, Edelweiss,
Bless my homeland forever.
***

That Germany annexed Austria with its agreement gave little solace to Austrians in the Third Reich's developmental years when they witnessed first-hand the repercussions of Hitlerian doctrines. Still, there is no denying the Anschluss was welcomed by the majority of the Austrian population and government for a host of reasons.

When structural changes within German forces reflected the Nazi state's ever-growing rigidity fueled by Hitlerian imperatives, cleavages within the German command became apparent. Western military operations were directed by the Oberkommando der Wehrmacht (OKW or Armed Forces High Command), who reported directly to Hitler. The Oberkommando des Heeres (OKH or Army High Command) was in charge of the war on the eastern front and was a rival to the OKW, but also reported directly to Hitler. Both forces had a high command structure responsible for reports to the Fürher, who delighted in pitting one against the other for forced results that matched his megalomaniacal initiatives. There was no love lost between the two factions. When over 850,000 Austrians were conscripted for various assignments within the Third Reich war machine for military operations, and Austria's economy was pressed to the limit, people began to realize that annexation was little different from occupation.

The population's significant Jewish contingent was summarily rounded up by the Gestapo (Geheime Staatspolizei), the secret police, under orders from the SS (Schutzstaffel). Austrians witnessed their tactics and fell prey to fear when they saw their society changing into a military state wherein you were safe one day, but the next, you got arrested because of an accusation, cast aspersion, or pointed finger. It became easier to believe the stories about stormtroopers, beatings and imprisonment, deportations, slave labor, and death camps. People were either frightened into belonging to the Nazi party or cowered behind closed doors attempting to maintain a low profile.

After her parents were taken and subsequently executed for consorting with and helping some Jewish friends, Anneliese Kaiser went to live with her grandparents in a small border village in the mountains where she spent many happy childhood summers. The horror of war had not permeated daily life in the mountains to the extent it had in the cities, and for a few years, life felt safe again.

She helped her grandfather with the few goats, sheep, and cows that comprised his herd and planted and harvested vegetables with her grandmother. She went to school and studied by kerosene lantern, reading aloud to her grandparents until she was distracted by their snores. Each weekend, they would all walk the two and a half miles to the church in the village. Anneliese found stability and happiness in her new life, despite that she missed her parents and would sometimes cry at night or in church for their loss. Overall, the sweetness of her grandparents and the contentment of a simple life brought her peace.

She thought her new life held no surprises until the day the military vehicles entered the village. She was in town with her grandfather purchasing flour and salt for her grandmother and some repair items for their little barn. The vehicles were loud and smelly. The officer marched around, smacking his leg with a riding crop, surveying the curious town folk who had gathered in the tree-lined square. Two of the soldiers went down each side of the village tacking up notices. The officer said nothing, re-entered his car, and left with two trucks loaded with soldiers, leaving a small vehicle with two soldiers in the town. Anneliese wanted to stay longer to see what else would happen. Her grandfather hurried her along up the hill toward home.

"We have a long walk, *mein Schatz*. We'll know soon enough."

"But when will 'soon enough' be, *Großvater*? I want to know now!" she protested.

"*Mein, mein*, the impatience of youth. What you do not know now, you will know tomorrow. *Komm Jetzt*."

Walking home, Anneliese chattered, sharing her speculations and questions. On their next trip to the village, they passed a newly constructed guard shack on the trail, several hundred feet beyond the village boundary. Its occupant exited and greeted them, demanding their names, identification papers, and their house location. Anneliese had her answer.

Many months later, a man approached her grandfather following the church service. They stood conversing in animated whispers. Anneliese crept behind them unseen. The man asked her grandfather to show some people the way through the caves, and the trails beyond that crossed the border into Switzerland.

Her grandfather kept shaking his head and said finally, "I am sorry, Otto. I cannot. I am not up to such climbing anymore, much less the *Höhle*. The Berge is too steep for me now."

"If you do not, they will be noticed by the soldiers here. Few in the village know the way like you. Besides, if any of us in the village were to be away for two days with no good excuse, it would make trouble! You live outside the village and come only once a week or so. Do you not see you should take them?"

"Do you not listen, my friend? I cannot. I..."

"I can take them!" Anneliese chirped. "I know the caves and trails well. *Großvater* showed me years ago, and for years we have had picnics, and..."

"Hush, child. I will not hear of it. Forget what you have heard this day. It will lead to no good. *Komm*!" Grabbing her hand and pulling her away, they joined his wife and trekked homeward. Her *Großvater* was unusually silent, and her *Oma* tugged at her braids like she did when she was worried.

When the weather was still nippy in the spring, and the wind rustled down from the mountains into the valleys, Anneliese reveled in her solitary walks to the village. Her grandparents were a few years older now and, depending upon their state of health, made the journey to church only when they thought they could manage the distance and the height of the climb home, altogether foregoing the mid-week walk to the village which they deferred to Anneliese.

"*Guten Tag Ihnen*, Herr Bergmann. Do you have any shriveled sausages today or perhaps trimmings? It is *Oma's* birthday this Wednesday, so I would like to fix her a special dinner."

"Ah, yes, and how does Inge fare after our frigid winter?" The kindly butcher rummaged through his icebox. "Look here, I saved you some big beef bones with much marrow for soup, some trimmings from pork belly, and all the chicken and goose scraps. There are only four sausages from the ends of tubes, and although they are curved and short, they will do with potatoes and onions."

"Oh *Danke*, Herr Bergmann. *Großvater* will love the sausages! *Oma* is always cold and has a bad cough, but her spirits remain cheerful. I will tell her you asked after her. And I will make a special fowl pie in pastry with vegetables for her birthday. Do you think if I boil the scraps and pick the bones, there will be enough meat for a pie?"

"*Oh ja, es gibt genug für zwei Kuchen!*"

"Two pies! *Vielen Dank!* You are truly kind to us. Here are our cheeses: one goat and one sheep. They are especially good at this time. Next week, I will have more, and the sauerkraut will be ready too. Do you have containers for me to fill? I cannot lift the heavy crocks. I have enough to give you about 16 jars or so. May I borrow your wagon to bring them? They will be heavy."

"*Ja natürlich*. Everyone loves your sauerkraut, Anneliese. It is so crisp!"

"I am glad they love it! I cannot cook so well as *Oma*, but I make good sauerkraut, pickles, and wild berry jelly and jam!"

"Everyone is good at something, child. Here, I have loaded this burlap sack for you. By the time you get to the top of the hill, it will feel like it is full of rocks!" The jovial butcher laughed so hard, his belly shook, and his face reddened. Anneliese thought he looked like St. Nicholas. She bade him a fond goodbye and headed to the greengrocer.

"Herr Fischer, good day to you!"

The kindly man held up a finger and disappeared into the backroom of the shop. He returned with a half-full sack. "Flour, potatoes with sprouts, wilted carrots, onions, and salt! Only a little bit, but something is better than nothing, ja?" he said, puffing his chest. "There's a carp in there as well, but you must eat it today or tomorrow; it will not last. I know you cannot grow root crops well up there, Anneliese. I will always save for you what I cannot sell. Now, what do you have for me today?"

With pride, Anneliese passed him the large burlap bag full of wool from her shearing.

"Wonderful! I can smell that it is washed. This will sell quickly and make warm clothes and blankets. I have several women who still spin always ask me for fleece. Good, good, Anneliese. Alas, it is a lost art, but here in the mountains, progress does not come so quickly, ja? Does your *Oma* still sew and embroider? I was asked a few weeks ago for linens like she makes."

"Her eyesight is still good, Herr Fischer, and I will ask her if she is interested. Thank you for the vegetables." In truth, Anneliese was more than grateful for the vegetables; she was ecstatic! She had all the makings of a fine birthday dinner for *Oma*, and *Großvater's* strength might be restored with some solid food for a change. Although Anneliese toiled in their garden and carefully fertilized the soil from decomposed animal and chicken litter, the garden had only a shallow soil depth before the Alps' limestone began. While that made the earth sweet, it meant that mountain homes like theirs could not grow root vegetable crops to feed themselves successfully. Cruciferous vegetables, however, did very well in their climate and kept satisfactorily in the root cellar.

"Uh, Anneliese. There is something I must ask you." He checked to ensure his shop was empty except for them, as he did not wish to be overheard. "A family is coming, I think by Friday—man, woman, and little girl. They were originally from Vienna and have traveled for a while on a circuitous route. My Astrid has a friend in Vienna who knows them. The friend suggested our border village to escape Austria and told them to contact me. You and your grandfather—above everyone in the village—know those *Höhlen* backward and forward. You herd your animals on the trails in all seasons, and you know the best ones to use depending on the weather. Can you help them?"

"Herr Fisher, you know the guard shack has a soldier in it around the clock. They know my family goes down and up routinely, but strangers to the village? That would be a telltale giveaway, and I am sure would end up with their questioning and arrest. There is no way to get to any of the trails or caves without bypassing that guard shack!"

"What if we had a plan to distract the guard? Then you could get them past the guard without being noticed, ja?"

"What plan? It would have to be foolproof, which means it must cast suspicion on no one. Let me think about it. If they come on Friday, can you keep them until Sunday without anyone knowing or seeing them? Ja? That part is up to you. And I want no one but you and Frau Fischer to know, particularly about my involvement... IF I decide to help. I have to think of my grandparents, Herr Fischer."

"Yes, yes, thank you, Anneliese. I will see to the rest and wait to hear from you. Saturday, then?"

"I don't know. I may be able to see you again on Friday to tell you one way or the other."

"Thank you, sweet girl. Thank you. They are good people, I'm told. I don't know much about why they need to leave, but so many people flee and become refugees. One more thing: I do not know if they are Jews."

"That does not matter to me. People have their reasons for wanting to escape the Germans. That is reasoning enough for anyone. *Guten Tag Ihnen*, Herr Fischer. *Denken Sie daran, kein Wort*; not one word!"

"*Ja, ja. Auf Wiedersehen*, Anneliese. And thank you."

As it turned out, Anneliese went to the town on her usual trip on Friday, pulling the cart of cheese and other items. She nodded to the now friendly guard who stood outside the guard shack smoking. He called a greeting, and she smiled and responded. "Bring me a paper on your way back!" he called to her. She smiled again and hurried along her way.

When she got to the greengrocer's shop, his eyes lit up. "Anneliese! I am glad to see you!" She frowned at him biting her lip, her back to Frau Huber's caterwaul greeting and questions.

"Anneliese, you are so skinny! Just yesterday, the women at quilting were speaking of your *Oma*. So, how is she these days? We don't see either of them at church. Is her husband well? Are you not lonely up there? Ach, for such a young girl, all work and no play, not good, ja?" On and on, she droned, not pausing to receive an answer to any of her questions. Anneliese turned briefly and nodded, smiling. "Is she deaf, Herr Fischer?" prattling on and chastising the man about her order.

When she finally left, Anneliese sighed with relief. "Herr Fischer, we must be more careful."

"Child, I was only glad to see you! Nothing to do with anything else. And Frau Huber, busybody that she is, I am sure was only expressing the same thing. Now, what do you need?"

"A paper or magazine—it is alright if it is used or old. It is for the guard in the shack. And any old or soft vegetables would be wonderful. I used all that you gave me last time, except for a few shriveled potatoes. I have some cheese wheels and jars of sauerkraut and jam."

"Excellent, Anneliese. Now, have you come up with a plan? If all goes as they hoped, they should arrive here after dark tonight. I can keep them for a short while if that is what you want."

"We must all keep to the same routine as much as possible, Herr Fischer. I will return to the village for church services and then go directly home as usual. If you and Frau Fischer can take the children on a picnic after church, you could stop at the guard shack. The soldier there is always glad of the company to talk to. You could use the boys' interest in the guard shack, his rifle, and radio as a distraction. Instruct Frau Fischer not to be nervous but to stand in front of the window facing the upper trail, and you try to stand near the doorway to block his view if the door remains open. Hopefully, he will be busy with the boys For once, let them misbehave!

"Tell your friends to hurry by when you have the guard's attention. They should hide in the woods by the trail when everyone is still at church service. They should have enough time to leave the village unseen with the service's length and parishioners taking coffee afterward. They must be in the woods and stay hidden until they see you and the family enter the shack. Do something like hanging a handkerchief from your pants or jacket pocket to signal an 'all clear' to them. If things go wrong, tell them to stay where they are if they do not see the handkerchief.

"If things go well and you can distract the guard, they should stay off the trail and follow along the edge of the woods until they are past the shack. They will come to an outcropping of rocks that they must skirt around. I will leave a kerchief on some brush covering a small entrance to one of the caves. They should take the scarf and enter, staying near the entrance but out of sight. No flashlights; no noise; just wait. I will come after dark and softly sing 'Edelweiss' just outside the cave entrance to let them know it is me.

"I will know if I have to get them from the woods because something went wrong with you if the kerchief is still on the brush by the cave. It can go right or wrong; we will not know until we try. Either way, they must be strong, be quiet, endure the darkness, and wait. It is the price of freedom. When compared to what others have gone through, not so high a price to pay, ja?"

The greengrocer listened intently to all she said. "That seems like it might work. My boys are curious about everything to do with the war, which will be an exciting thing for them. So, after, we should go to the picnic as planned?"

"Yes, I suggest the broad promontory on the right side of the trail just after the shack. It has a big view, and the guard will be able to see you there. It will look natural and be a likely place for a picnic."

"Good, ja. So church, shack, picnic. Only Astrid and I to know, besides the strangers."

"Yes, and make sure the children do not slip and mention your visitors!" Anneliese cautioned.

"They do not know anything, and the strangers will stay in the back room of my shop, not the house, so all will be well. I thought of that. The children do not ever go to the shop, afraid I will put them to work. Besides, I padlock the back door when I lock up the storefront each night." Herr Fischer clenched his jaw and said in a tight-lipped smile, "We are loyal mountain people of free Austria, you and I, Anneliese."

"Yes, but we must always be careful and aware. Not every-one shares our feelings. Are you afraid, Herr Fischer? I know I am."

"I too am afraid, child. But this is something we can do. It is always scary when you do something that no one else will do. But knowing it is the right thing gives you courage. Remember that. We will be alright. The plan is a good one. We stick to it, and all will be well." Anneliese hoped he believed what he said and that he was speaking from experience, not just trying to bolster confidence—his own, and hers.

Taking the offered sack, she headed to the butcher shop to return the barrow and begin her climb homeward. Anneliese lugged her sack up the hill from the village, her mind focused on devising a plan for the fleeing family. Her grandfather would be furious and hurt if he knew she was considering disobeying him. But how could she refuse? She knew all too well the fear and threat the family had experienced. She had asked herself what her parents would do and, knowing the answer all along, had concentrated her thoughts on making their escape a safe reality.

Humming 'Edelweiss,' she was enveloped by the image of her father singing it to her as she lay in bed before sleep. She smiled as she trudged onward.

Chapter Twenty-two
First Escape

Following church and greeting various people, Anneliese hurried away toward home. Everyone meandered outside, chatting on their way to the small village hall for the after-church social. She veered off the trail when she could not be seen when the trail snaked between two rocky faces. Knotting her kerchief to a fallen limb, she dragged it to the opposing hillside, placing it over an opening to a small cave entrance, partially hidden by insinuating undergrowth. Unless one knew of its location, it could and did usually go undetected. She continued on the trail to her grandparent's home, swinging her sack with an excited spirit.

The Fischers said their goodbyes, using the picnic as an excuse to skip coffee. They gathered their basket after church, each tying a sweater round their shoulders for the late afternoon spring chill. Herr Fischer had unlocked the rear door of his shop earlier that morning under cover of darkness, relocking it before their departure for the mountain trail. When they reached the shack, the guard met them with friendly greetings. Herr Fisher retrieved their papers from his vest pocket and extended them to the guard. He shook his head and waved them on.

"Well, actually, sir, I have a favor to ask. Might my children be able to see your post? The boys especially are interested in the life of a soldier and would be excited to see your rifle up close."

The guard beamed with unexpected pleasure. Not only was it rare that he saw *anyone* at this posting—except the skinny girl who spoke little—but he was unused to friendly attitudes from the town folk. "*Ja, ja, kommt nur alle.*"

The children tentatively followed the guard walking inside, Herr Fischer taking his wife's arm and following. The radio crackled, making everyone jump. The guard laughed, explaining to the boys that it was a normal occurrence, and continued explanation as to its function. Frau Fischer walked to the rear of the desk, positioning herself in front of the window revealing the upper trail. Herr Fischer stood by the open door. The guard then showed the children his rifle. It was then that Herr Fischer realized he had not hung his handkerchief from a pocket! The signal! In his anxiety, he had failed to remember!

With a flourish, he removed his handkerchief from his shirt pocket and shook it out. He mopped his face and blew his nose, placing the handkerchief in his rear pants pocket with the majority hanging out. All he could do now was hope that someone in the waiting family could see it.

After allowing the children to hesitantly touch the rifle, and doing the same with his pistol, the guard walked them to the far wall and pointed at the map, continuing the tour of his paltry guard shack.

Frau Fischer meekly interrupted, suggesting that they had taken enough of the soldier's time, and thanking him for his patience with the children. She offered him a sandwich and an apple from her basket. Herr Fischer bowed slightly, expressing his appreciation for the educational chat, and ushered the children outside between his daughter's curtsy and his sons' salutes, all of which made the soldier laugh with appreciation. The family continued up the trail to the clearing on the promontory and spread their blanket. Herr Fisher and his wife unpacked the picnic food while the children played catch. The scene viewed by the guard was of a normal family, children frolicking and parents watching from the blanket calling to their children. The carefree setting made the soldier reminiscent of times with his own family, unaware that the picture was an orchestrated facet of an escape plan.

Later that night, not too long after darkness had fallen, Anneliese dressed in layers and quietly crept from the cottage. She had provisionally pulled some extra hay from the mow for the animals to ensure they had sufficient fodder during her absence and filled the water tubs to the brim. She thought to collect and hard boil some eggs to place in her knapsack, together with a wedge of their homemade cheese and some apples from Herr Fischer. Reaching the outcropping, she saw that her kerchief was gone. Quietly, she hummed the melody of Edelweiss and, after a few bars, saw the kerchief fluttering from the cave opening.

"I am Anneliese," she said as she stood from her entry

crouch. "And you are?"

"I am Felix," said the tall man. "My wife, Amalie, and our daughter, Katja. We are the family Schwarz. Thank you for coming; I was worried something had gone wrong." The little girl peeked out from her hood holding fast to her father's leg.

Anneliese curtly nodded to the parents and knelt in front of the little girl. "Katja, that is a pretty name. Are you hungry, Katja?" The little girl's brown curls jounced as she nodded her head vigorously.

"I have a little food with me. It is not much, but it will stop your tummy from grumbling," Anneliese said in a hushed voice, smiling as she removed and distributed the meager fare to the family.

"What about something to drink?" asked Amalie. The plaintive sound of her voice made Anneliese look closely at the woman, who was wringing her hands.

"The water in these caves is safe to drink and is sweet from the limestone. It is filtered many, many times as it seeps through the rocks. There are cups by the back wall over there," she explained, pointing. "Did you bring anything with you? Bags or cases?"

"Just our rucksacks, and the clothes on our backs," responded Felix, looking worriedly at his wife. "It has been a very trying journey. Can you tell us how much longer it will take to get to Switzerland? Any details will help. We have been under great stress these last weeks. But we are grateful for your help, incredibly grateful, isn't that right, Amalie?" Katja looked at her mother and tugged at her coat.

"Grateful, yes, grateful. A cold, damp cave, a mouthful of cheese, no idea whether we shall live or die... grateful? I hate it! I hate it all, do you hear? Make it stop, Felix, make it stop!" Her voice rose and became shrill as the veins in her neck throbbed. She hugged herself and rocked back and forth huddled over her knees. Felix rushed to his wife, tentatively placing his arms around her, whispering inaudibly.

"Frau Schwarz, I understand. Now, you must *all* understand me." In a hushed tone, Anneliese continued, "Outbursts like that *cannot happen again*. Noise carries and we don't know if a patrol is nearby. Because you cannot see anyone does not mean you cannot be heard. We must be quiet at all times, speaking only in whispers. I know you are tired and afraid. The only chance, and I mean *only* chance you have, is to do *exactly* as I say. Others have put themselves in danger to help you, as have I. You must swallow your hardship, fight through your fear, believe that you can do this. If not for yourself, think of your child. Now, try to get some sleep. We have a long trek in the early morning." Anneliese got the stack of thin blankets from a hollow in the cave wall and distributed them, leaving the family to lie against the opposite wall. She watched them from partially closed eyes for a long while into the night.

The following morning, she led her group through the cave, negotiating the high and low passages carefully, encouraging them when the footing became slippery or the way narrowed, delighting in the little girl's wide eyes when she saw a few stalactites and stalagmites. At day's end, they rested.

"Tomorrow morning, I will lead you to a mountain trail we should reach by midday. It will be very windy on the trails. One of you should hold the little one's hand. *Never allow her to walk on her own*, as she could slip and fall hundreds of meters. Nothing could be done to rescue her, even if she survived the fall, which I doubt."

"You are a coldhearted girl," Amalie said with venom. "Have you no feelings?"

Anneliese was silent but watchful.

The following morning, Anneliese collected the blankets and stuffed them into her knapsack now empty of provisions.

"You are close now. Follow me and take hold of the child. I will go with you as far as the second trail, no further. After you have walked for about two hours, you will be met by a man called Jost. Just stay on the trail until you see Jost. I can only guess the time because you are slow.

"He will take you to a convent of nuns where you will have a bed and food. The rest will be explained to you by the Reverend Mother. *Never ever* speak of me or this journey or the others who have helped you, do you understand me? You must promise, or we will be placed under arrest because we helped you escape. You will be free, and we will be dead. And there will be no one to help others as we have helped you." She looked at them fiercely, and Amalie shrank and turned away.

Katja said, "I think you are brave. You saved us. Thank you. I will keep the secret on my life."

"You are a brave little girl, Katja, thank you. Now, go, go, and live for me; live for all of us! Be happy, sweet one." She hugged the little girl with tears unashamedly flowing down her cheeks, and looked up, nodding at Felix.

"Thank you, Anneliese, for giving my family a chance at a new life." He shook her hand. Amalie stood with her back turned.

"Come, then. God be with you." Anneliese led the group to the trail, waving as she turned back toward the first trail and the cave. She could allow herself little or no emotion during these trips. No one understood how much it took from her to risk herself by helping people walk toward a new life, when she had to walk back to her old one to await new anxieties. She worried for her grandparents, for their health, for their lives: they were innocent bystanders to the path she had chosen. She worried that others involved might crumple if questioned by soldiers, even if asked about unrelated, insignificant matters. People lost resolve when their lives or families were threatened. She worried when or if she would be asked to undertake this journey again and again and again. She worried if she had the fortitude to continue. She worried about being caught.

Worry was such a complicated word. It meant apprehension and fear; it caused uneasiness; it made one fret, agonize, and lose sleep. Worry was a state of mind that threatened all that she was, all that she did, and all that she loved. She had to find a way to free herself from that constant threat. But, how? She hummed Edelweiss, her only true comfort during the cold, lonely walk home.

It was a long road Annaliese walked from her days in the small Alpine Austrian village where she had lived with her aging grandparents, and from which village she had led people over the Austrian border, fleeing from the Third Reich. Those were dangerous days full of fear. She had adopted an unfeeling *persona* to masquerade her panic when questioned by soldiers, and an ascetic lifestyle and hardhearted manner to provide cover for her anxiety at being caught. The most difficult aspect of her life in those days was convincing broken, worried, and terrified travelers to entrust their safety to a young, barely communicative, emotionless girl.

She could show no sympathy to her charges because their fortitude and adherence to her instructions were the two things that would determine their success or failure. If she showed sympathy, it inevitably encouraged histrionics from pampered women, or crying from the children, or irrational demands from the men. She could not allow any interference; the mission required austerity and silence. Everyone's life depended upon their courage and ability to stick to those basic requirements, regardless of how difficult or frightening the conditions. Annaliese's steely reserve and self-denial was like a lantern showing the way through the caves and trails to freedom. She experienced no failures in her dedication to strike a blow of revenge against those who killed her parents and brutalized so many indiscriminately.

The last group she accepted occurred one week before she found her grandparents dead in their little hilltop cottage a mile or so beyond the border guard post. She pulled her sledge to the wooden building, eager to remove the straps from her shoulders. Hans opened the door.

"Hello, my little friend. It is very cold, ja? Come in and warm yourself. What did you bring this week?" Annaliese smiled shyly and extended a sack of small loaves of bread and a block of butter. She walked into the hut and gratefully accepted the mug of hot tea, watery from steeping too many cups from the leaves, but hot and welcome as it slid down her parched throat.

"Every week you make this walk up the mountain from the village, pulling that heavy toboggan. It is a long way to walk for anyone, but extremely hard for such a young, skinny girl like you! I see you still work early mornings for the baker sometimes, ja?. What about the butcher and the greengrocer?"

"I do mornings with the butcher and afternoons with the baker when they need help. The butcher lets me have the scraps for *Großvater* and *Oma*. Then I unload the crates for greengrocer, and I can have the split and badly bruised fruit and vegetables, if there are any. This week, he gave me potatoes that did not look like an old man's face! But I never know just when they will have work for me, so I go when there is work wherever it is!" Hans laughed.

"Here, I have some cheese left. Have a slice with some of this stale bread you brought me. It will help fill your stomach for what's left of the journey. You did not eat before leaving, did you?" She shook her head and accepted the chunk of cheese and bread slice. "You are a good girl."

"My grandparents are old. They cannot do work anymore, so I take care of the few vegetables we have in the ground during good weather, but the root cellar is empty now. There is no more livestock, so I am glad for the butcher's scraps. I can make soup for them. I must go. I have wood to chop when I get to the cottage, and the snow is falling thicker. Thanks, Hans. Stay warm."

"Be safe, sweet girl. When you come next time, bring me

something to read if you can find a book, newspaper, or magazine. My relief partner brings nothing for here. It gets very lonely and boring." He went back to his card game. The radio crackled, but no audible voice sounded. She closed the door and put her arms through the harness straps to begin the last trek uphill in the failing light.

Her grandfather sat frozen to a wooden chair with his arms bound behind him, his face a rictus of horror. Her grandmother was in a bloodied heap on the floor beneath her shawl, her apron and dress torn. Her hand still clutched a wooden spoon, likely in a feeble attempt to protect herself. Scuff marks and identical boot prints suggested a visit from soldiers. Annaliese surmised they intended to search the sparse cottage given the state of disarray. Clearly, her grandfather had been bound and forced to witness whatever the soldiers did to her grandmother. Annaliese hoped he died from heart failure—a quick and merciful death. She vowed vengeance on behalf of them both. Crumpling to the floor in tears, her wails were lost in the wind. It was the last time she would allow herself to cry. Her parents were dead, and now her sweet, unselfish, kind grandparents were dead, too. She was all alone in this nightmare of a world.

With deliberation, Annaliese packed her few items of clothing into one of the large sacks from her village trips. Usable foodstuffs went into her knapsack along with a sharp knife, fork, spoon, and a length of stout rope. She bound her skis and poles together with her snowshoes, tying a sack to each end for balance. She donned her hat, tying her kerchief over her head to keep it stable in the wind. Wearing two pairs of socks and woolen stockings, she tugged on her worn boots. A well-worn woolen tunic just fit over her dress; both were too short, as she had grown in height, but both still fit, as she was skinny. Looking around the cottage, Anneliese took a small metal pan, cup, and pot, along with one of the linen pieces her grandmother had embroidered, and her grandfather's big hunting knife and belt holster.

Placing her worldly belongings away from the cottage beyond the side of the empty little barn, she returned to the cottage, carefully lighting a fire in the fireplace. As the flames swelled, she wrapped her beloved grandfather in one of the quilts crocheted by the knotted hands of her grandmother, put on his hat and pulled it down over his eyes, kissing his cheek. "I love you. Thank you for loving me and taking me in. I am so sorry, *Großvater*, sorry for the trouble I brought to you. My heart will be easy knowing you will be with God. *Auf Wiedersehen*."

She lifted her grandmother onto the daybed against the wall, marveling at how light she was. Covering her with the quilt from the bed, she removed the cross her *Oma* always wore, slipping it around her neck. "I will keep this for you always, *Oma*. It will keep you close to me. Please forgive me for the trouble I brought to this peaceful place, a place where I have been loved and happy. Thank you. Thank you for loving me and for everything. I will always love you. I am sending you to God's care, now. *Auf Wiedersehen*." Bending to kiss her grandmother's white hair, a few sobs escaped her.

She looked around one last time, then walked to the fireplace, taking a piece of flaming wood and lighting the bedding in her grandparents' room, all the curtains, stuffed furniture, rugs, and anything immediately flammable. Closing the door, she walked to the barn setting the last of the hay alight. As she collected her belongings, she looked back at the blazing buildings, thinking of the Vikings and other peoples of the world who practiced cremating their dead.

"God's blessing upon you both," she whispered. Heaving her ski bundle to her shoulders over her knapsack, the two sacks balancing the load, she strode toward the caves, cognizant that these were her first steps toward freedom without worry. She felt only the sadness of loss.

The Germans may have thought her grandparents knew something of use to them regarding the apparent disappearances of persons of interest to them. The butcher told her that one of the people she had helped was a scientist that the Reich wanted badly. Perhaps they deduced that the village was a likely crossing point and decided to pressure townspeople. Blessedly, no one caved to that pressure, but instead acted like simpletons leading a bucolic life away from the war. Herr Bergmann reported that Hans, the friendly guard beyond the town, had been summarily shot on the grounds of dereliction of duty, as had his relief comrade who routinely did the overnight watch. His commanding officer used them as an object lesson, executing them in the village square, requiring everyone to witness the event. That action merely hardened the hearts and spirits of the people, 99% of whom knew nothing any-way. They heard tales of the same group of soldiers paying visits to other border towns and villages, spreading their nasty brand of cruelty and fear. Yet, the people they sought remained missing, and in a short while, the attention to the Austro-Swiss border dimin-ished, made more likely by the mountainous terrain and consistent-ly snowy, severe weather.

Chapter Twenty-three
The Convent

Kloster der Varlorenen

She lay in bed awaiting sleep, idly wondering what life might have been if she chose another path so long ago. She realized that her life was blessed to be in the care of the sisters. Each had, in her own way, mothered the young girl who appeared without warning. She mused that it was a healthy arrangement for both: Annaliese's parents and grandparents were dead--butchered by the Germans, and afterward, she needed patient care and understanding; the nuns had no children of their own as chaste brides of Christ, but still possessed hormones and the innate female needs of nurture. Her appearance at the Convent as a skinny wraith in the middle of the night was fortuitous for both Anneliese and, as it turned out, for the nuns.

When the ragged, skinny girl Annaliese, now called "Hannah," arrived at the gates of The Kloster, the kindly Mother Superior took her in without hesitation. Wartime created orphans, unwed mothers, refugees, those seeking political asylum, and many other needy categories. Dedicated to service under the pledge of St. Benedict [see Endnotes], the nuns and sisters provided succor to all those who sought help. At the time of Annaliese's appearance, three children aged 4-7 were in residence. Annaliese was eleven or twelve. The ravages of war visible in her eyes told Reverend Mother Alycia that she had seen horrors no child should suffer, but which many did in these troubled times.

Annaliese did not speak. Reverend Mother Alycia was familiar with this trauma. She merely ordered the sisters to prepare a bath and a bed in one of the available cells, assigning three sisters to maintain watch over her throughout the next several hours. She gently held Annaliese for a long time, rocking her while softly humming, until the girl relaxed in her embrace. Following the gentle ministrations of the loving nuns, Annaliese allowed herself to sleep. The next morning, she joined the small group of convent residents for morning prayer and breakfast. Sister Marta's open and friendly face elicited a smile from Annaliese as a plate of eggs and bread was placed before her.

"Those are fresh eggs, *Liebchen*, from our very cooperative chickens!" Sister Marta beamed and exclaimed, "Praise God!" when she received Annaliese's acknowledging smile.

As days passed, and Annaliese repeatedly declined to tell the Mother Superior her name or supply any information about her origins, a decision was taken and announced at vespers two weeks following Annaliese's arrival.

"We shall have a morning celebration for the naming of our newest daughter, Sisters. If you agree," and Mother Superior inclined her head toward the girl, "you shall be known as Hannah Blume. Hannah kept her promises to God in the Bible, and Blume is in honor of your love and care for our gardens, thanks to Sister Marta. As well, you are a beautiful flower that our Lord has brought to brighten our lives. Already, you have helped us in so many ways and made us smile. We welcome you as a child of God within our walls. You are no longer 'lost,' sweet Hannah. Thanks be to God." All the sisters repeated the phrase and then clapped and surrounded the smiling Hannah to hug her and kiss on the cheek or brow. So began the life of Hannah Blume at The Kloster.

Sister Marta, a large woman, was in charge of the gardens and cooking. Under her patient tutelage, Hannah learned much about herbs, flowers, vegetables, and trees. She pleased Sister Marta with her sponge-like ability to retain Marta's instruction, carry out mundane tasks without complaint, and faithfully to assume responsibility for the care and nurture of all growing things as reliably as she looked after the nuns and sisters' health and well-being.

Sister Mary Margret taught her routine first-aid procedures together with various treatments for common ailments. She helped her develop diagnostic ability through a keen eye to spot more severe problems or symptoms of life-threatening illnesses. The town had only an aging general practitioner. Dr. Weinstein was a kindly, old Jew whose family had perished in WWI. He had emigrated to their small village immediately afterward. Now in his late seventies, his effectiveness in caring for the townspeople relied on Sister Mary

Margret's professional medical knowledge and assistance. Sister Mary Margret's abilities and availability were critical.

Reverend Mother Alycia—Mother Superior—calmly and effectively led the small contingent of nuns and sisters of the Convent of the Lost, officially known as Kloster der Verlorenen. The Convent of the Lost was an outpost of the well-established Fahr Convent—part of the double monastery with Einsiedeln's monks. Fahr Monastery (Kloster Fahr) is a Benedictine monastery of nuns geographically and politically in the canton of Aargau, surrounded by the municipality of Unterengstringen (in the canton of Zürich), so is not far from the city of Zürich. Established in AD 1130, Einsiedeln Abbey rules the nunnery, governed in daily life by a Prioress appointed by the Abbot. The Prioress of Fahr Convent established the much smaller Kloster der Verlorenen during WWI, and Fahr Convent serves as its Mother House. Kloster der Verlorenen is run by a Mother Superior directly reportable to the Prioress at Fahr Convent. She, in turn, is reportable to the Abbot of Einsiedeln [Zürich].

Townspeople called it merely "The Kloster." Serving several mountain villages, their stone convent (a medieval outpost castle near three borders) was on a hillside just beyond the town's southwestern limits. It overlooked a lake not far from Zürich, in the northwest, with the Liechtenstein and Austrian borders closely east, and the German border farther north. The Convent of the Lost lay within the southeast region of canton St. Gallen, close to canton Glarus.

Her daily routine consisted of following the convent schedule for prayer and praise, taking meals together, working with Sisters Marta (in the garden), and Mary Margret preparing herbal remedies or assisting with the treatment of the town folk referred to the Convent by the aging town physician, Dr. Weinstein. He could no longer sustain a full day of work and increasingly transferred his patients to Sister Mary Margret.

As the Kloster was not a monastery, the nuns were not cloistered. They could, therefore—with Mother Superior's permission—leave the Convent for shopping or work purposes. Not all the nuns were "extern" sisters, only those whose talents were used in the town or needed to sustain the Convent. The Kloster had only three "sisters" who had taken temporary vows for several years [not less than three years and not more than six], whereas all of the eight nuns took solemn vows for life. Extern sisters helped shop, pass messages, assist with home care for the villagers, charitable works, and other commonplace but required tasks. Each sister was subsidiary to her "assigned nun," as determined by Mother Superior. However, all the women in service referred to each other as "sister," denoting their sisterhood in Christ's service. All lived within the convent walls; all wore habits; all lived lives of prayer, contemplation, and service to others and saw to their duties for convent operation.

All of the nuns at The Kloster took vows of stability (to remain members of their community), obedience (to an abbess, prioress, or mother superior), and conversion of life (poverty and celibacy). Their dress consisted of a tunic tied at the waist, with a leather belt from which hung either their rosary or a simple cross. Reverend Mother Alycia wore a large cross on a chain around her neck, a mark of her position as Mother Superior of The Kloster. Each professed nun wore a white wimple and black veil. In the winter months, each nun also wore a black woolen tunic overtop of their white one. The extern sisters had completed their postulancy in between six months to two years to test the life. They received the order's habit but with a white veil, signifying they were in the novitiate (a period of one to two years) or had taken temporary vows, awaiting petition to take permanent, solemn vows. The slight differences in habit allowed the townspeople to differentiate between members of their order. Although the Convent was enclosed by walls, it was a small community explicitly formed to serve the local surrounding villages and hamlets. Thus, the nuns within could forego strict adherence to speaking behind grilles or half walls to communicate with visitors or recitation of the full Liturgy throughout the day in church or a chapel. The nuns and sisters at The Kloster were not monastics in an enclosed community. They were much loved and respected by the people of surrounding towns and villages for their tireless support and care of all.

Hannah was schooled within the convent walls until the time arrived to apply to and attend university in Zürich. She had displayed a natural affinity for healing during her years with Sister Mary Margret and Dr. Weinstein. The good doctor had long since retired from practice to his small cottage by the lake, receiving daily visits and provisions from the sisters and villagers alike. On some occasions requiring his expertise, Sister Mary Margret would collect him to accompany her for a house call.

As the closest large city, Zürich was host to one of the best global universities. Hannah was accepted on full scholarship with limitations in recognizing her status with the Convent and several personal recommendations from persons of notoriety. After six years, she completed her Masters' degree, taking the Swiss national examination in medicine, which allowed her to practice as a doctor. Hannah completed the three-year mandatory training as an assistant physician and was offered a position at the hospital in Zürich but chose to return to her village as a private practitioner with hospital privileges. Frau Hannah Blume became Dr. Hannah Blume, and all the sisters and nuns rejoiced! Arrangements were made, and she took the premises previously occupied by Dr. Weinstein for her clinic in the village, in which building her office was also housed. One clerk, Sister Mary Margret, and one nurse comprised the staff to provide 6-day per week alternating coverage. This schedule allowed Hannah the freedom to make house calls depending upon the patient load schedule.

Long past the hour when everyone had retired, Hannah woke from her doze in the chair by the fire, which was now only glowing embers. She was chilled and supposed that was what awakened her. She heard a light tapping. Scuffling in her overlarge slippers to the door of her cell, she quietly called out. "Yes? Is someone there?"

"Apologies, Hannah. It is Sister Birgit. Sister Helga asked me to fetch you. There is a German soldier at the gate who asks for help from a doctor. Klaus ran from the Gatehouse and found Sister Helga, who was on night duty. She is with the man now."

"It is alright, Sister Birgit. Where are they now? I will dress and come."

"In the hall sitting room, I think. I'm sorry, I didn't ask, but that is where she might take him."

"Fine, I'll go there first. You tell Sister Helga that I am on my way, please." Hurriedly casting off her shift, she slipped into a long gray dress and pulled on her black cardigan, socks, and flat shoes, not bothering to unbraid her hair. Grabbing her medical bag, she dashed out the door, down the hall to the staircase, and arrived slightly breathless at the sitting room. There she saw Sister Helga sitting by the fire with a uniformed man in silence. When Helga saw her, she bowed her head and mumbled a word of thanks to God. She was clearly shaken by the unexpected event.

Hannah went to her immediately, giving her a light hug. "Thank you, Sister Helga. You did very well," she reassured the nun. Turning to the man, "How may we help you? Hauptmann, is it?"

"Yes, Frau? Please forgive the intrusion at such a late hour."

The Captain slightly bowed, clicking his heels from habit and politeness.

"I am Frau Blume, yes. I repeat, how may we help you at such a late hour, as you say. We are not accustomed to receiving visitors in the middle of the night except for rare emergencies."

"I understand. I, we, were told we could find the doctor here. I need a doctor immediately. Can you summon him? Much time has been wasted already."

"You look perfectly well, Captain. But, yes, a doctor is here." She thrust her hand toward him. "Doctor Hannah Blume. And where is the patient?"

After the initial shock, Hauptmann Müller gathered himself. "He is in the car and almost unconscious with a very high fever."

"I shall come and examine him. We may have to bring him to my clinic in the village. Do you have sufficient help to carry him, if necessary?"

"Yes. My driver and I can manage," he said, following her brisk pace from the hall to the wrought iron gate. He opened the rear door to reveal a man drenched in sweat, whispering in hallucination. Hannah and the Captain entered the vehicle, Hannah sitting beside the older man. She noticed from the ranking on his uniform that he was a high-level Stabsoffiziere. After a cursory examination, Hannah advised, "We had better go to my clinic in the village. I cannot properly treat him here. Give me a moment to explain to someone here." Without waiting for a reply, she jumped out of the car and ran to the gate where Sister Helga stood behind Klaus. After only brief moments, she was back in the car and ordered, *Schnell!*"

Hauptmann Müller and Hans carried the General into Hannah's clinic, gently laying him on the examination table. Müller whispered some instructions to the driver, telling him to wait in the car. When he turned back to Hannah, the patient's clothing was unbuttoned, revealing his bare chest and abdomen.

"Help me remove this uniform," she said, holding a sheet which she placed over him. Then, reaching for his jacket, "Hold him up." After removing his leather holster, jacket, and shirt, she donned her stethoscope, gesturing the Captain to the man's feet. "Get on with it, Hauptmann: pants, boots, everything." When he had finished, she nodded to a chair near the door. The Captain sat down, ever watchful. The examination, although thorough, took less than ten minutes. She took a blood sample and spent what seemed an excessive amount of time under the sheet in the General's nether region.

"Does he have appendicitis, Frau Doctor?"

"No, I am sure he does not. What has he said to you, Captain? About how he feels, I mean."

"Not very much. The General complained little about pain, so I thought maybe he developed an ulcer, or his appendix might be acting up. Sometimes, he gets dizzy, but only for a few moments. The General is stoic and a powerful man in mind, body, and principle," he said with evident admiration and loyalty.

"I see. Well, your general needs antibiotics and further treatment. I have given him a strong initial dose, and in a short time, he will come back to himself. In the meantime, we will try to break this fever, and I shall have a look at his blood sample. If he becomes fully conscious while I am in the adjacent room, quieten him and explain where he is. Call me, and I shall be with you in minutes. Do not cover him with a blanket at this time. Place the compresses where I show you."

"I will, Doctor. Thank you. He is an essential man," said the Captain, folding the General's discarded uniform and placing it over one of the chairs.

She allowed herself a brief assessment of the Captain and his general, then hurried off to her lab with her clipboard, scraping, and blood sample. After a confirming check in one of her reference books, Hannah was satisfied that she knew what ailed the General. She prepared herself for a serious conversation with the high-level German official.

When she returned to the exam room, the Captain was speaking softly with his commanding officer, who seemed fully aware of his surroundings and was intently listening. Hauptmann Müller nodded to Hannah as she approached. "May I present Doctor Hannah Blume. Doctor Blume, General der Gebirgstruppe Wolfgang von Richter."

Clutching her clipboard to her chest. "General," Hannah nodded. "Shall we speak in private?"

Looking at the Captain, "You may relax in the waiting room, Ulrich. Thank you."

Rechecking his temperature, Hannah stated, "You are considerably better than when we first met, General. You still have a temperature, but it is no longer dangerous and will continue to abate. As for the underlying cause of your visit ..."

"Yes, Doctor, it seems to have gotten the best of me. I hoped whatever was ailing me would run its course, but it seems to have gotten worse."

"Do you suspect what is wrong with you, General?" Hannah considered allowing the man to save face by looking away but instead chose to flatly stare at him.

"War makes strange bedfellows, shall we say? I have been away from home for an exceedingly long time, and my postings do not always guarantee suitable companions."

"Hmm, so it is possible, perhaps even likely, that the person from whom you contracted this venereal disease is infecting others. Also, you may have infected other paramours on your various postings. I need to know as accurately as you can recount--when you first noticed the problem, where you were geographically at the time, and with whom."

The General did his best to supply a medical history, sketchy at best with no definitive names, only estimated dates, and locations. With the preponderance of infidelity, prostitution, temporary relationships, etc. fostered by wartime, there was little chance to trace other sexual transmissions.

"Why seek a local doctor, General? Why not consult your army physician? Surely, he has much experience with this sort of thing. The amount of discomfort you must be in and clearly have endured for weeks, I think, would drive most men to seek help before this. Here, this will help with the pain," she said as she injected him. "And these will help in the days to come. The instructions are on the bottle. Do not take the tablets with alcohol unless you want to make a fool of yourself or subject your men to nonsensical orders."

"Are you saying I can no longer drink, Doctor?" the General asked with wide eyes.

Hannah laughed, "No, I don't care if you drink, General, just not as a chaser with the tablets. Water, juice, coffee, or tea would be better. Your blood shows a serious infection, and you need to faithfully take the tablets to help your body. Now, let's get to the treatment of these lesions," she said as she folded back the sheet to reveal suppurated sores over a considerable portion of his genitals and lower abdomen.

She explained that the initial loading dose of antibiotics she had given him should address the significant infection but would require further treatment. She needed further testing to ensure he had not contracted more than one disease in parallel. While the treatment for all venereal diseases was similar, some were bacterial, and others were viral; some could be completely cured; others were chronic but could be managed. Results of further testing would determine his status, degree, and stage of infection.

"I can have broader results for you in about two to three weeks. I am sorry, but the samples must be processed in Zürich. Perhaps your man can drive them there today for expediency. It is the closest place with the appropriate facilities. Meantime, I can treat these lesions for your comfort and give you instructions and some additional topical medication to hold you over between visits. If you have any signs of weakness, lack of coordination, numbness, swelling, fever, or a bloody or cloudy discharge from the penis, notify me at once."

"Please understand, Doctor, this is a sensitive matter for a man in my position. I need complete confidentiality. I could not risk an army physician and the accompanying medical records. Besides, we were scheduled for the car trip to this sector of Switzerland and several weeks or months in this posting. I hoped to last a bit longer, but the discomfort was, as you said, quite unbearable, and the other symptoms—mostly the fever—made this an emergency visit. I apologize for spoiling your sleep."

He twitched as she scraped and swabbed the worst of his abscesses, removing oozing and crusted pus and sealing the sores. "You will undoubtedly have continued pain during urination, but that too will ease with time and continued medication. You may resume normal duties the day after tomorrow. Today, if you wish to do so, you may work but only for a few hours. Take the rest of the day to give your body some rest to heal. And do not concern yourself; all doctors respect confidentiality."

"Thank you, Doctor. You have been kind and thorough. Ulrich will handle the payment. I assume you have no objection to cash?"

"No, I do not, but I have an alternate suggestion, which I hope will not insult. Because of the surrounding war, supplies are at a premium. Perhaps in payment or barter, you could expedite or locate some of the drugs needed in this clinic? For instance, penicillin—such as I gave you tonight—is perilously low. I could make a list, and you wouldn't have to concern yourself about future visits or records that could damage your reputation."

"You are bold, Doctor Blume. You are also clever and seem to understand the way of wartime beyond the confines of your quiet, little, mountain village."

"I am the only physician available for miles, General. The people I serve continually need help and treatment for a variety of reasons. Supplies dwindle; replacements are slow to unavailable. You would be helping this neutral country's citizenry, which allows you entry, residence, and operation, but still suffers the effects of a war waged by Germany. It seems a fair exchange to me. Ja? And, of course, I will remain at your disposal, as I am not going anywhere."

"Agreed. I will inform Ulrich about everything. He is the only one who has my complete confidence—besides you. Be aware, Doctor, my expectations are high and constant. Do not disappoint me."

Hannah stiffened. "I will keep my end of the bargain so long as you keep yours." Her eyes burned with passion. The General erroneously read that "tell" to mean that she was pleased with her arrangement. In reality, Hannah was glad to have another chess piece to save for her commitment to revenge.

Chapter Twenty-four
from Zurich With Love

Hannah made the last check on the Mayor's wife and new baby and then took her leave.

"Hannah, thank you most sincerely for staying with me. I know the obstetrician here is a good one, but I have confidence in you. Besides, you know my history of so many miscarriages intimately. I just did not wish to take any chances. As it turns out, you were of critical help in the operating room, so thank you, thank you." The Mayor and his wife gave Hannah a tearful goodbye. As an official in Hannah's small town whose wife had experienced many trials trying to bear him children, the Mayor requested Hannah to accompany them to Zürich. This was less a request but a veiled obligation and duty. She was fond of the pair and happy to comply.

Leaving Zürich in the Mayor's car (at his insistence), Hannah relaxed into the luxury of the leather. The Mayor had decided to spend a few days with his wife and newborn, more to convince himself that they were alright than to be of help and company. Hannah suspected that sweet Gerda might have preferred a few days' rest on her own. Still, their generosity allowed Hannah to stop at Fahr Monastery and visit with the Prioress on her way back to The Kloster. It was only a short ride, and the driver was happy to have three hours on his own while Hannah spent time at the Monastery.

"I am sure the nuns will invite me to the midday meal, Bernhard, so if you please, return for me about 3:00 PM. That should allow us to reach The Kloster and the village before dark." Hannah looked forward to her few hours at the Monastery. The Monastery's history dated back to the 1300s, with suppression around 1530 during the Reformation, renovations, closures, and eventual autonomy ending in 1932. Under the jurisdiction of the Abbot of Einsiedeln, the Prioress (an Abbot appointment) governed the daily life of the nuns.

With keen eyes, stern resolve, and an indomitable spirit despite her gentle manner, Prioress Mathilda was an apt administrator with wisdom that seemed to fly beyond the walls of her cloistered convent. She awaited Hannah's arrival behind the massive iron gates set into two-foot-thick walls that encircled the convent. "My dear Hannah. It is wonderful to see you again." With her arms outstretched, Hannah ran to Mother Mathilda and immediately burst into tears. "Why, my dear girl, what is this? Come, we shall have some tea and a talk." Walking with her arm around Hannah's shoulder, she called Sister Ana to prepare and serve tea in her office and Sister Brigitta to set another place for the midday meal. "You will stay, of course."

Once in the Prioress' office's enclosing peace, Hannah relaxed and apologized for the emotional reception. "It has been a rather harrowing few weeks, Mother. But Reverend Mother Alycia sends her love and respect, as do all the nuns and sisters. I confess I felt privileged to see you and spend a few hours at Fahr Monastery. Thank you for all of your help and support over the years."

"My dear Hannah, you are a light and a joy for my sisters at The Kloster. That you chose to remain resident there to look after them and the villagers is a particular blessing. That you also look after all of us is a blessing multiplied! It is we who give thanks to you! Now, tell me everything."

Hannah reiterated the late-night arrival of Hauptmann Müller. She explained her treatment of Muller's commanding officer, his ailment, their bargain, and the German interest in the operation of The Kloster and the complexion of its residents. Hannah mentioned that the General was at the hospital when she was overseeing the treatment and delivery of the Mayor's wife and child. Though she had no indication the General's visit was connected to her presence, she recalled wondering if he was checking on her residency details or history. Hannah discarded the notion and had redirected her focus to her patient and the reason for being there. However, she still questioned it in the back of her mind.

"They have searched the archives and the Reverend Mother's records. I do not know what they are looking for, but, clearly, they think there is something or someone at the convent of interest to them. The Hauptmann explained that since mountain troops are stationed in and around Switzerland, it falls to them to flush out any dissenters to the Reich and refugees they suspect might be of use or threat. I think it is all wrong and should not be allowed by our government because we are a neutral country!"

"Ah, my dear Hannah, neutrality can be maintained only with 'give and take.' That is the reality of global war and silent threat. It is an ever-changing landscape that must be carefully monitored and negotiated. How does Reverend Mother Alycia fare?"

"She is a rock covered in velvet! I do not know what we would do without her. The other sisters fuss and worry when the soldiers come. Reverend Mother appears with one or two calm words, and all is right again under Heaven. We remain close."

"Good, my child. That is how it should be." Pouring a second cup of tea, the wise Prioress said, "And the rest of it? What else troubles you, Hannah?"

Shaking her head in amazement, Hannah declared, "You must be the wisest woman I have ever known! How did you suspect there was more?"

"Only God knows, my dear, and He allows my Guardian Angels to whisper to me!" she chirped.

"Perhaps most important, I am fearful that my presence is the root cause of the Germans' attention. It might have something to do with my arrival and subsequent life there. I left Austria after helping many families and people escape through the caves and over the border trails. Some of those people were of value to the Reich; others suspected of treason or revolutionary ideas; some were also Jews. When I left after my grandparents were killed, I was taken in by The Kloster and nursed back to mental and physical health, you will remember. When I could finally speak about my past, Mother Alycia merely accepted me but never recorded my appearance. Subsequently, when she was questioned, she feigned specific knowledge about my arrival circumstances—the when and how of their questions. I got lumped in with all the other war orphans that sought refuge within those walls. Of course, a few opted to return for a novitiate, but most were placed in homes. I merely stayed.

"Mother did not lie, exactly; she simply did not reveal the details of my arrival or my age. One couldn't even qualify it as a lie of omission because she steered the conversation to explain the convent's operative circumstances in earlier days, the struggle for survival, the constant need to treat and feed the villagers, the influx of orphaned children, etc. She made a good case for lack of record-keeping, which seemed both unnecessary and time-consuming. Those nuns had no time to spare! You know what a small house it is and how overburdened they have been. I cannot help but think that my presence there might make them suspicious. After all, I didn't arrive as a toddler, but as a preteen! Not addressing my age on arrival, she did address my unique needs...you know, in terms of not speaking. So, I believe they accepted that I was not a child who could be easily relocated or placed with a family. During wartime, people need contributing family members, not a millstone that is merely another mouth to feed. It did help, of course, that I performed jobs for the convent and the sisters. My work at the clinic and in the village with Sister Mary Margret was very much needed.

"But did my very presence and circumstances cause our wonderfully sweet and committed Reverend Mother to commit a sin before God? And does my presence place her in any danger? All I can think of are my sweet, unsuspecting grandparents who were brutally murdered by the Nazis. I believe that happened because of me and what I was doing! And they didn't even know about it! I cannot allow the same thing to happen to Reverend Mother; I cannot be the cause of any hurt to come to The Kloster after all they have done for me. Do you understand, Mother?"

"I do, yes. I shall have to contemplate awhile before answering you fully, Hannah. But this I know: you are feeling guilt where none should exist." Nodding to Sister Brigitta, who was standing in the doorway, "We shall be along presently, thank you, Sister."

"Oh, I didn't hear her. Another blunder! What can I do to fix that? I don't want to expose the Reverend Mother in any way!"

"She heard nothing of any damage as she only just appeared. Besides, Sister Brigitta has taken a vow of silence. Now, we must go to the dining hall. Come, my child. We will finish our talk in the garden after we have eaten as we are all well here, and you have no patients to attend. Come now."

After their meal, they retired to the garden with cups of tea. "'Vengeance is mine,' the Lord told us, remember Hannah? I know you believe your life in Austria and the path you chose to help people escape the Nazis was motivated by vengeance for your parents' deaths, ja?" The Prioress and Hannah settled themselves on the benches in the beautiful garden, the lilting sounds of the nearby fountain complementing the soothing effect of the convent's ambiance.

"Yes, Mother, that is so. When I came to Switzerland after *Großvater* and *Oma* were lost to me, I thought I had left all that behind. Only recently, when Hauptmann Müller and I had a conversation about current events, I realized my passionate dislike of war and German tactics might be fueled by the need for revenge. I am basically living an alias life, Mother, thanks to the protection of Reverend Mother Alycia, who has ensured there is no connection between Anneliese Kaiser and Hannah Blume. I don't want her at risk because of my situation and weakness of character. However, Hauptmann Müller seems to think I have a strong, intransigent character that lacks all understanding for the life of a loyal soldier! But he is wrong."

"Aha! The last piece of the puzzle! But first, let me address what you feel. Revenge is much the same as vengeance, dear, as it usually involves a payback or reprisal, retribution of sorts. Is that what you think you are doing by helping people? Perhaps, you might look at it differently: your help deprives the Nazis of exercising brutality against people. It is a protective move on the chessboard of life. If you feel justification and satisfaction, so much the better because the true fuel for your actions is the spirit of brotherhood and love, and that is a direct command from God. It is so with all the sisters here and those at The Kloster, as well. It is the founding motivation for all our actions because we put our love for God first and foremost, and try our best to follow His commandments in our daily lives."

"I never thought about it that way," admitted Hannah.

"Next, you do not control Mother Superior Alycia or her actions. She chooses what to do or not do, based upon her prayers, contemplations, and commitment to Christ. If someone benefits, it is God's will that it be so.

"And finally, this Hauptmann Müller about whom you speak. He troubles you." She held up a finger to silence Hannah when it was clear that she was about to interrupt. "It matters not whether you have a fleeting attraction to him. It is the meat of your conversations and the opposing viewpoints that trouble you. Consider, dear Hannah, this may bother you because you question how such a man as he, who appears to be a reasonably pleasant, courteous, and loyal officer, could align himself with an evil man like Hitler, ja? May I suggest that he disagrees with Hitlerian initiatives but is bound by his oaths to be a good officer and soldier for his country? Not everyone agrees with their leaders, and when they do not agree, not everyone can distance themselves and enact a change. You must ask yourself: can this man simply stop being a soldier and officer? Would there be repercussions to, perhaps, his family or friends beyond those that would impact him personally? You don't know.

"If, on the other hand, he does agree with Hitler's orders and is defensive about the unconscionable actions taken by the Nazis as a whole, then you are justified in your opinion of him. I fully understand that you would find any attention from him completely unacceptable in that scenario He would not be a person worthy of trust, but a person to treat with awareness and a distant courtesy for your own protection and the protection of those you hold dear. Only you and he hold the answers to both alternatives, and until you know for sure where you and he stand, you can make no fair decision."

"You have set my heart at ease, Mother. Thank you. You always have sufficient wisdom to impart. I am not a child any longer, and I am embarrassed I did not see these things myself." Hannah hung her head.

"Now really, dear Hannah, you do go on! Do you not think that we all have our blind spots? We learn and learn and continue to learn as we live this life. Our lives here are relatively quiet, as we are cloistered. Yours is fraught with pressures that would fray anyone's nerves. Your schedule is a recipe for continual exhaustion because you do not know how to stop giving of yourself, even when it is to your detriment. I prescribe time off. I know, you object, because there is no spare time every week. It doesn't have to be every week, dear, but you must try to incorporate complete separation and rest at least once a month. Otherwise, you will begin to make mistakes and burn out. People need you, Hannah. The Kloster needs you; we, here at Fahr Monastery, need you. Your village people need you. Those who are taken in by the nuns at The Kloster need you not only for initial treatment and care but to help get them to us, where they can be sequestered."

Hannah's head jerked alert at that last statement. "What do you mean?"

"Reverend Mother Alycia will explain when you return home, Hannah. For now, it is enough that you know that we have a few Jewish mothers and their children here at Fahr Convent. Only Mother Superior at The Kloster and two of her nuns together with two of my nuns, and I know this; now you know it. We are expecting another few over the next months, and that is where you will be able to help. Now, no more questions; no more talk. I must retire to prayer, and you must go home. I had Sister Alia bring a box to the gate for Mother Superior if you would be so kind as to deliver it for me with my love."

The two women hugged and kissed; Hannah expressed her parting thanks again. As she walked down the stone hall, she turned back briefly and beheld the figure of the Prioress standing alone in the distance, the late afternoon's sun rays bathing her form as if in a golden aura. The benevolence of her smile washed over Hannah. That image would sustain Hannah through the coming months.

Hannah reviewed her conversation with the Prioress on the drive home. She felt so relieved, she dozed for over half the journey. On arrival, she was greeted by an unfamiliar German officer whose uniform Hannah had not seen previously. With a stern tone, he ordered Hannah to produce her identification papers and answer questions about where she had been, for how long, her purpose, etc., etc. While she was being interrogated, some of his men searched the car, removing her luggage and the box from Fahr Convent's Prioress.

"Against the car!" the officer ordered brashly, pushing Hannah. For her objection, she received a resounding slap across the face that made her lip bleed. "Search her thoroughly!" the officer commanded. Meanwhile, her luggage was opened, the contents scattered on the grassy berm. The box, too, was opened under suspicion of the contents being contraband.

The soldier roughly searched Hannah, pushing her cheek firmly to the car's bonnet as he ran his hands over her body. He then flipped her and, using both hands, investigated her front side, prolonging his probe of her chest and nether region. Hannah said nothing, only glared at him defiantly.

"What is this?" demanded the officer, gesturing to the contents of the convent box splayed on the grass.

"They are Bibles sent by the Prioress at Fahr Monastery to the Mother Superior of this convent. You surely cannot find fault with the Word of God!" Hannah said vindictively. "I live here; I am the doctor for this convent and the village. My medical bag has sensitive instruments and medicines. If anything is out of order or broken, I shall make a formal complaint to General der Gebirgstruppe, who, among others, is a patient of mine. Do we understand each other, Leutnant? Your uniform tells me you are SA, the Sturmabteilung Storm Troopers. Am I correct? I want to make sure you get full credit for the way I have been treated."

During this exchange, Klaus had slipped through the partially opened iron gates and was rushing to retrieve the scattered Bibles, many of which landed with open covers in awkward positions. The imposing Sister Marta followed with her wheelbarrow, demanding, "What is the meaning of this? This is a house of God, including the land upon which you stand! You dare to defile it?!"

Unaccustomed to any resistance to the violence of his overpowering tactics, Sister Marta and Hannah gave him pause. Just then, Hauptmann Müller and the General arrived by car, Müller leaping out of the vehicle before it had stopped entirely.

"*Leutnant! Was ist das?* Doctor Blume is under the General's protection, so unless you want to be Korporal, release her immediately! *Gib mir deinen Namen und deine Abteilung sofort*! [Give me is your name and division at once!]

With an arrogant attitude, the Leutnant scribbled the information, tore the sheet from his chest notebook, and strolled to Müller. With only a slight nod, he handed the note over, never letting his insolent gaze fall from the Captain. When the General exited the vehicle, all the Leutnant's men snapped to attention where they stood, including the Leutnant, whose face reddened.

The General walked immediately to Hannah, ignoring all of the Brown Shirts. "Are you all right, Doctor Blume? My apologies, this should not have happened." Hannah was speechless and could only nod and breathe heavily in noticeable relief as she attempted to close her blouse despite that the buttons were missing, and the fabric torn.

Turning to the detachment of rowdy soldiers, the General quietly ordered, "Formation!" The soldiers hurried to make a straight line. Then to the Leutnant, his glare making clear his displeasure, "I shall revisit this at Headquarters. I can assure you this is not the end of the matter. Take this rabble and be gone from here immediately. *Jetzt!*" Not a few seconds after the General had delivered the orders, three more Brown Shirts came running from behind the gates to join their ranks. The Leutnant motioned to his men. They ran to their vehicles and sped away.

Hannah had the presence of mind to hurriedly thank the General and Hauptmann, rushed into the convent, and left Klaus and Marta to gather the contents of her luggage and the box of Bibles. As she ran down the path from the encircling wall to the building, she heard weeping and excited whispers.

"What has happened here?" she demanded, trying her best

to soften her worried tone.

"The Germans, they…" sobbed Sister Birgit, "they forced their way into Reverend Mother's Office, and …"

"And what?! Sister Birgit is Mother all right?" cried Hannah, half running down the hallway to the Mother Superior's Office. When she arrived, she saw Sister Sigrid and Sister Elke attending the Reverend Mother, who lay on the floor motionless and silent. Hannah's heart dropped. Rushing to her, she bade the sisters step back so she could perform an examination, yelling to Sister Birgit to fetch her medical bag from Sister Marta outside the gates.

Working quickly to gently palpate the Reverend Mother's body, she told Sister Sigrid to fetch clean cloths, towels, and hot water. Sister Elke was dispatched for blankets and one of the Reverend Mother's nightdresses, a soft veil without wimple, clean stockings, socks, and slippers. A breathless Sister Birgit arrived with Hannah's medical bag.

Aside from cuts and contusions on her face, some broken ribs, and abdominal bruising, the most immediate injury Hannah identified was a dislocated right shoulder. In short order, the Sisters Sigrid and Elke returned. After more careful palpation, Hannah was reasonably sure how Reverend Mother's shoulder had popped out and that there were no broken bones. The first thing needed was a shot for the obvious pain she was in, along with some gentle massage to try to relax her muscles. Hannah instructed Sister Sigrid to firmly hold the Reverend Mother's upper torso; Sister Elke bent over her legs and feet to keep them still.

"Mother, I know you are hurting, and I will try to hurt you no further. But I must see if this joint will go in by itself. Are you ready?" The stoic woman nodded and shut her eyes. While the shot was having its initial effect, Hannah realized that Reverend Mother's muscles were still bunched, contracted, and quivering. Her massage had not done enough, and gentle pressure to coax the ball back into the cup failed. Mother Alycia lapsed into unconsciousness. Gently and slowly moving the arm to about 45 degrees from Mother's body, Hannah applied the pull/pressure technique using the ball of her foot in Mother Superior's armpit. As gently as possible, Hannah pulled steadily on the arm, but only enough to allow the joint to pop back into place. The Reverend Mother regained mindfulness shortly after Hannah had reset her shoulder.

"Hannah! Welcome home, my child. I'm sorry, I must have fainted," she said weakly. Hannah examined the Mother's head, and a growing lump and blood confirmed her suspicion of a possible slight concussion when her head hit the stone floor. Hannah was sure that she had likely been pushed or thrown after receiving the striking blows because of her other injuries.

"Not to worry, Reverend Mother. I am here now, and you shall be fine, but you must rest and follow my orders. Do you promise?" Hannah tenderly stroked the woman's unbruised cheek; the other was bruised so badly that her eye was swollen shut as well.

"Yes, yes, my dear. But please do not let the sisters fuss. I shall be fine in a bit." She drifted off again in reaction to the shot Hannah had given her only a few moments before. Sisters Sigrid and Elke helped Hannah carry the Reverend Mother to the daybed near the fireplace. Sister Sigrid and Hannah removed her soiled and bloodied garments while Sister Elke stoked the fire until it blazed. Hannah gently cleaned her wounds, applying ointment or bandages where required, and wrapped her ribs with gauze and tape. They redressed her in the garments Elke retrieved from the Reverend Mother's cell. Last, Hannah placed Reverend Mother's arm in a sling.

Weeping throughout, Sister Elke—one of the younger nuns—said, "Oh, I hate them for what they have done to her. She is such a pure soul. How could they?"

Continuing her treatment, Hannah said, "No, no, Elke, do not hate. As I learned not hours before returning home, better it is to say we do not understand or approve, but not hate. Do not give them the power to make you less than you are, even for a moment. You love God, and God loves you, Sister Elke; hold fast to that, and in that, you will find the strength to pity them. Reverend Mother will be all right with time. God brought me home to care for her, and all of your sisters helped defray this ugliness by your support. It could have been much worse but for your presence and distraction. Now lead the others in the best support of all: prayer. Can you do that for all of us?"

Glad to have something constructive to do, Sister Elke nodded her compliance and rushed away.

"Sister Sigrid, stay by Mother's side and continue to apply the compresses. I must clean myself from my encounter with the Brown Shirts. I will return as soon as I can. She should remain asleep for an hour or a bit more. We don't want her to go to a fever. I will recheck her blood pressure and temperature once I am back. I will ask one of the novices to deliver a tray of tea outside the door.

I want no one in here but you for now. Do you understand?"

"Yes, Hannah. It will be so." She positioned a chair beside the daybed and the table with the basin and cloths.

"We shall have to get her to the hospital after some rest and once the swelling abates. I want to make sure there are no breaks or other complications, so you must encourage her not to use her shoulder when she awakens." Following Hannah to the door, Sister Sigrid locked it once Hannah crossed the threshold.

On the way to her cell, Hannah fumed. The Germans! Was there no end to them! Again, and again, these gentle nuns were subjected to reckless aggressiveness and vulgarity—all in a House of God under the justification of war! 'Oh, God, help me to stand firm but prudent in the face of such injustice!' she fervently prayed as she ran a bath to erase the feel of filthy, insinuative hands from her body.

Chapter Twenty-five
Persistance

Responding to a gentle knock at the door to her room, Hannah beheld an embarrassed Klaus standing with his hat in his hands.

"*Entschuldigen Sie bitte, Doktor,*" the man said apologetically, "but the Captain insists on seeing you. The nuns and sisters are at evensong, and I did not know what to do, so I came to your room. Please forgive me."

"It is all right, Klaus. Since I cannot see him in my robe, tell the insistent Captain, he will have to wait for me to dress. Show him to the Courtyard Garden. I will meet him there. Thank you, Klaus."

In a fit of pique, she tore off her robe and quickly dressed. Running a brush through her wet hair, she grimaced into the mirror, wondering, 'What now?'

"*Guten Abend*, Doctor. Or should I call you Frau?" The Captain rose as she walked toward him, clicking his heels, and inclining his head.

"*Hauptmann was führt Sie hierher. Was bringt sie hierher*? My day has been very tiring, and I need my bed."

"I apologize. Your hair is wet; did I interrupt your bath?"

She shook her head. "I had just dressed in nightclothes. Can you please get on with it? Why are you here again? The hour is late."

"I was ... I hoped ... would you care to have dinner with me tomorrow evening, Hannah."

"What?!" she exclaimed, her eyes flashing. "That is the height of insult after your men searched my car, dumping the box for the Reverend Mother onto the ground, and body-searched me! Yes, that's right," she said to his shocked expression. "They checked every curve and crevice of my body with great enjoyment--front and back! It was not until they left that I discovered they had mistreated the Mother Superior. She was punched in the face and had contusions; she was also tortured such that her shoulder was dislocated, and she has several broken ribs." She continued her cold recapitulation of the soldiers' behavior.

The Captain collapsed onto the bench. "I gave no such orders."

"They were German soldiers! Your men!"

"I will look into this immediately, I assure you."

"Isn't it enough that you people have stressed the sisters and nuns by your presence within their walls with repeated searches? What in the world do you think you will find in a house of God? These women are gentle souls, committed to a life of service and love. They know little of the outside world, much less are they prepared to deal with the cruelties your soldiers dole out with no thought for the damages they wreak. There is no excuse for this, and I shall file a formal complaint!"

"I am so sorry, Doctor. I have no explanation, but I shall get one. I will stop by to see you tomorrow. Please give my apologies to the Mother Superior, and accept my personal apologies for your unpleasant and unnecessary search on your arrival home. Until tomorrow." He stood, clicked heels, and walked away briskly. At the gate, he looked back at her slight figure as it receded behind the wall.

Shortly after the episode, Hannah arranged the appropriate tests for the Reverend Mother. The news was positive: she had no broken bones, chips, or tears; she suffered only a slight concussion and no apparent severe bleeding associated with a more traumatic brain injury. Her muscles, while still sore, would mend nicely. Her sight was not compromised, and her bruises, while a remarkable shade of yellow and purple with threads of red, were dissipating. The woman had remarkable resilience despite her mature age. Armed with nothing more than a sweet smile, she managed to run The Kloster from her daybed in the office while following Hannah's strict and supervised instructions for continued rest. Sister Sigrid's watchfulness allowed Hannah sufficient time to leave the convent to work at her clinic for afternoons, once she attended the Reverend Mother and completed paperwork for her office while observing her patient.

The driver hovered in the covered entry shivering. Eventually, the door opened, and an umbrella appeared, almost opening in his face. He jumped down the steps, slightly bowing, holding his hand out for the umbrella as the rain pelted him.

"Hauptmann Müller has a car for you, Doctor."

Dr. Hannah Blume frowned but passed the umbrella to the driver. Together, they dashed to the waiting car. The door flew open, and a gloved hand extended. "Doctor Blume?" the familiar baritone asked.

"Hauptmann Müller," passing her Doctor's bag to the offered hand and climbing into the vehicle unaided. The driver hurried to the front seat, shaking the umbrella before passing it behind him.

"To the café, Heinz, and take care. The visibility is terrible in this downpour." Hauptmann Müller then shut the glass panel, assuring them privacy.

"I have the information I promised you, Frau Blume. May I call you, Hannah? It is easier and less formal for a private conversation."

Wiping her leather bag with her handkerchief, she answered, "As you wish, Hauptmann Müller." She did not look at him.

"You may use my given name in like manner. It is Ulrich."

Silence.

Continuing with a frown, the Captain explained, "A new officer from the SA has arrived in town. His name is von Ramstein. I am sure you know that the Abwehr and the SA are not compatible divisions of the Army, and..."

In a snappy tone, she said, "Is this an excuse or an explanation, Hauptmann?"

"*Eine Erklärung, keine Entschuldigung*," the Captain responded. "I make no excuse for what happened to you and the Mother Superior. It was unnecessary and wrong. Again, I offer my apologies, even though Generalstabsrichter von Richter nor I issued such orders or were aware of the severity of the incident. That is, not until you and I spoke about it. I have since informed the Generalstabsrichter, and he is very displeased with von Ramstein. I suspect he got his commission only because of his name. He is not a gentleman nor has undergone proper training."

"Ah, ja? I should hope you and the General are displeased. You should also be embarrassed! I am still furious if you were wondering. Why did you direct the driver to a café?"

"To make good on my invitation to dinner. Surely, Hannah, you must take time to eat."

His remark drew a smile. "Yes, I confess that a meal in a café will be better fare than the leftover soup at the convent."

With that small bit of conversation and her relaxing attitude, the Captain sighed relief. "I am told that the Käsespätzle and Rouladen or Schnitzel are their specialties. But, of course, you may order whatever you like."

They arrived at the café and, in short order, were shown to a corner table at the rear. Ulrich ordered a Rosé wine. "I know this wine, and it will compete with any white or red they serve, so it will complement whatever you choose to order. *Zur Freundschaft*! Enjoy!" Smiling, he raised his glass in a toast.

"To friendship? That is unlikely, Hauptmann. Better we say, *Zum Frieden*, to peace." Hannah sipped her wine.

"You must understand, Hannah, we are at war. Things happen in war that would not otherwise be the case. We don't wish for this to be so, but situations develop, actions are taken, and inevitably people get hurt, including soldiers—not just civilians."

She scoffed. "Just how does that rationale apply to routing civilians out of their homes, subjecting people who object to searches to beatings or even imprisonment, separating families, and much, much more? You Germans are in a neutral country, yet you treat the Swiss as if we were an occupied nation! Your presence in Switzerland has guidelines—privileges and restrictions! You push the first to the limit and disregard the latter. Do not expect me to capitulate just because you are a man of power in German ranks, Hauptmann!"

"You have no understanding of the life of a soldier, Doctor."

"I understand that soldiers are all about the devastation and taking lives, while doctors are about saving and preserving life. We are at opposite ends of the question, you, and me. We can never be friends."

"My hope is that one day your opinion might change." Ulrich sipped his wine looking directly into her eyes. "I have made it my personal mission while in your country."

"*Verliere nicht den Schlaf und warte.*"

"My dear Hannah, I will not lose sleep waiting because I sleep soundly every night. Let us set sarcasm and warring tongues aside for a few moments. Please, just consider this: If you disagreed with another doctor on a case who was a specialist and therefore considered superior to you, would you deem that doctor evil or wrong because they pursued a course of treatment with which you disagreed and did not recommend?"

"I see where you are going with this," she said levelly. "But the scenario you suggest is not at all the same as what we face, and you know it. Brutality—whether under the guise of wartime or exhibited in peacetime—has zero approval in my world."

"A soldier does not always agree with the orders he is given. But as a soldier, he has taken an oath to protect and defend his country and its people. His superiors—those judged more suitable to consider decisions in war and peace—are his superiors because of more education, experience, or a host of other credits. So, the soldiers of lesser rank follow the orders given by their superiors even if they disagree because they are not privy to the whole picture, parallel plans, information that may speak to the success of an initiative overall. It may not sound simple, but it is simple when reduced to how an organization operates successfully. It's no different in governments, companies, schools, hospitals, even families: someone is the boss, the superior, the leader; everyone else is below the superior and must follow orders or plans. If they do not, they are considered disloyal, or worse, a revolutionary or traitor. Surely, you can see this."

"These days, Ulrich, I see many things, most of which I do not like. I am not free to oppose what I consider wrong, speak out to try to influence change, and make any change whatsoever. My options are minimal. Life has become a trade-off: one does what one can to ease the pain or suffering of others, but one must keep silent to make even a small contribution toward what is right. Surely, you can see this."

They placed their orders and sipped wine in pensive silence until dinner was served. Conversation throughout dinner was sparse and limited to Hannah's explanations about the differences between the nuns and sisters, everyday life within the convent walls, the limitations wartime had placed on her clinic's inventory, and comments unevocative of their individual passions about life and their professions. Once or twice, Hannah allowed herself to laugh, though she quickly squelched it.

"Thank you, Ulrich, for dinner; it was delicious and a great change from Sister Marta's soup. I would appreciate a lift to the convent if you have the time. I have an early day tomorrow."

Hauptmann Ulrich Müller emptied his wine glass and left bills on the table, holding Hannah's chair. Outside, he reached for her elbow to assist entry to the car. She pulled away without so much as a glance. He sat in brooding silence until they arrived at the convent.

"I had hoped this evening would be different, Doctor. I am sorry; perhaps it was a bad idea. Do assure your Mother Superior that I shall do my best to ensure she has no further, unexpected trouble. Thank you for coming. Good night, Doctor."

As she disembarked the vehicle, she turned and said, "Ulrich, everyone is entitled to his own opinion, but not to his own facts. Good night, Hauptmann Müller, and thank you for dinner."

Chapter Twenty-six
Réalité

"Do what you can with all you have,

wherever you are."
-Theodore Roosevelt

As they came to understand the German war machine, the much-feared "SS"—the Schutzstaffel—began as a Nazi Party bodyguard detachment for top leaders and personnel. It developed into a paramilitary arm of the Nazi party overall. It completely replaced the "SA"—the Sturmabteilung (Storm Troopers or Brown Shirts – mostly a band of violent thugs as distinct to a serious military force), which had been much larger than both the SS and the Wehrmacht in the beginning days of the Hitlerian regime. The SS further flourished, becoming the organization that ran slave labor and death camps, Sipo (Security Police), the Gestapo (State Police), Kripo (Criminal Police), and all intelligence agencies including the "SD"—Sicherheitdienst (the security and intelligence service of the SS responsible for neutralizing resistance to the Nazi Party). Essentially, the SS implemented Hitler's Final Solution. Blackmail, disinformation, arrest, imprisonment, deportation, and murder became commonplace methods. Survivors were consigned to slave labor and death camps.

Originally, Herman Goering formed the Geheime Staatspolizei (Gestapo). It comprised professional policemen in the main and the "official secret police" organization for Nazi Germany (as well as German-occupied countries), later to be under the control of Heinrich Himmler.

In 1939, Heinrich Himmler was in control of the Reichsfuhrer-SS and Chief of the German Police. The Reichssicherheithauptamt (RSHA), which administered all security agencies and operations in Nazi Germany (as well as in occupied Europe), was under Himmler's direct control, as well.. Its mission was to fight all internal and external enemies of the Third Reich.

Part of the Oberkommando der Wehrmacht (OKW or Armed Forces High Command) reported directly to Hitler, Hauptmann Müller, and General der Gebirgstruppe Wolfgang von Richter were assigned to the Abwehr (a German intelligence organization from 1921-1944). Its ranks were comprised mostly of officers, and it focused on intelligence gathering. Posted in Switzerland and overseeing mountain troops since 1940, they were a part of the Foreign Branch (Amtsgruppe Ausland), concerned with foreign intelligence, the evaluation of captured documents, analysis of foreign press and radio broadcasts, and liaison with the OKW and general staffs of all the services. Additionally, they coordinated with the German Foreign Ministry on military matters based upon their findings. Thus, theirs was a commission more of the intellect as distinct to the implementation of violent methodologies.

Except for Hitler's fear of individual people and organizations mounting a coup to overthrow him, it seemed as if the Third Reich and its forces were an ever-growing, undefeatable power that spread like a plague penetrating every layer of life.

"I appreciate your explanation, Reverend Mother. Of course, I will do anything you ask of me in honor of all your love and care since I came to the gates of Kloster der Verlorenen, those many years ago. I lost my family; I lost my country; I lost my safety and security; I lost all life direction. You and the others restored me here at the Convent of the Lost. You gave me back my life; no, excuse me, you gave me *a new* life. That is a debt I shall forever owe, and one for which I shall be forever grateful." Hannah's face unashamedly bore tears, but they were not tears of embarrassment or discomfort of any kind. They were tears of joy and love.

"My sweet child," whispered the Mother Superior as she extended her hands to Hannah. "I have prayed long to ensure that asking you to return to what you did in your former life was not too great a sacrifice to make, given how far you have come from those early days.

"But your accomplishments and position make you an ideal candidate to help with the new group we expect shortly. You go routinely to Fahr Convent to care for the sisters' health. If we can concoct a way to transport those we hide to the larger and more appropriate monastery, we would save many more lives.

"The longer this war goes on, the more the complexion of our wayfarers changes. We are but a temporary stop, an outpost for the Prioress and her many nuns' good works. She also has the backing of several important people and agencies, to say nothing of the insulation that comes with being overseen by the Abbot."

"I will do it, Reverend Mother. But I must ask that I be in on the planning. I do not wish to risk anyone's life at all, though I realize we will all be at risk despite our best efforts. It's just that I do have some connections of my own and experience with this sort of thing from my early childhood in Austria. Since I shall play the conduit, I should also be part of the entire process. Do you agree?" Hannah squeezed the Mother Superior's hands, bending her head to kiss them in affection and obeisance.

"Yes, Hannah. I agree, and I thank you. We have enough time before anything becomes necessary. Thank you, also, for bringing me the box of Bibles. They will be put to good use both here and in the villages.

"Did you know that the Prioress hid some fruit in the false bottom? It was enough for each sister to have an orange and lemon apiece! Such a treat; we haven't even seen citrus fruit in a very, long time!" The two women laughed together at the ingenuity of the Prioress and pleasure for the sisters.

"It was worth being a spectacle for the soldiers to watch that despicable search. They obviously found my revulsion more interesting and merely overturned the box to tip out the Bibles! So much for the training of the German soldier!" Hannah said in disdain.

"But, my dear, they weren't soldiers, didn't you know? I know soldiers can be harsh too, but these were Brown Shirts, a particularly vile and ruthless group of men who delight in abuse of all kinds. They are brutes of the worst order. Men like that are usually cowardly. Not soldiers, Hannah, no, not soldiers."

"I have never seen their kind before, Mother. I only guessed from the stripe decals that the leader might have been a *leutnant*, but it was only a guess. They did look a bit ragged, more like vagabonds. Hauptmann Müller and the General saved the day. They were horrified and disgusted too. The men are new to this area and from a division that neither officer likes. They will look out for us, at least to a point."

Knowledge of the escalated atrocities committed by the

Third Reich spread among the Austro-German population and regular military. As updates slowly dribbled out, other countries' governments and populace were shocked into recognition of the Third Reich's power and ultimate threat. More and more at-risk people dared to escape, seek asylum, or go into hiding. Ghettos were a scant step up from the camps, and camps were rapidly adopting various applications of the "final solution."

"We must do everything we can, Reverend Mother. Even the little we do might allow a few souls the freedom they deserve. It may be only a droplet in the ocean of injustice, but many droplets can begin a current. If the current gets strong enough, other people will notice it. That is what we need: a swelling current of awareness for the rest of the world. We will do our little part knowing that we are part of something right and good and demanded by God."

"All we need now, my sweet, is God's help and direction. He will keep us safe in His arms." Rising, Mother Superior stroked Hannah's bowed head.

Over time, Hannah and the Convent of the Lost assisted in the placement of 16 Jewish women and two refugee families to Fahr Monastery under the care of Prioress Mathilda. Their creative methods spanned from an orphan's group tour of the double monastery to short trips for medical care for the nuns and sisters to a string of various mountain cabins to being hidden in vegetable carts to a hidden compartment in the boot of Hannah's car when transporting either Hauptmann Müller, General von Richter, (or both), the Mayor and his wife, and many other creative methods and ruses. She was exceedingly bold by risking such gambits but carried with her the faith that she was doing God's work and would be successful. And successful she was until the end of the war when the need ceased.

She and Hauptmann Müller shared a companionable but somewhat impersonal relationship until he and his general were reassigned and left Switzerland. She never heard from him again, although she received a blank note posted from various cities in Germany or throughout Europe for several years on the anniversary of her disappearance from Austria. Inside the notecard was a pressed, dried flower.

Hannah lived out her days at The Kloster der Verlorenen until the age of 66, when she succumbed to a particularly bad bout of pneumonia. She is buried by the fountain in the gardens of The

Kloster, next to the Reverend Mother Alycia. *"Unsere Blume"* ["Our Flower"] is the only inscription on her gravestone.

No records have ever come to light connecting the Swiss Doctor Hannah Blume of The Kloster der Verlorenen to the young Austrian girl named Anneliese Kaiser, who thwarted the Nazis from a small, somewhat remote, mountaintop village in western Austria. She helped 18 refugees escape from Austria to Switzerland through caves and via mountain trails.

The nuns and sisters of Kloster der Verlorenen and Fahr Convent, together with the ever-changing roster of civilian help, and all others who worked with Annaliese Kaiser / Doctor Hannah Blume saved a combined total of 41 people from the clutches of their pursuers. They all lived, and they all remembered.

With the Convent Garden in bloom, and as part of the celebration of spring, the nuns and sisters of The Kloster gather to pray and sing. Their sweet *a capella* voices can be heard beyond the walls as they sing in honor of their special "flower":

DEAR ANGEL, EVER AT MY SIDE
Frederick W. Faber, d.1863 / Adapted from Day's Psalter, 1563

Dear angel, ever at my side,
How loving you must be
To leave your home in heav'n to guide

A little child like me!
2
Your beautiful and shining face
Is always very near;
The music of your guiding voice
Is ever in my ear.
3
My eyes see only here below,
But you are by my side,
And you have God before your eyes;
I need you for my guide.
4
My guardian angel, help me now
To give to God my love,
To serve Him in this world below
And come to Him above.

Chapter Twenty-seven
The Coming of Bayth

She sat sipping the cool wine spritzer as she reviewed the menu. A refreshing breeze blew through the open French doors of the international restaurant from the generously sized balcony. Beautiful greenery and hanging flower baskets swayed gently, their scent softening the air. Beyond, the dark skyline of Middle Eastern mosques and buildings starkly accented the purple sunset of the waning sky.

One of the first tables on the balcony held four men, some of whom let loose with raucous laughter. Shortly afterward, they clinked glasses, one of the men signaling the waiter for another round. The man who sat with his back facing her kept shaking his head in response to cajoling from the others. Bethany could tell that he seemed to be the butt of their jokes only by intonation and body language. Two men were Caucasian, one of them in a khaki wrinkled linen shirt with matching trousers, the other in an entirely black outfit. The third man, an Asian, wore a short-sleeved striped shirt and tie. The Caucasians were perspiring heavily; the Asian, while verbally animated, looked as cool as a cucumber. The man with his back to Bethany wore tan trousers and a long-sleeved pale blue shirt. His mane of long, thick, black hair tousled in the breeze.

For a moment, Bethany wondered, toying with the thought that the man's garb and hair resembled someone from long ago of whom she had been very fond. No, it was improbable; what was wrong with her? Entertaining such thoughts, remembrances though they were, could lead only to heartache. She was done with drama, complications, and disappointment.

The man with the black hair raised his right hand to rake his hair back from his face. That gesture! On the middle finger of his right hand was a large silver ring with a faceted blue stone that shone as brilliantly as a diamond. It looked just like the ring Amir wore. Bethany's heart skipped a beat. She recalled Amir telling her that the unusually colored blue stone was scarce, rarer than diamonds with excellent dispersion. Benitoite was named for the San Benito Mountains in California, where it was discovered, although it was initially thought to be a rare bluish-purple sapphire. It remains rare as supplies are limited, and sources are not easily identified. Amir's ring was about 10 carats in size, remarkable and highly unusual.

The waiter arrived to take her order. Bethany decided to take an unlikely chance. Scribbling her room number on the rear of her calling card, which had only an embossed "B" on its front, she instructed the waiter to present the card to the man in the long-sleeved blue shirt with long black hair, along with her compliments and a bottle of chilled Rosé wine and four glasses. Rosé was Amir's favorite wine. Below her room number, she wrote: "Benitoite?"

She told the waiter she had changed her mind and would order room service instead, placing an order for delivery, including bottles of wine and sparkling water. She presented a beautiful smile and a hefty tip to ensure he followed her instructions. She briskly left the dining room.

As the evening passed into nighttime, Bethany chided herself. Perhaps the man was not Amir, after all. If it was Amir, likely he had no interest in responding, or else he would have appeared by now, wouldn't he? Moreover, if it was him, what exactly did she expect of him? Or herself, for that matter! Stupid, stupid, foolish girl! As she was walking back and forth tormenting herself, she heard a knock at the door.

Her bare feet padded silently to the door, and she said softly, "Yes?"

"Bayth?"

Bethany opened the door and smiled, backing up a few feet. "Come in."

"I wasn't certain it was you, but then it had to be you, didn't it? Benitoite—you remembered. And what are the chances of an embossed "B" served up with my favorite wine? People usually gift a red or a white, not a rosé. Very clever."

"I wasn't certain it was you, either. Your companions were loud; I couldn't hear your voice over their laughter. I decided to take a chance." She backed further into the room as he entered and closed the door.

"You look just the same …wonderful …are you good? Happy? What are you doing in this part of the world? I met up with James not long ago at a conference; he told me you had been traveling and researching a new project. That would make it almost two years now, wouldn't it?"

"Yes, approximately. That's why I am here. I hope to wind up some of the last bits here in Turkey, and the last of it in Syria or Jordan."

"So, how are the boys… and Alistair?"

"Ah, the boys! They are well, happy, and settled in school. We spend school holidays and summers at Waverlee with the extended family. Papa has taught them to ride and sail; Uncle Nick and Uncle Andy have taught them to shoot properly with all the respect and responsibility of that pursuit. Mum's brothers –Luke and Matthew—have had them to the States on occasion over the years. So, they have a bevy of strong, good men as role models since Alistair's traveling disallows much personal time with them. He loves them in his way and has always been good about providing for them. Did you know he re-married?" She moved to the table to pour wine in two of the glasses.

"No, I had not heard that," he replied, accepting the glass of wine and sipping.

Smiling, Bethany explained, "Yes, in a remarkably short time after our divorce, he married a genuinely nice woman, Thyra, who is enchanted with his lifestyle and all the trappings that go along with it. I'm glad for him that he found an appropriate partner, given I wasn't."

"Bayth," Amir said consolingly, "you must not think of yourself in that way. You grew apart as your aims matured, that is all. It happens sometimes."

"Yes, you're right, of course," shaking her head as if to clear her thoughts. "And what of you, Amir? To what or to whom have you devoted your time since last we were together?"

Amir reached to take her wine glass and place it on the desk beside his. Turning to her, he said softly, "Bayth, I have loved only you these past years." In two steps, he was standing in front of her. He placed his hands on her shoulders. "One cannot ignore a connection like ours."

Looking up at him and wanting to kiss him, Bethany instead laughed, turning from him, saying, "No, I grant you, we forged an almost immediate link, didn't we?" Walking onto the terrace, she said, "Come, Amir, fill me in. Archaeology has always been your first love, as it is James's. Where have you been, and what have you found that stirs your soul?"

He followed her, taking a seat opposite, placing her wine and his on the small table between their chairs. "History, hmm, let me see," he said, recounting the recent past as requested. "Only because of the timing was I unable to attend your father's special ceremony. We were just wrapping up the dig, and you know all the work involved down to every detail to safeguard provenance. I wanted so badly to attend, but it was impossible. Tell me about it."

"You would have loved it, Amir. He was awarded a beautiful silver trophy as a lifetime achievement award. The announcer's recitation of some of his remarkable attainments surprised even me. I knew about the FEI Ranking List, that he'd held 2d place in the Gold League and was a British Showjumping National Champion for years, but some of the other things he's done and championed blew me away. Papa was never one to call attention to himself, well, at least not in terms of how accomplished he is, I mean. He gets plenty of attention from all his mischief and antics; just ask Mum! He had no idea what the family had planned until the arena lighting changed to a dimmer illumination with stars floating and a spotlight trained on the ingate. I was so very proud of my boys!"

The first to trot into the arena was James on a black Vindicator, son bearing the Waverlee flag; next was Marcy on one of Demiluna's showy granddaughters. Then came Bethany's eldest son, Simon, holding the Union Jack pole and riding a high-stepping black gelding, also by Vindicator. Bethany rode a mare out of Demiluna's line, followed by her second son, Noah, riding a substantial dark bay by Vindicator, bearing the British Showjumping banner. Trotting the perfect distance behind, James' daughter, Vanessa, rode a gorgeous black bay mare from Obsidian and Demiluna's lines, followed by Bethany's uncle, Andrew, on a prancing black stallion, also by Vindicator, with the Stars and Stripes aloft. All of them trotted to the orchestra's rendition of *Rule, Brittania*!

"The audience stood and clapped as they made a full circuit, ending up in two lines, either side of Papa, as the announcer called out, "Vindicator and Thomas Brandon, the honorees."

The room got darker with only stars flickering around the arena and the barest of illumination but for a broad spotlight on the ingate. In strode Bethany's uncle, Nick Lawson, in full military regalia proudly leading the famous Vindicator, Waverlee's current foundation stallion.

"Now, Obsidian, you might remember, was his original show horse and foundation stallion, but that was in Papa's heyday. His son, Vindicator, is his spitting image in looks and talent as well. Papa rode him to some of his most outstanding achievements. Even though both of them have a bit of age, neither looked old at all, rising to the occasion."

The orchestra changed to Land of Hope and Glory as they entered and walked to the Family Honor Guard's head. At Nick's signal, a flustered Thomas Brandon walked between the horses' row to where Vindicator stood proudly waiting. Nick changed hands on the lead, and after assuming the position to head Vindicator, saluted.

"I thought both would burst into tears as Papa nodded and shook Uncle Nick's hand," a tearful Bethany related.

Lord Brandon first patted, then nimbly mounted Vindicator to begin his circuit around the arena as the orchestra played the beautiful and poignant, I *Vow to Thee My Country* from the Sir Cecil Spring-Rice poem from 1908. It was set to music in 1921 and was (and remains) a patriotic favorite.

Bethany was breathless with the retelling. Turning to face Amir, he saw tears streaming down her face, her expression alight with the memory. She continued, "As he finished the circuit, we all filed behind him to trot out the end gate. It was a crazy time, and we were all in high spirits for hours afterward." Bethany chuckled, shaking her head, wiping away her tears.

"Listen to me going on so. I'm sorry, Amir. I guess remembering it made me excited all over again, but I wanted to share it with you so you'd know what it was like being there. You're so close to the family, after all, and I always seem to tell you what's in my heart without any filter." Taking a sip of her wine, she said, "Blame it on that special connection we have!"

Laughing together amiably, Amir reached for her glass. "There's a touch more if you'd like it," he offered.

"Yes, please. My appointments tomorrow don't begin until after lunch and prayers, so I intend to sleep in a bit. For sure, the wine will help me do that."

Returning to her, Amir placed both glasses on the table between the chairs. He held his hand out to Bethany. As she arose, he engulfed her in his arms, whispering into her hair, "Bayth, it has been too long." Music from the hotel ballroom below wafted throughout the garden beneath the balcony. Amir moved them into the rhythm of a slow dance.

"I have always wanted to dance with you, did you know that?"

Too astonished to speak, she shook her head.

"I have dreamed of holding you again in my arms and dancing for hours. Then…"

"Then?" she asked. "You are still a Muslim, Amir, with beliefs that disallow anything between us, and I am still a divorced Christian woman. I will not be a party to the detriment of another man. My experience with Alistair is enough for one lifetime."

"Ah, Bayth, Bayth," he crooned. "What if I told you that things have changed for me?"

"I would hope you have a convincing argument that explains a life change not exclusively attributable to me." She stepped away from him, backing up to the railing.

They stood a few moments in silence. Then Amir explained his ongoing struggle with some of the faith's tenets into which he was born.

"I am not relying exclusively on my research, Bayth. I have consulted several trusted Imams, as well. "Further, The Quran in Sura 5:5 says: Likewise, you are permitted to marry chaste believing women [Muslims] or chaste women among the people who were given the Scripture [Jews and Christians]." (Maududi, vol. 1, p. 427)

"Thus, since you are a Christian woman, we are free to marry. Although it is not encouraged, most Muslims agree that divorce is permitted if a marriage has broken down, and generally, Muslims are allowed to re-marry if they so wish. However, there are differences between Muslims about divorce and remarriage procedures: Sunni Muslims do not require witnesses, whereas Shi'ah Muslims need two. The Sunni husband must state his desire for a divorce on three separate occasions with a waiting period of three months. In contrast, the Shi'ah Muslims must have two witnesses, followed by a waiting period before the marriage can end. If a woman initiates a divorce, it is called *khula*, and there must be a waiting period to ensure the woman is not pregnant.

"Where I misspoke when we earlier visited this subject, is that Imams merely *report* that the Prophet Muhammad said that the most detestable of things before Allah is divorce. This means that many Muslims who experience marital difficulties will try to resolve their issues. Also, many Muslims make a contract before

God called a *nikah* to remain together for life. Divorce would mean breaking that contract.

"You, however, nor I have made such contracts — not me with Allah, nor you. Although technically you initiated a divorce...a *khula*...you *are not* a Muslim, and Alistair *is not* a Muslim, and we know you are not pregnant. The two years' traveling more than qualifies as a waiting period, don't you think?

"And remember, a marriage under Islam is a social contract that carries with it the implication of creating children and stabilizing society, even though a man is allowed to have several wives. It is thought that responsibility staves off the likelihood of particular desires and sinful behavior. On the other hand, women are disallowed to have several husbands, as you may have suspected. I cannot dispute that Islam is patriarchal and does not treat women equally.

"Christianity — even Biblical Christianity with all the constraints of that age— does a much better job of equality. I think Mary of Magdala's presence as an apostle of Jesus Christ, and his inclusion of several women during his ministry, is an example of that. The overriding principle within Islam is that women's education fosters unrest and encourages women to resist subjugation to their husbands as their superiors.

"Amir," interrupted Bethany. "I have been patiently listening to your summary, but let's not spoil the evening by theological orations, which change nothing except my mood!"

Placing a staying hand on her arm, Amir said, "Bayth, please bear with me for a little while longer. This is important to me, and I hope to you. Surely, a few minutes more of patience to cover what has happened in the years we have been apart is not too much to ask?"

Bethany nodded and sighed.

Continuing tentatively, Amir said softly, "Of course, fornication and adultery are considered grave sins, as they are in Christianity. However, we have committed neither. *Zinā*[36] is sexual deviance, according to Islam. We have not coupled from the front of our bodies; I have not entered you; neither of us has forced the other. We have expressed our desires and shared certain intimacies, but we are neither fornicators nor adulterers in the eyes of our individual faiths.

---

36   Zinā' (زانء) or zina (زینی or الزنا) is an Islamic legal term referring to unlawful sexual intercourse. According to traditional jurisprudence, zina can include adultery (of married parties), fornication (of unmarried parties), prostitution, rape, sodomy, homosexuality, incest, and bestiality. Although the classification of homosexual intercourse as zina differs according to legal school, the majority apply the rules of zinā to homosexuality, mostly male homosexuality.
https://en.wikipedia.org/wiki/Zina

"Well, that was a mouthful," Bethany teased. "I've listened to you attentively, Amir, and while what you have said makes sense from a sort of 'technical' perspective, are you sure your beliefs are not compromised? Would they become compromised if we pursued a relationship? In other words, I think it all depends on what you truly believe in your heart of hearts, despite what the rules or religious leaders say."

"I have tried to be as thorough as I can, given the unusual circumstances of then and now. I cannot change our past, Bayth. What I can do is apologize for misunderstanding the possibility of our ever being together because of your status as a Christian *divorced* woman. I was in error, and I have been berating myself, giving you that impression ever since I learned the correct specifics and ruling. Will you forgive me?"

"Before my association with you, I never had cause to even think about such things. If I ever married, it would likely be arranged and be the usual businesslike contract. One would hope that someday, partners would come to a degree of fondness for each other, if only through familiarity. Love is possible, of course, but unlikely in those circumstances by my reckoning.

"I feel bad because I believe without any ego that I could have been some small help to you during your disputes with Alistair, but I shut us down. It was difficult for me to do as I loved you deeply, but I honestly believed I was doing the right thing for you and me. I feel like a fool, but I had to make this right between us, even if you wish never to see me again, Bayth."

"Oh, Amir, are you blind? Can you not see and feel how your presence affects me? I was crestfallen when we had that last conversation, I admit. And I, too, loathed asking anything of you that would compromise the essence of what you are, even if it meant that I had to deny myself loving you. Thank you for telling me and explaining it all." She lightly kissed his cheek.

"I was unsure if I should come tonight when I understood the message on your card. It was bold of you to write your room digits. I did not know if we would say 'hello' again or 'goodbye' forever. But I felt I had to come."

"Had you not, your absence would have sent an irrevocable message," she whispered.

"Bayth, you have not said whether or not you have forgiven me. You have also not said whether or not there remains anything between us other than friendship." Amir looked pensive.

"You silly old poop! Sometimes your sense of decency drives me crazy! We shall always be friends, Amir. We shall also be lovers, just as we have been lovers since our time together in the cave. We will give ourselves time to see what each of us wants for the future, so we will not visit the subject of union until we are both comfortable doing so. We have much to think about insofar as that is concerned. Still, we must restrict our physical love as we did behind the waterfall to support each other's principles, agreed? Even though my divorce takes adultery off the table, fornication is still an ever-present temptation, so we will just find a way around that. Are you game?" Bethany's face was ablaze with both mischief and joy.

"My Bayth, I accept you; do you accept me?" a sheepish Amir asked, unable to mask his anticipation. He began to breathe rapidly. "Bayth?"

"I see you; I hear you; I accept you, Amir," Bethany said, smiling broadly. "There is nothing to forgive."

Laughing together, they walked hand in hand inside. Amir scooped Bethany into his arms and spun round and round. He fell onto one of the beds with her in his arms. They lay quietly together for a few minutes, just looking into each other's eyes. Slowly, tentatively, they kissed. Their kisses shortly revealed passions long repressed. Bethany abruptly broke away. Taken aback, Amir was temporarily confused. Had he pushed too fast, too much? It had been years, after all. Nevertheless, he loved her so much and had kept silent for so long.

"Now, my tall, dark, and handsome Muslim lover, let's try all we can do just short of fornication!" she giggled as she drew her caftan over her head.

And they did, for over two hours.

The following day, Bethany readied herself for the meeting she had arranged with Professor Aydin, the acclaimed and wealthy Turkish archaeologist and collector, thanks to James paving the way for her. She wore an ankle-length black skirt with black stockings and low-heeled shoes, a white shirt buttoned to the neck, a black pashmina, and a black headscarf and veil. When Bethany arrived at his walled estate, she exited the car and mounted the steps to an impossibly white edifice that seemed to radiate. Removing her shoes once inside the entry door, she followed the manservant to what she presumed was his study or reception room. The servant announced her, and she entered.

"Ah, Ms. Maxwell-Brandon; good of you to be perfectly punctual unlike other of your countrymen!" said a smiling man who stood behind an ornately carved mahogany desk, indicating for her to proceed into the room. She politely inclined her head, keeping her eyes downcast, saying, "Beyefendi."

As she neared the desk, she was aware of his scrutiny. From his form of address, it was apparent he knew she was a divorced woman. She stole a glance at him, noting that he indicated the chair to the right of the desk, adjacent to a small desk to the side of which stood another man dressed in white tunic and trousers.

"My assistant in whom I have the utmost confidence will remain during our meeting," explained the Professor. Bethany understood that practice to be culturally proper, as she was an unknown, unaccompanied female. She was not surprised. When she heard the faint squeak of his desk chair, Bethany was free to sit. Primly erect in her chair, hands folded in her lap, eyes downcast, she awaited her host's initiating conversation, as was the custom.

"I appreciate your nod to our customs and culture. You will find us—even the orthodox among us—used to Western visitors and very tolerant. You may address me as Mustafa. May I use your given name? I see no need for formality since your brother, James, is among my closest and most respected associates." The Professor keenly monitored Bethany, noting the smallest of smiles sneak to her expression.

"Mustafa bey," she said softly, finally bringing her gaze to meet his, "I thank you for seeing me."

"Oh!" he exclaimed. "James is blonde and fair with eyes the color of a winter morning, but yours are like the richest Columbian Muzo emeralds! Odd for twins, no?"

"We are fraternal twins, Mustafa *bey*, and genetics always has its way," she replied with a smile. "I am the eldest by three minutes."

The Professor was delighted by her reply and commented, "You are both fair-skinned, but I see you follow your father's coloring. Thus, James is more like your mother?"

Bethany's hand flew to her *hijab*, conscious that one of her curls must have escaped.

The Professor laughed with amusement. "No, my dear, do not be concerned. The trend here is for women to have long hair, neatly and tightly drawn back when wearing a hood or head-scarf. Your short, curly dark hair is not compatible with a headscarf. There is no need whatsoever for embarrassment; in fact, we have relaxed the need for *hijabs* most recently, except for attendance at mosques, but I do appreciate your respectful garb."

Bethany relaxed somewhat, although she could feel the bloom of color in her cheeks. Her host had researched her and probably had seen a photograph of her short, curly hair. "My mother has green eyes and red hair; my father has black hair and hazel eyes. All my mother's brothers have blonde hair and blue eyes like James and my grandfather. I seem to have bits of both my parents' coloring."

"Yes, my son and daughter are very different in looks as well."

"*Onun ismi ne?*" Bethany inquired.

"His name is Mehmet, and her name is Deren." The Professor smiled in recognition of Bethany's politeness in inquiring about his family, impressed that she knew at least a few words of his native tongue.

"Do either share your love of history?"

Shaking his head, the Professor said, "Not really, at least not in the same way as I would choose. Mehmet's concentration on history relates to the solar system as an astrophysicist studying electromagnetic radiation, specifically gravity waves and gamma-ray bursts. He pursues the mystery of the creation of our universe and others. Deren is a teacher of Art History at the university, a far tamer profession but still exhilarating. Thus, she has an interest in and knowledge of my collections."

"My goodness, your children have chosen highly respectable professions. You and your wife have just cause to be proud of them," said Bethany in genuine compliment.

"We are pleased indeed. Likewise, your parents must share similar attitudes about their offspring. Your reputation precedes you, Bethany, and I am delighted to find you as informed as information warrants. Now, what is it that you want from me? James did not elaborate."

"Mustafa *bey*, the Director of Egyptian Antiquities, allowed me to view and photograph their pages from the Magdala Book. He provided me with a copy of its translation, as well. I am advised that you possess four partial pages of the relic."

Bethany drew a deep breath and continued. "Might you allow me to view them? Of course, I would like to photograph them for research purposes and would be extremely interested in a copy of any translation you may have. I am aware that many translations of the combined materials are available, as the information is in the public domain, even if the relics themselves are under private ownership and care." Bethany's heart pounded, hoping that she did not unintentionally push too hard.

"Is this an official entreaty? In other words, what organization do you represent?" the Professor asked with a poker face.

"None, *beyefendi*. I inquire for myself alone and my project of creating a volume rich in photographic imagery accompanied by short fictional stories exploring ordinary women accomplishing extraordinary things throughout history. I recognize that thematically, this might not be welcomed in certain circles. However, in the case of Mary of Magdala, I hope to debunk her historically accepted label as 'prostitute' for 'female apostle.' Because I am not an authority and merely speculating and proposing a point of view based upon historical record available from many translations, the story relating to her remains fictional."

His explosive laugh took Bethany by surprise. "And just how do you intend to do that?"

"By letting her words speak for her, with your help. I have thoroughly researched Josephus and other ancient historical accounts for factual representations of the period and pursued the translation and contextual differences between the scriptures, synoptic gospels, canonical gospels, and the translations of Mary's Gospel in the public domain. I need a counter comparison, if you will, to include her words from the missing pages in your possession. In a more inclusive form, I believe her Book will supply the balancing view of her time and part of the ministry amid early Christianity. Can you help me? *Will* you help me?" She looked at him intently, trying to gauge his reaction.

After a long and considered silence, Profesör Aydin clapped his hands together. Bethany jumped in her chair, further confused by his assistant's approach with a tray of coffee.

"I deplore answering a question with a question, but in this case, it is relevant, my dear. I am of your father's generation, and I would ask you something of importance to me: What were your first impressions and reactions on arriving here at my home?"

Instinctually, Bethany knew this was a test of her character on several levels. She realized she could show no hesitation despite his question's irregularity, which on its face seemed unrelated to the subject at hand.

"It was multi-faceted. The visual impression was that of a gateway to *Cennet*, or what paradise might look like. My reaction was one of wonder and peace, thinking that this could be a place of spiritual contemplation. I acknowledged that your kindness extended to me only because of my brother's relationship of respect with you. My concern was that you would refuse, as is your right, on the basis that my project is not sufficiently worthy of accommodating my request. My hope was that you would view my proposal without prejudice, understanding that my project is designed to inspire hope and empowerment for women everywhere." Looking at him directly for only a moment after finishing, Bethany respectfully lowered her gaze.

"Hmm," the Professor said while looking at her steadily. "Your first impression is precisely the vision I kept in mind when building this place. Your reaction pleases me. The acknowledgment and concern are both correct at the base level. Still, just as the archaeologist must have extra sensitivity to his dig and belief in the integrity of his potential find, one such as you must demonstrate perception, conviction, and principled commitment to an undertaking of this complexion.

"Therefore, based on your previous work and your intentions for your current work, I shall fulfill your hope and give you my permission, as you have all the prerequisites for my support. Now, let us conclude our business with coffee, and you can regale me with stories about James, which I will undoubtedly use to embarrass him in the future!"

Discarding all notions about propriety and cultural postures, Bethany laughed out loud, accepting the cup and saucer from Profesör Aydin's assistant. "My sincere thanks, Mustafa *bey*," she said, lowering her head and eyes. Removing her veil and taking a sip of her coffee, she smiled and said in a conspiratorial tone, "I will be only too happy to accommodate your request. Just before James and I entered university," she began.

"Listen to me, James. After all the digging I've done—excuse the pun and shame on me for using that term with you—I've learned there are differences between The Book of Mary, or the

Gospel of Mary and the Gospel of the Beloved Companion, as in the public domain. I need your experience to differentiate between them and what we found on the dig, albeit that was threadbare by comparison. I will give you all my data to help, but I do not want to utilize quoted information from translations that *seem the same but are not the same, specifically*. And because of my limited understanding and expertise, I might quote something that makes a difference in syntax, symbology, meaning, whatever. Get me? Mixing them up will only disqualify my volume from having academic validity, value, and impact. That would defeat my fundamental aim in doing this project. I need scholarly accuracy.

"What we found in that ossuary may or may not be a part of the existing gospels in the public domain, and each of those may be from one or the other gospel. Do you see? I know you and the other experts posit that our find belongs to Mary as a fragment of the missing pages, but..." Bethany paced the room as she fleshed out her proposal and plea to her brother, James.

"Ok, ok, Bethy. I get it. While I can help, I am not the one to whom you should give your pitch. Of all my contacts in the scientific world, I'd suggest you speak with Uncle Andrew. His linguistic skill and knowledge of ancient languages are far superior to mine. Don't forget, he amassed some of the best minds in the world to reliably examine The Message. I'll bet he could get one or two of those associates to help. Love of George, they might do it for free if you can excite them enough about the project's relevancy! Those that are still alive and kicking are likely retired and perhaps bored to death. They might be eager to exercise the old gray matter on a new and exciting project, no?"

"Brilliant, James! I did consider Uncle Andrew, but it never occurred to me that he might be able to strongarm one of his past associates to help. Do you know where he and Aniela might hang their hats nowadays? Last I heard, they had a flat in Switzerland as their base but were traveling in the Galapagos."

James scrunched his face in thought. "I tell you what: let's call Mum right now. I'd wager she knows." Brother and sister hugged while James initiated the call. After getting the information from their mother, Bethany telephoned her Uncle Andrew.

"Look, Uncle Andy, I know the timing is not great, and you're probably tired, but just tell me when I should call back. I need to speak with you at length, as I need your help." Bethany looked toward James and winced.

"No, no, it's nothing bad; in fact, it's something I think will excite you," said Bethany hopefully. "Ok, got it. Until then, and Uncle Andrew, forgive me, but thanks. Love you. Bye."

Bethany jumped into James' arms. "I think he will do it! He said, 'Anything for you, Bethy,' just before we rang off! But I did awaken him, silly me. But we'll speak in a day, and trust me: I am going to use everything I've got to convince him to join up!"

"Yes, I'm so sorry, honestly. My enthusiasm got the better of me." James grimaced. "I never thought of the difference in time zones. Poor Uncle Andrew hasn't got a chance."

Both twins grinned at each other.

Chapter Twenty-eight
On Becoming

"I'm going to need more wine," a breathless Bethany said to her assembled family, "before I can continue. I confess I'm so excited I can hardly breathe!"

"Darling, tell us everything... your phone call was hardly revealing! We've all come together straight away as you asked, and we're excited too. It appears as if you've got good news?" Marcia questioned a rosy-cheeked Bethany, the others gathering around the refectory table in the kitchen.

"Yes, at least I think I can safely say, 'yes,' in fact, a resounding 'YES!'"

"Come on, Bethy, give!" James ordered impatiently.

"Well, to start, Nat Geo reviewed the galleys of my new book before the meeting, having thoroughly examined and evaluated the enormous number of photographs I submitted to them earlier. They took provision to invite a tame publisher they've used previously for any volumes that have come out under their umbrella.

"It seems they were stunned by my photography which—when buddied up to the accompanying short stories as a representative component of the overall theme—more than pleased them. It energized them! Ideas were popping during the meeting, some of which put me quite off balance.

"Because the format is heavy on the visible side with short stories portraying the inspiration, emotion, and intensity of some of the expressive photographs, they're seriously suggesting a sequel! And the publishers believe that such a book *or books* would or could be useful as reference and educational tools in schools, civic, or philanthropic organizations—not just on someone's coffee table! The aspect of that last possibility is continuous, with the right marketing, of course, backed up by acceptance in the marketplace!

"As the two Board representatives agreed and stated at the meeting, I have only 'just scratched the surface.' There's a whole world out there, countries and cultures past and present, stories to be unveiled, ordinary women accomplishing extraordinary things to be brought to everyone's recognition and attention as a vital part of fully comprehending humankind's history. It fits well with the social evolution we're currently undergoing, which is, I am sure, the main thrust of their argument in terms of successful marketing. They want to be seen as one of the leaders of the egalitarian movement for humanity by presenting a meaningful and inspiring depiction of women's evolution and their contributions. Of course, that concept was my thrust when I pitched the book to them in the first place. In fairness to them, NG has always followed its mission: to educate its readership impartially by featuring parts of the planet and all its inhabitants—animal, vegetable, mineral—for the benefit and appreciation of humankind. In that regard, they have been singularly successful and principled, in my view.

"It all traces back to my journey. Self-discovery was torturously slow during my time with Alistair. I'm not blaming Alistair, mind you. I allowed what happened to happen, so that's on me. And it was not *all* bad, mind you. It deteriorated with time until we grew irreparably apart as man and wife or partners. Not everyone is as successful as you lot, you know.

"Then I experienced something new and wonderful during my sequestered time with Amir behind the waterfall. He opened up feelings and new vistas for me that I had long since believed were beyond my life. That grew in the immediate aftermath. We then backed away from each other for quite a while because of moral and religious convictions. We both accepted the rightness of the need to sort out our feelings and dreams individually without the other's influence. When we finally reconnected years later, we discovered that, despite the hiatus, none of our attraction or shared passions had diminished.

"Following that, as you know, I completed my initial phase of research, followed by writing the fictional accounts with just sufficient historical inclusion as to make the stories believable. In other words, a 'this could have happened in this way' kind of moment. This phase meant another postponement for Amir and me to explore what might be or become between us.

"You see, the images of Middle Eastern women with Semit-

322

ic weathered faces free of all adornment in a coarse headscarf of plain cloth, for instance, is as revealing and legitimate today as it was in the time of Mary Magdalene. In some outer villages, they still draw water from ancient wells! The stark portraitures expose an authentic depiction behind which are centuries of history, little of which has changed or modernized in certain areas and cultures. In some, it's almost as if you can hear the questions they pose or the words of experience they utter.

"Of course, for other eras like the 15th and 16th Century France portion, I had to research period clothing and fine fabric and have it sewn into germane designs of that time. I hired models and used current landscapes to portray the mood I sought for whatever images I included to amplify the story. The same goes for the Blue Woman section. Civil War, WWI, and WWII bits were easier to manage, but the same principles applied.

"The planet was my most valuable partner. For example, it provided legitimate background from the craggy mountainous terrain of northern Italy into the boundaries of Switzerland, Liechtenstein and Austria frequented by ancient Teutonic tribes in the time of the Romans. The barrenness of vast stretches of land in the Middle East during the time of Christ *or* the rolling, green gentility of the French countryside and gardens—all of it was then more or less as it is now, lending credibility to the photographic journey presented that accompanies the fictional short stories. I wore many hats: photographer, writer, artistic director, negotiator, and on and on.

"Depending upon what power, message, emotion, or starkness I wanted the photograph to reveal, I employed both black and white as well as color photos. The entire exercise was challenging, thrilling, and grueling. But I learned a great deal about myself in the undertaking. What's more, I gained an appreciation for our species and our conjoint history. More than ever, I find myself a champion of women... then and now.

"Apparently, that has some significant validity in the social and political development of our current day world. One of the men closed the meeting by saying that my work was 'one of the most impactful works of our time and evolution.' Can you imagine that?

"Forgive me; I've gone on too long." Breathless, Bethany apologized to her silent, spellbound family. "Uh, they're planning a book launch for a select group of attendees. I would love it if you could all come. I'm calling the book **MEMORY OF ECHOES**." There were a few moments during which only the ticking of the mantelpiece clock was audible.

James said, "Bethy, you never cease to astound me. If you were half as passionate during your presentation to that initial meeting as you have been with us, I am not in the least surprised at their resounding reaction! Good for you, old girl. You've really accomplished something here, and all of it on your own: reaching deep within yourself, having the grit to see the project through, instinctually knowing the fitting and most powerful way to present an unbiased interpretation, and backing it all up with your passion for what is true, right, and fair. My heart is bursting with admiration, at the moment."

"And mine is bursting with pride, sweetheart," said her father in an impassioned whisper.

The dam broken, everyone spoke at once, offering exclamations and congratulations. As seemed to be his role in family gatherings, Nick popped a champagne bottle, filling the glasses Lauren held on a tray. The family laughed, reminisced, and toasted Bethany's achievement.

"Your father and I lead a quiet life these days, Bethany," said Marcia thoughtfully when conversation quieted. "At one time, my veterinary practice was exceedingly busy and challenging, as were his legal practice and the responsibilities of his political appointments. But these days, we are content for our children and extended family to have their 'moment of fame or attention.'

"Life, in general, is blissfully mundane and moves from whether the roof is leaking to one of our grandchildren's graduation from this school or that to what to plant in the upcoming spring garden, and a host of other routine life tasks and demands. Everyone's life is similar, in the main. We don't lead the kind of lives Hollywood presents of English gentry to the viewing public. We lead everyday lives, grow thick around the middle with deeper creases on our faces beneath graying hair. We've done what we've done as an outcropping of our abilities, interests, and dreams, some of which accomplishments were stellar, others fairly uninteresting... just like everyone else. But we've also had a lot of dullness, drama, sadness, and disappointment in our lives, as well—also like everyone else.

"But it strikes me as I bathe in the love of our family and the pride expressed in you that the years you spent bringing this project to fruition is noteworthy, particularly since you began at a weak point in your life. The endless hours you invested flabbergasts me since much of it was either exploring inhospitable parts of the world and its cultures and fraught with technical difficulty.

"I wonder if you realize just how significant the last few years have been? I grant you no one knows the ins and outs of it all but you: the doubt, the problems, the exhaustion, the planning, and dedication, to the lack of your personal safety in some instances. Still, I would venture to say that in my unprejudiced view of it all, *you* are like the women you feature in this spectacular volume. *You* are an ordinary woman who has accomplished an extraordinary thing. I marvel at your accomplishment, my love. You began a broken and unhappy woman; you are now an archetype of the very theme you sought to unfold."

Everyone stood as Lauren called out, "Hear, hear... to our Bethany!"

"And," came a voice from the archway, "to my Bayth!" A tall, slender man with long, black hair, dressed in a slightly wrinkled chambray linen shirt and beige trousers, entered the room and embraced a shocked Bethany.

"Amir..." she whispered.

Chapter Twenty-nine
Bayth

"And so, as becomes apparent, despite where they currently reside, the pages in the Berlin Gnostic Codex (Papyrus Berolinensis 8502), discovered in the late-nineteenth-century somewhere near Akhmim in Upper Egypt, was purchased in Cairo in 1896 by a German scholar, Dr. Carl Reinhardt, and taken to Berlin. The codex is believed to have been copied and bound in the late fourth or early fifth century. It contains Coptic translations of three significant early Christian Gnostic texts: the Gospel of Mary, the Apocryphon of John, and the Sophia of Jesus Christ. The texts themselves dated to the second century initially authored in Greek.

"Unfortunately, they were not translated and published until approximately 1955 due to various reasons, not the least of which were two World Wars. By that time, the Nag Hammadi collection of Gnostic writings were recovered.

"Although the Berlin Codex assisted and augmented the translation of the Nag Hammadi texts, the Berlin Codex contains the most surviving fragments of the Gospel of Mary. I say 'fragments' because the manuscript is missing pages 1-6 and 11-14 from those documents.

"Still, the named 'Mary' is the person we have for years called 'Mary Magdalene' or 'Mary of Magdala.' Considering that two other small fragments of the Gospel of Mary from separate Greek editions unearthed in archaeological excavations at Oxyrhynchus, Egypt, together with pieces of the Gospel of Thomas, we can conclude that the Gospel of Mary was well distributed in early Christian times and existed in both in original Greek and a Coptic language translation.

"The pages revealed on these Slides 22-26, alongside their amplified translation, show some of the text from missing pages

11-14 of the original Coptic in the Berlin Codex. I thank Professor Mustafa Aydin of Turkey for sharing these treasured relics through his gracious and professional cooperation. The other contributors are listed on each relevant slide and in the Notes Section at the rear of your packet.

"Slides numbered 27 through 39, and their parallel amplified translations represent the findings of Drs. Nigel Rutherford, James Brandon, and Andrew Stanton, together with other respected scholars, named for partial aid or augmentation listed on Slide 40 and those following within the noted section. I am sure most of you will recognize their names and the strength of their reputations. This most recent archaeological treasure found in Syria by those mentioned above on their recent highly publicized excavation augments the already significant texts in the public domain as a partial representation of the missing pages of Mary's Gospel. I thank them for their willingness and professional courtesy in sharing these relics and their associated data.

"As part of your packet, you have copies of only some images used for this address featuring Biblical times through other eras to WWII. Photos of people, portraits, in particular, are current; however, their faces' lines and expressions depict ravages survived from a lifestyle not dissimilar to their ancestors. Costumes or uniforms photographed are legitimate representations of museum pieces, painstakingly reproduced by expert seamstresses and displayed by hired models with depictive hairstyles appropriate to the time. Reproduced historical photographs accompany real-time photographs of respective locales for comparison, accepted artistic effects allowed.

"As occurs in the developed storyline of **MEMORY OF ECHOES**, the protagonist re-establishes herself both personally and professionally as a result of life experiences and the inspiration she derives from compiling a photographic and short-story looksee into the lives of her forebear "sisters," historically speaking.

"After all, ladies and gentlemen, it was only in the mid-19th century through the suffrage movement that women received the right to vote in elections by the passage of the 19th Amendment to the Constitution of the United States. Women also worked for social reforms and broad-based economic and political equality but had to fight and march to change voting laws of their time to allow them to vote. Further, it wasn't until 1964 and the 24th Amendment's passage that poll taxes were outlawed--a major barrier to

African American voting. That was only 100 years ago for the former Amendment and only 56 years for the latter! Some would argue that women still suffer inequality in many areas, despite the changes accomplished by our Western societies. Globally, excepting a very few remarkable instances historically, that remains true.

"**MEMORY OF ECHOES** is both a homage and a message of hope to women everywhere: from every ethnicity, from every culture, from every society, from every religion. It is a banner that proclaims encouragement for women's empowerment—much deserved, much fought for, seldomly acknowledged in many walks of life from today looking back to yesteryear.

"I hope that it will touch your heart and mind. I dream that it will inspire change in humankind's outlook and arouse transformation.

"Now I see it's Noon," Bethany said, checking her wristwatch, "marking the conclusion of Part I of my presentation for the launch of **MEMORY OF ECHOES**. I will now entertain questions, after which we will take a one and a half-hour lunch break beginning at 12:30 PM. Part II, which begins at 2:00 PM, is a private viewing of displayed images in Ballroom 2, followed by a brief reception in Ballroom 3, beginning at 3:00 PM and concluding promptly at 4:00 PM. Thank you."

Having gathered her notes, Bethany nodded to the projectionist in the overhead office and strode from the stage. The applause surprised her. Once behind the curtain, she bent at the waist and gulped in several deep breaths, allowing herself to lose composure.

"Hey, Beth, come here," said her Uncle Andrew, drawing her into his strong arms. "You did wonderfully, sweetheart. I thought your father would pop the buttons on his shirt, and Marcy hasn't smiled so much since you and James were wee tots!"

"Was it ok? Did it sound professional and convincing?" Her words tumbled out of her mouth at breakneck speed.

"Whoa, whoa, girl. It was, in a word, terrific. I must say I was most intrigued about that little French Madame. What a clever girl she was!" Andrew grinned as they walked toward the gathering of family awaiting them.

"You are incorrigible!" Bethany said, smiling.

After kisses, hugs, and too many questions and compliments, the Brandon/Maxwell-Brandon/Stanton/Lawson/Graham contingent went into their reserved small, private dining room for lunch together.

Awaiting them was another archaeologist dressed in pale linen trousers, a navy sports jacket, and a long-sleeved blue shirt. Holding a champagne flute aloft, he said, "*Mabruk bayt eunyana*, congratulations to our Bethany!" She ran to him and kissed him full on the lips.

"My Bayth," the man said quietly, brushing his hair back from his face, his blue ring sparkling almost as much as his dark eyes.

"Dr. Amir Najjar, *beyefendi*," she responded, smiling up at him.

As the family looked on, Tommy whispered as he hugged his wife to his side, "So, how do you think she is going to structure her name? Want to lay bets on its going from a double-barrel to a triple-barrel name?"

"You're on," said Marcy. "But I reckon she'll give no recognition to Amir's family name, nor will she continue to use Maxwell before Brandon. It will simply be Bethany Brandon."

Nick Lawson leaned in. "Couldn't help but overhear, chums. Can anyone get in on this?"

"It's 100 quid apiece; winner takes all," warned Marcy.

"I'm in, with a bet she'll use initials between her given name and Brandon as her surname, you know, 'N.' and 'M.'" chimed in Lauren Graham. "If you agree, Nicky, you and I can split the bet's terms."

"It's ok with me, but I wonder if Beth might use 'Baythani' instead of 'Bayth'? It depends on whether she prefers 'Bethany' or 'Beth,' doesn't it? Amir uses both names."

"Good night, Nicky!" exclaimed Lauren. "We're not going to complicate this any further! You're either in or out of our joint bet; if not, fork up for your new idea."

Nick just shrugged. "I was just pointing out that..." reaching for his billfold.

"Sometimes you overthink things, Nick Lawson. Come here and kiss me, you darling man," Lauren said, smiling, knowing just how to end the conversation.

"What *is* this? The whole bloody world is in it now?" complained Tommy.

"Oh, quit your sniveling," quipped Andy. "Aniela and I are in for 200, but we wager she'll use 'Bayth' in her name, either as a first or middle."

"Well, well, well," said James.

"Given I convinced her to be part of my team, my good wife and I will each chip in 100 pounds, making the total 800 quid, right? But our bet differs from all of yours: we think she'll go by 'Bayth' professionally from now on--nothing from her former life whatsoever. No first name, no middle, no surname, no hyphenated marriage names, no initials. After all, this new book of hers is entitled, '**MEMORY OF ECHOES**' with the author as 'Bayth.' She's finally found herself, and we reckon she'll make a name for herself as just 'Bayth' under her own steam."

"Right then! Bets are sealed; everyone pay up!" Tommy reached for his wallet.

"Not to throw a damper on things, but when is the jig up? Who sets the date when the bet expires and who holds the pot?" Nick asked.

Collecting the notes, Thomas Brandon said, "Amir, of course! He can't participate in this bet because he is a possible influencer in the result. Likewise, he cannot know the bet's terms. But he *is* the most likely candidate among us, don't you all agree?" Everyone nodded. "As to the expiration, let's give it, say, two months after this book launch. She will have had feedback, publicity, and interviews by then."

"And the time to decide her future course," said Lauren, winking at Nick.

"Yes, indeed," Nick said, smiling, "What say you, my darling? Time to take our leave? After viewing the exhibit and attending the chit-chat session, a turn around the gardens at Waverlee is in order, methinks. They have always held magical solutions to all sorts of dilemmas over the years." He reached for Lauren's hand, saluting goodbye to the others. Tommy and Marcy smiled at each other in knowing memory.

"Right, then, to the business at hand! Amir, my good man," called Tommy, walking briskly toward Bethany and Amir. "I need you to do us a favor," he grinned, turning back to the assembled family with a wicked waggling of his bushy eyebrows.

Chapter Thirty
Equilibrium

The foals and yearlings frolicked in the pastures, exuberant with the energy of spring. The bright green grasses and fullness of the trees' leaves painted a glorious picture of renewed life and all of its potential promises. Bathed in that security, Bethany took up her pen.

"My dear Alistair," she began. It had been too long before she had the courage and clarity to write him this letter which she always intended to send as a means to level the playing field to ensure his and her freedom and subsequent happiness apart. Co-parenting was a part of their longtime future. So was the need for healing without recrimination. They both deserved that, and Bethany knew that Alistair's pride would not allow him to address either in any extensive way. 'I, however, can, should, and therefore will,' she thought to herself smiling. As she penned her thoughts unhampered, her mind flitted through their early years together.

"Surely, you as well as I recall that our time together was not all bad. We began our journey together full of wide-eyed idealism fueled by passion and excitement. Then, it was 'you and me against the world.' What wonderful dreams we had!

"What sometimes happens is that when people pursue their ambitions, the associated demands of their path exacts more and more of their time and energies, and they are drawn into the exigencies of moving ever forward, ignoring the core reason that inspired them to walk that path in the first place. They forget or find themselves too busy to nurture that special place within. In our case, our relationship eroded, fading away bit by bit, until we were faced with an abyss between us impossible to breach.

"I want you to know that I accept and admit my complicity in this. I am sorry for the things I did that annoyed or angered you; I am sorry for the things I did not do and ask you to understand that, in both cases, I could not do otherwise at the time. I gave our lives together the best that I had to give. It was not enough. I needed you to help me save us.

"We began as partners in a joint venture, and we separate as partners in the failure of that endeavor—very different people from when we began. Now, all that remains is for us to accept things as they are and move forward cooperatively as concerns ensuring a balanced life for our wonderful boys. If you can derive any satisfaction from the memory of 'us' at all, let it be that together we produced a marvelous blessing for the world in our boys."

Discarding all the antipathy that marred the discussions leading to their divorce proceeding, Bethany outlined some of the upcoming dates and plans affecting Alistair's participation in the boys' lives... if he so wished and could arrange his schedule accordingly. She closed the letter with a genuine wish for his continued success, personal happiness, and re-establishment of a life he desired with the rewards he sought.

Acknowledging that he was like many other professional men but not a 'bad' man, her anger and disappointment with Alistair blew away with the spring breeze. She smiled as she realized they were both free. He deserved happiness as much as she. Signing the letter "Always, Bethany," she applied sealing wax and stamped the envelope. Placing the brass stamp, stationery, and pen into her letterbox, she rose from the veranda table and flung her arms to the sky, to greet her new life full of anticipation. Her eyes scanned the horizon and briefly, she wondered if Alistair would even notice the letter "B" and speculate if it signified "Bethany" or "Brandon." She chuckled to herself, realizing she did not care. Her chuckle grew into lilting laughter as she realized it could also denote "Bayth."

BIBLIOGRAPHY

1. Convention for the Amelioration of the Condition for the Wounded and Sick in Armies in the Field. Geneva, 6 July 1906, issued by the International Committee of the Red Cross, online: https.//ihl-databases.icrc.org/ihl/INTRO/180?OpenDocument
2. Moser Jones, Marian: The American Red Cross from Clara Barton to the New Deal, Baltimore 2013, p. 159
3. Hutchinson, John F.: Champions of Charity. War and the Rise of the Red Cross, Boulder 1996, pp.150-160
4. Makita, Hoshiya: The Alchemy of Humanitarianism. The First World War, the Japanese Red Cross and the creation of an international public health order, in: First World War Studies 5/1 (2014) pp. 117-129
5. The Work of the American Red Cross During the War: A Statement of finances 1919, p.5
6. The Work of the American Red Cross During the War. A statement of finances and accomplishments for the period 1 July 1917-28 February 1919, Washington D.C. 1919
7. The Work of the American Red Cross. Report by the War Council of appropriations and activities from outbreak of War to November 1, 1917, pp. 75-81
8. Gilbo, Patrick F.: The American Red Cross: The First Century, NY Harper and Row 1981
9. Davison, Henry P.: The American Red Cross in the Great War. NY Macmillan 1919
10. Coplin, W., American Red Cross in the World War. Philadelphia: EA Wright Co. 1923
11. Civil War Trust. Civil War casualties. http://www.civilwar.org/education/civil-war-casualties.html
12. Hacker, JD. A census-based count of the Civil War dead. Civ War Hist. 2011; 57:307-348
13. Wilbur, CK. Civil War Medicine. Guilford, CT; Global Pequot Press; 1998
14. Rutkow IM. Bleeding Blue and Gray: Civil War Surgery and the Evolution of American Medicine. NY Random House; 2005. Pp. 21-28
15. Lister, J. On the antiseptic principle in the practice of surgery. Br Med J 1867; 2:246-248

16. Bell AM. Mosquito Soldiers; Malaria. Yellow Fever and the Course of the American Civil War. Baton Rouge, A: Louisiana State University Press; 2010, pp. 41-44

17. Buist JR. Some items of my medical and surgical experience in the Confederate Army. Southern Practitioner. 1903; 25:574-581

18. Prostitution, sexuality, and the Law in Ancient Rome: Thomas A. McGinn 1998

19. The Julian Marriage Laws, Article, University of Oregon, online

20. Views of Ancient People on Abortion: Kourkouta Lambrini, Maria Lavdaniti, Sofia Zyga, Health Science Journal online

21. Barton, Carlin A. The Scandal of the Arena. Representations 27 1989, pp.1-36

22. Carter, MJ. Gladiatorial Combat: The Rules of Engagement. The Classical Journal 102.2 (2006) 97-114

23. Josephus, Flavius (1981) The Jewish War. Translated by Williamson, G. A.; NY Penguin

24. Clontz, T.; Clontz, J. (2008) The Comprehesive New Testament. Cornerstone Publications ISBN 978-0-9778737-1-5

25. Bowman, Steven (1987) Josephus, Judaism and Christianity. Wayne State University Press ISBN 90-04-08554-8

26. Gray, Rebecca (1993) Prophetic Figures in Late Second Temple Jewish Palestine: The Evidence from Josephus. Oxford University Press. ISBN 0-19-507615-X

27. Hillar, Marian (2005) Flavius Josephus and His Testimony Concerning the Historical Jesus. Essays in the Philosophy of Humanism. Washington DC: American Humanism Association. 13-66-103

28. Flavius Josephus Eyewitness to Rome's first-century conquest of Judea, Mireille Hadas-lebel. Macmillan 1993, Simon and Schuster 2001

29. Jackson, Wayne; Demons: Ancient Superstition or historical Reality? Apologetics Press; April 1998; pp. 18-31

30. I. Miller, Robert J.. The Complete Gospels: Annotated Scholars Version. Polebridge Press. 1992

31. Susan Haskins (30 September 2011) Mary Magdalen: Truth and Myth. Random House

32. King, Karen L.; The Gospel of Mary of Magdala. 2003 Polebridge Press ISBN 0-944344-58-5

33. Crossan, J.D.; The Birth of Christianity. Discovering What Happened in the Years Immediately After the Execution of Jesus. San Francisco; Harper Collins 1998

34. Brock, Ann; Mary Magdalene, The First Apostle: The Struggle for Authority. Cambridge; Harvard University Press 2003

35. Haskins, Susan. Mary Magdalen, Myth and Metaphor. NY Berkeley Publishing Group, Riverhead Books 1993

36. Higgs, Liz; Unveiling Mary Magdalene, Colorado Springs: Water Brook Press, Division of Random House, 2001

37. Lockyer, Herbert. All the Women of the Bible. Grand Rapids, MI: Zondervan 1967

38. Pagels, Elaine. The Gnostic Gospels; NY Random House, Vintage Books Edition 2003

39. Robinson, James M. Ed. The Nag Hammadi Library in English. The Definitive Translation of the Gnostic Scriptures Complete in One Volume. NY Harper Collins 1990

40. Lester, Meera. Mary Magdalene Book; F+W Publications Company 2006

41. Mead, G.R.S.; Pistis Sophia; 489694BV00002B/176/P CPSIA, USA

42. DeQuillan, Jehanne; The Gospel of The Beloved Companion; Editions Athara, 09000 Foix, Ariège, France 2010

43. Leloup, Jean-Yves. The Gospel of Mary Magdalene; Inner Traditions International 2002, Rochester, VT2002; English Translation and Notes by Joseph Rowe;

44. The Gnostic Society Library; http://gnosis.org/library/marygosp.htm

45. Encyclopedia of World Biography, Magdalene, Mary; 2004 The Gale Group Inc.

46. Carroll, James; Who Was Mary Magdalene? Smithsonian Magazine, June 2006

47. Cox, Wade; The Origin of the Wearing of Earrings and Jewellery in Ancient Times; 1997 Christian Churches of God, Woden, Australia 1997, 2001, 2011; www.ccg.org

48. The New Interpreters Study Bible, New Revised Standard Version with the Apocrypha, Abingdon Press 2003 ISBN 0-687-27832-5

Merrill, Selah, 1837-1909, Galilee in the Time of Christ, Boston : Congregational Publishing Society, ©1881, (DLC) 05003468, (OCoLC)5049454

Clarke, Adam. "Commentary on Luke 8:2". "The Adam Clarke Commentary."

https://www.studylight.org/commentaries/acc/luke-8.html. 1832

Tabor, James D, "The Jesus Dynasty: The Hidden History of Jesus, His Royal Family, and the Birth of Christianity,"

April 2007, Simon & Schuster, ISBN: 074328724X

Smith's Bible Dictionary, ISBN: 1565638042, ISBN13: 9781565638044, by William Smith, 1990, published by Hendrickson

Books by Callie McFarlane
The Hidden Series:

A Clear Destiny	Book One	2011
Betrayed	Book Two	2020
The Lantern	Book Three	2021

Thank you for your support by purchasing and reading my
books. Every
author depends upon feedback from readers and I invite
your
comment to either my email or website.
(graywoodstables@yahoo.com)
(www.karenkatrinawood.com)

Blessings and Smiles,

Callie McFarlane

CPSIA information can be obtained
at www.ICGtesting.com
Printed in the USA
LVHW020017110821
694977LV00003B/343